FREEBORN TRAVELLER

Graham Fuxon

small world media

SMALL WORLD MEDIA
2 Great Strand Street
Dublin 1
Ireland

www.smallworldmedia.ie

First published as a trade paperback, October 2007

Trade enquiries to
087 955 1504 (Ireland, Europe)
07816 146 567 (Britain)
info@smallworldmedia.ie

ISBN: 978 0 9554634 1 9

A CIP record for this book is available from the British Library

Cover, book design and typesetting: SMALL WORLD MEDIA BOOK SERVICES
Photography: Gemma Sayers

Back cover photograph: The Seventh Lock, Dublin, 1963. The wagon belonged to the author. The poster-carrier "Justice for Itinerants" is a member of the Republican movement. The two in hats and overcoats are armed Special Branch men.

Printed by La Grafica Nuova S.c.r.l., Torino

AUTHOR NOTE

The release of Irish State papers on the Puxon affair, including letters between Bertram Russell and Charles Haughey has renewed speculation in the controversial events surrounding the early years of the Travellers' civil rights movement.

Publication of the correspondence did little to throw light on my arrest at that time nor on the covert involvement of the IRA. My motivation for writing this docu-novel therefore has been to clarify what happened and by so doing to chronicle the birth of the Travellers' struggle. Organisationally, this has manifest itself since in the activities of the Traveller-led Minceir Misli, the Pavee Point community centre and the Irish Travellers Movement.

Forty years on, recognition as an ethnic minority and the rights this would entail are still denied in Ireland, while in Britain severe difficulties have been put in the way of the nomadic life by the Criminal Justice Act of 1994.

Meanwhile, the now legendary stand at the Cherry Orchard squatters' camp has its echo in the ongoing Siege of Dale Farm, in Essex. Here a thousand Travellers, some the grandchildren of people at Cherry Orchard, continue to thwart the attempts at ethnic cleansing by a hardline Basildon council, while across Britain the notorious bailiff company Constant & Co. cuts a swathe of destruction through the lives of British Gypsies.

Despite all the harassment, as Dale Farm spokesman Richard Sheridan says, Travellers continue to triumph over adversity. In the 1960s owning only bender-tents and wagons and circulating in a few counties, many now travel in the best trailer caravans and make trips to all corners of Europe.

Readers may like to know that Pop's Johnny Connors went on to lead the Gypsy Council's campaign against evictions in the British Midlands and Venice Manley (aka Denise Hanley) later opened a Gypsy school in London and followed her career as a singer.

I was tasked with organising the first World Romani Congress, became for ten years general-secretary of the International Romani Union and currently assist in the Dale Farm campaign.

Grattan Puxon
July 2007
dale.farm@btinternet.com

To Sasha

1 At the kerbside a pony idled in the shafts of a flat-cart. On it, legs dangling, sat a boy. His face pinched with cold, he was watching the queue forming outside the cinema. The Gala cinema, with its cheap façade and alluring pink-lit foyer, provided a social focal point for the sprawling post-emergency Ballyfermot housing estate. Three-bobs' worth of picture-house fantasy inside, the windy reality of mass unemployment on the pavement out front.

People were moving on the broad pavement, tiredly dressed housewives accompanied by small children, lugging the weekend groceries from the general store. While men loitered around the now unlocked doors of Hennessy's Bar, the big patterned windows of which shut out too much casual observation of too many unsatisfactory lives temporarily geed-up by alcohol.

It would be a great night at Hennessy's.

Ballyfermot lies on the western, inland fringes of the city, far from Dublin Bay, the docks and quays, the fashionable thoroughfares and all the commercial ballyhoo. The extensive housing scheme, which has obliterated the old, one-street village that gave it its name, was at this time a dormitory town for the mostly poor and unemployed. Some wag had recently called it The Workless Republic.

The green, number nineteen double-decker buses that served the estate used to terminate at the Gala. A few carried visitors up to the Cherry Orchard Fever Hospital, a little further into the rural hinterland, where two big, empty fields stretched away to the edges of Palmerstown village.

The local jobless that raw autumn were hoping a few more factories would open on the nearby Ring Road. You could see the construction going on there, turn-key deals for foreign companies. But no-one could say when they might be occupied. Meanwhile, some of the adjacent land had been taken over by Tinkers. The barrel-top wagons and low bender-tents stood in clear view of the road, and their washing lay haphazardly across the sparse hedges along the Grand Canal.

It was the early nineteen-sixties and nothing much was happening anywhere in Dublin.

When the breeze got up suddenly, bringing another wet scattering, the boy jumped off the cart and ran to the queue, an anxious eye on the man in the box-office. With his jacket held above his head, he started gaiging for coppers, working his way down the shuffling line.

In a short while, the people had gone in and Paddy took up his post, alone, beside the picture-frames. As he waited for the odd latecomer, chinking his pennies, his father emerged from the pub. Mikey stood blinking at the rain, sliding two bottles carefully, almost reverently, into his loose coat pockets. Then he stumbled to the curb, retrieved the hanging reins and placing a boot on the wheel-hub, sprang deftly onto the cart. The pony began a lurching turn while the man, upright above him like a charioteer, stood as solid as a sailor back on board. He seemed pleased with himself, in a very uncertain way, apparently oblivious of his torn, damp clothes, his blighted circumstances, oblivious even of his son.

Nobody on Ballyfermot Road gave him or his pony a second glance. Travellers like Mikey Ward were driving these little, painted carts up and down the Dublin streets all day, crying and calling through the neighbourhoods as they went about their trade, hawking for old iron and rags. Their womenfolk, wrapped in heavy, plaid blanket-shawls, often a babe at the breast, assembled each morning at the Gala bus stop for the ride down to the city centre, where some begged for a living on O'Connell Bridge. It was Paddy's eyes alone therefore that were fixed on the standing figure in the cart.

'I won't always be doin' this,' Paddy thought, looking after his father. Then he turned his face again to the framed pictures of the film-stars and wondered whether, to be honest with himself, he would ever be anyone, anywhere, other than who and what he was.

The street-lamps came on, their light glinting off the wet road. Beyond the illumination the cart was already shrinking into the dusk. When it was finally out of sight Patrick went to buy his cigs and crisps at the shop and headed homeward through the darkened streets, in the midst of which loomed the huge schoolyard and long buildings of Our Lady of the Angels Elementary, the biggest school in the whole of Ireland. Paddy had never spent a day in it. Now eleven-years-old he feared those high, iron gates as if it were a prison.

Beyond the last road, in the pitch dark, lay the rising, humpbacked land the Travellers called the California Hills. Here, hidden in a wilderness of crumbling banks and bramble thickets, the Wards and others had made their temporary camp.

In the morning, amid the noises of the bivouac and the crackle of a newly kindled fire, Mikey lay in a deathlike slumber on a bed of straw, well back inside the low tent. Behind his head are stowed his tool-box and slender T-shaped anvil, untouched since the Wards landed here from County Galway. The tinman's trade is all played out and obsolete. He will sleep on while the rest of the family busy them-selves at preparations for another survive-as-you-can kind of day.

Three paces from the open end of the tent, Mikey's wife Eileen lifts a tin bath onto bricks set in the fire and fills it with water from a churn, leaving a drop for the kettle of tea. She sits back easily on her haunches, pushing the bushy black hair from her eyes. It reveals a coarsened but still handsome face, marred by a vivid burn scar on her right cheek.

Nan, her eldest daughter, slender, dark-haired like her mother, hauls the nearest sibling from the tent and puts the babe into her mother's arms. Behind the girl, the other tots loll on a pile of old coats close to Mikey's feet, waiting their turn to be washed and fed. Eileen will scrub them white, there in the open air, though the dirt may swallow her work before the tea is boiled. She imposes a fragile order, following a pattern and a purpose that belong to the Travellers' world, a world utterly apart from the council houses and gated gardens on the other side of the unfinished road.

'Patrick, hurry on will yer and get a pint o' milk before your father wakes,' Eileen commands. 'And a loaf.'

The boy takes the silver florin and begins to cross the camp, back towards the Gala and the shops.

2 The young Englishman had been standing for a long time on the rolling leeside of the ship, watching the gulls and the sea. Now he caught his first sighting of the low, dark line of mountains under a mantel of rainclouds. The approaching land looked a little forbidding.

He was a fresh youth, with spiked blonde hair which overhung his duffel coat. Carrying a haversack, Steven Aiken looked the sort who in those times you might have seen on a Ban-the-Bomb march. A small black and white CND badge winking on the navy-blue coat confirmed this impression.

An hour later, the B&I ferry was wallowing in the sheltered waters of Dun Laoghaire harbour, and he came down the gangplank, a lone English lad in a throng of Irish homecomers. It had been a rough crossing but as he disembarked, he experienced a thrill of relief. His escape was complete. He was free. They could not follow him to the Republic of Ireland.

A light rain blew as he followed the crowd through the customs shed and into the railway station. A little steam train carried the boat passengers into Dublin.

In O'Connell Street he bought a postcard and went into the General Post Office and sent it off to Denise, his girlfriend. On his way back across broad O'Connell Bridge, a row of ragged children almost barred his way. He saw them out of the tail of his eye, squatting on flattened cardboard boxes. Before he could get past, a woman rose to her feet and put her hand out. With the other she held a baby close against her under a shawl. Her face, hard and careworn but not unhandsome, showed a livid scar.

Steve fumbled in his pockets for coins. He gave her an English shilling. 'God bless you, sir,' he heard her say.

The guest-house Aiken found at the top of Harcourt Street was close to the busy South Circular Road. Settled in he dozed off immediately. When he awoke, it was night. He got up and looked out of the window. A big double-decker rolled past. The traffic was noisy and continuous. He switched on the bedside light and yanked a book out of his haversack. But he could not read for the memories. His mother dead; he could not get over it. He peered around the unheated room. An oversized wardrobe, washstand and shadowy, papered walls. In its own black shadow a crucifix. He had known his mother was dying, and she herself had known it. Yet to each other they had said nothing. All their lives they had said nothing. He saw how crazy that was. He had not told her he was in trouble over National Service, of his resolve to keep out of the army. He could not worry her, not when she was so close to death. Not ever now.

Extinguishing the light, he tried again to sleep. It was the sudden banging of a car door which next disturbed him. He was still on the run and not so certain now that the long arm of British law could not reach him even here. He tried to forget his mother. After all, he reasoned, the death of his father in the war no longer bothered him. He must get over it. His fear of arrest, the alarm and accumulating anxiety, all this he strove hard to suppress, thinking instead of Denise. Of what they had done, all they had shared. Now he would have liked to have told her what he had just been through; how he had so narrowly evaded the Military Police. He could tell Denny everything and that comforted him.

3 Steve had come down to the breakfast room, his night fears gone and famished as only a young man can be. As he waited, an old priest seated himself nearby, red neck above a white collar. The serving girl darted over, a plain girl with plain legs. At home, he might not have given her a second look, yet here alone as he was he felt a mild attraction. He looked on with relish when she came back and unloaded the breakfast in front of him. Ireland might be a great adventure, if only he knew how to get it started.

Walking through the morning streets, Steve found himself hurrying as if pursued. He was out of step and needed to slow down; Dublin had its own pace. So he made himself stop altogether when he came across the Grand Canal, and looked for a while at the old waterway here on its inner-city stretch, with locks and a towpath under dipping trees.

He needed to find a job before Denise came over and called into the Dublin Branch of the National Union of Journalists. His apprenticeship on an East Anglian weekly hardly qualified him for work in the Irish capital but he paid his dues and got a new Press card. On the inside it said Recognized by the Garda Siochana, which the woman in the office told him meant guardians of the peace. She knew of no job vacancies but gave him a list of daily papers, some magazines and an agency called the National Press Bureau. Over the next two days, he tried all the papers and got the impression, though no-one spelled it out, that to get on here you had better be Irish and preferably have a knowledge of Gaelic. Being English was a handicap. Finally, with little optimism, Aiken visited the National Press Bureau. The office was off Burgh Quay, hardly a stone's throw from O'Connell Bridge.

4 Brendan Carey looked up from his typewriter, regarding Aiken with mild curiosity. Not that he was surprised or nonplussed by the young man's entry. People barged in the door all day, sometimes to his advantage. They brought news and rumour, or laid on him their mimeographed press releases.

He waved his visitor into an old lounge chair by the wall. 'Can you wait a bit?'

Steve watched as Carey resumed tapping on the big, iron-framed Olivetti.

'What have you got?' he said, when he had finished, pulling off his spectacles. He was twice Aiken's age and in a blue gabardine suit looked the quintessential reporter. Steve offered the same particulars which by now he had repeated a dozen times. He did not mention that he was a deserter from the British Army.

'You're an odd one coming over here for work.' Carey's head shook slowly. 'This, my friend, is the land of the jobless, full of boozers and losers.'

The pessimism in his voice made Steve want to keep the interview short. 'Any scope for a freelance?' he said, now as more of a gesture.

Carey said nothing, continuing a disconcerting examination of Aiken's smooth youthful face. He was inundated this week and in need of some help. He felt inclined to take the young Englishman under his wing.

'I don't market articles for a commission, or anything like that,' he said. Steve remained silent. 'But I could maybe do with someone to cover some routine things. Have you done any court reporting?'

Aiken assured him he had. Carey took a phone call before addressing him again. 'Would you care to come for a drink? I can tell you what I want and show you around a little.'

The newsroom at the Irish Times was a cavernous den of clacking typewriters and insistently ringing phones. Nobody took any notice of the two visitors as they sidled between the close-set desks. After Carey had dropped off some copy, he led the way next door to the Pearl Bar, a regular hangout for writers and journalists.

A barman approached and came back with two beers. Steve's eyes lit on the framed caricatures of Dublin literati. He wanted to smoke but did not like to take out his tobacco tin.

'I never got as far as a newsroom yesterday,' Steve ventured. 'I think I ran into some prejudice.'

'You may do' said Carey, giving a tolerant smile. 'Nothing personal.'

'Would I be resented working in Dublin?'

'Only by the ignorant. But we're a very nationalistic lot and you may feel at bit out of place at times.' Carey sipped his stout and Steve followed his example.

They both took cigarettes from Carey's packet of Sweet Afton. Steve gestured to the pictures on the wall. 'So who comes in here?'

'Our local celebrities. Quite a few but you wouldn't know them, except Brendan Behan maybe.'

'The Borstal Boy,' exclaimed Steve, quoting a title.

'Right. Fortunately or unfortunately caught up in The Patriot Game,' said Carey, pleased.

They continued drinking and then Steve asked in a more plucky tone, 'What's the cracked plinth I saw this morning in St Stephen's Green. The statue knocked off it.'

'Great observation,' Carey replied. 'Well, a lot of old statues were removed. Queen Victoria and the like. But it wasn't enough for some people. The IRA blew up a few since.'

'I'm against bombs,' the English lad stated. 'Especially nuclear bombs.'

'Banning the Bomb is right,' Carey agreed. 'We only go in for reasonable sized bombs over here. Not that I condone those physical force fellows. I'm not of that ilk.'

Carey went on to describe with some glee how a customs post on the border had been demolished and was going into detail about the troubles in general and then the famine; even bringing in Oliver Cromwell. Steve found it too much to taken in at one go, a little boring and very confusing. But listening to Carey it occurred to him that he had never talked before with an Irishman about Ireland. Now he was getting the inside story.

'Isn't that all in the past though?' said Aiken, 'What's left to object to?'

'Object to? Only the occupation of the Six Counties.'

'I mean here in Dublin.'

'Well, I don't know. Anti-British? A lot of it's symbolic I suppose. Some don't like your Nelson Pillar.'

Steve was beginning to realise that Ireland was a minefield of ill-buried hurts. Carey called for another round and ordered sandwiches. After a while, the Englishman said: 'I wasn't going to tell you this. I'm on the run. I should be doing military service.'

'Not a loyal subject of the Crown?' Carey laughed.

'More of a rebel,' answered Steve, and in good humour they left.

But walking back with the bureau chief to his small office, Steve was still not sure he was going to give him any work. Carey sat at his desk again, shuffling through some papers. Steve resumed his place in the old lounge chair.

'Could you cover something for me this afternoon?' Carey said hopefully, handing Aiken a court charge sheet. Steve studied the list. The cases were mostly traffic offences, the kind he was used to reporting on in England. In the margin beside some of the defendants' names had been scribbled a plea and the fines imposed.

'I was up there this morning,' explained Carey. 'All I want you to do is phone in the results. They make fillers. All the papers use them.'

The job sounded simple. Aiken was to work on a casual basis and be paid two pounds ten for the half day. He set off immediately for Kilmainham District Court. In the following week, he covered several court sessions. There were some petty larceny cases, a drunk and disorderly, and two charges of begging against women described as itinerants. He had trouble understanding the women. The younger of the two burst into tears, covering her face with her tangled hair. The elder swore when they were sent down to serve a week in jail. Steve thought this harsh and wondered at the precarious situation of the women who sat on O'Connell Bridge. He saw them every day, with their small children, but had no notion where they went when evening came and they vanished from the central thoroughfares.

Usually, he did his writing-up in view of the bridge in the office near Burgh Quay. Sometimes he preferred his room at the guesthouse where he set up his own portable type-writer on the washstand. When the copy for Carey was done, he wrote letters to his girl in England. He told Denny he worked for a national agency and urged her to join him in Ireland. At the bottom of the page he drew a heart and coloured it red.

1 He had told Carey that Denise was coming over soon so he was looking in the classifieds for a flat. Carey warned him Dublin landladies were an intolerant lot and that being unmarried the couple would be sure to meet disapproval.

'Keeping the girl waiting is it?' said Carey, mocking his youth and hinting at his own view of the matter.

This oblique suggestion that he ought to marry Denny surprised and confused Steve.

'Too young?' The older man prompted, letting him off. 'Sure we're all late marriers over here and the bachelor girls are not keen to marry. They want to show off a bit first.'

Carey had not finished opening the mail. He stood up, sorting the envelopes. Steve picked up a brown packet and read on the cover Report of the Commission on Itinerancy.

'Itinerants – the bureaucratic word for Tinkers. The erstwhile makers and menders of pots and pans, who presently only make a nuisance of themselves, according to most.'

'The women on the bridge there,' said Aiken. 'I'd like to do a story on it.'

'A feature and we'll get pictures,' Carey encouraged, taking the yellow covered publication and skipping through it. He had no time for lengthy government blurb.

'Go and find some Tinkers. Talk to them.'

2 The Englishman read more of the Report of the Commission on Itinerancy in between hearing cases at Kilmainham Court. Afterwards, still looking for a home, he walked down Old Kilmainham Road through a dilapidated quarter around Bow Lane. On waste ground beside the tiny Camac River stood a hut and by it an up-tilted cart, surrounded by bottles. Nearby an old house had a For Sale notice fixed to it. The crumbling stonework was covered in wisteria whose fading blooms cascaded in abundance almost to the street. Further up the hill was the boarded-up hulk of the Railway Tavern and venturing through the coach arch he followed a sandy lane that led upwards to the back of the vine-clad house. He liked its raised garden on the plateau of land high above road level. Above again towered the walls of Old Kilmainham Hospital. Returning to the street, he saw on closer inspection that the house was no more than a ruin. But he was sure that he could make something of the place. After all he might be in Ireland for years.

Aiken passed by the hut and the cart again and went into a bar in Bow Lane. The bar was dark and neglected like the rest of the neighbourhood. He ordered a stout and a sandwich and then made a telephone call to the estate agent. His enthusiasm for the property rose when he heard the owner was asking just three hundred pounds and that he could meet Mr O'Keefe the next day.

As Aiken stood in the gloom eating his sandwich the barman was drawing the cork from a bottle by means of an old-fashioned contraption screwed to the counter. He opened a second bottle. Out of curiosity, the Englishman turned to look at the single other patron, who had come in while he was phoning. The man met his eye and acknowledged him by a nod.

'You're not from around here are you,' he stated affably, raising his glass.

'I might be moving in,' Aiken answered, his gaze on the man's face, darkened in the poor light. 'Are you?'

'Across the way,' the other answered, indicating with his lifted arm. Pop's Johnny could not himself see his hut from where he sat but judged the stranger could. 'That home-made looking place is mine.'

Steve glanced out the half-curtained window. He had already noticed the hut. He knew now the man must be an itinerant, one of the people he was supposed to be writing about.

'See the house with the creeper. I'm going to buy it,' Steve said emphatically.

The barman stood between them putting the bottles of porter on Johnny's table.

'Join me for a drink young man,' he said. He had Steve summed up as a harmless visitor.

'You ordered two,' said Steve, coming over.

'I like a pint and they only have bottles in here.' He pushed one towards the youth and refilled his own glass.

'I'll tell you right off. I'm a newspaper reporter,' Steve said, sitting down opposite him. 'I'd like to talk to some of you people.'

'About what?'

'About yourselves. Your lives. Any problems you have.'

'We've plenty of problems,' Johnny said cheerfully. 'A world of problems. You can take your pick of them.'

'How d'you manage then?'

'Oh, I get by, collecting scrap. All sorts of stuff people throw out. Would you believe that? I make a few bob to feed the wife and children.' Johnny rubbed his unshaven chin. 'I was in Wales a good while and Birmingham. That's where the money is. I haven't been back long meself.'

In the next hour, helped by the beer and Johnny's easy manner, the two established a lively rapport. Steve learned a lot about the

Travelling people. Johnny claimed they were the original inhabitants of Ireland, here before the Celts. He said they were the first metal-workers on the island and had a secret language of their own.

'The scholars says it's only a bastardised Latin. I say it's a whole lot more than that.'

'I think you're something of a scholar yourself.'

Pop's Johnny grinned pleased with the compliment. 'I'm a seven-week scholar, that's all. Seven weeks in school. The nuns started me off and I've educated meself. There's not a book I can't read.' Steve looked at the Traveller in genuine admiration. He hoped they would be friends as well as neighbours. He was soon talking about himself. He spoke freely and felt better for it. Johnny was the first person in Dublin he told about his mother dying. It brought up again an anguished sense of loss. He changed the subject to his desertion from the British Army.

'Then you've come over here to put all that behind you,' Johnny said with sympathy.

'With luck we'll be near neighbours.'

'You in that leaky old house. You'll be a lot worse off than us.'

'I'll fix it up.'

'You'd be better off in a wagon. You could park it up there on the land while you put the place in order.'

Steve was attracted by this idea though he did not know what kind of caravan Johnny meant.

'I know a man who's selling one.' Johnny went on. 'I'll take you to him right now, if you like.'

'Okay, why not?' Aiken smiled. 'My name's Steve by the way.'

'They call me Pop's Johnny.'

Getting to their feet, the two shook hands. They walked to Johnny's camp and the Traveller fetched his pony from further along the wasteland and hitched it to the cart. There was no sign of his wife or children and Aiken did not ask. Johnny talked and joked all the way to Ballyfermot. For Aiken it was the beginning of an odyssey.

3 They passed the Gala and continued through the top of the housing estate. On the far side of the last street, a narrow, mud-crusted track led between a break in the brambles and through into the hideaway camp known as the California Hills. The brambles rose steeply, bearing high up a crop of dusty blackberries. Above, a solitary horse stood against the grey skyline. As they came along, several ragged children stepped out of the bushes and ran ahead of Johnny's cart.

Before they had entered the camp, Johnny stopped the pony,

jumped off and started to scramble up the hillside. Steve clambered in his wake. On the windy heights more ponies came into view, rag-hobbled, feeding on the rough grass. The children collected nearby, in silence, as Connors pointed out the sights to Aiken. They could see the Liffey and beyond the river the trees of Phoenix Park, and pale in the midst of the trees the big columned house that was the residence of President Eamonn de Valera.

The camp was quiet when they came down, almost deserted. The children had stayed on the hill. Some low tents lay close to the track and away on the far side of the ground several caravans were grouped. The smell of smoke drifted towards them; a dog got up lazily and began to bark. As they passed the tents, a small girl emerged carrying a baby.

Johnny led Steve to the caravans where a fire burned. At the side of a half-built caravan a man stood on a chair, balancing his paunchy body as he worked with a saw. A boy was walking around him collecting up the falling pieces of wood. When he saw Johnny coming, the big man climbed down to meet them.

'He wants to take a look at Tom's wagon,' Johnny called, indicating Aiken.

The other made a response, eyeing the young man. The boy meanwhile had run away out of sight. A Traveller in shirtsleeves poked his head out of another caravan and descended the wooden steps, paint-brush in hand. He seemed not to mind the chill air.

'New cover. New paint on it. Everything in proper order. Come and have a look inside, fella.'

Steve went ahead of him up the steps and stuck his head in the door. As he put a foot inside, the caravan swayed on its springs. He paused getting his balance. Then he looked around avoiding the wet paint. On his left stood a slim iron stove, its four feet resting on the plank floor. On top of the stove was a heavy, black frying-pan. A chimney went up through the arched roof. Set in the rear was a high bunk bed, with a little window above it, and below a locker space filled by a tumble of bedclothes. He guessed children slept in there. He touched the roof above his head. It was lined with blanket material behind hoops of plywood. The whole impressed him. Though giving limited room it seemed snug and homely. He turned around, aware of the man in shirtsleeves behind him on the steps. A knife lay in the frying-pan and he bent to see it. This was no ordinary knife. It had a carved, horse's-head handle. The blade was short and curved. He coveted the thing. He wanted to have the caravan and also wanted this knife which he picked out of the grease.

The owner had retreated to the fire and was waiting for him.

The fat man sat enthroned on his chair.

'Can I buy this knife off you?'

'That old peg-knife?' the vendor of the caravan smiled. 'That was made by an English Gypsy man. Sure you can have it along with the wagon.'

'Have a proper look,' Johnny coached, touching his arm and leading him back to the caravan. Steve kept the knife in his hand.

'Look at the cover and the lock underneath.'

His head went down with Johnny's and he saw the small front wheels attached to a lock that turned beneath the body of the vehicle. The undercarriage, from which the shafts ran out, and the wheels and axles, had all been neatly picked out in yellow and red paint. He was not yet comfortable with the Travellers but he loved this caravan and every detail of it.

A round of good humoured bargaining began. Pop's Johnny acted as middleman. In the end a price of forty pounds was agreed. As is the custom, the purchaser was handed a pound back for luck. The older man got up from his chair and hung a medal of St Christopher on the door, also to bring luck to the new owner.

They were still talking, now congratulating Aiken, when a woman came up. She had a kettle in her hand.

'I've ne'er a drop of water,' she said. 'Is any of you goin' out?'

'Send a child to the houses. I've no time to fetch for ye,' the seated man answered.

'I won't,' she answered sharply. 'Wouldn't it be the height of imprudence to go botherin' the houses after what's happenin'?'

'You've no water here?' asked Steve.

The woman made no response only stared at him blankly.

The man kicked a stick into the fire and said no more, and she walked away with the kettle complaining.

'There's nothin',' Johnny told him. 'No water, no light, no toilets. And they're tormentin' us to leave. Didn't a whole mob come up once and make us shift. I'll be well out of it. I'll go back to England presently.'

'Who made you leave?'

'The people from the houses. Oh, it was a while ago. They threatened to push over the wagons.'

'Why?'

'It was mostly over the horses,' said Johnny, looking at the other Travellers. He had perhaps said too much. 'Tramplin' the people's gardens. But what are those scamps doing only cuttin' off the ponies' tails, maimin' the animals. The young fellas out of Ballyfermot ride them half to death and afterwards we have to find them.'

Before he left, Steve got Johnny to obtain an undertaking from the two men to bring the wagon to Bow Lane.

Back at the start of the track, Steve noticed a Traveller was now working on a little anvil. Behind the man, several small children were crawling over a bed of straw at the entrance to the tent. A babe sucked hungrily on a bottle. Under the stranger's gaze, the tinsmith stopped and looked up.

'The tools of the tinman,' he said pleasantly. 'You won't see many of these any more.'

Aiken stepped closer. 'What are you making?'

'A few little mugs, that's all.' Sitting back on his heels, he held one up.

Steve took it in his hands, examining it. He wondered how the man could put in such a fine seam.

'Keep it if you want,' the Traveller said. 'I'll have the double of it knocked out in a minute.' Then he laid down his hammer and extended his hand. 'Michael is the name. I'm a cousin of Lawrence Ward, the man they call the King of the Tinkers.'

'Thank you very much.' Steve shook his large, grimy hand. The generosity impressed him. 'Why do they call him the king?'

'Oh, didn't he win that title in a fist-fight at Ballinasloe Fair?'

A girl of about ten, dark-haired like her father, now stood at his shoulder. She picked up the baby and the bottle and moved away. Michael returned to his task, placing another sheet of tin-plate over the anvil. He began tapping deftly with his hammer.

A woman appeared on the track, carrying a sack. She came forward briskly, showing proprietorship over her bit of territory and her tent. A boy trotted up and laid some sticks on the embers of the fire. The mother collected the little ones around her skirt and handed out cuts of bread. All the while the girl watched the intruder out of eyes which were almost Indian in their depth. At first, the English boy found these eyes disconcerting. He wanted to ask the girl something only he could not bring himself to do so. Instead he looked again at the mother and as she turned her head saw on the broad face a livid scar and recognised her as the beggar woman who had stopped him on O'Connell Bridge his first day in Dublin.

Dusk was falling as Aiken walked back through the Ballyfermot council house estate. In the sky the Evening Star had risen. Passing by the lighted houses, he wondered at the hostility hidden there behind the curtains. He liked the Travellers, the immediacy of their lives, their simplicity and frugality. He liked the way they did things, overcoming the odds. They were outcasts, existing on the fringes of the city; on the run like himself, theirs was a journey without a fixed destination. Almost everything about the Travellers appealed to him. They had affected him as nothing had before. Of all possible lives, this was the kind of life he would like to lead. He itched to consort further with these footloose, landless folk. He wanted not only to write about it but share their open-air life. His star was on a peculiar trajectory and here Aiken believed was where it might come down.

Waiting at the bus stop outside the bright lit Gala, he looked again at the little peg-knife. The knife would be his talisman.

4 Brendan Carey was highly amused at the eccentricity of the young Englishman.

'I sent you out on a story. I didn't say you had to go and live with the Tinkers.'

'I'm not. I'm just telling you. I'm buying a house.'

'And you want me to advance you fifty quid for the deposit? Is that right?'

'Thanks.'

'I didn't say I would.

'Well, you look as if you will.'

'Alright. Cheque or cash? I don't think I've that much money on me.'

'Cheque to Mr O'Keefe. That would do it.'

Brendan got out his cheque book and began writing. 'Associating with Tinkers will get you into trouble. But there'll be a story in it.'

'Oh I'm prepared to bet on that. 'He tore out the cheque and handed it to Steve. 'I don't know what I'm aiding and abetting here. When's your girl arriving?'

'I'm waiting on a letter.'

'What's she going to say about all this?'

'She's ready for a bit of adventure – I hope.'

'She must be crazy. Crazy about you, anyways.' Brendan came out from behind the desk and opened the door for him. 'Good luck with it.'

Aiken went straight from Kilmainham Court to the house in Irwin Street. The owner was waiting. He saw the inside for the first time. The hall was full of dust and fallen plaster. The stairs were broken.

In a room on the left of the front door an iron gas cooker stood detached from the wall. The place was a wreck. But Aiken had wished himself into this and would not back out. He gave O'Keefe the cheque.

'You're gettin' a freehold you know. '

'When must I pay the balance?'

'Three months. Is that fair? I'll have my solicitor draw up the conveyance. You'll have to come to the office so. Have you a solicitor yourself?'

'What does it mean freehold?'

'It means young man that you own the land. No ground rent. No lease to bother about. Yours for ever and I wish you well with it.'

5 The day that Tom Wall was leaving for Liverpool, he brought on the barrel-top wagon from the California Hills. He had the loan of a strong wagon-horse. But when they tried to get the wagon through the coach arch of the shuttered and abandoned Railway Tavern, the arch was too low. Tom, his stout brother Luke, aided by Pop's Johnny and Steve, toiled for two hours scraping narrow trenches in the hard gravel for the wheels to run through. Finally, they pushed it under the arch and up into the back garden. The tall, barrel-top wagon now rested in a conspicuous position on the high bank above the chimney pots of the sombre row of stone houses.

In the distance, beyond the roofs of Thomas Street and the St James's Gate Brewery poked the grey spire of Christchurch Cathedral. There was a view of the suburbs melting away towards the foothills of the Dublin Mountains, which in the early autumn air appeared as a soft, irregular purple line, capped by low running clouds.

When Aiken had finished looking at the view, he got the others to help pull the shafts around so that the door of the caravan faced this magnificent panorama. Luke chided them for the arrangement saying it was a mistake to have the wind on the door. But the young Englishman wanted it that way. Playing the squire, he led the Travellers to Kavanagh's Bar in Bow Lane for a drink they all well deserved.

The barman had watched the Tinker's wagon go up the road and reappear on the plateau in front of the ivy-covered walls of the Old Kilmainham Hospital. Steve talked to him, while the others went to a table. He was interested to hear what the old-timer had to say.

'Were there houses on this wasteland?' he asked.

'Never. It was a field once. They call it Cromwell's Cabbage Patch. And that's what it was I believe.'

'And the big place up there behind?'

'Old Kilmainham Hospital,' the barman said, drying his hands on a cloth. 'Not the kind of hospital you may be thinking. That up there was a hospice for old soldiers. '

'British soldiers?'

'Irishmen, sure. Old pensioners who'd served the British Crown. They used to come down and drink in here.'

Now he took Aiken to the window, anxious to show him something else.

'That mill you see on Old Kilmainham Road. See the roof of it there? 'Twas taken over by the Volunteers in 1916. Oh yes, Bow Lane was in the thick of it. Those lads were firing all day at the British soldiers on the hospital wall. Not the old fellows mind you. Fresh troops who'd been in France brought here to put down the Rising.'

'How did it end?'

'How could it end? They all surrendered didn't they? But they'd held out for near a week.'

The barman went back and started washing glasses again. Aiken sat with the Travellers. The brogue and their jargon fascinated him. He didn't understand everything they said. However, as the table became crowded with bottles, he believed he might eventually know it all.

Tom Wall rose first, unsteadily. He had a boat to catch and with much emotion bid his brother farewell.

'Good luck forever!' he bawled from the door, flinging up his arm. Then he saw the English lad again and coming back, planted a noisy, beery kiss on his head.

A while later, making an oblique journey to fetch his haversack from the guesthouse in Harcourt Street, and pick up some food, Aiken was back, alone, at the wagon. It was night now and by the light of a single candle he cut bread with his Gypsy peg-knife, then collected wood in the darkened garden and lit his first fire in the tiny, compact stove. He heated water in the tin mug Michael Ward had given him and sat sipping his tea. He thought of the barman's story, imagining the wagon caught in the ghostly crossfire of the Easter Rising. Only now in place of that long ago acrid cordite, a faint aroma of beer wort drifted across from the Guinness brewery at St James's Gate.

Aiken had formed a bond with the Travellers and slept better than he had for a long time.

6 Next morning, Aiken walked up Bow Lane in a spell of morning sunshine. He felt caught up in a new romance that enhanced his feelings for Denise. He was certain there would be a letter waiting for him at James Street Post Office. There were two. Outside, he tore open the one which had her handwriting on it and read with a sudden thrill that she would be arriving on Friday morning.

A long manila envelope Aiken carried back to the caravan. Inside he found a copy of his mother's will. The formal, legalistic language somehow befitted the dead. Yet the words came sadly alive when he reached the phrase 'Steven Richard my only son and heir'. He threw the papers onto the cot bed and, seeking a distraction, went out into the garden to look over his little kingdom.

There were in the garden two ancient, unpruned apple trees and a walnut sapling; a whole tangle of gooseberry bushes and some withering raspberry canes. In a shadowy corner by a side wall he found a big patch of rhubarb. These discoveries conjured a fantasy about living off the land. He and Denny would grow vegetables up here, keep a goat and chickens. They could be nearly self-sufficient. In his enthusiasm, he barely considered how Denise, with only one good leg, would bear up to the life he had in mind.

During the week, Aiken went on a shopping spree in O'Connell Street. He bought two pairs of Belfast linen sheets, two plaid blankets and sundry small household items, doing his best to imagine what Denise would need. He would sleep in his sleeping bag until she came, keeping the linen for them. They were going to be sharing the cot-bed in the caravan. Happily laden, he headed home on one of the ubiquitous green buses that ran along the Liffey quays.

1 Her hair, from which she had just rinsed the henna, dangled wetly across her face as she attempted with her weight to snap shut the suitcase. Even as Denise completed these final preparations for departure, she continued to argue with herself over her reckless investment of so much hope in Steve.

His precipitate departure should have warned her. He had left to avoid his responsibilities and while she agreed with his opposition to compulsory military service she could not dismiss the thought that he might be on the run from her too.

As she struggled simultaneously with the physical and metaphysical, two children ran shouting along the corridor outside her room. When they rushed in to say goodbye, she put her arms around them, feeling in this last hour that she was abandoning her two charges. In response the girl, a plump eight-year-old, held tightly to her nanny's waist. The boy, two years younger, resisted her embrace, kicking moodily with his heel on her metal leg.

They left her as quickly as they had come, surrounded by her last belongings packed into a collection of wicker baskets. Many of her things she had already sold or discarded.

After a last breakfast, she was driven away from the white clapboard farmhouse in the family car and in no time was waving hard from the train window. Then the train rattled under a few bridges and glided onto a high brick viaduct. She looked down, a little giddily, at the small muddy river, the meadows and the freshly ploughed fields, at the whole sloping landscape rolling slowly away. A few crows rose in low flight. She looked back to them regretfully. The crows would stay on here, on the land that had nurtured her. In the closed compartment she was already separated. It was a big gamble she was taking leaving the security of a home and a job, and the people she knew.

Through the summer Denise had come to confide in Steve Aiken completely. It had been a heady, intoxicating experience getting so close to a boy. Now on the train she experienced gross, if momentary, misgivings. He had never taken her home. Yet they had become unique to each other, blindly and willingly exclusive. She had the testimony of his letters in her bag. For better or worse, she had to be with him. She could neither explain nor deny it, Steve had become a necessity. Her lover had fled to Dublin. And there, in pursuit of love, she must go.

2 Denise had grown up not knowing who her birth-parents were. She knew her mother had been unmarried and had recently made efforts to trace her. Other than the tantalising fact that both were alive she had been unable to prise anything from anybody. She had been adopted by a middle-aged couple who for her ninth birthday, in a time of post-war shortages, had bought her a second-hand Raleigh bicycle. It had a basket on the front. Once able to ride, she took off on it, screeching around the neighbourhood like a banshee. One day, while riding two abreast with a friend, she had been struck from behind by a car. Her right leg had to be amputated below the knee. She spent months on crutches and underwent painful training before she could walk, still in pain, with an artificial limb.

Now the huge, vaulted glass shed of Liverpool Street Station, noisy with hissing steam and taxis, claimed her as another insignificant incoming passenger. Having laboured on the Underground to bring her baggage to a left-luggage at Euston, Denise Hanley spent the afternoon at Roehampton Hospital getting her leg checked. They replaced a worn screw and gave her a dozen stump socks, a year's NHS supply. By six o' clock she was back at Euston Station, buying her ticket. When the overnight Holyhead train pulled out of the sooty terminus it was already dark.

Now and again, she heard Irish voices in the corridor. Ireland still seemed an extraordinary, distant place. Yet somewhere ahead the great locomotive roared on through the night, pulling her inexorably from her roots, her past, towards an unknown future. The speed, the strangeness of the journey and the foreign destination, all heightened her excitement. Tomorrow she would be with Steve; and seeing her own reflection in the darkened window, she recalled her first encounter with him.

She had been singing at a jazz club in Ipswich when this boy came in and stood by the wall near the band. As they looked at each other, something had been awakened that was not just physical attraction but a mutual acknowledgement exclusively theirs. After the club closed, she had spotted him again in a coffee house and Steve had turned and caught her examining him. Neither had looked away. Whatever it was her green eyes said, his seemed unflinchingly to answer. In a few moments, quite stupidly, they were smiling at each other. Lost and found; it had all happened in the instant and the unknown.

When by accident they met again Steve sat sunk over a café table, ignoring Denise and the cup of in front of him, and leaving her looking at the top of his head. Only after much coaxing, she got out of him what was the matter; his mother had just come out of hospital after an unsuccessful operation. She was dying of cancer.

'I'm hardly company,' he said almost inaudibly.

'Don't for goodness sake apologise.' She took his arm.

'On top of everything my call-up has come through. I'm supposed to go for my medical.'

'You are in a bad way.'

For a while they had sat in silence, his troubles seeming to take up all the space. But before he left her, he had asked very tentatively if they could go out when he finished work. In the cinema that evening, their bodily proximity became pleasurably uncomfortable until, clasping hands, their heads touched and they kissed. Under the projector's smoky beam they kissed again. Emerging arm in arm, she had stumbled on the red-carpeted stairs, leaving him behind. Her right leg dragged and she felt suddenly and painfully exposed. It became a performance to reach the bottom.

Denise had felt humiliated and certain of rejection. The magic between them, such an unsubstantial thing, must be broken. But in the street Steve took her arm. It was his turn to offer reassurance. Only suffering a sort of ignominy, she pushed him away. They went along the closed shop-fronts, without hope or direction. Then in the final extremity of her anxiety she got the better of herself. She knew she did not want to go home. She wanted to go with him.

'It's okay,' he said. 'I was in too much of a hurry.'

Approaching closing-time they were still drinking in the backroom of a pub. He had seen her limp and now she told him the full story. Unaccountably, it made him feel guilty. Feelings arose he could not utter. It was as if he would rather not have known. He began gulping down his beer attempting to drown the knowledge that the girl beside him was a cripple. They fell into a painful silence, able only to watch the other young people around them. There was a hop going on in the next room. Some couples had already left their seats in the snug. Wanting somehow to be part of the mob, Steve and Denise got up too.

The ballroom was thumping to a rendition of Forties swing. The two hesitated at the door. Then Steve drew her after him and in a moment they were holding each other in the close press of bodies. They shuffled through the waltzes and stood out the dances she could not manage. Denise was flushed and non-caring. She looked at Steve, glad she was with him. She looked at her watch and realised her last bus had gone. Last drinks had long since been called in the bar and the band struck up the Gay Gordons for the finale of the night. They dived between the prancing legs and fled out into the street.

He had grabbed her hand and dragged her, half-willing, into a clattering gallop down the windy street. She did not how she kept her balance in this mad, exhilarating charge which brought them to the side-door of a lofty printing works. Panting while Steve fetched out his keys, she allowed herself to be led inside where all she could see in the momentary flare of a match was the end of a huge rotary press. Somehow, she remembered, they climbed a metal ladder to a platform above the machinery. It was pitch dark and cold, and the works reeked of oil. Feeling paper under foot, she had sat down and reached out for him. They were too intoxicated with drink and the newness of each other to notice the discomfort of their hideaway.

There was a shivering delay as both removed some of their clothes. Then in the luxury of this blind privacy, she felt his body against her naked skin. By then it was too late to think about the risk of what they were doing.

Afterwards, he lit cigarettes for them, unaware of her dissatisfaction. That so much keen emotion, such arousal, could be so shortly spent had been a disappointment. Yet he was very close and she had to be content with that. In a while, Denise lent forward and unbuckled her prosthesis. She would not sleep with it on. Then, on impulse, she took his hand and guided it to the metal and leather, explaining the parts and functions of the artificial limb. Steve had already come into contact with its hard edges. But now his hand went forward unwillingly until his fingers lay on the moulded socket. Finally, at her prompting he touched the scared, folded flesh of the injured leg, aware of the extent of her vulnerability and her trust. She had brought him to the most unprotected area of her reality. She had let him in.

3 The train clattered on through the night. Somewhere between Stoke-on-Trent and Crewe, Denise was shaken awake by the ticket collector. She tried to sleep again, lying full-length across the seats. But the compartment had grown chill. Instead she sat up sleepily, watching the vague humps of mountains. Then came a vista of wide waters, dimly reflecting the platinum light of a high-riding moon. Soon the coaches were running alongside Colwyn Bay. She had slipped back into sleep when the long train came to an abrupt halt on the quayside at Holyhead.

For a while all was quiet. There was the B&I ferry under bright electric lights waiting to make the crossing to Dun Laoghaire. Porters came on the scene, shouting to each other in Welsh. Carriage doors began to slam. Having touched up her face in the narrow mirror, Denise let down the window and called to one. The crowd outside jostled forward and she followed her porter up the gangplank. Every part of the ship filled rapidly with returning migrants; the bar was packed. At daybreak, accompanied by wheeling gulls, the ship manoeuvred out of the harbour and into a choppy St George's Channel.

From the stern, Denise observed the little hill of Holy Island slowly receding in the silver dawn. It saddened her to think that somewhere in all that land mass were her natural mother and father. She was following her heart and, in this susceptible interval, the child in her craved a parental blessing. Alone at the rail, she closed her eyes and cried.

4 Outside the house in Irwin Street Denise gazed in at the crumbling front. She surveyed in dismay the poor, two-storey building and the mass of dying creeper. Steve was too busy paying the taxi-man to notice her reaction. He kicked open the unfastened door and carried in her baggage.

'Before you tell me how bad the place is,' he said in the gloomy hall, 'wait till you see what's in the garden.'

She put her head around the door of the one downstairs room. The walls were damp and peeling.

'You must have been mad to put down money on this place,' she commented, following him cautiously up the steep, narrow stairs. She crossed the dusty upstairs parlour as he disappeared out the back door.

The odd shape of the old stone house appealed to her, as did the weed-filled garden and the Gypsy caravan, when she reached them. She stood behind the dry-stone wall which Steve had topped with rocks from the lane. The view from up there was something splendid and she admitted so aloud.

Through the whole afternoon she slept curled up in the built-in bed. The new bedclothes soothed her tired limbs and the slight movement of the wagon lulled her. Steve stole a look at her now and again. She was like a treasured new possession. When evening fell, he lit a candle and sat beside the bed.

Much later, with a sense of privilege, he got in beside her. She was his own, his girl. He could hardly believe such a thing could be.

Eventually, they were both asleep, in the contented slumber of the reunited.

In the wee hours the peace of this first night was suddenly interrupted. Both awoke as the occasional gentle motion gave way to a violent lurch. The wagon was rocked on its chassis. Steve lent over Denise and put his head half out the small back window. The movement stopped abruptly. He heard crashing footfalls but it was too dark to see what made them.

'What is it?' the naked girl whispered from the covers.

'Don't know,' said Steve, clambering down from the bed and pulling on some clothes. As he did so the little room shook again. He relit the candle and its pale flicker played over their alarmed faces.

When he lumbered to the door the candle fell from the candlestick. Through the chill night came the sound of hoarse breathing. Now holding the candlestick like a club, he negotiated the steps and reached the ground between the shafts. A stooping figure moved dimly behind the caravan - it was a donkey using the back-rack as a scratching post. Denise heard Steve raise a shout to turn the animal out of the garden.

The donkey belonged to Pop's Johnny Connors. He came looking for it the next morning. As he passed the broken gate, smoke was sliding from the tall, tin chimney. Denise was sitting on the front ledge, sipping a mug of coffee. A little abashed by the presence of the girl, he called over her head to the Englishman.

'I see you've your missus with you now, God bless her.'

'Will you have a coffee with us? I have some made.' Denise smiled at their visitor. As she got up, the Traveller noticed her gammy leg.

'That donkey nearly pushed the wagon over last night,' said Steve, descending the steps with a mug in either hand.

'I'm real sorry,' said the owner. 'He's a stupid old creature. I'm going to sell him shortly. But I can tell you I had a bigger ass around my place an hour ago. Didn't that Corporation fella Big Bill come nosing around. He wants us to shift.'

'Where will you go?' asked Denise. They both looked at Johnny with concern.

'Me old daddy's above on the Ring Road. I'll be moving up there in a day or two.'

'What kind of place is that?' Steve asked, thinking of the California Hills where he had met the other Travellers. Johnny told them about the new ground near the factories. Steve fetched his copy of the report of the Commission on Itinerancy. He read out to them both the words of its chairman Chief Justice Walsh where he recommended local councils provide houses and caravan sites for the itinerants.

'He says they shouldn't go on moving you from place to place.'

'You tell Big Bill that,' replied the young Traveller, passing his empty mug to Denise. 'Sure we only go around in circles.'

In a minute, leading the donkey down the track, he turned and saluted them. They saw him emerge on the road and a woman came out of the hut, followed by a little girl. From the elevation of the garden they continued to watch the activity on the wasteland.

'How can they raise children in that?' Denise was indignant.

'They shouldn't have to,' remarked Steve.

5 Having returned one morning to chivvy the Connors, Bill Redmond took a walk up the track to investigate the new arrival. Parked up there on the patch of land above the Railway Tavern, the thing was to him like every Tinker's wagon, a provocation. He tramped into the unkept garden and rapped hard on the back of it.

Through the rear window Denise spied the large man in an overcoat and cloth-cap. He carried a stave in his hand.

'Come out will you. I want to talk to you.'

When Steve appeared Redmond was brusque, demanding an explanation for the presence of the caravan.

'I'm buying this ground and the house.' Steve pointed to the tarred flat roof. 'The caravan is just temporary.'

'Temporary or not, you're not supposed to bring it up here,' Big Bill scowled at his latest victim. The young Englishman was worried by his bullying attitude.

'You can ask the owner if you want,' he said reasonably.

'Listen, young fellow. You're over from England aren't you? You don't understand. The owner can't give you permission to live in a caravan in this garden. The Corporation has planning laws. Regulations. You can't just plant yourself here like some Tinker – which you evidently aren't.'

'What can I do then?'

'What can you do? You can get this caravan off here. I'll give you a week. If you're still here when I come back you're in trouble.'

Without waiting for further argument Redmond turned and left. Steve watched him descend the track in his big rubber boots. Denise had heard every word and together they pondered the ultimatum. She thought they should get rid of the caravan and camp out in the back parlour. But it was dark and dungeon-like down there. Steve had to tell her the agreement with O'Keefe allowed them to move into the house only after the conveyance.

6 With Steve away next morning at Kilmainham Court, Denise fretted. In England his absence had unbalanced her. Here she saw things more clearly when left alone. She had swept and cleaned, sewn curtains for the caravan windows and hung her baskets from the roof-benders, storing in them her few personal items. But she was tiring of the privations. All they had was a standpipe tap and an outside privy in a corner of the garden. The need to avoid infection had been instilled in her at the hospital. Now keeping her body clean was becoming a daily chore, and already her stump felt sore. To heat water she had to negotiate her way down stairs and light the gas stove, which was none too safe; or get sticks and boil a kettle in the parlour grate. She was trying again this morning to make something of their home but saw all she had planned was in practice imposs- ible. The walls crumpled under her touch and the rotten plank floors threatened to give way every time she took a step. Dust and plaster lay everywhere. Even the electric wiring had long since decayed. Of the three oil-lamps he had purchased, the glass chimney on one had already been broken. His letters had left too much to her imagin- ation and the vision she had conjured had been shattered. Now they were faced with eviction.

Before one o' clock she retreated to the caravan. As she stared miserably out of the door watching the low-flying clouds, Denise wished she had come less hastily to his side. At least they might have planned and prepared better, like a normal couple.

Just before the rain started, and turned into a downpour, Steve returned. Dismayed by her mood, he stoked the small stove and cooked, while Denise lay on the bed venting her complaints. Every now and then he dived out in the rain and brought up wood from the pile under the caravan, salvaged from the Railway Tavern.

Soon, however, they were trapped inside by the streaks of water falling down the door and the muddy pools spreading on the ground around the wheels. The wagon grew warm and the rain beat a comforting tattoo on the arch of stretched canvas above their heads. Then came the first flash of lightning. Cheered by their new predica- ment, they lay on the bed and made jokes about Noah's Ark.

'Look at us!' Denise nudged him with her elbow. 'I'm happy we're together, yeah. But what's going to happen?'

Steve said nothing. The house did not matter to him. He only knew he did not want to be part of the British Army on the Rhine. Denise unbuckled her leg and it slid to the floor with a bump.

While they dallied the afternoon away, the rain hissed in the stovepipe and the wind rattled ceaselessly at the window.

The water had now collected in lakes at the base of the loose stonewall and on the tarred flat roof of the house below. Little rivulets of brown water ran steadily from between the stones, adding to the dark reservoir floating on the tar. For hour after hour the earthen bank softened and eroded, while inside the house leaking drops pattered on the plank floor. About six in the evening, the young couple in the caravan, listening to the incessant rain, heard an ominous rumbling and then a crash. Part of the loosened wall, top-heavy from Steve's added rocks, slid and fell the few feet onto the house. A rending and cracking followed as the combined weight of stone and water broke the rotten rafters and cascaded like an avalanche through the roof. The plastered ceiling of the dingy parlour showed a gaping hole.

For a few terrifying moments the caravan on its high-sprung wheels seemed to topple forward, as if it too might roll forward and plunge them below. The young couple clutched each other. But it didn't happen.

Eventually, the storm subsided to a drizzle and night came on. From what they could see when they ventured out to take a look, the house was no longer inhabitable.

7 Down on the wasteland, the Tinkers' hut had also suffered damage. Before morning, the Connors abandoned the leaky shelter and built up a huge outside fire. While Johnny dried himself, Catlin held a damp blanket to the blaze. Her drawn face showed years of hard going. Their small daughter Kitty came out and shivered beside them. The two baby boys, swaddled in coats, were asleep under canvas in the cart. Johnny fetched porter from Kavanagh's Bar and they drank from the bottles in front of the big fire, their backs to the wind and rain.

Hastening their departure, Johnny and Catlin loaded what they had left onto the trap. Johnny tied the donkey to the back and lifted Kitty on top, where the children were accustomed to hang on. They moved off slowly, he at the pony's head and Catlin behind, scolding the ass. The wreckage of the shack and the scattered embers of the fire were left for Bill Redmond and the Dublin Corporation.

Turning from Bow Lane onto the Kilmainham Road, Johnny could see Tom Wall's old wagon still defiantly in position. From the road, the broken roof remained out of view. He wondered how long the English people would stay there and envied them their security.

On a whim he stopped the pony.

'I've got to say a last word to those people,' he told Catlin.

'It's bad luck to say goodbye!' she called after him.

Shy of the English pair, he hesitated at the half open gate. Then he saw the tumble of fallen stones that had been part of the wall. Steve raised a hand in welcome.

'I thought you were gone.'

'I'm on my way,' he said, surveying the house. 'You look as if you've been bombed.'

'It felt like it,' Steve said.

'Why don't you come with us?'

'Up to Ballyfermot?'

'You could get us in the papers.'

Steve looked at Denise, unsure how she was taking this. She stood motionless in the half-door of the wagon, watching the two men.

Johnny placed his hand gently on Steve's shoulder. 'I think we're gonna need you.'

The young Englishman glanced away over the broken roof. Fellowship was being offered, a kind of brotherhood of the road. Perhaps a cause. He wanted these things.

'We'll come,' he said simply, without reference to Denise. It was a pact between men.

The Traveller walked away. Then he waved from the road as he started the trap.

'Is this the best we can do?' Denise asked.

'We're not committed, Denny. We don't have to stay there.'

'I think you are. I can see it in your face.'

1 The mare's hooves struck hard on the cobbles as she hauled the tall wagon, creaking and clanking, up the incline of Old Kilmainham Road. In a few minutes, they were passing the courthouse and the long, high walls of the disused Kilmainham prison, which hid the execution yard where leaders of the Easter Rising had been shot by the British.

After moving his own paraphernalia to the Ring Road, Johnny had returned to Irwin Street riding his father's grey mare. The reliable Dolly had stood in the shafts, straining to wrench the sunken wheels from the confines of Aiken's waterlogged garden. Then she went, a little sceptically, slip-sliding down the back track, through the Railway Tavern arch and out into the freedom of the street.

Now the three of them were on their way, Aiken proud to be with the jolly, whimsical Traveller. Denise too was game, her mood lifted by the movement of the horse and wagon, the sense of adventure and relief at getting away from the ruined house. As they jingle-jangled down the broad Naas Road alongside the Memorial Park, she saw with different eyes the ordinary Irish people on the pavement. Becoming familiar to her in the past week, she seemed again to be leaving them behind. She might now be allying herself with different people, the Travelling People. Johnny was taking them to their land.

Soon they were in the narrow privacy of Bluebell Lane and running by Bermingham's scrap yard and piggeries, the odours of which stayed with them until the caravan emerged onto the new Ring Road arterial. By the time Dolly had brought them to the far side the encampment was in sight. More caravans, tents and shacks came into view from the Grand Canal Bridge. In two adjoining fields sloping towards the canal, Steve counted eighteen wagons like his own. It was a bigger gathering than he had expected to see and the prospect delighted him. Denise wondered, with a little trepidation, how the Travellers would take to her.

Just inside the muddy gateway, beside a pile of scrap, an old man and two youths were digging a hole next to a half-finished hut. A black bitch rolled with her puppies on the wet grass. The mare ambled up the field and, under Pop's Johnny's guidance, swung the wagon into position close to his store of bottles, stacked neatly in a line of hessian sacks. Before the English couple had descended, self-consciously, to the turf, Catlin greeted them from the door of a caravan close by.

'What d'you think of this one?' she called shrilly, waving a cloth.

'Can I see inside?' Denise approached and Catlin gave her a hand up the carved steps, while Steve admired the interior from the door. Catlin told them how Johnny had ordered this custom-built square wooden caravan from Newry, in County Down. It had arrived from Northern Ireland on the back of a lorry only the day before.

'Cost Johnny two hundred and fifty pound,' Catlin said, expecting to impress. 'We've been waitin' on it months.'

Kitty stuck her head out of her new berth beneath the bed, pulling the crisp, flowered curtains around her face and grinning wildly. Behind her, the two boys giggled uncontrollably. Catlin seated her visitors on the side-bench and insisted they take tea. She had new Delft to show off.

Steve looked around again, noting the neat fittings and pretty paintwork. This was far superior to his wagon. He had to adjust his estimation of Pop's Johnny Connors.

'Are yous taking up travelling' then?' Catlin teased, as she set the cups.

'I don't think we know what we're doing,' answered Denise, looking at Steve. 'But we should have a caravan like this.'

'Wait a bit and Johnny'll sell it to you. '

'You must be joking.'

'Ah, we're always choppin' and changin' don't you know.' She held out a piece of bread for Kitty.

When Johnny returned from putting Dolly out to grass, he led them to meet some of their new neighbours. They shook hands at another caravan with Old Pop Connors, a man with one eye, and Johnny's mother Maggie. The old couple were shy and rather humble with them. At the MacDonalds' fire, a savoury steam, mingling with the smoke, arose from an oval pan hung from a blackened kettle-bar. Mary MacDonald, a ruddy-faced matriarch, crouched on one knee ladling the stew into a tin mug, which she passed to one of the smaller children. She held her large, hot face back from the heat, regarding the visitors as they entered the close family circle.

'Move over you little ones and give the people room,' Mary ordered, pressing back her ragged, grey hair. She seemed short of breath. 'Will ye take a taste of me stew?' she managed, smiling. 'Sure three more'll make no difference with this lot to feed.'

Not yet accustomed to the banter and etiquette of Irish Travellers, Steve and Denise accepted the bowl of food handed to them. Johnny politely declined. Mother MacDonald, concealing her private observations, began breaking bread from a flat round loaf she had baked that morning under the embers.

They ate awkwardly standing before the clannish audience. But it felt good to be included. Glancing now and then at the ring of faces, both envied the strong family bond. The ragout of bacon ends, potatoes and cabbage, seething in the greasy gravy, tasted delicious.

The homemade flat cake was better than anything they had bought in the shops. The warm company and hot food were altogether welcome to the newcomers at the end of the long day.

The MacDonalds occupied two barrel-tops and three tents, one tent standing close to the wheels of the nearest wagon, the others pitched a short distance out. A young woman had now come up to the fire and was warming her huge belly. It was evident her baby would be born any day. Her face showed a knuckle-sized bruise under one eye. Mary, wheezing with the asthma that was the great affliction of her life, told her visitors she shared one wagon with her husband, John, and two of her littlest children, Amie and May. Her eldest son Terry, married to Rosaleen, owned the second wagon. Her big Johnny and the other boys slept in one tent, which they put up themselves. Wack, whom she described as her wildest, had the other bender with his wife Maisie. 'Another grandchild on the way,' Mary ended indicating her daughter-in-law.

The three were strolling back between the fires when Old Pop drove down the field with Johnny's donkey in harness. Coat collar turned up against the weather, the old man was going out late to weigh in a load of rags. He raised a battered hat as they passed.

'I'll take you to meet the Donohues tomorrow,' Pop's Johnny promised, leaving them at their wagon.

'Are there a lot of them?' asked Steve

'There are,' said Johnny. 'He's a wonderful man Old Pat Donohue. His brother Joe they call the Gaffer on account of him bein' the Travellers' spokesman. He's there beyond by the canal.'

'I'd like to meet him.'

'You will, brother. Tomorrow.'

When later the young couple lay together in the caravan the camp grew quiet. Only an occasional muffled voice, a distant bark, reached them on the damp night air. In the serene stillness of this first night the flame of the oil-lamp, creating its own glow and shadow, gave up a tendril of sooty smoke.

'All those people out there but you hear nothing,' said the girl.

After a pause she asked in a low, serious tone. 'What're we doing here, Steve?'

'Denny, you can see for yourself. They need us,' he replied, unable to offer a better explanation. In truth, he was not sure himself and was suffering second thoughts. He ought to lie low in Ireland; not draw attention to himself by moving in with the Travellers. He arched over her and blew out the lamp.

'Steve?' Denise said in the dark.

'What?'

'We are partners aren't we?'

'In everything.'

'Don't get ahead of me then. Okay?'

She lay there thinking, needing his reassurance. She had come so far for him; and was with him now in this strange field. She could not understand his ambition, what it was he wanted. She saw that she was exposing herself to too many new hazards, jeopardising her health. The silence around them became complete. In the middle of the night, a baby woke up somewhere close by and started to cry. It cried incessantly.

2 A vaporous mist invested the caravan standing alone on the canal bank. Primitive horse-heads painted in black and brown along its dripping tarpaulin, here an unusual rendering of a Gypsy totem, glinted wetly in the dull light. Inside, Joe sat reading a newspaper beside an oil-lamp, while Olivine busied herself at the stove preparing his breakfast.

Olivine's sturdy daughter Mary, a child by another marriage, was already out at the canal filling two pails with water. Her brother Tom had been up an hour since, looking for Tiger, Joe's piebald gelding which had wandered away in the night. Only little Joey, his own son by his doting Romany wife, was still in the bedcovers. Joe Donohue, a man in his forties with a head of black hair that as yet showed little grey, kept an eye on everyone and everything. He kept Olivine and his two step-children in a state close to servitude. They fetched and carried like drudges.

Donohue had been the only Traveller to speak out at a public hearing held by the Commission on Itinerancy in Ballyfermot two years previously. His careful speech, delivered before Judge Walsh in the packed assembly hall of Our Lady of the Angels school, had won him distinction and raised the hopes of those then stopping with him in the California Hills. In a locker draw he kept a copy of the Commission's report and a letter from Judge Walsh. But he was a man afflicted by chronic caution.

'Ma, there's someone for Joe,' Mary called, standing up from a bucket of wet clothes.

The top of the wagon door swung open and Olivine looked out. She saw the young man approaching through the mist. In a moment Donohue showed himself.

'I know who you are, young fella,' Joe said, looking sharply at Steve Aiken as he came closer. 'They told me an Englishman had pulled on.'

Though Donohue spoke freely enough about himself while Olivine made tea, it was an uncomfortable first encounter. Joe's father had been a chimney-sweep who in the First World War had signed on in the British Army. He himself claimed to have served in the Free State Army and was proud of his family's military record. Mentioning nothing of his own dislike of the military, Aiken told him he wanted to help the Travellers by publicising their situation.

'We don't want no publicity,' Joe told him bluntly.

Rebuffed, the Englishman tried to find out what Joe intended to do. But Donohue offered no clue.

'Won't you go to City Hall?' Aiken prompted.

'Didn't I talk to Judge Walsh himself? He's the head over it.'

'But Walsh can't stop the Dublin Corporation,' the young Englishman warned. He realised Donohue would resent any usurpation of his own assumed leadership, but although still unsure of the role he might play in the camp, did not like the other's evasive manner. He felt frustrated.

'What will you do if they come to put you out?' he asked, scarcely concealing the challenge.

'Ah, they won't do that. I've as good as the Judge's word on it.'

'Does Big Bill come here?'

'You know about him? Well, he drives by, that's all.'

Aiken could not pin him down and knew he was irritating the man they called the Gaffer. Finally Joe said, 'I don't know what your intentions are, young man. Only don't you go doin' anythin' without telling me.'

3 When he regained the bigger field, Steve found Denise surrounded by a flock of children. They had gathered at the shafts of his caravan, a shoving, animated pack. Denise was being mobbed. But what struck him more than the children's uninhibited gaiety was her evident pleasure. Denise stood in the press of small bodies, her arms gesticulating, voice rising above their shrieks, thoroughly enjoying herself. She had no need of rescue.

Seeing the man approach, the children's ranks broke and scattered. Steve recognised Amie and May MacDonald, who toddled away in the rear on their chubby legs. The bold Kitty Connors was standing her ground and waving at him. Some of the boys now stopped to gawk from a distance

'Run along you others,' Denise urged as Steve came to her side.

'Not one of them is going to school,' she told him when they were seated in the caravan. Her face was bright and excited. 'I asked them all, one by one. Most of them have never been, even for a day. Except Tuckerlaly.'

'Tucker what?'

'Tuckerlaly. He's Mary MacDonald's nine-year-old. That's his nick-name. They nearly all have nicknames. The nuns put him into school here in Ballyfermot. But he didn't stay.'

'Why not?'

'Because the other kids wouldn't leave him alone. They called him a dirty Tinker.'

'These children grow up with a great education on the road. And they have a lot more freedom.'

'That's just romantic rubbish, Steve,' Denise retorted, paying attention to further childish yells. 'You can't get by today without reading and writing.'

She got up and looked over the door. A boy with cropped hair was running behind another in reins. She felt for these little outcasts, wild and wilful as she had once been.

'Joe Donohue can read. He learnt in the army,' Steve said.

'How did you get on with him?' She was still intent on the children gathering again outside.

'He won't do anything. Mostly brags about himself.'

Denise was watching the children. Their needs stirred her. She turned to Steve, her face inspired.

'We should start a school!' she said emphatically. 'Right here on the ground.'

It was the answer to his doubts. This might get things started. Denise had surpassed herself. He knew he ought to go back to Joe Donohue but instead he searched out Johnny Connors.

'A school could force the issue,' Steve told Pop's Johnny. 'Nobody can deny the children need education. The Corporation won't know what to do. Big Bill will have to leave us here.'

'I'm for it,' said Johnny. 'We'll all pitch in for whatever's needed.'

He was away before Aiken could talk to him about Donohue.

Meanwhile, Denise had gone to the MacDonalds to tell the ailing mother of her project.

'I'll be grateful if you can take a few of them off me hands,' Mary told her. Her unmarried son Johnny was listening. He was on his way out to get sticks and offered to take Steve with him.

'We'll find something to build a school,' Johnny MacDonald assured Denise.

To Aiken's chagrin, Pop's Johnny had left so he and the young MacDonald had to go without Connors. Aboard a four-wheeler lorry, they headed for the refuse dump behind the Red Cow, a poorly frequented bona fide, a mile or more from the Ring Road towards Clondalkin. They passed the old inn and turned into the tip. It proved to be a treasure trove of discarded building materials; everything they wanted lay around for the taking. Helped by Steve, the young Traveller began to pile the long lorry with lumber and firewood.

'Will you be the teacher?' Johnny MacDonald asked, a little in awe of the educated Englishman.

'We'll try to get some students up.'

'The nuns might do it,' Johnny suggested. 'They come round to teach us the catechism for our first communion.'

On the way back a barrel-top caravan lurched out of a side road. A crate of bantam chickens, now squawking in protest, had been strapped precariously on the back-rack.

MacDonald drew the cart parallel and hailed the other driver.

'Jimmy-o! What are yous all doin' out here?'

'Up from Naas,' the man called back, his hand on the brake wheel. 'Lookin' for a place to pull in.'

He sat bent on the wagon front, his craggy face hunched down into his crumpled overcoat. Two children peeped over the door.

'Follow us then,' said Johnny cheerily. 'We'll all at the Ring Road and we're puttin' up a school.'

'Jesus,' said the man, much amused and rubbing his chin. 'I need a bit o' schoolin' meself.'

When they reached the field an anxious Pat Donohue, standing by the open steel gate, told them that Big Bill had just been on the field.

Jimmy Hanrahan, up on the wagon, looked crestfallen. Nowhere was safe.

'What did he say?' MacDonald asked the older Donohue brother.

'Nothin'. He only stared at us like the idiot he is.'

'Well then,' said the youth and urged his pony forward again. The Hanrahans came on, less enthusiastic now, to pick out their patch among the crowd already settled in beside the factories.

As the load was being thrown off the cart, Pop's Johnny saw the Englishman and strolled over to apologise.

'To tell the truth,' he said, grinning impishly, 'I wasn't in the humour take you to Joe and Olivine this mornin'.'

Connors stood a while with Steve and Johnny, examining their findings. The story of the intended school had already gone around the field.

'Not a lot of good stuff,' he pronounced disparagingly. 'Are yous willin' to go out again?'

MacDonald walked the four-wheeler to his mother's fire and put off the firewood, then turning the weary pony around started for the gate.

'Drive to Bill Bermingham's,' Pop's Johnny commanded.

4   The ill-smelling yard in Bluebell Lane, stacked on every side with wrecked car bodies, offered a helter-skelter of fenders, hubcaps, axles, engines, old batteries and other spares, which made up the mainstay of Bill Bermingham's business. You could also find house-doors, drainpipes, butts, building bricks and blocks, and pieces of wooden furniture, all carelessly exposed to the recent rain.

Contented honks and squeals came from the pigsties beyond, as the three moved on to the cottage door.

A heavy-bellied man with oil-grimed hands opened to them, pressing himself back to let them through the low doorway.

'Come on in, lads. Find yourselves somewhere to sit. Johnny, get that chair over.' He treated them like a delegation.

Bill's bulky wife came out of the back room and set a kettle. Every now and then as they talked, she studied the young men seated in her steamy kitchen.

'One of you Johnnies,' she said, fascinated. 'Tell me - is it right you've built a school? What's the Corporation goin' to say about that?'

'Not up yet, auntie.' Pop's told her, for once bashful. 'We were hopin' Bill would give us a couple of those old school desks.'

When they had drunk their tea Bermingham led them back out and helped manhandle items onto the four-wheeler. He gave them planks, a door and three window-frames, in which most of the glass was intact, and added some cans of nails. They picked up eight old Board-school desks. Then Bill went back to the cottage and came out again holding up to view a huge Irish tricolour flag.

'Wouldn't it fly grand on the school? Proper thing,' Bill exclaimed, handing this final gift to Aiken, who happened to be nearest him.

A police motorcyclist stopped to watch the high-loaded cart come out of Bluebell Lane and cross the Ring Road. Revving noisily, he swung his machine in an arc and pulled up in front of the pony's head. Cursing loudly, young MacDonald struggled to control his animal.

The three waited for the expected questions. Aiken regretted he had not got his press pass in his pocket.

'Where did you get this lot?' The guard peered through his goggles, black boots planted on the road.

'From Mr Bermingham, sir,' said Connors.

'And where do you intend goin' with it?'

'Just up the Ring Road. Right there, officer.' He indicated the distant collection of wagons, from three or four of which a lazy smoke was rising. 'Sure, its only firewood.'

The guard looked doubtfully at all three.

'Get on with you then and don't be blockin' the road,' he said, losing interest, and kick-starting the bike, swung it around and shot off in the direction of Kilmainham Barracks.

'Big idiot,' exclaimed Connors.

'Pig-faced bastard,' MacDonald spat on the road.

'A harmless old shaydog,' Johnny Connors retorted in fun. 'And him like a big bluebottle riding a pair of scissors.' He gave Steve a dig in the ribs.

Old Pat Donohue, propped at his habitual post by the gate as the load came in, raised his short pipe in salute.

'You fellas, come over here a minute,' he croaked, starting towards his newly enlarged hut. The black lurcher bitch followed at his heel.

While MacDonald drove on up, the others scrambled off and went after the older Donohue. Stooping at the door they found themselves in a surprisingly roomy interior. A table was set with china and on the walls around hung family photographs and holy pictures. Two windows let in the afternoon light, while from a corner a brazier radiated a muggy warmth. There was no Mrs Donohue for Pat was a widower. Instead at the table, her arms akimbo, sat Denise Hanley. The old Traveller stood beside her, only too ready it seemed to share the hosting with the friendly English girl.

Both now hastened to place food before the guests. A soda loaf and a wedge of cheese were fetched from an orange box that was a cupboard; ham and a pound of butter out of a shopping bag hung on a beam. There were some apples that rolled across the table.

'Would you ever lift that kettle?' Pat gestured to Denise. The spout was already spitting gobbets of water onto the hot metal.

The door-curtain swished back and in came two of Pat's grown sons. They hailed the company and sat down in silence. Their father was spooning tea and sugar into the kettle-pot. Denise rose at his side, picked up the kettle in two hands and commenced to fill the cups. She did it with a flair, confidence and show of good humour that had big Chap and Francie looking on open-mouthed. Only yesterday the girl had been an outsider, a total stranger here.

A lively talk sprung up and Denise repeated what she had been saying around the camp. When she had finished, Old Pat laid a hand on her head.

'This is a wonderful young lady,' he said, smiling down at her. Denise felt that caress of approval like a drop of gold.

Pat Donohue informed the little gathering Big Bill had been up to the Gala and that all the Travellers from the California Hills would shortly be shifting to the Ring Road. Michael Ward, with his bender tent, had already landed while the school-builders had been out.

The Walls would likely follow tomorrow.

'He won't run us off here,' Johnny Connors boasted.

Since he had just heard they were leaving the old ground, Aiken was sceptical. But he said nothing to spoil the new defiant mood.

In the evening light, the two strolled up the long field hand in hand, passing by the multiplying campfires. Now happy, Denise confided to Steve her instant liking for Pat Donohue. He had spoken to her at length about his sons, his late wife and their life in a house in Barrack Street, Mullingar, a town in the Irish midlands. His wife had died of pneumonia.

From behind the half-built factories a wintry sunset peeped, pink and gold between the trees. At the caravan, Denise had one more novelty to reveal. Seated on the edge of the high cot bed, she put a recorder to her lips and blew a cheery little tune.

'This is for my singing class,' she told her admirer.' Wait till you hear the lyrics.'

1 After the three Walls brothers have moved over from the California Hills, a trickle of Travellers, put out elsewhere in south Dublin, continue to arrive at the Ring Road. Here is their last hope for winter quarters. Seeing the big school hut under construction, its newly-sunk corner posts pointing like portents of hope to the leaden sky, most believe they may be left to spend the Christmas on this land.

In imitation of the school-builders, the new arrivals, taking what they can from the Red Cow tip, hasten to put up their own shacks. Soon a row of makeshift-huts and kitchen lean-tos arise alongside the hedges close to the half-completed factories. Dogs bark over bits of new territory, children argue and cry, and Jimmy Hanrahan's bantams screech away in fear for their lives, as the new parties subdivide the precious acres.

Only that unshakeable feeling of impermanence, which is the Travellers' mindset, keeps a few old-timers and their children under stick and sheet.

No longer the last in, the English couple begin to feel less like newcomers. They too are settled in for the duration, however long that may be.

2 Aiken went out almost daily, with Pop's Johnny or one of the MacDonalds, for churns of water. Sometimes, if no workmen were about, they filled them from a standpipe on a nearby building site. More often the task meant a four-mile round trip. Groceries, and peat briquettes for the stoves, had to be fetched from the shops near the Gala cinema.

Only once the young reporter had put in a half-day for the National Press Bureau. It had meant catching several buses. When told of the school his chief thought it a cockamamie scheme but he liked the write-up Aiken brought in. It was published, together with a picture, in a Dublin evening paper.

The optimistic mood on the field was still apparent when early one afternoon a silver Mercedes-Benz, a rare sight in Ballyfermot, turned in at the gate and, crawling across the grass, stopped outside Pat Donohue's hut. The small dapper figure who had emerged from the big car was now talking to Old Pat.

Embolden by their numbers and believing the man could only be the harbinger of bad news, a group of men quickly surrounded the grey-haired intruder. If he represented officialdom they were game to confront him on their ground.

'You obviously don't know me,' he said, standing badger-like before the squad of Travellers. 'Liam Grady, your senator at your service. Clann na Poblachta. The People's Party. I'd like to get to know you and I want to be of help.'

They closed around him now, shaking the proffered hand of friendship, laughing at themselves; still not sure who or what he was but only too ready accept his alliance. Pat ushered the elderly senator into his shanty parlour, and all filed in behind. As they jostled in the confined space, Steve Aiken arrived. The small, eager faces of children bobbed at the windows.

Pat seated Grady and stayed at his shoulder. Those that could sat with him, forming an informal council. Last to enter, Denise Hanley lent with her back against the door, as silent and as incredulous as the others.

'When I saw in the paper what you were doing,' began Grady, his voice a husky rasp, 'taking over this field, putting up your own school, I was reminded of what Ireland, the Republic, is supposed to be about. I was reminded of some principles which, in our day, have been badly neglected.'

He looked from one to another. As yet they only half understood his message. Grady tried again: 'You Travellers are our kith and kin, part of the Irish nation. Your have long, too long, been deprived of your rights. I will, if I can, see that changes. It has to be changed.'

Now there was a stirring and restlessness in the little room.

'Are we gonna be put out?' a voiced asked from the back.

'What he means, sir, is can you stop the Corporation?' Pat Donohue stated quietly.

'I haven't finished,' Grady answered, a little flustered by such a dire question. He seemed for a moment at a loss.

All turned to look at Aiken as he ventured to intervene.

'Mr Grady, senator, I'm sure I speak for everyone here when I say we'd love to have you open the school. Would you do that?'

'I will. I'd be honoured,' he answered simply. 'When would that be?'

Eager to clinch the deal, and seeing no need for ceremony, the company rose instantly and bore Grady up the field. In mounting excitement, children and adults came from all sides, some for a curious peep, others bearing holy pictures to hang upon the walls. Grady drew them all behind him into the school. Before the impromptu opening got underway, Joe Donohue, summoned from his wagon by the canal, and having donned a clean white shirt, took a seat beside the senator. The larger crowd, a small sea of bright intent faces, were ready to hang on Grady's every word.

The old politician recommenced his speech in a pose he might have adopted before Dail Eireann. 'The Irish State,' he said, rising to his feet, 'was established to champion the welfare of all its citizens.

That's what we in Clann na Poblachta believe. Anything less is an unforgivable betrayal of Republican ideals.'

As he continued much of his high-flown speech was lost on his audience. But by degrees they began to grasp the spirit and intention of it. Never had Travellers been addressed in this manner and there came welling up in these men and women of the road a new belief in themselves. Backs straightened and knowing glances were exchanged. Mothers held their children tighter. A noble lesson was being taken to heart. They might henceforth be more than chaff in a cruel wind. Affected himself by the mood he had created, Grady stopped. Perhaps he expected applause. Joe Donohue full of a sly self-importance, passed to him his smudged copy of the Report on Itinerancy and pointed to the preface.

'Let me read you the words of Chief Justice Walsh,' said Grady, looking at the opened page. 'One overriding consideration dominates the entire background to the itinerant problem. This is the simple fact that the humblest itinerant – that's you! – is entitled to a place in the sun.'

Grady looked at them and, now jocular, added, 'I don't see much sun, d'you?'

A snicker went around the room. Smiles and naïve, open faces, awaited his departing message.

'My advice to you all is stick together here and keep them to their word.'

Everyone was suddenly noisy. He had uttered an incitement to resist eviction, thrusting responsibility back on them. Many had hoped for something different. A sober Michael Ward called from the ranks:

'Mister, can't you stop them shiftin' us? We've nowhere to go.'

'I'll do what I can. But it's going to take time. The Corporation is very set in its way as you well know. We're going to have a hard task changing them. I wish I could say otherwise.'

The Travellers were disappointed. But Joe, his face flushed with pleasure stood now to thank Grady.

'You are the first great man to come among us Travellers. We appreciate you comin' here today.'

Grady had something else to say. He reminded them they had not yet chosen a name for the school and, after a short debate declared it would be called St Christopher's. Finally, he told them: 'What I have in mind is to speak to the Irish Civil Liberties League. See what support they can give. This can't be left to an Englishman. You need some local volunteers.'

In a minute, standing beside the emptying school, the English pair watched the Travellers going with their new leader to the gate. Joe Donohue had already reached the silver car. Aiken had not spoken at the meeting and now felt left behind, almost shunned. He had made notes for a report but could not bring himself to ask Grady for a lift. It was another hour before he got to a public telephone to dictate his copy.

Casey assured him he would take the item right away to the Irish Times, but expressed reservations about the senator.

'Liam Grady is a complex man,' Casey warned. 'I wouldn't wish him on you. He's been a thorn in everybody's side.'

3 It was difficult to follow the track in the pale light that hovered over the long, cold strip of water. Bats dived and swirled close around, while on the far field, indistinctly seen, grey figures moved among the groups of caravans. Voices reached them, once a shout, on the thin night air.

When they stopped, Steve drew her to him and she relaxed, accepting him back after the tension of the day's events. They could be close again if only she could tell him what was on her mind.

Seeing she had something to tell him he touched her upturned face. But still unsure she did not wish to be coerced.

'Not now,' she said, drawing a packet of cigarettes from her coat pocket. They lit them together.

'What Grady said got to you didn't it?' she said, turning the conversation away from herself.

'He wants these civil liberties people to get involved – whoever they are. He thinks I'm interfering where I shouldn't.'

'D'you think he wants them to take over the school and everything?'

'Maybe it would be better.' Steve took a drag on his cigarette, then flicked it away into the water. 'In the end it's for Travellers to conduct their own fight isn't it?'

A rat scurried down the bank and plopped into the dark water. A moment later, a wild duck paddled out into the middle and, squawking loudly, half took off, leaving a trail of bubbling ripples.

They strolled on again slowly in the direction of the Seventh Lock.

It was the furthest she had walked for a long time and her leg was beginning to hurt. But the towpath was utterly deserted, the new night lonely, and for a whole hour they had the world to themselves. The moon was rising as they turned back towards the camp.

'So what haven't you told me?'

'Nothing that can't wait,' she replied. 'It's just a little thing. Maybe nothing at all.'

At the Grand Canal Bridge, the couple were overtaken by a man on a moped.

4   Picking his way through the unfinished factories, the late-night visitor was now stumbling unseen along the inside of the dark field. Then he hurried forward, almost ran, towards the isolated red embers and stopped abruptly beside two black tents. Beyond rose the outlines of huts. As yet no dog stirred. No voice broke the night quiet.

'Hello, anybody awake there?' he called into the half-open mouth of the nearest tent. 'I've a message for you. For you all.'

After an interval, a woman's voice answered, 'Who's that? What d'you want? We're all in bed here.'

'I've come to tell you something,' the man said, adding in a bolder, insistent tone, 'It's that important.'

The tent moved and the woman, muttering first to herself, bawled for all the camp to hear, 'Paddy, get up out of there and see what the man wants.'

A sleepy Patrick Ward emerged from the other tent, rubbing his fist in his eye.

'Get Donohue. Quick, d'you hear?' his mother's voice commanded. 'No, wait. Tell the English fella there's a man here.'

The lad, pushing his shirt into his big trousers, looked disinterestedly at the buffer. All that distinguished him in the limited light was his cloth-cap. Without a word Paddy ran off into the dark on his bare feet.

No more communication passed between the stranger and the woman in the tent. Left to himself, the mystery man hung uncertainly by the remains of the fire. Only long premeditation on his mission now kept him there.

Finding Aiken's wagon empty, Paddy woke Pop's Johnny. Together they returned to the benders by the far-side fence. The conference by the Ward's smouldering fire was short. The man would not give his name. He said what he was doing could cost him his job.

'The Corporation is going to evict you,' he whispered. 'I know because I work for them.'

'The holy terror!' exclaimed Michael Ward, who had pulled himself out of his tent.

'When will they come?' asked Johnny, suspicious of this night intruder.

'Next Tuesday or Wednesday,' the man replied, with a certainty that struck alarm into his listeners. 'Early mark. That Bill Redmond has been doing the rounds of every depot getting a gang together.'

'How d'you know it won't be Monday?'

'Monday Molloy, that's the Housing Manager, will be briefing them. The guards will be there. Believe me, it's to be done like a military operation.'

'Why are you tellin' us?' queried Pop's Johnny, feeling the weight of doom descending.

'I'm a trade union man. I think it's a sin the way you people are treated.' Then he added. 'Oh, they know all about what's going on here. About your Englishman. They have it on for him.'

They let the informer go without so much as bidding him good-night. Pop's Johnny was doubtful. He might be a Corporation spy. As queerly as he had appeared, the man threaded his own inconvenient way out through the fence, passed the shadowy factories and regained the Ring Road. He mounted his moped and with a pop-pop-pop of the two-stroke engine, vanished up the unlit road.

5 As if invigorated by the threat of eviction, the encampment seemed to shake off the old indifference to fate and the weather, and now stirred with renewed life.

A knot of young men stood in animated talk around Pop's Johnny's fire.

'It makes no odds if the Gaffer won't come with us,' Johnny was arguing. 'We'll all go down there anyways and say our piece. Sure we've nothin' to lose now we're certain they mean to put us off.'

Chap Donohue looked doubtful. He wanted his uncle Joe to lead the delegation to City Hall. But the younger men were already fired up. Johnny turned with a questioning face to the Englishman.

'I've promised to help with the school,' Steve told him, feeling that like Joe Donohue he was letting them down. 'You don't need me. This is your show.'

'What'll we tell them? That we'll buy the field off them?' Johnny joked. 'We can all put in two quid apiece.'

'Ask them to put in a standpipe and start a rubbish collection,' Steve suggested. 'You could offer to pay rent.'

'Big Bill can be the rent collector,' said Johnny MacDonald, full of mirth.

Suddenly, above the raucous laughter at Johnny's fire, came a piercing, exuberant yell. Then another yell as Wack MacDonald, on the roof of the school, let the large, green, white and orange flag fall from his hand and take the breeze. The Irish tricolour, nailed to a pole, flattens and flaps, cracking like a top-sail.

Balanced for a moment above them, Wack launches a kettle-bar like a spear and jumps after it to the ground.

Soon an assortment of carts and traps are assembling out on the Ring Road. Young men and women impatient to be off.

Maisie MacDonald planting herself in the well of the gig behind Wack, rocks to and fro, crooning to her unborn child.

At the last minute, some of the old women, wanting a ride into town, decide they will come along. Eileen Ward, pressing in beside Maisie, out of sorts after a night broken by the Moped Man, hugs close the babe in her shawl. With no buses passing the camp, she too, is ready to join Pop's Johnny's protest to City Hall.

Just before the line of vehicles moved off, the tingle-tangle of a hand bell sounds across the field.

With Steve holding open the door, St Christopher's is filling with eager youngsters, prancing in agog to claim their desks for the first lesson. Immediately she is inside, Catlin's Kitty, small as she is, appoints herself Denise Hanley's help. She lifts little ones and slots them into the front row, she upbraids Paddy Ward for laughing, and dabs at the chalky blackboard with the corner of her coat. Nothing is going to quench the zealous energy of this precocious little girl.

Still clutching the bell, Denise finds herself before a bank of gleaming, upturned, expectant faces. The children are packed in three to a desk and standing along the walls. A hush spreads through the room as, uninitiated as she is, all await her performance.

'We're going to start with a singing lesson this morning,' she says pertly, as if a routine had already been established. 'You can all sing can't you?'

'Yes!', ''Cos we can!', 'You bet!' come their shrill responses. A deafening chaos follows wrecking the untrained teacher's small core of confidence and defying all hope of order. She thinks of ringing the bell but it would only add to the din. Steve stands there helpless. Bedlam continues until little Kitty Connors climbs up on a desk and bellows, 'Shut up! Shut up all of yous!'

6 The cavalcade of horse-drawn vehicles was now wending its way towards the city centre. The carts were already rattling between the stalls in Thomas Street market, their wheels almost running over the feet of the crowd that jammed the road. The crashing of horseshoes on the cobbles frightened and excited all who beheld them.

The startled people looked after the column of wild Tinkers, wondering what they had just seen.

Pop's Johnny Connors, reins in hand, thrilled by the bumpy ride and the public attention, felt himself empowered. He looked back at

Wack MacDonald, standing upright like a warrior in the second trap, dangerously close behind. Whipping their ponies into a reckless canter, they were out to lash the Dublin Corporation.

Behind Wack, in the bucket of the shaking trap, young Maisie held a hand to her swollen belly as an aching spasm gripped her. She could only hang on grimly against her panic. But at last the jolting stopped and the carts stood in line below the mullioned windows of the Corporation offices in Dame Street.

Whilst Eileen stayed with Maisie and the ponies, hitched to a row of parking meters, the crowd of Travellers charged up a broad flight of steps into City Hall.

Two ushers running forward to meet the onrush were swept aside. His people at his back, Pop's Johnny announced they had come from Ballyfermot to see the City Manager. These words restored a little dignity.

A clerk was fetched and, staying his distance, heard the request repeated. He padded off down a corridor leaving the mob to wait. When he reappeared he holds up three fingers. Three only will be allowed into the inner sanctum.

The whole lot marched forward again, nudging each other gleefully, making the two-finger sign behind the retreating back.

All the same, at the large, panelled office door the majority found themselves unceremoniously closed out.

The man behind the massive redwood desk eyed the delegation and demanded their names.

'Foley, sir,' said Johnny Connors, looking across the desk. A chrome plate inscribed Sean Fogarty, Assistant City Manager, rested against a glass inkwell.

'And you?' The man jabbed the butt of his fountain pen at Wack.

'Joyce, Paddy Joyce, I am.'

Johnny MacDonald gave his right name.

'And what do you have to say?'

'Your Mr Redmond has told us we have to shift,' Pop's Johnny began. 'But we've nowhere to go, sir, and Senator Grady says we should be allowed to stay.'

'You know as well as I do you've no right on that land.' Fogarty was already hostile. 'Your Senator Grady has got nothing whatever to do with this. He is only misleading you. The law is the law, d'you hear?'

'Surely sir, we've a right to live somewhere,' Connors tried again. 'Didn't Judge Walsh say so?'

'You've no right on the Ring Road site. That's an industrial zone. Factory land. Nobody is allowed to live there. Use your common sense.'

Wack MacDonald was staring at Fogarty's pink face, his fists clenched behind his back.

'Are you gonna leave us alone?' He held the man's watery eye. 'We're not gonna shift again.'

'You'll blasted well go if I say so!' The desk got a ringing flat-hander.

'Gammy feen,' young MacDonald muttered.

'The instructions I've given will stand. That's all I've got to say.' Then to end the meeting Fogarty added, 'Good day to you.'

Alone in his office, the Assistant City Manager flicked a switch on his bakelite intercom.

'Get me Housing Department, your Mr Molloy.'

As they tumbled down the steps outside, Brendan Casey was there to meet them. A photographer was getting pictures of the carts.

Doubled up in the gig, Maisie, suffering more urgent contractions, now begged Wack to hurry on with her to the Coombe laying-in hospital. Most of the other women had left already for O'Connell Bridge.

Angered by the failure of his City Hall mission, Johnny called out to Brendan, 'Wait a bit and I'll give you twice the story.'

He asked Johnny MacDonald and the Donohue brothers to go easy but drive the ponies, including his own, with the rest of the boys, back to Ballyfermot. Then he walked with Casey towards the Liffey telling him how the Travellers had been treated by the assistant city manager.

On the bridge, Eileen Ward and the other women were sitting with their children on the flattened cardboard.

'Get up off them boxes,' Johnny ordered. They got up and taking a pencil from the reporter he wrote several crude posters and handed them out to the children. Some Dubliners stopped to watch.

Johnny began to address the little crush. 'You may look on, sure. We're here every day in your faces. But when is Ireland goin' ter stop treatin' us like dirt?'

After minute, pleased with himself he remarked to Casey. 'Our biggest blow for freedom since the Battle of Augrim. Only you won't have heard of that one.'

Brendan Casey admitted as much and desiring to hear more suggested he and Connors adjourn to a bar. With Eileen Ward left in charge of the protest, they soon had pints drawn at a pub nearby on the north quays. The bridge was visible from the big plate window.

'I've little schooling,' Johnny said, offering Brendan his cigarettes. 'But me Old Daddy taught us a lot.'

'Where are you from? I mean the Connors.'

'There's different Connors. We're from Wicklow and Wexford. You've maybe visited Augrim in County Wicklow?'

Casey said he had not and neither had he heard of a battle there. He urged the Traveller to tell his story.

'Wasn't me Old Mammy Mary-Anne on the bridge at Aughrim when a big sergeant came along. Will ye get off this brudge he says and stop annoyin' the people. I will not says she until I have what I need. Well, the sergeant ups and slaps her a belt in the face and goes on his way.'

'And?'

'She went back to the woods there by the river where all the Travellers were stoppin' and the camp was in an uproar. The police were after burnin' all the tents and everythin' the people had. 'Twas the final last straw when me Old Mammy told them about the sergeant, so didn't all the Travellers go into Augrim and beat the police out of their own barracks. They destroyed the place and there was not a constable in it until they sent re-enforcements from Arklow town.'

'When did this happen?' asked Brendan, aware others in the bar were listening.

'I couldn't tell you the year. In me Old Daddy's time is all I know.' He took a sup of his pint and then said: 'Sure a few got locked up over it but we survived that battle. We're the survivors. We'll outlive yeas all.'

'D'you intend to clobber the Corporation?' asked Brendan, convinced now that Tinkers were, as their reputation had it, a violent lot.

'Sure, this is only a skirmish.' Johnny answered, keeping an eye out of the window. 'Your politicians, your policemen, your mobs of vigilantes. They may all come and go. Nobody can destroy us. Nobody can save us either. Sure, we just go on as ourselves.' He lifted his pint. 'We're the undestructibles.'

Brendan liked the Traveller's blarney, his philosophy, and was willing to drink even to what was to him the incomprehensible.

'And what if the Russians drop the bomb?' Brendan challenged in jest. 'Won't we all be dead on this island?'

'Ah, but the Travellers are everywhere,' retorted Johnny. 'Somewhere we'd survive. We may not win the war. But we can't lose it either. That's impossible.'

Out there on the bridge meanwhile, three guards were pressing through the people towards Eileen Ward. Boards went into the air over the stone parapet and sailing down into the river.

Through the window the two saw the Travelling woman rise up tall to face them.

1 'It's no good me not telling you,' she said, her hand on his, as if to keep him. 'I'm pregnant, Steve.'

They had come to Trinity College, the largely Protestant university in the centre of Dublin, hoping to meet students. But instead of hunting up helpers for St Christopher's, Denise had to her own surprise, suddenly let out the secret that she had been keeping to herself for days. Even as she told him part of her was in denial. There might be nothing to worry about. It could just be stress that had upset her monthly cycle. She glanced around the half-empty refectory and then leant her head nearer to his.

'I've missed my period. It's two weeks overdue. I think I'm pregnant.'

A panicky confusion swept over Steve as he grappled with the implications. Foolishly they had never taken precautions. Never even talked about it, and now it seemed the inevitable had happened.

'Didn't know about the ban on contraceptives did we,' he whispered, feeling like a fool.

'If I do have a baby are you going to make it legitimate?'

'Let's go somewhere else,' he said. 'This is too public.'

As if nothing had changed, he took her back to Trinity's vaulted stone entrance where they perused the college notice boards. The Chess Club, Poetry for People, The Fabian Society; there were scores of notices. Undergraduates in college scarves milled by. Aiken's eye went to a poster for the Trinity Players and they crossed the flag-stoned yard to a basement theatre. The inner door was closed. A note on it read Dress Rehearsal 4 pm. Aiken tried the handle and the door opened, and descending some stairs, the couple entered the unlit auditorium. Here was the seclusion they needed.

A thin line of light guided them to the back row. In the closed dark-ness, Steve could detect the slight odour of her body, now part of the most intimate experience of his life. Her fecundity was a powerful presence. Denise opened her coat and the warmth of the embrace they shared lent to both the relief and reassurance each craved in their new situation.

'I'm all for helping and I love doing the school,' she said quietly. 'Only we've got to get a proper place to live if I'm going to have a baby.'

She held his hand tight, trapped in her warm, unseen lap.

'I'll be able to pay off on the house. I'll have money soon. We can still do it up.'

'Oh, Steven. Face facts. That house is a dead loss.'

A silence descended between them. Aiken did not want to face facts. Nor was he being honest with her. The loss of the house was no loss to him. He wanted to stay with the Travellers. In this short time he had entered into the lives of the Travelling People, entered their world, and found with them something he needed; something he would not now give up. That much she sensed, and shared to a lesser degree, without him putting it into words. But she wished bitterly that for this once they could escape from the Ring Road. He had promised they would spend a whole day away from the encampment. They sat in the darkness in silent struggle, lost to each other.

'You relish defying authority don't you?' she said suddenly, her words echoing around the unseen walls.

'I have to challenge them, yes.'

'Why?'

'I don't know. But it's something I have to do.'

'You want to force the Corporation to take care of the Travellers?'

'Yeah.'

'Why, because nobody took care of you?'

'That goes for us both, Denny. Motherless aren't we.' Tentatively, he put his arm around her again.

'We're like the babes in the wood.' she said, happier with him now.

'Got to take care of each other. Got to take care of the baby, yeah?'

They kissed again with instantly returning ardency for each other.

'Let's get out of here,' she said, rising first. 'We can come back for the rehearsal.'

They came up the stairs from the theatre, frowning for a minute against the daylight. Then marching out the college entrance, reached the sanctuary of an island on College Green and still holding hands slumped together onto a bench.

Close by at the base of a statue lay a whiskered tramp, his trouser-bottoms tied with string. The sight of the old vagrant, asleep amid the noise of the traffic, amused them and touched their pity. Aiken placed a half-crown near his head.

'May bring us luck,' he said as they went on their way.

Pleased with themselves, they decided to go into a restaurant.

Rashly they were spending money set aside for a house payment to O'Keefe. But this was a day to be extravagant and they had never yet eaten out in Dublin.

For a time both concentrated on mouthfuls of the luxurious meal. An occasional swift survey of the room full of animated, civilised Irish diners, added to a sense of wellbeing. Aiken raised the wine bottle to replenish their glasses, giving her an inquiring sideways look. She dismissed the quizzing with a small shrug and sunk closer to him on the padded bench. She would keep now to simple, uncomplicated body language.

A waiter removed their plates and brought them the bill.

'I've somewhere else I want to take you, Denny,' he said, wanting to be in charge.

He led the way to the elegant shops in nearby Grafton Street and let their affluence work its influence on her. Happily window-gazing, she was anticipating a surprise when they halted at the lamplit window of a jeweller's shop. Steve jolted her arm and pointed. Shining under a spotlight were rows of wedding rings on velvet trays. For a second perplexed, she glanced up smiling into his face. He had no words to say but gave her a little signal with his eyebrows.

'You want me to wear a wedding ring?'

Aiken nodded his head. 'Both of us.'

'But without being married?' She smiled, a little mocking smile, but was pleased.

They went into the shop. They came out laughing, the rings in little boxes in his pocket. They sashayed all the way down to the quays at O'Connell Bridge. An effervescent, carefree mood bore them across the broad bridge, now devoid of Travellers, and along the north embankment where together they walked out pluckily onto the boards of the humpbacked Halfpenny Bridge. Here the young couple stopped, in the middle of the cast-iron structure, eyes wandering for a while down the long vista of Georgian buildings, broken only by the massive, whitish stone of the Four Courts. Dublin looked magnificent under its eighteenth-century mantle.

Below the bridge slid the murky, grease-laden waters of the Liffey. On the ebb tide, the river was moving fast. A barge floated down from the Guinness wharf, noiseless in its ongoing to the bay. Seagulls swirled above, crying over them.

Their hands lay on the chill iron. An icy draught blew on their backs. They looked at each other. What they would do and say now would matter supremely. It would matter for the rest of their lives.

'Keep this true,' said Aiken, his voice earnest. 'I mean us to stay together.'

He slid the ring onto her finger. She took his from the box. He looked so unexpectedly anxious. She did her best to meet his eyes.

'Steve, I won't ever hurt you,' she said, out of some spontaneous response to what she saw in his face.

Solemnly he donned the gold ring and they kissed with cold lips.

2 When they got back to the Trinity Players Theatre the stage was brilliantly lit up. Resuming their place at the rear they noticed that further along the wall a second couple had taken seats. A scattering of other students were intent on the intermittent entertainment of the dress rehearsal.

Hearing the director call a break, Aiken slid along the row and asked for a light. As he lit up, the couples introduced themselves.

'I'm Andrew Meachen. This is my wife Tracey. We're from Minnesota.' The man, in his thirties, smiled through a full chestnut beard. Some handshaking followed, complicated by the cigarettes.

'May we talk to you?' said Denise, encouraged to know they were Americans. She liked the look of Tracey, a blonde, heavy-breasted woman only too ready to be friendly.

After a few minutes of conversation the wife said: 'I admire you. You're real Bohemians going off to live with the Gypsies.'

'Not Gypsies most of them, Irish Travellers,' Steve corrected, not wanting her to be frivolous.

They were reduced to whispering as the actors were called back to the stage. Andrew Meachen suggested the four of them go somewhere else and they crept out together as if already joined by some conspiratorial bond. In the Americans' red Ford station-wagon they rode the short distance to Donohue's, a popular singing pub. The two women sat chatting with their backs to the dark woodwork under a large mirror while the men fetched orders from the bar.

'I'd be fascinated to hear some Tinker music. I heard they have great musicians,' said Andrew, his brown eyes shining and benign.

But Aiken looked at him dubiously and for the moment said nothing. A kind of shame had come over him about himself and the Travellers. Since hearing Denise might be pregnant he was not sure he had his priorities right after all. Nor could he be altogether comfortable with these strangers, older than him and better off. He wondered if Andrew had done his military service. So many Americans were in Vietnam.

'There's a lot happening,' he explained, wanting them to understand this was not about folk music. 'We could be evicted any day.'

'We saw the children with the posters on O'Connell Bridge,' said Tracey. 'Did you organise that?'

'They organised that themselves,' replied Aiken, with some satisfaction.

'Nobody was arrested,' Denise told the American girl. 'They let the women off with a caution. I think they wanted to stop the begging more than the protest.'

Wide-eyed on hearing of the makeshift school, Tracey Meachen at once expressed a wish to help. She was very keen to come to the rescue of the handicapped girl and of the ragged children she had seen on the bridge.

'I've trained as a Montessori teacher,' she said, swinging back her long blonde hair. 'I've not much experience but I definitely want to be part of this, if you'll let me.'

Andrew said he was doing his doctorate degree in Irish folklore and would like to meet some musicians. He would include something about the Tinkers in his thesis.

'When could you start?' Denise asked Tracey.

'Is tomorrow soon enough?'

There was pause and then they all laughed together in relief as if some formality between them had been completed.

Aiken sat back now content to let the talk go on without him. The music started and he listened to the raucous voice of Luke Kelly and the plunk-plunk-plunk of Barney McKenna's banjo. The Dubliners sung some rebel songs, which re-aroused in the Englishman his spirit of defiance. He had a youthful desire to do battle with the enemy and drive them from the field. He knew this urge was an irresponsible one but it felt good. It tasted good like the black stout he was swallowing.

Denise was reminded of those carefree evenings when she had sang at the folk club back in Ipswich. The stump of her leg was sore from all the walking but she knew the Americans would drive them up to Ballyfermot. In Tracey she believed she had a new friend.

She was drowsing on Tracey's shoulder in the back seat as the station wagon drew up outside the house in Irwin Street. The two men got out to look it over.

'Look what the Corporation has nailed to my door,' said Aiken, pointing to a large new notice:

Dangerous Building. Keep Out.

'Someone said they would get me,' he told Andrew, not hiding his bravado. He cared nothing at this moment about the Corporation's hostility nor the unexpected and final end to any possibility of moving back to live at Irwin Street. He did not however relish telling Denise, who was now asleep in the car.

Denise came to herself only when they arrived at the open gate of the benighted camp, forlorn and silent. She awoke to hear the American girl exclaim:

'God, is this where you live!'

3 The Leyland lorry, breaking ominously through the fog on the canal bridge, slowed and shuddered to a halt at the roadside. The cab door opened and the bulk of Bill Redmond ponderously descended and went out of sight.

Ever since getting up, Pat Donohue had been listening for the sound of motor-lorries and now feared Redmond's arrival signalled the start of the eviction. The Corporation bailiff had cruised by often, each time looking peevishly towards the caravans. He had been keeping a count. Now it was Tuesday morning, one of those days on which the Moped Man, risking his job, had sworn the Corporation would come.

The old Traveller was wondering what the man could be doing, if not taking a leak, when Bill re-emerged and started across the road. In the crook of his thick sleeve wriggled one of Pat's black puppies.

Redmond had scooped up the runaway from the gutter and was taking the trouble to return it.

Pat, sweating under his shirt, greeted Bill over the fence.

'That's surely your good deed for the day,' he called, scrutinising the big man as he approached.

'Keep 'em in the field won't you', Redmond advised in his brusque manner, unhooking the puppy's claws and handing him over the hedge.

Pat's lurcher bitch was jumping excitedly at her master's waist.

'He's after wanderin' away there,' the old man excused himself.

'You'd best all of you be wanderin' off,' Redmond muttered, about to turn away.

'You can have him if you like,' Pat said, thinking to detain and question the Corporation bailiff.

'Too small sure,' answered the other, already waddling away.

Old Pat raised his voice, 'You're welcome to the pup, honest to God.'

Not bothering to face around, Big Bill lifted his hand dismissing the offer. He recrossed the road, the cab door slammed and with a grind of gears the lorry pulled away.

Rebuffed, Pat stared after it, his face still filled with surprise. He concluded there had been a delay; perhaps a full postponement of the eviction. But the Travellers still had to worry about tomorrow. Eventually he turned and walked up the misty field. The bitch came too, foolishly wagging her tail. Giving the puppy to Denise would be his consolation.

'I won't take it from its mother,' the English girl insisted from the caravan door.

'Keep him for a while anyways,' Pat urged, lifting the little thing to her and smiling a winsome, crooked smile. He was old and grizzled.

Pat had brought good news and she agreed to mind the pup for an hour before school opened. It quivered on her lap, snuffling its wet nose over her skirt. In her present belligerent mood this babyish interest upset her and she put the puppy on the floor with a saucer of bread and milk, where it lapped hungrily, stepping into the food in its trembling haste.

Ignoring the puppy's antics, Denise took up a mirror and was examining her face. Seeing a small pimple on her forehead she attacked it with a vicious squeeze. Then peering absently at her reflection wondered whether bad blood might be a sign of pregnancy. She commenced examining the whites of her wide stretched eyes but for what she did not know.

Since waking she had done nothing but worry about the growing possibility that she was pregnant. What peeved her was that she had just let Steve leave without sharing her feelings with him.

The puppy, scampering away impetuously from the spilled saucer, bumped into her metal foot. It lay flat and started to whine. Looking down at it, Denise could not suppress a qualmish sympathy. Still displeased, she bent and fondled its woolly head, aware as she did so of the gold ring hanging heavily on her finger. For the first time giving the pup her full attention, she caressed its coat with slow, deliberate strokes. The pup responded, cocking up its rear and pointing its sharp little tail. Now, feeling the soft shivering warmth of this small, living animal she began to realise she might like being a mother.

But a negative thought then made her leave off stroking the pup. Steve loved her, of that she was sure, but it did not qualify him for becoming a dad. He was just not formed enough in himself for the responsibility. For all his talk and ambition, he was a needy thing, sometimes, like this mother-deprived pup. So her heart closed and she hoped, against her own nature, that she was not carrying his child.

She picked up the hand-mirror again. But having stared once more at her face, a little hatefully, she tossed it back into the basket. Coming to Ireland – a great escapade! All the blame she took upon herself. What a futile talk they had had last night. Ought they now to abstain? They were young and inflammable. She let out a groan. She could have kicked the puppy. She wished she knew, for sure, whether or not she had conceived. Ignorance had become her greatest torment.

4   Seeing the flag clinging limply to its pole over the wooden building in the midst of the Ring Road field, the American teacher hurried up the land in her galoshes and knocked on the door. The noise from inside added to her first-day nerves. But after a short wait, aware of being watched by the camp, she pushed the door and let herself in.

A classroom confronted her which at the front seethed with children while at the back a homemade stove, presently neglected, roared hotly and was leaking smoke. Seeing Denise, she raised a hand, expecting a greeting, but the other was too absorbed with her clamorous pupils. The children, out of their desks and on their feet, were working themselves up. They had shut the English girl into a tiny space close to the blackboard, and were bellowing out letters of the alphabet while Denise, on tiptoe, chalked them up.

Tracey continued to hesitate, hands over her ears, bewildered and grinning stupidly. For an age nobody seemed to notice her there.

She helped out, the best she could, for the remainder of the morning before the two women retreated together to the caravan.

While water boiled on the miniature stove, Tracey unwrapped some salami sandwiches, delicatessen food which Denise was glad to share.

Everything they did in the cramped space was of necessity at close quarters. Denise liked her new friend's broad, matronly figure, now leaning so comfortably close. The American woman, unaware of her own attraction, did not reciprocate on that physical level. Forced into proximity, she shied a little from the metal leg. However, the intimacy of the snug interior helped create a comradeship between them and they talked without inhibition..

'Don't you find these children too much sometimes? They've no discipline at all,' Tracey asked, truly curious.

'The kids, the noise. It's bloody impossible,' her friend answered. 'But this morning, I don't know, I've been in such a horrible state of mind and they take me right out of myself.'

Needing a confidante, Denise told Tracey what was bothering her. She showed her the wedding ring, candidly relating the story behind it.

'What will Steve say if you definitely are having a baby?' Tracey asked coolly.

'He says it's okay,' Denise answered and added wryly. 'I can see he only half means it though.'

There was a silence which Tracey broke in a gleeful voice saying that she and Andy were delaying having children. They had gone to Belfast where Tracey had been fitted with a diaphragm at a family planning clinic.

'That's what I should do – or should have done,' Denise said quickly, rising to fill their mugs. She felt inferior.

They sipped the hot coffee and spoke of plans for the school. Tracey talked about the Montessori method and how suitable it might be for the Ring Road children.

Steve came back loaded down with groceries. Denise took the large raffia basket and grasped from him a bale of peat briquettes. He perched himself awkwardly beside her, and reached for the leftover food. Seeing their glances meet now and again, he was ill at ease and thought the two women had formed a conspiracy.

'I hear you may become a father,' the American said, catching him unprepared.

Aiken felt himself reddening like a boy. He darted a resentful look at her.

'We don't know for sure,' he said stiffly. 'Denise hasn't been to a doctor yet.'

'And what if she is?' Tracey insisted, covertly pleased with her own impudence.

'I'll feel great,' he said, feeling only embarrassment.

Denise listened to this exchange, subtly increasing the pressure of her knee against his thigh. Tracey had cut to the point but she could communicate with her mate on a more carnal level.

'I couldn't rear a child in a place like this though,' Denise threw in, encouraged by the American's straight talking.

'Of course not,' Steve rejoined, defending himself against both the women.

Catlin Connors put her head in the door to say the afternoon class was waiting and kicking up a row. 'Maisie had her baby last night – a boy,' she told them cheerily, before disappearing back down the steps.

The two young women went back to the school, leaving Aiken alone with his typewriter. Unable to work, he lay brooding on the dishevelled bed. He could not fathom why he felt so bothered. It was not that she might be pregnant, might have a baby. That was still almost an abstract and far in the future. Finally it came to him. Denny, whether she was aware of it or not, was already playing the mother. My God, she was garnering to herself all the rights, privileges and prerogatives of child-bearing and motherhood. And Tracey Meachen had a big stake in this. The American was egging her on. The male in him had became suddenly wary of their female powers. He wanted to stick with the Travellers on this field. Here with them, he was coming to believe, might lie his whole life's destiny. He had convinced himself it was only with them he could follow a new-found road, his true path. Yet he loved Denny and would willing die for her. He recalled when she had first arrived, just a month ago; had lain innocently asleep in this bed. The sight of Denny, the magic presence of her, had made him want to protect her forever. It had nothing to do with her handicap. No, her courage cancelled that out. Her sheer loveliness drew him to her. But now there was a power in her eyes which laid claim to him in a way he resented. He fantasised her swelling with child, his child. The picture was both gross and alluring.

For relief, Aiken got off the bed and occupied himself tidying up the caravan. While putting things away, his Gypsy peg-knife came to hand. Burdened with so many unresolved feelings, and though not usually superstitious, he squatted on the floorboards and gave the knife a spin. If it stopped pointing at the bed, his destiny was with Denny; if towards the door, well, he could not bring himself to think he would leave her but it would mean he must stay with the Travellers. He watched the knife slow and slide to a halt. The blade pointed at the fire.

More troubled, he picked up the knife and putting it aside, went to join the women and children in the school. He could no longer bear his own company.

1 'Me ma has been taken,' said Patrick Ward solemnly, hanging onto the school-hut door. He looked up at her out of a tear-stained face.

Denise bent over the distraught boy, pushing him gently ahead.

'What's happened, Patrick?' she asked when they were in the empty classroom.

'I should've been taken meself but I ran off.' Patrick's eyes were round with anxiety. He was on the edge of crying again now that he was in sympathetic hands.

'I couldn't help her. I couldn't do nothin'.'

'I believe you,' said Denise, wondering what was coming. Her own concerns were temporarily eclipsed.

'One of the guards hit me a belt in the back.'

The American teacher, who was helping out on the school's fifth day, stood shaking her head. She could not believe what she was hearing.

'What happened to your mother?' Denise coaxed.

Exhausted, the boy slumped into one of the desks, then raising his head looked from one to the other.

'Let me tell you first', he implored, more agitated. 'I was with me ma in O'Connell Street. We weren't on the brudge. We weren't doin' nothin' only lookin' at the people. Didn't we go on then into the market to get the spuds and these two shayds came up behind us. The first I knew I got a clout in the back. I took that much of a frit I ran off. When I went back to look for me ma she was gone. She'd been taken. I know they have her locked up somewhere. I just had sixpence to get home on the bus.'

Tracey guessed he was hungry and fetched out a sandwich.

'Thanks,' he murmured and took a bite quickly.

'Me ma was taken in Moore Street. She weren't on the brudge,' Patrick repeated, distressed.

There were other children at the door now waiting for the afternoon class. When Tracey went to let them back in she came face to face with Joe Donohue. He had brought his son Joey, his hair combed and in clean Wellington boots.

'You've room for one more, I hope miss,' he said civilly, seeing the American close-up for the first time.

Tracey bent towards Joey, saying: 'Where have you been all the week?' Then to the father, 'Don't you have other children?'

'The others have jobs to do, miss', he answered, a little ruffled. She was not awarding him the deference he expected.

As Joey was taken from him, Donohue said, 'I'd half a mind not to let you have this one.'

'Why?' said Tracey, annoyed.

'You can't have a school in Ireland without there be religion in it.'

Tracey, rather troubled by this remark, let him go without attempting a reply.

Meanwhile, Patrick lingered on the fringes of the class, mournful and alone. After a while, Denise sent him to bring more wood for the stove, believing he would be better occupied with something useful. Soon the schoolroom warmed up again. The steel-drum brazier, fed with sticks, threw out a tremendous heat.

Tracey was introducing her teaching materials to some of the girls. They liked the Cuisenaire Rods, which she let them play with for a while before starting lessons in addition and subtraction.

There were not enough sets of the coloured rods for the boys and they complained.

'I'll fetch me dad's anvil if you like,' Patrick offered, quite cheered up. 'I've watched him makin' yokes. I could teach 'em somepun.'

Denise was pleased with this initiative but decided the hammering would be too loud. Instead she suggested a different lesson. Paddy went around the field with little Joey Donohue and they came back with armloads of scrap metal. Put in charge of some smaller boys, Patrick began to teach them to identify and sort the different pieces.

'This is ali,' he told them, showing them aluminium. 'You can lift a whole world of it with one hand.'

Then he bent the rod to demonstrate how soft the metal was.

They learnt the different values of copper, lead, zinc, brass, nickel and other alloys. How much a stone, a hundredweight, would fetch at Bermingham's yard. They all had fathers and uncles in the scrap trade and when they reached Patrick's age would be helping out.

This orderly instruction however did not last long.

Two of the boys gave up listening to Paddy and crouching on their knees in a corner, started breaking some cast-iron. The hammer blows screeched on the dull, friable iron, liberating a salvo of sparks.

The other boys gathered round and the hot sparks hopped dangerously in the air between their heads.

Denise wanted to ignore the noise, reluctant to bring an end to Patrick's efforts. But Tracey had already lost patience.

'Stop that! You're disrupting everyone else.'

The heads bobbing near the floor, intent on the work, took no notice of her command. Tracey looked on, helpless, until distracted by the appearance of a woman in the doorway. She was waving a stick in one hand and had a boy grasped in the other.

'I'll hit you such a beatin',' the woman was shouting at him, almost lifting the boy from the ground by the collar of his outsized jacket.

'Don't hurt him on my account,' Denise called. She did not recognise the woman but was already acquainted with the boy. 'We let them run off their energy outside.'

Everyone stopped what they were doing and watched the confrontation. But it was quickly over.

'Lord, you won't get them teached that way,' the mother said, quieter now, only looking at the two young woman in dismay. She released her boy and he ran away.

The children saw that the teachers in the Travellers' school had meant what they said; they were free to come and go as they wished. Denise Hanley had also told them that they owned the school, a concept no-one could truly grasp, including herself. However, a rough and ready class self-management was beginning to evolve with a few of the older pupils imposing restraints on the disruptive ones. St Christopher's was swiftly taking on a life of its own, far different from the regime at Our Lady of the Angels Elementary.

But this was just a little pioneering experiment in a hut. Denise also saw that the American teacher, trained for the job, would soon impose her own scheme of things. Only it gave her a secret satisfaction to know she would always be closer to the Travellers than Tracey because she was living with them and shared their privations.

There was one necessity to which the crippled English girl could not adjust. Denise had watched the first afternoon the comings and goings from the back hedges; the sight of others squatting among the nettles was rather comic. The leg would not allow her to hunker down easily, so it took some courage to walk to the rear of the field herself and go into those hedges, aware that everyone knew her business.

She and Steve had gone through the ritual the last few evenings but now the camp had grown larger the hazards were increasing. The ditches stunk and the ground defied safe footfall. The host of hardy children ran free, the smallest half-naked, defecating where they pleased.

'I can't just hop out in the night when I need to,' Denise told Tracey, who so far had managed to wait until she got home.

2 Alerted to Patrick Ward's crisis during the afternoon, Aiken set off to go to Kilmainham court. He would be able to find out from the court if Eileen Ward had been listed. But on reaching the camp gate he was surprised to see Andrew Meachen's red station wagon still on the road outside.

He guessed the American had been invited into Pat's hut and followed him there, hoping to get a lift.

When he entered, Old Pat, his brother Joe and Andrew were engrossed in conversation around the table. The room was full of tobacco smoke.

'I'd say Monsignor McQuaid might get involved.' Andrew was telling the Donohue brothers. 'I hear there's little the archbishop hasn't got his fingers in.' When he saw Aiken he said, 'We're just saying the Church ought to be helping.'

'Always talk to the top man,' said Joe. Then looking disparagingly at the Englishman: 'I suppose you might be a Protestant, young man.'

'I'm not anything,' Steve responded. 'We're just trying to teach the three Rs.'

'Has anyone approached the local priest?' Andrew asked.

'We was goin' to Mass in Ballyfermot one time,' said Old Pat, knocking the doddle out of his pipe on the side of the table. 'They'd only have us standing at the back and we'd have to leave pretty sharp.'

'I know for a fact the Pope is takin' an interest in Gypsies,' said Joe, who had been reading the Catholic Standard. 'In Italy, sure, they have chaplains just for the Travellers.'

He got up to leave.

'There was a great priest in Mullingar one time,' Pat put in, letting his brother pass.

When the Gaffer had gone Pat said, 'This man has the best Virginia tobacco.'

Andrew, taking a pouch from his pocket laid it on the table. 'You can finish this for me. I have a fresh tin at home.'

'You're a decent fella,' said the old Traveller, giving a gummy smile.

Aiken was keen to go on to Kilmainham and broke in to say: 'Paddy Ward's mother was arrested today. She might have come up at Kilmainham court.'

Andrew got up at once and Pat, sorry to lose his visitor, cleared the cups from the table.

'The guards are too hard on the women,' Pat said. 'Sure what else can they do only go around the houses or stand on O'Connell Bridge. The hawkin' is all played out. Nobody wants to buy a peg or a pot from a Tinker no more.'

'Well,' said Andrew, 'From what I've seen here you've plenty of the pioneering spirit. This is like the Wild West, the horses and the covered wagons and cooking on the open fires.'

On the way to Kilmainham, Meachen confided to Aiken: 'I like old Pat's language and his manners. He's a brilliant old man.'

When they got to the court Aiken searched the lists only to find

Eileen Ward's name was not on it. Andrew waited while Steve phoned Brendan Carey. No Ward had appeared at the other courts and they brought this news back to the Ring Road. The school was finishing for the day. Patrick Ward took his mother's absence with stoic resignation. He lingered on with the teachers. He had nothing to go back to but a poor shack full of hungry siblings.

3 'Why don't you come home with me today?' Tracey said to Denise as they closed up the school. 'Have a bath and a rest.'

'I suppose I could,' Denise answered, half reluctant to leave the camp at this time of danger. 'Yes, I would like a break.'

She went to the wagon to tell Steve. He had the stove going and was about to cook something. He immediately wanted to come.

While Tracey waited, Paddy Ward sidled around the corner of the school and stood dumbly by the wall. Hiding behind him was a girl a little under his height, her crown of black hair visible.

'School's finished now, Patrick. You know that,' said Tracey. 'You two can come tomorrow.'

'Mi sister,' said Patrick, falteringly. 'She mayn't come. She's to mind the littluns while me ma's gone.'

Nan came out from behind her brother and stood in bare feet before the American woman. In her arms, swaddled in a shawl, lay a young infant. The girl looked tired and hungry.

All three stared at each other, the dire message conveyed without a word spoken. Having no more food with her, Tracey did not know what to do.

'Can I give you some money?' she offered, starting to feel in her coat pocket.

'The shops'll be shut,' said Patrick.

But the girl stepped closer, holding the child a little higher. Tracey saw now that it was a baby of about twelve months.

At that moment Denise returned with Steve. After a quick explanation, they all went back to Steve's wagon, Nan loping along in the rear with her bundle. Denise climbed the steps and filled one of her baskets with the food Steve had been about to prepare, together with some bread and a few other items.

Nan took the basket and looked into it. Then turning her large dark eyes on the English girl, she said softly. 'Please, do you not have a drop of milk you can give me for the baby?'

The two women realised at once the predicament the girl was in. The baby would be crying all night if milk could not be found.

'Wait,' said Denise. 'I'll see what I can do.' And she hastened away towards the MacDonalds, reluctant to make such a request at their fire but no knowing who else to turn to.

'I'll bring milk tomorrow,' Tracey told the girl as they waited, knowing it was not much of an offer at this moment.

Denise came back with a half-full milk bottle and gave it to Patrick to carry. He had already taken charge of the basket.

'You'll have to put some water with that,' she told Nan. 'He looks big enough to eat some bread soaked in milk.'

'I will try him,' said Nan, attempting a smile and rocking the child now as he started to stir. 'His name is Larry.'

They watched the two young ones walk off towards the far trees and the row of huts. Dusk had closed in now and the campfires gave out a localised glow. In a few open wagon doors, oil-lamps had been lit and candles shot little glimmering rays from the low, hooded tents. Around these spots of illumination darkness was quickly settling.

At the Meachens' spacious flat on St Stephen's Green Denise went straight to the bathroom and locked herself in. She stayed in the bath a long time, soaking her stump. Her backlog of dirty washing, including stump socks, jogged in a washing machine close by.

The two men lounged in opposite armchairs in the big drawing room from which tall Georgian windows overlooked the well-lit park. Aiken took some press cuttings from his pocket and passed them to the American.

'This isn't likely to change anything,' said Andrew, looking at a picture of the O'Connell Bridge protest. 'It's all about who you know here, contacts and quiet diplomacy. Demonstrations will never do it.'

'I don't agree.' Steve responded. 'People feel empowered by standing up for themselves. Doing it for them is pure paternalism.'

'Ireland is run on paternalism. You must know that. No neat division here between Church and State. The Church has the last say every time.

Aiken shrugged, unable to argue against the facts but feeling uncomfortable with about Meachen's views.

Tracey brought in food and sitting them at the dining table said to Denise, 'Would you like to see my doctor?'

'I've got to know haven't I', Denise replied, her hair wet and a little shy in front of Andrew.

'Having a baby, would that affect your handicap?' Tracey asked.

'I've been told walking on this leg will gradually push my pelvis out of line,' she answered. 'I could end up in a wheelchair. So yes, the extra weight of a baby, a full term baby, would probably be a strain.'

'You're remarkable,' said the other. 'I wouldn't be as brave as you.'

'Just facing reality,' Denise responded. 'What else can you do?'

'There's no-one with more courage than Denny,' Steve put in, catching her eye.

The two women went on talking about pregnancy and having children. Hearing them gave Aiken a strange thrill. He felt a new and poignant blood-bond with Denise. When the subject changed to the Travellers his composure returned and he joined in a conversation about what had happened to Patrick and Eileen Ward and how Nan had been left to act as mother to her little siblings.

'You men, the both of you,' said Tracey, looking at her husband as she cleared away. 'You say the Travellers have a great way of life. But I don't see that. You have to admit it must have gone downhill for this last generation.'

'Johnny Connors says the life is far different in England,' Steve explained. 'He says they're all going around in trucks and modern caravans and some Travellers there make good money.'

'Maybe,' Tracey answered. 'But here they're just stubbornly hanging on to more or less nothing. It's the children I'm thinking of.'

Although he did not say so, Aiken felt her thinking was dominated by notions of rescue. It was clear she wanted the Travellers to give up their way of life and settle in houses. In this she had the zeal of a New England missionary.

Alone in the kitchen, Andrew said to his wife, 'Put some food together for the Ward children. Denise can take it with her now.'

It was nine o' clock when Andrew brought them back to Ballyfermot. Before they could get out of the station wagon, Old Pat emerged from the gate and approached them like a shadow.

'Your Moped Man has been again,' he said softly into the car window. 'The Corporation is comin' in the mornin'.'

'But he was wrong the first time,' Steve quibbled, hoping there might be more delay.

'I asked him why they had not come afore,' Pat answered. 'He said some of the men were not willin' for the job after what has been in the papers. The top people got a frit from the protest. But they've got the men now and they'll be comin' for sure.'

'Right then,' said Aiken. 'Can you and the boys get a fire built at the gate?' Then winding up the window he asked Andrew to turn around and drive to a phone box near the Gala.

As they drove away again, Pat stood back in the gateway, a lone guard over the camp. Denise sat hunched and silent on the back seat with Tracey. She reached for her friend's hand. This is what Steve cares about, she thought, resentful of his enthusiasm for the coming fight.

From outside the cinema, Aiken rang Carey and alerted him to the eviction. Carey had still heard nothing about Eileen Ward. A woman answered when Aiken called Liam Grady.

'Senator Grady is not home yet,' she said. 'Would there be a message?'

'Tell him they're evicting us from the Ring Road tomorrow,' said Aiken. Then raising his voice he repeated, 'Evicting us. Please tell him when he comes in.'

'Oh dear. I am sorry. What will happen to the school?'

'We don't know,' said Aiken, distressed. 'Ask him to be there if he can will you?'

On returning to the Ring Road, they found Pat Donohue and his sons piling wood and kindling near the entrance so that a fire could be lit first thing.

When the Meachens had gone, Denise felt coldly exposed in the doomed camp. The two went forward slowly, stumbling often on the bumpy, sodden turf, with Steve carrying a box of food that included bottles of milk. At this moment, Denise could hardly credit that she was here by her own choice. Although the caravan, next to Pop's Johnny's, must be waiting ahead, nothing seemed to be where it should. Through a silvery hole in the clouds, faint stars shed a distant light, insufficient to guide them. A chill, damp draught blew up from the canal. Soon they came to the dying remains of the MacDonald's fire. The wagons, including their own, were somewhere to the left beyond. Now the school loomed up just to the right. From the window a pale light shone out onto the wall of darkness. Together, they altered direction to investigate.

Through the window they could see children at the desks. Candles throwing weird shadows, dramatised their ghostly presence. In front of the others, her upper body illuminated, stood Kitty Connors. She was pretending to read from a book held between the flickering rings of light. Her childish voice floated like a lullaby out into the night.

The English girl, peeping in on this scene, fell at once under its spell. To these children she could relate; here too she belonged. Quietly pushing open the door and hoping not to disturb the children the two stood still. But seeing them in the shadows, Kitty let down the book as if caught at some mischief. A row of little faces, eyes wide, wondering, peered at them in the candlelight.

'We're only after playin' at school,' Kitty explained, apologetically, giving a husky laugh.

Denise went forward and hugged the girl, who had been her chief help.

'Time for bed all you little ones,' she crooned over them, ushering them out and watching their small, neat bodies file through the door.

Here were her school and her children, she thought, with an unexpected hunger in her womb.

While the children dispersed in the dark across the field, she and Steve carried the milk to Nan's hut. Her mother had not returned.

Eileen Ward had spent yesterday morning calling, following a round of better-class houses. Getting a sight of her burned face some closed the door on her, others took pity. Whatever way it had gone, by noon she had barely seventeen shillings collected. Most of the clothes people had given her were useless and she had discarded them along the way. A half loaf of stale bread also went into a dustbin. Carrying her newest baby in her shawl, a string bag in one hand and with Paddy at her side, she was tired and could not bother with inferior trifles. Bringing home sound food and cash was the essential part of the task.

Her Galway shawl over her head as protection against the sudden dousing rain, Eileen walked now in poor spirits up O'Connell Street. She was heading towards the open-air market in Moore Street where she could get a cheap cut of meat from one of the butcher' stalls and all the vegetables she and Patrick could carry.

Patrick, his face pinched with cold and boredom, trailed along wearily beside this mother. His nose was running.

'Can't we stop a bit, Ma?' he begged her, pulling on the fringes of her shawl.

They sat down in a doorway out of the rain. Eileen gave breast to the baby, hardly raising her eyes to the passers-by. Her string bag was at her side.

Two nuns, swaddled black creatures belonging to the Little Sisters of Charity, stood further along holding out their collection tins. They had taken up a position on the corner at the entrance to the fruit and vegetable market, where the crowd was thickest. One held up a large black umbrella.

Patrick glimpsed them through the moving crowd and watched how the people dropped coins into the tins. He jogged his mother's arm and pointed.

'Look, ma, how they get the gred!' he exclaimed in his high boy's voice.

'They're allowed,' his mother said patiently. But her heavy eyebrows knit tight and she observed the nuns with envy.

Patrick wiped his nose on his jacket sleeve. He wished the gaigin was as easy as that for his ma. He wished he could help. On a bold impulse, he touched and tugged at a man's coat. The man looked down at him through his glasses.

'Give us a penny, mister,' said Patrick, squinting up in the rain, holding his hand out.

The man got out change and pressed sixpence into the boy's hand, smiling thinly and hurrying on. Patrick gave the coin to his mother and she let out a low laugh of appreciation.

'But don't be doin' it again,' she cautioned, her brown face creased and serious.

'Why not?' Patrick asked.

'Because we'll be taken over it,' she told him earnestly. 'They knows we was on the brudge afore. They knows yer ma too well.'

At the same time it was tempting to make up the pound she needed there in the street. And suddenly she changed her mind.

'Alright Paddy, if ye want to help.'

She rose carefully to her feet, adjusted the shawl and took up the bag of food. The baby felt heavy after all the walking. 'We'll walk on so and you can see what you can get. Only watch for the shayds d'you hear?'

Eileen calculated they would be safer asking as the two of them moved along. It was less conspicuous. They could also reach the market. For a few minutes Patrick dropped back behind her ample skirt, importuning everybody who came his way. The coins began to weigh in his jacket pocket.

Eileen was holding out her hand too, bending in a supplicating manner. Her scarred face wore a blank, callous expression that masked her real feelings.

In the market two guards loitered on the look out for pilferers. They had concealed themselves in a shop doorway, in their belted raincoats, heads above the passers-by. They spotted the Tinker woman and the boy, and watched them slyly. As soon as it became apparent they were begging, the two stepped down into the street.

Patrick felt a blow on his back. He lurched forward towards his mother giving a hopeless little cry as he ran against her. Eileen turned quickly.

'Run, son!' she said, putting the bag between Paddy and the first policeman. She stood still, stricken but determined, her body a rock blocking the way. In seconds Paddy was in a side alley and out of sight.

Not prepared to humiliate themselves with a chase after a small boy through the market, the two guards shepherded Eileen into another side street. The party progressed in silence through wet back ways until the river was reached. Close by the Four Courts, with their tall dome and towers, the dark, malevolent Bridewell, an old stone lock-up and police station, awaited them.

The ancient studded door half opened to receive the four. Eileen Ward, frowning under the electric light, stood by resignedly, gently jogging the babe for mutual comfort. The two guards, ignoring her, were talking over the counter to the duty sergeant.

Eileen was ordered to hand over her bag and put out all her loose belongings. The change clanked on the counter, making a small, precious spread. With the coins Paddy had given her, she had almost twenty-five shillings in silver and copper. The sergeant counted the money and scooped it into an envelope, together with her hair comb. The bag also disappeared behind the counter. Then she was led upstairs to the cells. She stiffened, holding tight to her baby, as the iron door slammed on them.

Then the bitterness spilled out.

'I told you, Paddy. Now we're done,' she said to herself, blaming her absent son.

She felt broken and lost, sinking into a depth of misery. Then she reminded herself that they would give her something to eat soon.

There was a single steel cot-bed with a mattress on it. In a corner a white toilet bowl gleamed obscenely. Otherwise the cell was bare. Graffiti had been scratched into the walls as high as a man could reach. She sat on the bed, feeding her baby. Bless her, she thought, not a peep out of her all day and she's no idea where we are.

After a long interval the light went on. Near the ceiling a grilled window let in the street noises. Eileen lay in her damp clothes on the narrow bed. The baby, after crying a little, slept innocently against her breast. The two were covered only by a blanket and her spread shawl.

In the night Eileen awoke several times. The light was out and the room colder, the smell of mildew and urine more pronounced.

No-one bothered with her until morning. About six the light came back on. A while later the door was opened. An old uniformed officer came in, his craggy face made an almost pleasant smile.

'You'll be gettin' cocoa shortly,' he called from the threshold, and ambled away leaving the door ajar. Eileen moved herself stiffly. Then she got off the bed, leaving the baby asleep, and used the toilet. It was a novelty.

She drank the hot, watery cocoa and got a piece of bread and margarine. Then, following his jangling keys, she was taken down-stairs by the elderly lock-up man. There Eileen was confronted by a different duty officer. Familiar with the police routine, she expected now to be charged and booked. She would be up before the justice this morning and most likely go to prison. This thought numbed her. But she fretted for Paddy and Nan, and the small ones left with Mikey. The babe, hugged close to her body, must any road stay with her.

'Well, woman out you go, you,' the broad-chested guard told her briskly, making large eyes and pointing his pen towards the huge outer door. 'Go on, get out of here!'

It took the Travelling woman a moment to realise she was being released. The inset door had now been opened. She was free to go.

She took a step forward and then turning sharply to the counter, her face filling with anger, she said, 'What about me money? I had twenty-five shillings took off me here yesterday.'

'Ill-gotten gains, woman. You forfeit that.' The officer flashed a big, false smile then remonstrated with her. 'Think yourself lucky and don't be on the streets again. We have your name here now.'

'I want me money,' she said, placing her baby on the counter. 'And I want me bag of food. I won't budge from here without them.' She gave the guard her fiercest look. 'What d'ye think the chillen are goin' to eat?'

The baby started to cry, and the cry became a bawling wail.

The officer reached under the counter and fetched out her string bag. 'Take it!' he said thrusting the bag at her.

'I will not!' she answered, taking up the child. 'You're robbers, the whole blasted lot of yous.'

Two guards now got hold of her and started hauling her towards the exit. 'Your money goes into the garda benefit box. We thank you,' the duty officer called after her as she was shoved out the door.

Not a penny in her pocket and eight miles home, Eileen Ward began to trudge up the quays in the semi-darkness. A mist was rising from the Liffey. A few early Mass-goers passed her and she came to a chapel. Frightened but desperate, she found herself putting out her hand and begging for help. A few coins came into her hand. 'God bless you,' she said several times over, her voice dead.

Now and then she looked over her shoulder, fearing the approach of a police car up the lighted quays. When she had two shillings she crossed the river by the Queen Street bridge, walked up to Thomas Street and caught a bus to the Naas Road. Sitting on the lower deck, watching the fog streak by, Eileen pondered her situation. Mikey would scold her over the whole thing and they would have a row.

From the bus stop, she walked on through Bluebell Lane, almost swallowed up here by the thick, clammy mist. The pigs were squealing in Bermingham's yard and she could smell their swill. Coming out the other end and nearing the canal, she was alarmed to see the squad cars with their red lights turning. Big shadowy lorries stood in line along the Ring Road. The eviction was about to start. Eileen hurried forward, clutching her baby.

2 Johnny Connors was banging on the front of Steve Aiken's wagon. 'The shayds are here!' he called up to the closed, unlit curtains.

Steve sat up, resting a hand on Denise. He was tired but came quickly alert now and shouting an answer, clambered from the high bed, making the barrel-top shudder.

He found his clothes and put them on, saying a few words to arouse Denise.

'I'll follow you,' she said, still drowsy.

The sight of the lights on the road thrilled and frightened him. He did not know what to expect.

Johnny came back down the steps of his wagon and they hastened together across the dark, foggy field towards the gate.

'You'll see somethin' now,' said Johnny, starting to leap and sprint over the mist-covered ground. 'We'll run 'em off the field this time.'

Outside the open entrance the low headlamps of a squad car burned onto the fog. A second car, engine quietly revving, was slowly closing up behind it. Down the unlit road towards the canal hunkered the hulks of covered Corporation lorries filled with workmen. Nobody had yet emerged from these vehicles.

On his haunches in the wet grass, Francie Donohue was trying to get the fired started. A match fizzled and went out.

Johnny squatted at his side. 'Get some paraffin,' he urged as Francie's brother Chap came up to them.

Suddenly the figures at the fire were drowned in a brighter light. A television crew had switched on two arc-lamps mounted close to the fence. Silhouetted in the artificial glare, the four defenders lifted the steel gate between them and brought it closed.

Big Bill, lit at the open window of his truck, blinked at them stupidly.

As if from nowhere the Mercedes-Benz glided out from the Ring Road's black tunnel. It rolled forward stealthily through the eerie atmosphere until it was close to the gate. Liam Grady ducked out, one hand on his blown white hair, caught like the others in the arc-lights.

He came to the gate calling loudly to the Travellers gathering at the fire, 'Don't mind 'em, lads! You hold steady.'

Wack MacDonald, working himself up for the fray, clapped his hands. 'The man is here!' he bawled into the dark behind. Other figures came running up.

Aiken climbed the gate and reached to shake hands with Grady. Their breath hovered in the fog, a ghost of enmity between them. Then the lad got down and, gripping himself, walked over to Bill Redmond. He looked up at the large face in the cab.

'They hate you for what you are doing.'

'I don't care a Tinker's cuss what they think.' Big Bill stared down at his protagonist. 'I've got a job to do.'

'We'll only go onto another piece of ground.'

'You - you've no place in this. You'd better take yourself off.' Then extending his arm, he pointed to a black car. 'But don't be talkin' to me. Talk to him.'

'Who?'

'The man in charge. Mr Molloy, the Housing Manager.'

Grady was already at the kerbside conversing with a grey-suited municipal official. Two heavy police officers, swagger sticks under their arms, stood close by

With his Mercedes-Benz blocking the gate, the senator was saying affably: 'I'm not here to stand in the way of the Corporation. But surely you're not going to send your men in there to evict women and children. Hasn't Ireland seen enough of this sort of thing in the past?'

Molloy, looking round with annoyance at the Telefis Eireann crew which was just closing in on them, told him: 'Don't you know this is a problem we have all over the city right now. I don't why you'd want to be involved. These people are simply trespassers. Trespassers, senator. The land is needed for development and they have to go.'

Molloy tried to move away, signalling with his arm to the men in the lorries. But like a Jack Russell terrier Grady was on his heels.

'Be reasonable. Sure, you can give them more time.'

'Haven't I given them a great deal of time already? They've been on this land months.'

Most of the workmen had dropped from the lorries now and were assembling on the roadside. They stood mute but attentive when Grady switched his appeal to them.

'Listen, you fellas,' he said, unabashed by his own short stature.

'There are families in there just like your own. They've been hounded all their lives. Now Mr Molloy says they can leave voluntarily. Wouldn't it be only decent to let them have time to get up and give the children something to eat?'

The men shifted their feet, looking glumly towards Molloy. They were clearly discomfited and did not like the task ahead.

'We're quite prepared to wait until two o'clock,' said Molloy, thrusting his hands in his pockets. 'That's if we have an undertaking from these people to leave by that time.'

Pop's Johnny, with others at his back, was listening to these negotiations, going on without their involvement. From the gate he called:

'Sir, mister, you there. You've not told us where we can shift to.'

Molloy turned away and pretended not to hear, disdaining to acknowledge Connors.

At the fire, Mary MacDonald bent her ruddy face to light a cigarette.

She had come down the field with a big kettle, which was now half buried in the flames. The men standing around her, spreading their hands to the heat, were growing tense and anxious.

'Well?' queried Pat Donohue as the Englishman came back to join them.

'They're not coming in till two o'clock.'

'And then what?' asked Pop's Johnny.

'It's up to us. Shift or stay our ground.'

Mary handed him a mug of tea. 'I've enough tea mashed for the whole Corporation, Big Bill and all.'

On the grass nearby Maisie had set out a tray with a dozen cups and mugs. Mary began to fill them, the girl putting in the milk and sugar. She meant to give them to the boys at the fire.

'Maisie, go on over and offer the tea to the workmen,' her mother-in-law ordered, tipping a little water into the fire. The water hissed and rose in a small cloud of steam.

Maisie rose from her knees and walked slowly forward with the tray.

'Will yer have a drop o' tea?' she hailed them boldly through the fence, raising the tray to her breast.

'We don't like doin' this,' one said, taking a mug. A few others accepted the tea, others hung back without saying a word to the Tinker girl behind the hedge.

When she got back to the fire, the tea was cold but some of the lads drunk it anyway. The mist having lifted, the morning was gradually lightening and they were driven back up the field by a faint drizzle.

A small amount of traffic now moved back and forth along the Ring Road, heralding the commencement of a normal day. The television crew, idle for the past fifteen minutes, were ready to quit.

But the number of police cars outside the field had increased.

3 Looking over the half-door of the caravan, Denise surveyed the dismal scene. Fires smoked here and there as families scratched together a last breakfast. A few ponies were being led about, wet-flanked and as ill-spirited as their owners. The hotch-potch of an encampment, under a mantle of low cloud and teasing rain, was already in a state of disintegration.

No smoke, she noticed, issued from the tin chimneys of the wagons. Like her own, the stoves had this morning been left cold for fear of accidents during the moving.

Seeing the police had not yet entered the ground, she strapped on her leg and cocking up the hood of her duffel coat hurried through the rain to Catlin's door. Mrs Connors was packing up her Delft,

while little Johnny and Paddy slept on under the bed. Kitty sat sucking her thumb, waiting for a piece of bread.

'I can't abide this shifting about,' said Catlin, helping her up the steps.

'They seem to be delaying,' Denise replied, turning to look over her
shoulder towards the road. In the distance, through the haze of rain,
a barrel-top was lumbering up from the canal. Joe Donohue, the
Gaffer, was the first to move.

'I don't care what they do. Paddy is sick. I won't shift this wagon.'

'Are you doin' the school?' Kitted piped up, jumping down and now
holding on to her teacher's knee.

'Why don't we?' said Denise, taking Kitty's hand.

But Kitty broke away from her and was out the door, down the
steps and running towards the school, yelling to the other children
as she went. When Denise caught up with her, the desks were filling
up and more children arriving. A crowd began to jostle in behind,
glad to get out of the rain. Mary MacDonald with Tuckerlaly and her
small ones brought all those who had earlier gathered around the
fire at the gate. Half the camp was now jammed into the school-hut.
Jokes were cracked and there was an air of superficial cheer. No-one
knew what to expect next.

They watched from the windows, faces anxious. Old Mike O'Brien
passed in the rain, with his pony. He would not join them.

Pat Donohue cried out suddenly that Big Bill was going to his hut.
But he calmed himself and remained with the rest.

'I hope the bitch flies at him,' he shouted, raising laughter.

The consensus was that the horses should not be yoked as this
would be giving in to the Corporation.

After some while there came a wave of uncertainty as to whether
they should stay in the school. Mary was fighting an attack of
asthma and close to panic. Children were scared, some crying. Yet
even as those inside began to doubt, other people were coming to the
door and pressing in to join them.

Among them came Steve Aiken, who shouldered through the crush
towards Denise.

'What's Grady doing all this time?' she asked, hot-faced.

'The last time I saw him he'd moved his car and was taking a nap
in the back of it.'

Complaining of the confined space, Denise put a hand on his
shoulder and he steadied her with both arms as she climbed onto
the seat of a desk.

'Good morning everyone,' she called out, feeling a little crazy.

Every head turned and some one shouted back, 'Good day to you,
missis.'

'How about a song? You'll all know The Wild Colonial Boy.'

Ready to enjoy the fun, Pop's Johnny started to sing the song with her. The rest quickly joined in, a ragged harmony of voices. It galvanised them and in great spirit another song, and another, followed until a hammering at the door interrupted. A few of the Travellers pressed back and Big Bill shoved his bull-like head into the room.

'When are y'all gonna pack up? It's gone twelve.'

The singing died out but no-one answered. Ignored for the first time in his life, Bill Redmond tamely closed the door.

Her arms raised to start them again, Denise began singing We Shall Not Be Moved, wanting to bring to the Travellers' cause a little of the spirit of the American civil rights movement. Steve sung with her but nobody knew it properly and the thing petered out.

The chugging of a tractor was heard from close by on the blind side of the building.

Eileen Ward came to the window, her livid scare close to the glass. 'The man has a chain in his hands,' she warned. 'He's gonna put it around the school.'

A commotion followed while Pop's Johnny, helped by Aiken and others started piling the iron-framed desks against the door. The children sat themselves on the floor and a few cigarettes were lit. As everyone listened they could hear Big Bill running out the chain.

'You'll have to bring it all down on our heads,' Catlin called out. 'We're not movin' for yous no more.'

Molloy's white face now appeared at the window.

'I want Mr Aiken to come out a minute.'

Steve did not move, wanting to stay with the others. He did not want to unblock the door.

'Go on,' said Old Pat. 'Talk to the man.'

The desks were lifted back and reluctantly Aiken squeezed out.

He found Grady and Joe Donohue standing with Molloy, who had an umbrella up. There were guards nearby. The tractor had gone to the top of the field near the factories. At a distance it looked like a harmless toy. A miniature Big Bill could be seen lifting a sledge hammer. The white plaster board wall of Michael Ward's hut sagged and collapsed. The little Ward children were running about there demented.

Elsewhere, a few people were half-heartedly packing up. Scrap metal and bottles were being loaded onto carts. The guards strutted about everywhere hurrying them on. An old woman tottered across the ground, seeming to care neither for the rain nor her fate. As Aiken watched, she passed unnoticed behind Molloy's umbrella.

The shining tops of wagons and huts, empty of owners who had retreated into the school, appeared permanently abandoned.

Molloy stopped talking to the others and said to Aiken, 'I'm told you're responsible for this building. I won't say again it should not have been put up in the first place. I'll just repeat we've given you extra time and we want this job finished.'

'Did you tell your men to knock down those huts?' Aiken said angrily.

'What about those government promises?' Joe Donohue put in, making up a little for his late arrival. His wagon was already at the gate.

Grady pulled out a large white handkerchief and turned away, blowing his nose noisily.

Aiken hoped the singing, minutes ago unified and defiant, would break out again inside the barricaded school.

'There's no land whatever in the city we could give you,' Molloy quibbled, losing patience.

'These evictions must stop,' said the senator. 'This is clearly the intention of Judge Walsh.'

'Only recommendations,' Molloy shook his head. 'The Corporation has not even discussed them.'

'Leave us just a month,' Donohue coaxed him. 'We'll pick out a place. Sure, we could go back to the California Hills.'

'Where's that?' asked Molloy. 'If you go out in the country you'll have no further bother from us.'

'Would you give us the four weeks?' the Travellers' spokesman persisted.

Molloy shifted uneasily, shaking his umbrella. He had come out alone onto the field and would sooner have been back in his car.

'If you people go quietly as agreed with Senator Grady here,' he said. 'We'll see what we can do. That's a promise.'

Molloy walked away, confident he had now got what he wanted.

The people in the school came out only half believing what the Gaffer was telling them. They knew they could have held out longer.

When the school was almost empty old Granny Connors, her face under a shawl, came in and lifted a holy picture from the wall. 'Joseph and Mary preserve us,' she whispered to herself, looking at the papers from the uplifted desks that now lay scattered and trampled on the floor.

Pat put his pipe between his teeth and hobbled down the field without a word to Joe. He and his sons began to salvage what they could from their broken hut.

The rain had mercifully stopped as the first wagons moved through the rutted exit. The Ring Road filled with a tangle of vehicles, manoeuvring every-which-way. Sometime in the afternoon, the line sorted itself out and a column stretched back half a mile to the road-fronts of the new factories.

All the while, Pop's Johnny paced in and out between the barrel-tops, exerting himself, telling the people to stay together. When his own wagon was on the road he went back with Dolly and fetched Steve's out of the field and placed it behind his own.

Standing on Johnny's flat-cart, the two were fastening the flag-pole to the back-rack of Steve's wagon when the Mercedes-Benz drew up alongside.

Grady called up them, 'You're a guerrilla army now. Think of that. Keep circling the city and don't be giving up!'

'We could have held them up all day,' Johnny told him. 'We'd no right to give up there.'

'Ah,' said Grady half apologizing as the Irish flag unfurled itself on the breeze. 'Wait till I get some of the boys out to you,' He drove on, shouting back, 'See you on the next spot!'

The guards, who had played no major part in the eviction, now closed on the flank of the mass of horse-drawn vehicles and as the column began to roll forward, spacing out as it advanced, two police cars drove slowly on ahead.

Through the rear window, Denise watched the following horses and under them the growing trail of white tracks from the many iron-shod wheels. Behind lay the two empty fields and the abandoned school, now an insignificant shed standing in the littered grass. The workmen were on the land clearing up, tossing everything onto the abandoned fires.

Denise had hardly thought of herself all day. That she might be pregnant had gone from her mind. But the failure of Tracey and Andrew Meachen to show up for the eviction was a bitter disappointment to her. They had let her down.

Steve was sitting on the front ledge holding the reins and having some difficulty in keeping Dolly close to the kerb. Johnny had assured him the mare was used to shafts and would follow his wagon. But Steve had never had charge of a horse before and was acquiring a new skill.

The two police cars, which had dropped back for a while, crawled past again on their right.

'See the squad cars,' Steve said over his shoulder to Denise, at the same time tugging the reins on the skittish mare, 'They want to run us right out of Dublin.'

1 The first of the tall barrel-tops tacked up to the crossroads, a chill wind blowing down on them off the Dublin Mountains. Behind, seeming to float in the early evening light, came more green-covered wagons, gigs and painted carts. The vanguard of the long, straggling line was about to make its unwelcome intrusion into the suburb of Walkinstown.

The heads of the horses nodded heavily as they plodded forward, unwilling to catch up; atop the carts, the bowed shapes of Travellers, the tired children holding on. Their dogs trotted down the pavements, on the move, still keen for the road.

Womenfolk, bothered by their fretting children, were calling for a stop so they could make a meal and the men, who had been frustrated by the presence of the Garda Siochana, cast about now for a place to pull in. Some led their ponies by the head. It was not that they had come far but it had been a long day.

Ahead of them stretched Walkinstown Avenue and to the right and left the Long Mile Road, down which traffic was passing on its way in and out of Dublin. The right turn led straight to the city boundary and out into the country

Johnny Connors, pulling his wagon-horse to halt, took a look up the wide intersection.

'That's the best we'll get into this night,' he told Catlin, pointing to a long lay-by on the far side. She was standing behind the half-door, Kitty at her side, attentive to her husband's gestures.

Chap Donohue got out on the road and holding up the traffic, helped the first four wagons to follow Johnny's across the intersection. Caravans and carts now followed until a good many had pulled in close against the sparse hedge that divided the lay-by from a low, gorse-covered hill which rose behind.

Pleased with himself for bringing his wagon in, Steve got down leaving Denny to hold Dolly's head. He walked back to the corner to watch the others come in. The sight of so many horse-drawn vehicles on the move together was an inspiration.

Pop's Johnny Connors came up to join him.

'Will they all get in here?' Steve asked, looking down the crowded lay-by.

'They'll get in but they won't stay,' the other answered. 'Some'll go on tomorrow, you'll see. This is a bad old spot.'

The Englishman had been certain they were going to stick together. He was counting on that spirit of resistance which had been so strong inside the barricaded school. Would it now evaporate? Even as he watched wagons were coming up in front of them at the crossroads. Each one as it wheeled right seemed now to be a loss. They would head out of Dublin and down the country in a day or two.

Determined to prevent a break-up, Aiken turned away from the on-coming column and started to run up the avenue. A strip of ground at the bottom of the gorse-covered hill extended from the junction towards a row of semi-detached houses marking the edge of the sub-urban estate. The land was protected by a barbed wire fence. He looked for a gate. But there was none.

'Johnny! Here a minute,' he shouted, much resting on a quick decision.

Johnny met him at the fence and the two of them started jerking away at a rotten post. When the post gave way, Steve twisted back the loose barbed wire, while Johnny hurried to the intersection to catch some of the stragglers.

Within minutes the first Travellers were on the new ground.

When Steve went back for Denny and his own caravan, he was relieved to find people were already abandoning the lay-by. Nobody wanted to stay at the roadside with the traffic passing close.

Denny walked Dolly up the road and onto the bumpy grass and the couple watched as the new camp assembled. Mikey Ward was throw-ing his sticks and canvas off his cart and the MacDonald boys had started to erect a tent beside their father's wagon. After the wanton destruction of the huts at the Ring Road, a lot of people would be back under canvas this night.

They could see other ponies following Dolly and Johnny up the hillside where they would be hobbled on the high top-land. Close to the road, children were scavenging for wood, taking out more of the broken fence.

By about seven o'clock a kind of normality had been established and Denise and Steve were in their wagon having a makeshift supper. All of a sudden, before anyone had spotted it, a police car drove through the gap. It bounced over the turf into the midst of the camp, disgorging blue-uniformed guards. They stalked towards the nearest caravan.

Jimmy Hanrahan was stooped over a wooden coop battening in his bantams.

'Stand up ye bleeder when I'm talking to you,' the leading officer commanded.

'I beg your pardon, sir,' Jimmy straightened himself, wishing after all he had gone on to Naas.

The inspector beckoned to other people with his swagger stick. Some came forward reluctantly, intimidated by his manner and rough language.

'You have one hour – all you knackers.' He scowled into their faces, his men at his back with their chin-straps down. 'If you're still here when I return I'll see you're burned out of it, begob I will.'

The party of guards ducked back into their car and it reversed out as suddenly as it had arrived, leaving a cloud of stinking exhaust smoke.

The Travellers stood around at a loss, shocked by this latest threat. The unexpected reappearance of the police had robbed them of their will.

Joe Donohue walked over to Aiken's wagon, the common menace drawing them together.

'The man's breath stunk of whiskey,' Joe remarked. 'They mean to do somethin' bad if we don't move for them.'

'Let's go and phone the papers,' said Steve, not knowing what else to suggest.

The two, ill-matched but now allied, walked up the dark, unfamiliar road together towards the lights of the Cherry Tree public house.

'We're well off the highway,' said the English lad. 'D'you think the guards would carry out such a threat?'

'Sure they do it down the country often enough. But most of the boys take a frit too easily,' Joe responded. 'We'll see whose got the nerve to stand their ground tonight. I'll not shift agin.'

On either side of them loomed the big suburban houses of Walkinstown. There were lights in the windows and cars parked along the pavement.

'We're too near the houses,' Donohue commented. 'There'll be complaints and won't that give Big Bill the excuse to come out to us soon enough.'

When they reached the Cherry Tree, Donohue urged Aiken go in alone. 'Likely as not they won't serve me,' he said, standing in the shadows.

'Shall I bring out a couple of beers?'

'Never touch it, thanks all the same.'

Aiken called Brendan Carey from a coin box in the lobby. As he did so he kept his ears open for any talk of Travellers in the noisy public bar. He could have done with a drink himself but came out again without having spoken to anyone.

Within an hour Carey's Morris Minor appeared outside the camp. Carey could hardly credit what they told him about the threat from the guards. But as much concerned for Steve and Denise as for the Travellers, he stayed with them at Joe's fire.

'You were on the news,' Carey said 'It was me tipped off RTE and left them to cover your eviction. This morning's papers have followed up and the Corporation is hopping mad about all the publicity.'

Denise stayed out for a while by the fire, rubbing her eyes from tiredness and the annoyance of the smoke. The cloud cover had almost gone and in a while there was a bright, clear sky. The stars looked like nuggets of ice.

When nine o'clock passed and the guards did not reappear Carey drove up into Walkinstown's main street. He returned to tell them nobody in the area had heard anything about plans for a vigilante attack on the Travellers. While he spoke a single car passed down the road, menacingly slowly but sped away.

'I doubt they'll come back now,' Carey said at last. He wrote down his home telephone number for Aiken.

Denise shook his hand vigorously and, still a little reluctant to be left on their own, they let him go.

Laying awake in the caravan in the unfamiliar suburban stillness, Steve could hear the crack of Joe's dying fire. From the hill came the braying of a tethered ass. He could see three stars high above the back window. Denise said in a despondent tone. 'What use is it us being here? We'll only be moved again. Honestly, I don't think I can hack this.'

Steve spread the covers over her. 'I'm too tired, Denny. Just shut your eyes and we'll see what tomorrow brings'

To his surprise she obeyed. But he found he could not himself unwind and a few hours later in the pale moonlight he got up and put on his clothes. Sitting in vigil on the shafts of the wagon, he kept watch on the avenue. The rest of the camp slept on, seemingly unfazed by the intimidation which the young Englishman found so disturbing. After a long cold wait, someone crawled from Mikey Ward's tent; it was Eileen. She squatted at the ashes and with a bit of newspaper caught a light for her butt of a cigarette.

'That's a chilly mornin',' she called quietly.

'I'm worrying about the Corporation and the police.'

'Ah, don't mind those swine,' Eileen responded, now rekindling her fire with a few twigs. 'You'll get used them afore you know it.'

'D'you think the Corporation'll leave us a while?'

'Not at all. The man there was only coddin' us.'

Steve knew that having lost their plasterboard huts and straw bedding, she must have slept practically on the bare ground. The Wards had little left but Mikey's cart and pony. Eileen, he thought, might have the tongue of a trooper but she had the heart of a mother. She would suffer anything for the survival of her children.

Grudgingly the daylight increased and Steve eventually gave up his watch. As he moved about getting the stove started to boil the kettle, Denise stirred in the bed.

'I'm going to go and see if I can salvage any of the school,' he told her, handing her up a mug of coffee.

Without further words he went to find Pop's Johnny. The two men set off on a flat-cart for the Ring Road. At the old camp they found Terry MacDonald had got there ahead of them and the three watched a gang of workmen going the rounds of the broken shacks. In a few minutes they set fire to the school. Smoke and flames started to stream from the roof.

'They're burning Wack's hut,' Terry said. 'All his yokes are in it.'

He told them his brother had gone off last evening to visit Maisie's people in Clondalkin. He'd shut up his hut leaving their clothes and all the bedding inside. The couple wouldn't know of their loss until they returned from the village.

The three walked back over the fields now under clouds of drifting smoke. The smell of burning refuse was everywhere. Fire had engulfed the school and the desks were burning fiercely; soon only the iron frames would be left. As they turned away, a broad cloud-column rose at a slant behind them.

They passed the ashes of what had been Old Pat's shack smouldering near the gate. Nothing remained to be saved.

'Molloy got his way this time,' Steve commented while the two carts jogged along empty. 'We shouldn't have listened to him.'

Terry called from his trap. 'Wack's going to kill somebody when he finds out.'

2 When they got back Andrew Meachen's red station wagon was parked on Walkinstown Avenue. Tracey repeated for Steve the explanation she had just given Denise.

'We did come to the Ring Road yesterday and saw what was happening but the police wouldn't let us through the gate. We were well upset.'

'I called the police this morning,' her husband put in. 'I guess they were quite helpful. They knew where you were.'

Denise looked at him with incredulous eyes. The American had been treated civilly. What a contrast with their ordeal of last night when a swaggering bully of an officer had tried to terrorise them into moving their caravans again in the dark.

She tried to describe last night's scene and told how Molloy had given his word they would be left on the next ground for at least a month.

'It wasn't a promise,' Steve corrected her. 'But yes, he gave us that impression. I've just come back from there. The school's gone. They've set it on fire.'

'O God!' Tracey's mouth fell open. 'What happened to the school things? My Cuisenaire rods?'

'They're in here,' Denise assured her, reaching her hand into the space under the bed and pulling out a box.

'Can we do something with them this morning?' she asked, her eyes wide and naïve.

'Where?'

'In here and in the car. Just three or four children at a time maybe.'

So Denise took heart and the two young women began to improvise. They started with some of the small ones who had worked with the arithmetic rods in St Christopher's. But it was chaotic inside the station wagon. Denise got out and played her recorder, with her pupils perched on the shafts. The two men, a little reluctantly, shepherded a party of children up the hill. There was a game of hide-and-seek around the gorse bushes but the bigger boys, unwilling to be corralled, went off on their own. They came running back to show Steve and Andy some mushrooms they had found.

Below on the margin of level ground, the camp was at a standstill. The men stood about idle, afraid to go out. Some of the women were debating a trip around the houses in Walkinstown. Olivine Riley advised against it. 'If we go botherin' the people sure they'll call the guards out and we'll be taken.'

About noon Pop's John proposed going to a soup kitchen in Ballyfermot. There was a centre serving free meals where they could get hot food for all the children.

'The nuns'll fill up a whole churn for a shilling – or whatever you can give.'

'Is the food any good?'

'Potatoes and stew mostly, if you don't be late. Then you may only get the rice puddin'.'

'You guys go,' said Andy, eager to return to his warm flat and his studies. 'I'd best take Tracey home.'

The Catholic Social Service Centre was a low one-storey concrete building, scrawled over with graffiti. The queue, not yet large, was moving patiently through the open double-doors.

Nuns in starched white headgear ladled the hot stew into the saucepans as each was placed before them on the table, now by a child, now by a man or woman, from the line of listless faces. It was obvious to Aiken that many of the people out of the houses, while more secure in the bricks and mortar of the council estate, were little better off than the Travellers.

Johnny's turn came and he lifted his milk churn onto the table.

'Gracious, we can't give you that much,' said the nun, her white headdress nodding. 'Whoever is it for?'

'It's for the Tinkers, ma 'am,' he told her humbly. 'For all the children in the camp. We couldn't get out to make a bob today, not one of us.'

She regarded him with a pursed expression. Aiken stood behind Connors not saying a word in case his English accent should lead to complicated questions.

'Oh, now in that case we'll do our best for you,' she said. 'Bring your can around here.'

Johnny moved the churn past the people in the front of the queue and placed it on the floor. Everyone watched as the nun, with some difficulty, poured in the stew from a huge steaming cooking pan. Then she beckoned to Johnny to carry it away.

'Have you any contribution to give us?'

'I have,' said Johnny, giving her a grin and searching in his pockets. He put a few coins on the table.

'God bless you,' the sister chimed, scooping up the money and turning to the next of Dublin's needy.

Back at Walkinstown, the children came from all over the camp, holding up their crocks and tin mugs. Catlin Connors, in good humour, had rolled up her sleeves and was baling out the stew. Some of the children stayed near her wagon, gobbling the gravy and biting up the big pieces of potato. The English couple ate too, standing in the open. Several women with pots and pans asked to get helpings for smaller kids. In the end most of the camp ate and the churn was empty. It was a communal meal.

Eileen Ward limped over afterwards. Like the others, she had not ventured to go calling, fearing the arrival of Big Bill. Her teeth, brown and broken, were paining her and she complained of feeling unwell.

'We'd have starved this day but for the nuns,' she confided to Denise. 'I'd ne'er a crumb of bread for the chillen nor meself.'

3 Denise was waiting with a jar of urine stowed away in her raffia basket when the American couple came next morning to take her to the doctor.

On the way, Tracey confided to the two of them, 'I've some ideas how we might get the school started again. Not right away but when things have gotten better. We'll talk about it after, okay?'

Denise made a half-hearted reply, worrying now about the impending consultation.

Within half an hour they were driving through the higher-class streets of Dublin. The Georgian houses, with their columned porches painted in varied colours looked smart, even opulent. The private surgery in Fitzwilliam Square was only around the corner from the Meachens' flat on St Stephen's Green.

Andrew dropped off the two girls and took Steve back to his flat.

The doctor, a stout man in his middle years, regarded his new patient with dispassionate eyes while the American sat in the waiting room. He asked Denise a number of questions and entered her in a file as Mrs Aiken.

'Would you please take your coat off and lie down on the couch,' he said, coming out from behind his desk.

'I have an artificial leg,' said Denise. 'Shall I take it off?'

'Oh, in that case, yes.' He stood by with the nurse, who could not conceal her embarrassment.

Denise pulled up her pullover, and the doctor touched her abdomen sparingly with his cold fingers. 'Nothing really to tell from here,' he said, now more kindly in his manner. 'Do you want me to look at your leg?'

'I have had some soreness lately. Yes, please do.'

Removing the sock, he was shocked to see the redness of the stump below the knee. It was badly inflamed.

'You must take better care of this,' he said. 'Should we find you are pregnant, Mrs Aiken, it's going to mean extra weight and stress. You appreciate that?'

He explained that because of the amputation he wanted additional tests done. The nurse took charge of the jar of urine and extracted blood from her forearm.

As he showed the two girls out, the doctor told Denise to ring the surgery in a few days for the pregnancy and blood test results.

At the Meachens' flat Tracey handed around small plates and offered them cake. Denise, worrying to herself, had little to say about the visit and let Tracey expand on her plans for the school.

'Andy felt so bad about the Ring Road - well we both did - that he made some phone calls right away. He got through to Archbishop McQuaid's office, whatever that's called officially. He'll tell you himself in a minute,' she said, looking at her husband.

She continued, 'Just by chance I went into Bewley's Café. They have wonderful fresh coffee and cakes. This is some I bought this morning. Oh, I didn't tell you but I'm a lapsed Quaker. Just as Andy is pretty much a lapsed Catholic. We're not really religious, not your Bible Belt Americans, but we do have our affiliations. Anyway, when I went in there I chanced to hear that the business is owned by Quakers. Victor Bewley is the head of it right now. And I asked to see him. And to cut this short he's very sympathetic. A very nice man and very ready to listen.'

'What's he going to do?' asked Denise.

'He's invited us to come to the Quaker Meeting House one Friday and tell everyone about St Christopher's and what we hope to do.'

'That's something.'

'It is,' said Tracey, 'only you can't do anything here in Ireland without the Catholic Church. And this is where Andy comes in.'

'I've been able to contact people close to the Archbishop. They've advised us to approach a nuns' teaching order. They've given me the details. But I get the impression they'll talk to them too.'

'I don't like the sound of nuns,' said Denise.

Denise could see they meant the whole project to be taken over by the Church. She objected saying: 'St Christopher's was built by Travellers and they're supposed to own it.'

Steve was upset that all this was being discussed behind the backs of the camp. At the same time it all seemed irrelevant to the immediate crisis at Walkinstown Avenue.

'Either the Church does it or the Travellers don't have a school,' said Andy shortly. 'Face it, you guys, there isn't a choice.'

'We don't have a piece of ground we can stay on. That has to come first,' Steve said. 'And to be honest I saw the school as a way of getting that. They've burned St Christopher's but I think we should rebuild it even if it's only temporary again.'

Andrew's voice was belligerent now: 'You're putting the cart before the horse. It's a wrong tack to go defying everyone and stirring things up.'

'What's your tack then?'

'Get a proper committee together, involve the Church - and the Quakers. Put the thing on a proper foundation.'

'The Travellers are getting kicked around the city. They'll be kicked right out of it while your committee is yammering away about what ought be done.'

Tracey turned to Denise, 'Do you want to go on living with the Travellers – what if you're pregnant?'

'Steve does, I don't,' she said bluntly. 'But I still want St Christopher's to be the Travellers' school - not something that's done for them by the nuns.'

'It's their school and their campaign, not anybody else's,' Steve said pointedly, 'Nothing should be decided without a meeting at the camp.'

They had reached an impasse and as the argument continued the disagreements becoming more personal.

'I'm losing it here. This is stupid! What's the matter with you two?' Tracey burst out finally.

No-one spoke for a minute and then in a bid to retrieve their friendship she said to Denise: 'Look, we've got a camp bed we can put up in here. You can stay over anytime you like. I'll be glad of your company.'

Already annoyed by Andrew, this offer from Tracey further upset Steve. He did not want to be separated from Denny.

4 While the four were away from the Walkinstown camp, two cyclists rode up to the broken fence and asked for Joe Donohue.

'Senator Grady sent us,' said the taller of the pair, a broad-built man who introduced himself as Frank McManus, chairman of the Irish Civil Liberties League.

His companion, Tommy Bowden, a squat fellow sporting a beret, said he was a car mechanic by trade and a founder member of the group.

'I live in Palmerstown. That's where we have our meetings.'

'We came by way of the Ring Road,' said Frank. 'It's shockin' what they've done to you, burning the school an' all.'

The connection with Senator Grady impressed Donohue but he remained wary of the two strangers. Getting offers of help from settled people was a new experience. The sight of their bicycles, now propped against his wagon, gave him no great confidence.

While they were talking Pop's Johnny sauntered over to the fire wanting to be in on the discussion.

'Will you fellas to be here when Big Bill comes back?'

'Who's Big Bill?' asked Tommy.

'That's the Corporation bailiff – the man that does all the shiftin'.'

'We know what he did at the Ring Road,' Tommy said.

'And a hundred other places,' said Johnny. 'He spends his life tormentin' the Travellers.'

'What we have in mind,' Frank McManus now explained, 'is to organise a picket.'

'What does a picket do?' asked Donohue. Then noticing some young lads collecting around, he turned and raised his voice to them: 'Run off you boys and don't be crowdin' the men. '

'Our members will be out here each day with placards. They'll walk up and down the road.'

'Like we did on O'Connell Bridge,' Johnny said. 'I'll come out and join in meself.'

'We'll ask the Corporation men not to cross the picket,' Tommy told them.

'We've a big flag that was on the school. Will I give it to you to hold up on the road?'

Johnny fetched the flag and handed it over. The two stayed a few minutes longer. Before they pushed off Donohue asked after Senator Grady.

'Liam is not well,' Tommy replied. 'I doubt you'll see much of himself for a while so.'

'He's a great man,' said Johnny. 'Tell him we intend to best Big Bill no matter what.'

Bowden twinked his bicycle bell and they were off down the avenue the way they had come. The Gaffer watched them go, feeling flattered and disturbed. The situation with the camp was getting more complex by the day.

5 They were big lads in heavy black boots, with the manner and stride of soldiers. Pop's Johnny nicknamed them the Recruits. Six Civil Liberties men turned up next day, all on bicycles, and were now marching in pairs along the fence each shouldering a placard with the words "Justice for Itinerants".

Bowden draped the big Irish flag over the barbed-wire fence. It was beginning to get ragged.

They had started the picket without more than a tentative wave to those inside. Only when Pat Donohue sent them out tea did the lads start to fraternise with those they had come to support.

'I've no place to bring you fellas into,' Pat told them. 'Sure me hut was burned by Big Bill. I've only the old bender but bring yer bicycles onto the field and we'll put a cover over them if it rains.'

'Right, we will so,' Frank McManus responded, gathering the others around him.

They wheeled their bikes over the rutted ground at the gap and piled them beside the two tall bender-tents which Pat and his sons had erected. A fire burned between the tents, sending a thin trail of smoke out onto the road.

While their were talking Aiken joined them, introducing himself and shaking hands all round.

'We hear you bunked off from the British Army,' McManus said.

'I didn't go for my medical and came over here instead,' Steve replied modestly.

'Good man yourself,' said Tommy. 'One less in the British forces is a plus for us.'

The youngest of them, a lad who had just introduced himself as Eddie, pulled a small red book from his pocket. He showed it to Aiken.

The young Englishman had never seen a copy before but he knew right away from the embossed red star on the cover what it was: Mao

Tse-Tung's Little Red Book . Eddie put it away again as if he didn't want everyone to see it.

The Recruits resumed their picket without inviting anyone from the camp to participate. They kept it up for several days.

6 Only two of them were manning the picket a week later when the Corporation came. At eight in the morning three covered lorries discharged a large gang of workmen on Walkinstown Avenue, while half a dozen police cars queued along the kerb.

Big Bill led a posse onto the ground without meeting any immediate opposition. But seeing Pat's black bitch rise up, they walked past the first benders and gathered around another tent further along.

Bill lifted the flimsy green cover and jerked it back over the hoops.

Maisie lay there on the straw suddenly exposed, clutching her new baby. Wack sprang up and seizing a kettle-bar, screamed at the bailiff: 'Now you're gonna get it – you pig-faced bastard!'

The irate young Traveller swung the hooked iron perilously close to Redmond's head. By a deft shuffle the big man got himself out of range.

'Put that damn thing down!' the bailiff bellowed, his hands spread in the air.

The long bar now lay back over his shoulder as Wack balanced it for another strike. It sang past Big Bill's eyes.

While Wack continued to menace his trembling Goliath, the whole camp closed around the two combatants. All mingled together, workmen, Travellers and guards, eyes on the fight as if the battle for the camp was to be settled by single combat.

As the Gaffer, many expected Joe Donohue to intervene. But he only stood there, head cocked on one side. He hesitated too long and two guards started to move in on Wack MacDonald to grapple him from behind.

Just before this could happen, Maisie arose from the tumble of straw and bedding and placed herself, with her baby in her arms, between the guards and her husband. Wack's sister Rosaleen, also carrying a baby, came out of the crowd and stood at her side.

The appearance of these barelegged, shivering Madonnas with their babies had an instant effect. The guards and the workmen were uncertain what to do. Then a new arrival stepped forward into the circle and planted himself next to the girls. It was the Moped Man, who had tipped them off at the Ring Road.

'Let's just consider what we're doing here,' he shouted, his eyes raking the crowd. 'I'm Sam Caswell – some of you know me. I'm a caretaker at the flats in Pond Street. We're all members of the union, right? And the union should be here to tell us what to do and what not to do. The Corporation whether or not it owns this land can't order us to put these people out. We're not the Black and Tans.'

He gestured to the half-fallen tent at his feet. The tarpaulin cover and the sticks lay on a bed of straw, a wrecked Nativity.

Everyone was intent on his speech. Caswell had a peculiar charisma. Molloy, the Housing Manager, looked on, stony and sour, for once short of an answer.

'That's right, Sam!' A tractor driver who had left his vehicle to join the throng spoke up. 'For one here, I'm not going on with this job until the union rules on it.'

The mutiny leader rounded on the Housing Manager. 'Mr Molloy, I'm asking you to allow us half an hour to consult with head office. We've a right to that.'

Before Molloy could open his mouth, Sam called to the workmen, 'Who is the union delegate here?'

A man at the front raised his arm and there was a brief exchange after which the Corporation workmen began to break away and in twos and threes they walked back to the road, deserting Molloy. In a minute, a tractor was chugging up Walkinstown Avenue with the union delegate on board. He would telephone union headquarters in distant Parnell Square.

Steve and Denise, who had been following it all with the Travellers from the fringes, came forward through the loosening throng. Joe and Pop's Johnny, Pat and others were enjoying their own audience with the Moped Man. Maisie and Rosaleen, rocking their babies nearby, were the teenage heroines of the hour.

'There's a lot yet you don't know about me. And there's a thing or two you don't know about your William Redmond. That man has a history,' Sam Caswell was telling the Travellers.

He said he had previously been a member of the Parks' Department himself and had got word from someone there a couple of hours ago. 'I took the morning off to come here in my own time and try and stop the eviction.'

The two young mothers moved away to the sheltered side of Terry Macdonald's wagon. Mary MacDonald, breathing asthmatically, waddled over and peeked at the infants. The grandmother wheezed, tried to smile for them, broke off and went into a fit of coughing. She put some shoes on the grass for Maisie.

'Come up in the wagon and sit in the warm,' she told them. 'I've the stove burnin' just to spite that Molloy. Be rights they can't shift us while the fire's lighted.'

Meanwhile from the road came the sound of an engine and the tractor hove into view, its big wheels rolling. The delegate was back with a message from the Irish Municipal Employees' Trade Union.

He came onto the ground to tell the men, 'They want to discuss this with the Corporation. Nothing can be decided immediately. '

Sam shook his head, dissatisfied, saying: 'Boys, there's already a resolution on the minute book. Sure, it was passed a whole eight years ago.'

Molloy, who had by this time recovered his wits sufficiently to put up some opposition to the agitator, tried to intervene.

'Don't listen to the man. He doesn't know the first thing about it. The Corporation has every legal right to remove these trespassers from this land. Any eedjit knows that.'

'Let me tell you then,' Sam raised his voice. 'Wasn't I sent to Keogh Square? We were supposed to shift some caravans out of a yard there – just like you today. When we got there and saw how the people were situated we refused to do it. At the very next union meeting wasn't this resolution passed unanimously?'

He held up a piece of paper waving it in Molloy's face and then read it out, emphasising each word. 'No member of this union is to enter any property or land acquired by the Dublin Corporation for the purpose of carrying out evictions or any form of forceful removal for any purpose whatsoever.'

'Never heard of it,' quibbled Molloy.

'Here it is in black and white.' Sam again raised the paper. 'And this was backed by the Workers' Union of Ireland.'

Even while Sam Caswell was speaking, the same tractor driver was shouldering his way out from the meeting.

Sensing desertion, the Housing Manager called after him, 'Where d'yous think you're going?'

'Home,' said the man and went on.

Molloy rounded on the rest, the spittle on his lips. 'That man will be disciplined. And anyone else leaving may face dismissal.'

The other drivers with the Parks' Department tractors backed away from Molloy and stood about behind their vehicles. The rest of the workmen scattered, putting some distance between themselves and their boss. With the morning ebbing away, Sam Caswell was obliged to return to his job.

All the while, Eileen Ward had been loitering by her tent, watching for Big Bill's next move. She had heard much of the talk and seen the men break up. But she knew Big Bill would stay loyal and her eyes were fixed on him.

'I'll scald his nasty face,' she muttered to herself, stooping and screwing her black kettle deeper into the embers of the fire. In a minute, a belch of steam leaked out under the heavy lid.

Her husband Mikey, in an old overcoat, stood at the other side of the fire. He was sipping tea, letting on to help Paddy break sticks. He did not want to hear Eileen. His wife in a fury was a worse danger than the bailiff.

And now, with the attention of the whole camp on him, there was Redmond himself attempting to lead a gang back to the work of the eviction. As he got closer, Eileen put her hand on the handle of the kettle. Only it was too hot to lift and before she could try again using the edge of her shawl, Big Bill strode on past towards Terry MacDonald's wagon.

The bailiff lifted the shafts in his two large hands. But unable to budge the wheels he dropped the poles again and bellowed for help.

Most of the Corporation men ignored the appeals of the foreman. Then two older cronies, rounded up by Molloy, came forward and put their shoulders reluctantly to the back of the barrel-top.

A bunch of boys stalked behind as the three strained to shift the caravan. More children were soon dancing on their flanks, jeering, enjoying the fun. 'Gee up there!' yelled a little lad.

Three Jack Russells rushed at the men's heels while Pat's black bitch barked in excitement and jumped at Bill's waist.

Maddened to extra exertion, Redmond got the wagon in motion. It lurched after him, his two helpers lending their weight behind. Confounding all who watched, the caravan rolled slowly forward towards the gap.

The Travellers were laughing. No-one had yet gone for their horses. Without pony-power it looked for a while as though the number of vehicles scattered over the ground could not be dragged out by this small crew. However, within an hour four more caravans were standing on the road.

Molloy cajoled other men to participate and gradually the tide of the contest turned. More guards had come onto the ground and a few older folk on the Travellers' side judged that the game was up.

Jimmy Hanrahan, worried for his bantams, fetched his cob. After that, sticks were pulled, tents began to fall, and wagons and carts, by ones and twos, started to leave under their owners' command. By the afternoon the camp was in motion and rapidly dissolving.

The majority, following the Gaffer's example, trekked back around the corner into the lay-by on the Long Mile Road.

A few lots kept on going, seeking a respite in the quiet of Clondalkin, Naas and County Kildare. They slipped away almost unnoticed in the commotion.

7 In the dusk of the evening, Wack MacDonald took his brother Terry's trap and drove the pony hard all the way back to Ballyfermot, the iron kettle-bar on the boards at his feet.

He stopped off at Hennessy's near the Gala to buy drink and as the trap bowled on through the poorly lit estate, jerked off the bottle caps with his teeth, taking gulp after gulp of the black stout. A few clouts on the pony's rump from the kettle bar sent the animal into a humpy gallop which brought it on in a sweating trot down the night-darkened streets.

Wack was well intoxicated by the time he found Bill Redmond's house.

With no attempt at stealth, he got out of the trap, hitched the pony to a lamppost and paced quickly up the dark path to the side of the house. He banged on the door with his fist, hefting the iron bar in his right hand.

A large woman wrapped in a housecoat half-opened the door. 'What's this racket in aid of?' she demanded, regarding the ill-dressed young Tinker in the light of the doorway.

Wack shrunk back, surprised by her size and quick aggression.

'Bill's not here. He's out,' she bawled, and suddenly swung the door shut.

'I'll fuckin' kill him if he comes to us again,' Wack roared back through the closed door. 'Tell him that.'

Sobered a little he retreated up the path back to the gate.

A while later Bill Redmond, coming home from the Walkinstown eviction, found himself in a domestic confrontation. With flesh enough and sufficient spirit to argue with her burly spouse, Yvonne was waiting for him in the kitchen.

She watched him lumber in and slap down his cap. 'Guess who's been here just now.'

'I don't know.' Bill sat down heavily, wanting his tea. He laid his weary arms on the table.

'One of them Tinkers. A young fellow. He cursed me out.' She pointed the bread knife at him.

'I won't have them comin' here,' he pronounced, sitting up and taking notice for the first time.

'Well, you have. And he was lookin' for you. Wanted to kill you, that's all.'

'Kill me?' Bill gave out a shallow chuckle. 'Is that right?'

'Well, I don't like it. And I don't much like what you do.'

'I can handle them.'

'Supposin' I can't, if they start comin' around here, breakin' the windows or whatever.'

'They wouldn't have the bottle. '

'That fellow who was here would. I'd say he'd had a few bottles an' all,' said Yvonne, tossing back her stringy hair. She turned to the stove and lifted the whistling kettle.

Bill was considering whether to tell her what had happened in Walkinstown when she set a mug down and stirred in the sugar for him.

'The job was no bother up to this. I could talk to the Travellers half decent. I gave them a day or so then they'd move as good as gold. No messin'. I'll admit they gave me a bit of bother today but...'

'Yes, now there is bother and it'll get worse,' his wife told him.

'Jesus, there's some of them got houses through me,' Bill continued to muse. 'Give up your wagons Molloy told 'em and you can have a house. Didn't that Jimmy Gavin let us burn his wagon not six months back? His wife was all for a house.'

'Oh yes, you and Molloy are gonna have all them Tinkers settled down. I don't think so. Where are you gonna put them? Nobody wants that trash in Ballyfermot that's for sure.'

'Sure we have some of them already. We've the Fureys and the Keanens. No trouble whatsoever.'

'Those musicians? Oh, they're a different breed. I'm talkin' about your bog Tinkers. Up from the country. You'll never tame that lot. Anyways what right have they got to be in Dublin? Trespassin' where they like, horses everywhere.'

'We'll shift the lot of them right out of Dublin.'

'You? You'd be better out of it. It's goin' beyond reason. The neighbours are talkin' about it. There's even people speakin' for the Tinkers. That senator what's his name was on the wireless.'

'Senator Grady,' Bill put in. 'Everyone knows him. And nobody listens to him. He belongs in the past. An old fool talking about the IRA and the flying columns.'

'He'll be handin' them out guns next,' said Yvonne, herself laughing now. She had had her say and they settled down to their tea in a better humour.

8 The two Recruits hung about at Joe's dismal fire. Donohue had tired of their presence on the lay-by and had said nothing for a while. Olivine, after making them tea, was ready to go to bed. Mary, her swarthy daughter, malingering somewhere between the tents and the wagon, still watched them, the young Eddie Logan in particular.

Eddie's brown eyes shot about too, once encountering those of Mary as she moved into the bright light of Joe's Tilley lamp hung above the wagon door. Mounting the steps, she gave him a quick smile behind her stepfather's back.

Frank McManus, the big man, stood with his hands thrust into his greatcoat pockets, his mop of hair hanging forward as he hunched awkwardly by the low-blown embers. He was leaving it to Eddie to keep up a bit of conversation.

'What d'you think then, Joe?' Eddie was saying, 'Should we be here in the morning?'

'Oh, don't trouble yourselves. There's no reason to. They won't put us off this lay-by for a while.' Joe turned, looking into the vault of darkness along the Long Mile Road. They could hear a pony clattering up the road. Then the trap was caught for a moment in the headlight of a lorry and Wack pulled the trembling animal to a standstill close to the fire.

'Couldn't catch the bastard!' Wack shouted, standing up and staring down drunkenly on them from a great height.

The pony's blown sides heaved and foam was dripping from its mouth.

'You should put a blanket on that beast,' said Joe, solicitously. He had no notion what Wack MacDonald was bawling about.

'I'll beat his brains in the next time, I swear to God,' said Wack less loudly. Regarding the strangers he said, 'You fellas didn't do a whole lot this mornin'.'

'What would you have us do?' McManus asked, squaring his shoulders in his big coat and looking up at him.

'Kill Big Bill!' retorted Wack, laughing at his own audacity. He expected nothing but would taunt them for the sport.

McManus kicked at the dying fire with his boot, his eye on the lively little flame that came to life. He wanted to do something to bolster their ebbing prestige.

'We ought to take that up,' he said, still gazing into the embers.

Much as he hated Big Bill, Joe disliked this talk of violence. He knew it would be the Travellers who would have to answer for it.

1 'Holy Mary, Mother of God! A child will be killed stone-dead if we don't leave this road.' Catlin Connors was at the end of her tether.

Little Kitty had just been pitched against the bed-rail and was clinging to her mother, scared out of her wits by the sudden lurching roar of a great articulated lorry that was now rumbling away over the cratered tarmac. Along the line wagons heaved, their canvas tops sucked taut, chimney smoke descending everywhere.

Living at the side of the Long Mile Road had become intolerable with giant lorries on the move, up and down, all through the daylight hours and into the night. Diesel fumes darkened the air, putting an acid taste in the mouth. Unable to endure any more of it some Travellers were leaving.

'We'll shift so,' said Johnny, holding on to their two small boys.

Old Mick O'Brien had gone on that morning for Lucan, leaving only a score of caravans on the lay-by. A few bender tents remained on the grass verge, exposed by the thinning line of wagons.

Later in the morning, Johnny went along the line to talk to the three Wall brothers, Catlin's uncles. Joe Donohue was there when Steve Aiken joined them. He had known the Walls since his visit to the California Hills to buy Tom's wagon and now felt included in their circle.

'That's agreeable to us,' declared Luke Wall, when the suggestion of moving was mooted.

They began to discuss some land near the Seventh Lock. It was an old paddock where a few of the fellows had ponies turned out. Johnny and Luke went off to look at it. They came back with a favourable report.

Aiken saw that when Joe, Johnny and the Walls were in accord the rest were likely to follow. And around midday, the men fetched horses from the hill behind and yoked them.

The caravans and carts began to come off the lay-by three and four together, clattering away for the run to the Seventh Lock.

Over the next several hours, they flitted up the Long Mile Road and disappeared into the wintry lanes, where the ponies' hooves were muffled among the dead leaves. The desolate, sullied fields beside these back lanes, littered here and there by abandoned cars and poisoned as development crept closer, would not be farmed again.

Getting there in the afternoon, Steve and Denny passed the Seventh Lock Lounge Bar and went over the humped canal bridge and turned into the small paddock where the earlier arrivals were already assembled. Steve pulled his shafts close to one of the sheltering oak trees near the gate then went with Johnny and two of the MacDonalds to view the surrounding terrain.

They walked for a way between tall, dried thistles and sunken rocks. Decomposing paper, mud-encrusted rags, tins and bottles lay in the withered grass, the debris of the spreading city.

Not more than half a mile to the east of the paddock Steve could see the Ring Road. There against the grey horizon stood the familiar steel girders of the unfinished factories, and the two fields sloping away to the canal.

Shielding his eyes, Johnny MacDonald exclaimed, 'Sure, we're no distance from where we started.'

The four turned back, a cold wind tugging at their coats. Across Dublin the rain clouds, cut with a whitish light, drifted southwards towards the mountains.

Denise was unpacking some of her baskets. She had lost count of how many times she had done this task since coming to Ireland. One of her suitcases was full of dirty clothes and she intended, if wood could be found, to build a big fire and wash everything in a tin bath, like the Travelling women did. She glanced at the clouds, hoping the rain might hold off.

Through all the latest upset and turmoil, Denise had remained stoically uncomplaining. She did not want to become dependent on Tracey Meachen, she was part of the camp, and willing to cope and copy. But she would not become a Traveller as Steve seemed to want.

She could hear him in the lane with Johnny Connors. They had Dolly yoked with a set of chains and were dragging up a car body. They intended to barricade the front of the paddock.

The work went on into the dark by which time several car wrecks had been brought up the lane, packed with rocks and bound together with barbed wire.

Steve came back full of enthusiasm over these defences.

'See the car in the gate. We can move that to get past,' he pointed out to her, keen and boyish in his militant role. He wanted her approval.

Looking over his shoulder she saw the ring of fires that now jumped and flared in the darkness. Families were gathering about them for a late meal. It was a warming sight and she felt part of it.

A whole week passed taking them into late November. A mood of cheery optimism pervaded the camp. The men went out ragging and collecting scrap again. The women, walking to a distant bus stop, were calling in better-off neighbourhoods, as far as Ranaleigh and Terenure. They came home a back way, bearing their loot over the fallow fields from the Ring Road.

Through the day the camp at the Seventh Lock was left to the children and old mammies.

2 Denise, clever with her hands, sat inside the caravan weaving a rush ball. Rushes she had pulled from the canal lay on the small floor space at her feet. She found the work soothing. Tracey had not come to the Seventh Lock and Denise had given up trying to teach.

His back to her, Steve stood awkwardly at his typewriter, which he had balanced on the bed. He was finishing the article about the Commission on Itinerancy.

Having tugged through the last strand, Denise put the ball on the bed near him. With a little bell inside it would make a baby's rattle.

'I've got to phone the doctor,' she said to his back. 'I can't put it off again.'

'Right,' he answered absently, his mind on the composition.

'Come on!'

'Just a bit,' he said, fingers over the keys. 'We can walk up to the pub.'

They put on their coats and started up the lane. The wind blew at them through the tattered hedges. There was an old stone cottage standing alone behind a wall. Denise looked wistfully into a garden of dead weeds and wizened red rosehips. She saw the door was overgrown and the windows boarded up.

'Look, here's the place we need,' she said, gripping his arm. 'A home for us. It's near the Travellers and we could make a schoolroom in it.'

They stared for a while at the cottage and suddenly full of hope, turned and hugged each other, both wanting to nourish a momentary dream.

Steve kissed her hair saying, 'We'll look on the way back and see if the roof is solid.'

But he saw that the cottage was in reality only another derelict building probably awaiting demolition.

Beyond the stone bridge, the lane took a bend to the left. Back from the canal, shadowed by tall bare trees, stood the Seventh Lock Lounge Bar. Mikey Ward's pony and flat-cart were tied up outside.

Denise stopped herself for a moment. Her heart beat hard. 'I'm scared, I'm just scared to know,' she said, holding onto his arm again.

At two tables in the saloon bar Travellers sat drinking, glasses and bottles clustered in front of them. Eileen Ward was there and some Travellers they did not recognise. The young couple had no wish to get drawn into a midday drinking session.

However, Mikey had already seen them and waving his arm called: 'Over here, lad!'

They moved forward reluctantly, two locals watching with disdain.

Steve had the pennies for the telephone in his hand.

Mikey ordered fresh pints saying to the Northside Travellers, 'You should meet this fella'. He's the one trying' to get us stoppin'.'

They smiled a little hazily at Steve and then Denise. Somebody got up for chairs.

'Sit by me, dear,' said Eileen, taking charge of Denise. They were the only women in the bar. Denise looked out of the window at the canal.

While they continued drinking another man came into the bar. Aiken recognised him by his cloth cap. It was Sam Caswell, the Moped Man. He rose to order the newcomer a pint.

'I've got the greatest news for you now,' Sam said standing close to the Travellers. 'The Corporation is in a pure uproar. The fellas are close to striking.'

'About us?' queried Mikey, a little too drunk to take it in.

'About a lot of things,' said Sam. 'You're one big item. The eviction work has been condemned by the unions. Thoroughly condemned. They are sayin' nobody can be ordered out. But they may still find volunteers to do their dirty work.'

'They'll find 'em,' said Eileen, despondently.

'It's goin' to take a lot of sortin' out. Meetins and discussions and more referrin' back. You may get your month anyways.'

Though impatient to go to the phone, Aiken was curious to learn more about Sam Caswell. He asked him to which union he belonged.

'Never mind which union,' he said out of the corner of his mouth. 'I'm the real Red McCoy. Workers Party of Ireland. That's why they hate me in there.'

Seeing the impression this made on Aiken, he added; 'I've been a lot of things in my time. I'll tell you one day if you care to hear.'

While the talk at the two tables continued, Steve took a slip of paper from Denise and went to find the coin-box. In his absence, Eileen saw that Denise was worrying about something and moved her chair up.

'I had to go to the doctor's,' Denise answered to her enquiry not meaning to tell her all.

'God bless you. I hope it'll be a boy', the Travelling woman exclaimed, guessing immediately.

'I haven't had the result yet.'

'Ah, now dearie, don't mind me. The first is a worry of course but I'd hardly remember that would I? God willin' all will go well for ye.'

'Thanks,' said Denise quietly. 'I don't know what I want. I'm hardly ready for this.'

'Course you are, dearie.'

Nobody at the table noticed their conversation though that did not lessen the English girl's discomfort. When Aiken came back she looked up at him, her eyes wide. But he took a chair before attempting to tell her the message.

'Here's to you both!' exclaimed Mikey Ward to the English couple and three of the men lifted their glasses. Caswell drank too and Aiken took a sup from a second pint that had been waiting for him on the table.

Finally Steve bent close to her and whispered the one word – positive.

What she had wanted to hear Denise did not know. Her emotions were all mixed up and she tried to conceal them. Seeing she wanted to leave, Steve helped her to her feet and abandoning the gathering with the briefest of excuses, they went out into the fresh air. The touch of their hands meant something more now with her pregnancy confirmed. It connected them in a way they could not have experienced before. They were in something big, big and not entirely welcome. They had become three and permanently attached.

He held tightly to her maddeningly potent hand. Yet as they walked back down the windy lane she was, with her unwieldy, awkward gait, also a stranger to him. When their looks met, once, their eyes flew away from each other.

He did not know if she was glad or sad, only that they were both in it together. Their steps stopped on reaching the humpbacked bridge. A little distance up the canal, the heavy wooden lock held back its load of water. They could hear a gushing leak, cascading noisily into the stream. The water coming down from it through the rushes smelt of decaying leaves.

When they faced each other Steve told her, 'The doctor wants us both to come in.'

'Did he say what for?'

'To do with the blood test. He wouldn't say on the phone. He said he'd explain it to us.'

Instead of paying attention to his words, Denise was taking a perilous step down the bank. Her leg buckled and she only just avoided falling. Steve, still above her, expected any moment to see her slip into the canal. But having regained her balance, she was tugging at a bulrush. As he watched, more fearful now, the head broke off and she collapsed against the embankment.

'I've got it!' she called gleefully.

Steve moved down to her and they scrambled up the slope together, she with the bulrush grasped in her hand. At the top she asked: 'Did you say there's a complication?'

'I don't know, Denny.' He was annoyed with her and breathless.

'I hope not. The doctor's going to tell us.'

In worse mood, they strode on briskly, heads bent against the wind. Denise carried her prize, the fine brown head of the bulrush. She was thinking of the baby but she had not yet said the word in connection with the quickening thing inside her. Language could be awesome.

They came again to the stone cottage behind its wall and tried the gate. When the gate would not budge, they had to content themselves with the view from over the wall. Both saw now that the chimney stack was broken and slates were missing from the roof. It no longer looked inviting.

3 The Meachens had gone away for Thanksgiving and the young English couple delayed going back to see the doctor.

Walking about the camp, Denise now saw the other women differently. Mary MacDonald, with whom she sometimes talked, had endured eight labours, losing two of her babies. It was hard to realise what she had been through looking at her large, worn body. Then there was Maisie breastfeeding at seventeen, two years younger than herself. She had seen the girl at the Ring Road, waddling about during her last days. That would be a trial for her walking on her artificial limb.

These past weeks it had been possible to pretend to be married and yet remain single. The babe denied this duplicity. A little bud was pulsing in her womb. She was not one, she was two, caught up in procreation. Like it or not her body was part of this wonder and this curse. Only nothing yet showed on the outside.

Sometimes she felt it was beautiful; she had a sense already of gestation taking over. Yet it was still in some measure abstract, like biology at school. Propagation, the thing animals did. But now it had happened to her. And it would involve her growing very large like Maisie had. Her adoptive mother had told her nothing about sex or childbirth; not a word. Nothing had been taught her taught at school. She had never been inside a labour ward. She worried at her lack of knowledge and preparation. Thank God the ordeal of giving birth was many months away.

4 Unable to sleep, Denise was distracted from thoughts about the baby early one morning by the sound of voices at the other side of the hedge. Someone out there swore. While Steve slept on, she raised herself and peered out into the dark through the back window. The grey forms of workmen were just discernable. They were stealthily removing the barricade, hauling at the barbed wire that held the car bodies together.

Their closeness and clear intent alarmed her. But just as she was about to shake Steve, the loud tooting of a horn announced the presence of a lorry in the lane.

Steve aroused himself and jumped up. They kissed in silence and dressing quickly he was out the door.

In a minute she saw a fire blaze up in a flash of flames. He had put a match to the paraffin-soaked wood near the gate and the fire was creating grotesque dancing shadows among the bare branches of the two great oaks.

A few yards away, the hedge began to tremble violently and from behind came the noise of scraping metal on tarmac as a car body was dislodged.

Suddenly there was a rattling of falling stones on the road. They were thumping into the hedge and clanging off the wrecked cars. A second and a third shower of rocks and stones followed immediately.

'Hey, fuck this!' a workman's exclamation broke from the other side.

More stones rained down, some falling short and dangerously close to Aiken. He picked up a couple and flung them high over the hedge, ducking quickly back under the wagon. He could see in the light of the flames that the workmen had begun to scatter, leaving the barricade unbreached.

Everything in the lane went quiet.

When Aiken crawled out a second fire had been lit close by the MacDonalds' wagons. Mary, face ruddy in the firelight, was minding her kettle. Pat Donohue and his boys had gathered with the MacDonalds, all now cracking jokes and laughing wildly. There was Joe too, hands in his pockets, watching the front hedge as if he expected a rabbit to jump out.

As Aiken walked over to join them another dozen young fellows emerged from cover behind two carts. They went towards the gate, whistling and catcalling, some with rocks still in their hands.

Realizing that the Corporation had retreated, many who had not yet flung stones, girls and women among them, also ran up and massed at the front, jeering and shrieking. The stone throwing started again, this time at short range, accompanied by fiercer yells and taunting.

The sound of engines came through the hedge. The lorries were being backed up out of range.

A lull followed during which the morning light increased and both sides broke off for breakfast.

In the interval the Civil Liberties' picket turned up, this time five lads on bicycles. They put their bikes in a ditch down the road and shouldering their posters mounted a picket outside the barricaded gate.

Eddie Logan, his bicycle clips still on his ankles, was soon at the hedge peeping through for a sight of young Mary Riley.

She and Teresa Maughan, shivering excitedly from the screaming and stone throwing, came forward in a while with mugs of tea for the picket. They pressed in close to the car bodies full of innocent girlish coquetry as they passed the tea and received their thanks.

Mary stretched a bare brown arm towards Eddie. Their fingers touched an instant around the hot mug.

'What happened earlier?' Eddie asked her, ogling the girl through the bush.

'The boys drove them off with rocks,' said Mary, giving him a quick, bashful smile. They flirted for a moment before the two girls ran away.

The five Recruits stood about enjoying the tea, their army boots crunching among the stones. Then Frank McManus led the squad back to the picket line. Behind him strode Tommy Bowden and Paul Mitchell, a newcomer. Again the lads glanced up the lane to where the Corporation gangs were reassembling. There was enough daylight now for battle.

They watched Bill Redmond climb into his lorry. If he went away the delay would continue. The engine choked and moaned and the Leyland crawled slowly forward. Bill's large face loomed through the windscreen. All at once the lorry picked up speed and came straight at them.

Eddie faced the lorry a second longer, flinging the mug at it in self-defence. McManus reached safety behind one of the oaks. The others too just scrambled clear of the oncoming vehicle.

Big Bill slammed on the brakes and the lorry slid on its tyres to within feet of the oak tree. His jumbo-sized posterior came out of the cab door and he climbed down weightily to the ground, hauling after him his huge link chain.

Frank McManus, galled by his own panic, had an impulse to do something violent. But a body of guards was now approaching and in a minute surrounded Bill's lorry.

Big Bill went to work quickly, grinding the gears as the chain snapped taut. Slowly another car body was dragged clear into the road, leaving the gate open.

Seeing the bailiff's intention, the Civil Liberties lads picked up their battered posters and placed themselves gallantly in the freshly opened gap.

In the paddock the Travellers, led by Pop's Johnny, pushed a four-wheeler across the exit and crowding behind it, started a new uproar of jeering and taunts.

Some hefted sticks and rocks, though more for show than intent. There were little children in their midst.

The guards and Recruits pressed close together elbowing for room against the four-wheeler and it seemed a point of combustion must inevitably be reached when a tall inspector edged forward through the pack.

The inspector bellied up to the cart, his big frame making way for Molloy, the Housing Manager.

'Listen up here,' the officer commanded, his swagger stick lifted. Everyone fell quiet. 'Mr Molloy will speak to you and you would be advised to take his words seriously. We don't want any misunderstandings here.'

'I am calling off this operation because I don't want to see anyone get hurted.' Molloy looked over the ranks of Travellers. 'But I'm giving you due notice now that you must leave this land within the next twenty-four hours. That is by noon tomorrow. If you are not gone by that time, if any one of you is still here, I have it from the inspector here that he will on my request order the guards to come in and clear you off.'

Nobody said a word but they watched in satisfaction as the inspector, accompanied by Molloy, led the guards and workmen out of view up the lane. Shortly, they heard the sound of the motors disappearing.

1 The police inspector, coming to the feet of the women, waved his silver-knobbed swagger stick over them as if it were a magic wand.

'I'm warning you all if you don't get up we'll have to move you by force.'

Nobody budged, only blanked him with the same hard expression he had seen many times on the faces of the Tinker women on O'Connell Bridge.

He tried again in a more wheedling tone: 'Come on out of it for your own safety. You'll not do yourselves any good sitting there.'

The guards had entered the camp and swiftly quelled the stone throwing, allowing Bill Redmond to lead in his much reduced posse. They were mostly non-union men, who tempted by the extra money had volunteered for the second attempt to evict the Travellers from the Seventh Lock.

By the time Big Bill lumbered over with the first caravan, he found his way blocked by this human wall. A few of the boys, seeing an opportunity to stem the defeat, had helped push Aiken's barrel-top into the gap. The English lad had then gathered women and children and urged them to squat down on the grass around the shafts. More quickly joined in, spreading coats and shawls beneath them, and were now gripping the wheels of the wagon to prevent it being moved.

'Are we goin' to get any help to shift these people, for Godsakes?' Redmond called to the guards.

The women at the front pulled in their legs, swaying back involuntarily and a ripple of tension ran through the mass of Travellers as a moment later the phalanx of guards advanced in among the prostrate bodies. Arms and legs were seized and the women shrieked. A lightweight Catlin Connors, lifted like a doll, bumped out, cursing and twisting in her wrath. Then Eileen Ward was torn from her seat, flailing her thick arms and shouting in protest. Maddened by the sight of this violation of their women, men lunged into the melee. In the midst of it all, there was Big Bill fighting to slosh off his attackers.

Suddenly freeing himself, the burly bailiff made a grab for Steve Aiken. Plucking him from the front ledge of the wagon, he half-dragged the English agitator out to the road like a trophy.

One of the guards now stretched down and grasped Denise by the ankles, but shocked by the feel of the metal leg let her drop and stared with surprise into her face.

'I'm bloody well pregnant too – so you better go easy!' she screamed at him.

Three officers combined to lift her clear of the other resisters and set her down in the lane. She got up and stood with several other ejected women, all brushing themselves down.

The Civil Liberties lads, in their army boots, were still displaying their posters and gawking at the fray.

'You're not much help,' the English girl complained.

'We can't do nothin' with the Special Branch on our backs', said Eddie Logan.

He pointed to two plainclothes men and then at the tyre marks on the road. 'Big Bill tried to run us down yesterday. We've had a bit of a barney out here too.'

His placard in one hand, Logan squatted down and picked up a fragment of a broken mug. It was a piece of the one handed through the barricade to him by Mary Riley.

2 By the time the two of them had moved around through the fields to re-enter the camp at the rear, the skirmishing was all but over. Their wagon had gone and another barrel-top was being run to the gap. The battle seemed about to be lost.

They went to the Walls' fire where Martin Wall was showing off a bruised head.

'I tore the coat off one fella,' he told those around him, 'before I got the blow of a baton.'

Already the Corporation men were returning for a fourth caravan. A small crowd still milled around them, mostly children, taunting them with names.

But as this caravan reached the road, a great cheer went up.

Aiken set off to investigate and found Sam Caswell standing with Old Pat Donohue outside the gate. Some of the workmen were climbing into a lorry.

'I just got here with a shop steward and the fellas in the municipal union agreed to quit.'

Several more Corporation men, vilified since the morning, came trudging out of the paddock followed by a party of girls, waving and hurraying, happy to see them walk off the job.

The older women, wrapped again in their dark plaid shawls, looked on gravely.

'Ah, but that's not all of 'em accounted for,' said Caswell.

They could see Big Bill with three workmen walking towards the Walls' caravans. Half a dozen guards strolled in the rear of this little work party ready to subdue any residual opposition.

'I have to push off,' Caswell said. 'If Molloy catches me here he'll be after gettin' me fired and me missis won't like that.'

'Did you see where the Civil Liberties people went?' Aiken asked.

'They've adjourned to the bar above, I believe,' the other replied, taking up his moped. As he rode off he called: 'I'll come back later, if I can, and see how you're situated.'

Luke Wall meanwhile had noticed Big Bill and his party heading in his direction and hastened to warn his wife. Bridget was up in the wagon fussing over a baby's bottle. The milk had boiled up and spilled onto the stove, giving off a nasty smell.

The baby lay on the bed, kicking his legs and crying irritably.

Bridget was refilling the pan when her daughter Ann ran up the steps.

'Your man's here. We're next to be shifted.'

'Next is it? I'll next his neck!' Bridget bellowed, watching Bill approach and meaning him to hear. She could see he had the guards with him.

Luke had turned to face Redmond, resigned to the inevitable, when Bridget's strident voice sounded again from the door.

'Go somewhere else, I'm not ready for yer, I've to feed the baby here. God save us, they won't leave us a minute!'

Bill halted at the tip of the shafts. His three men hung back, close to the guards.

'Now Mrs Wall, we'll be movin' this wagon so. I want you outside and any children that's in there.'

'Well, I'm not comin' out!' she shouted, ducking her head back out of view.

Luke mounted the steps and opening the lower door went in after her. Then his head stuck out, calling for his brothers. In two seconds Martin and Jerry climbed inside. And before Big Bill realised what was happening, several of the Wall children darted up the steps and joined those on board. Bill waited some minutes believing Luke would pacify his wife.

'Will you get this settled?' he asked. 'We've a job to finish.'

Bridget's hot face looked down. 'I told you, we're not comin' out.'

'This is the ridiculest thing,' said the bailiff to those around him, now mostly a gathering of Travellers. The guards were smirking.

'Alright so, you have it your way.' He grasped the shafts and ordered his men to the wheels.

The men's boots trod the mud but nothing moved. The weight in the wagon had driven the wheels into the soft ground. The crowd now watched in fascination. Everyone saw it could not be done.

All at once the top door flew open and Mary lent out with the steaming pan in her hand. It remained poised for the longest moment above the broad back of the unsuspecting bailiff. Then the milk came down in a scalding sheet, over his head and shoulders.

Bill let out a roar of pain and dropped the shafts as Bridget's voice rose shriller: 'You may have the milk – you won't let the baby drink it, you old sow-pig.'

Redmond stood there gasping from the scalding and another delay ensued.

A guard came forward to admonish the Travelling woman and advise all those inside to come out. His effort was half-hearted.

'This won't do, missis,' he said to the closed door. 'We can't have this continue all day.'

The Walls were not giving up and the workmen gathered close by were discussing what they should do.

One of them approached the caravan. 'Will you listen to us? If you let us finish the job just this time, we won't take part in any such carry-on again. You have our word on it.'

Luke pushed open the top of the door and asked the man to repeat this promise. When he had done so, Bridget climbed down the steps carrying the baby in her arms.

Everyone was clapping and cheering as the rest of the Walls climbed down.

'An awful way to pass the time,' Luke joked to the crowd, making towards a churn of water to splash his face. They had been suffocating up in the closed wagon with the press of bodies and the stink of burnt milk.

3   Old Pat Donohue was busy in the paddock, overseeing the dismantling of his own bender-tents and the evacuation of the last of the other tents and carts.

Outside, a few workmen were already erecting a stout new fence.

Most of the Travellers were in the lane reclaiming their barrel-tops. The wails of children, confused by the chaos, could be heard all up the road.

A body of men had headed for the Seventh Lock Lounge. Both bars were packed with an odd assortment of Travellers and workmen. In the hot lounge bar, the two Special Branch men, their open coats giving a glimpse of holsters, were drinking whiskies and listening to the talk around them. The cash register rang repeatedly.

When Steve and Denise entered the bigger saloon bar people were standing. In their midst there was Pop's Johnny doing a clog dance, the men and women around him clapping in accompaniment, happy and celebrating.

The Walls brothers cleared a pew and the young English couple joined them. The day's events made a lively topic.

In the lounge bar Joe Donohue, sporting his red neckerchief, sat with the Civil Liberties lads. Frank McManus was spouting politics.

'Slainte!' he said, seeing the others drink and giving up on his lecture.

Paul Mitchell, the newcomer to the picket, raised his pint. 'To Free Ulster and down with de Valera.'

Next to him little Eddie Logan was getting plastered.

Later in the evening, Brendan Carey came in to the Saloon Bar. He had Sam Caswell with him. Making their way between the tables, they stood at the Englishman's elbow. Sam offered round his cigarettes.

'Should be cigars,' he said amiably. 'You have the Corporation on its knees.'

'They had enough of it this day with us. So did we but,' commented Luke, teetotaller and about the only man still sober.

'We had the Special Branch here,' Steve said to Brendan in an undertone. 'They were watching the picket but I don't know why.'

Brendan gave him a wry look and then said to all at the table: 'You don't know much do you? There's two of the Specials in the lounge bar now.'

'What are they in here for?' the Englishman asked.

Brendan regarded them in wonder. 'You don't know? The Special Branch are keeping a watch on those fellas because they're known Republicans. Your picket, your so-called Civil Liberties League is just a Republican front organisation. '

Steve's face showed he still did not get it.

'I could put it in plainer language for you but not in here.'

Brendan, a little drunk, seemed to be enjoying a private joke with Sam. It was the height of amusement to him. Denise, already irritated by the thickening cigarette smoke, rose from the bench needing fresh air.

The three of them went into the hallway. It was too cold to go out into the lane but the noise from the bars was enough to prevent them being overheard.

'Your men in there with Joe,' Brendan thumbed over his shoulder, his face close to theirs. 'An IRA splinter group.'

'How d'you know?' asked Steve, excited by the news that he was keeping company with men who like him had the bottle to defy the British Army.

'Some of these lads got interned as members of the IRA,' Brendan explained. 'They set up this civil liberties group to campaign against the Offences Against the State Act. They're at odds with the IRA for ending its Border campaign and likely linked up with people in the North who've tried to get it started again.'

'This is scary. It scares me anyway,' said Denise. 'We shouldn't even be talking to them.' And she twisted out of his arm and headed for the door. He followed her leaving Brendan Carey behind in the hallway.

Outside Aiken was surprised to see the silver-grey Mercedes-Benz parked in front of Carey's car. It must have just arrived. Grady sat muffled up inside. At the sight of him, Denise wanted to run.

They left the ring of light outside the pub and hurried in the dark towards the Seventh Lock bridge. When they had slowed down Denise challenged him.

'You admire the IRA don't you?'

'I admire their courage, yes. But we didn't have a clue did we?'

'Look what happened today. We were sitting down. They wouldn't join in. Guns and bombs and killing people is all they know.'

Steve said nothing and as they reached the bridge Denise broke away from him again and lent over the stone parapet. A skein of mist stretched away over the smooth water. Looking down, Denise saw dimly below a white image of herself. In England she and Steve had been of one mind. Falling out with him hurt. But she had to think of the baby now. He was fixed on something else. Something dangerous. She tried to let go her worries but could not. She felt they were suddenly in the pull of some great disaster.

Low fires were glowing all down the lane, blobs of earth-born light in the surrounding darkness. They passed the lighted windows of caravans and here and there a bright Tilley lamp hung at an open door. The night air was loaded with the smell of drifting wood smoke.

Near their wagon, close beside the hedge, a candle flickered inside a tent. From the tent came the hushed voices of small children, settling themselves down to sleep.

'I'm going back to the pub,' Steve said on an impulse, letting her climb the steps alone.

'Whatever for?' she said, turning.

'Now Grady is there I want to find out more. Call it a reporter's curiosity. I've got to go.'

'You shouldn't be seen with them.'

'I've been seen all day.'

She pulled open the door and stepping out of sight called down to him, 'You go your own way, Steve. I'm going mine.'

4 Aiken found the whole party seated at a long table in the Lounge Bar. Liam Grady looked small and subdued. His white hair and elderly demeanour separated him from the younger men.

Brendan and Sam Caswell had left and there was no sign of the Special Branch men. Of the Travellers only Joe had remained with the Civil Liberties crowd.

At the sight of them all together, Aiken felt a sudden misgiving.

'Thought you'd deserted us!' Frank McManus shouted above the bar room din.

Steve got a chair and sat down. A pint was placed in front of him almost immediately. He realised as he supped at it he had drunk his limit already.

'We're talkin' here about where the Travellers should go next,' McManus informed him.

'What's the consensus on that?' Aiken asked, wanting to hear Grady speak. 'Sam Caswell says the Corporation may be facing a strike.'

'That's right and we've got to take advantage of that,' McManus pronounced.

'I'm game,' the Englishman looked around at their faces. Joe Donohue said nothing and was the only one who seemed unhappy.

'To the dear old Phoenix Park,' McManus raised his glass.

'Right on to de Valera's front lawn,' said Paul Mitchell, whose red hair gleamed with sweat.

'All the lot together, lads!' McManus commanded, beaming round at his comrades. 'A blow for liberty. Let's shame the blind old bastard.'

Aiken picked up his pint. He was in boozy collusion with the IRA. They drank a toast to the occupation of the President's garden. It felt a little crazy and unreal.

When the glasses were back on the table Donohue spoke.

'The Travellers are not able for it,' he said, without meeting an eye. 'The minute we land down there we'll be in jail.'

'You didn't say that before, man.' McManus was annoyed.

'I thought you was only coddin'.' Donohue sat up straight. 'I would-n't go into Phoenix Park nor would any of those belongin' to me.'

They all sat motionless staring at the Gaffer. The fun had gone out of it.

McManus scraped back his chair. 'Fuck Dev. We could have shaggin' well done it!'

Grady came to life then, asserting his authority. He had the tact McManus lacked.

'Joe here is the spokesman for the Travellers and Joe has spoken,' Grady said, looking first at McManus and then at the others. 'Let it be, fellas. You can't knock common sense.'

He turned to Donohue saying with a note of apology, 'You're clear-ly a man of realism, Joe. This crack went a little too far and talking like this in here was not smart either.'

'I'll speak to some of the others,' said Aiken unexpectedly. He wanted to show them he had influence among the Travellers. Getting up he was glad to get away from the contentious atmosphere around Frank McManus.

Passing through the hall to look for the lavatory, Aiken caught a glimpse of himself in a mirror; bloodshot eyes and a desperate unshaven face.

He re-crossed the Saloon Bar to the Walls and they listened to his tale of the IRA and the Phoenix Park caper, and the Gaffer's veto.

'The man's right, it'd be a foolish and impossible escapade. I'd not go,' Luke said with some contempt. 'We'll find our own spot and they can march up and down there. I'm not sayin' we don't want all the support we can get.'

'Can you suggest somewhere else? Another park maybe?'

'Sure we can't stay in the lane. The guards'll be at us.' Luke thought for a minute then said, 'If those fellas want to help us we could try gettin' into the Lansdowne Valley. There's a park there. That'd do us.'

'Up the IRA!' put in Martin Wall, who was well inebriated by now. 'That'd be a knock on the nose for Big Bill.'

Aiken felt more than satisfied with his mission as he went back to relieve himself in the lavatory before returning to the mob in the Lounge Bar.

1 The morning light that had since an hour struggled through the rear window now began to waver over the interior surfaces, playing restlessly across her face, as the high-sprung wagon shifted backwards. Aware of this movement Denise opened her eyes. She could hear the clatter of hooves and the grating of the wheel-lock beneath the floorboards. A horse was being backed up into the shafts.

Then came Pop's Johnny's voice through the door: 'We're movin' on so.'

Denise raised herself on one elbow. 'Where're you taking us?' she called, realizing that she was alone.

'To the Lansdowne Valley. Hasn't he told you?'

'Nothing, I've been dead asleep here.'

''Twas all agreed in the pub last night.'

In her sleepy state the sudden activity bewildered her. The caravan was in motion but through the rocking green curtains she could not get a glimpse of either Dolly, the big mare, or Johnny himself. All she could do for the moment was to lay back and let things happen. It was like her nighttime train journey to Holyhead, she was being drawn inexorably forward by the will of others. Only this time the journey was not for love. More likely, she thought, it had to do with some plan of Grady's. She was, as she guessed with a shiver, in the hands of the IRA.

As if to confirm that notion there came in a minute the tinkle of a bicycle bell passing up the lane.

When Denise came to herself again the caravan had stopped. She could smell the strong whiff of pigs. Steve came in, dishevelled, his face still unshaven. He told her they were outside Bill Bermingham's in Bluebell Lane.

'The lads are out here. I'm helping them get some tools.'

'Which lads?'

'The Recruits.'

'Oh Christ, those!'

'I'll tell you what's going on when I come back.'

Before she could utter another word he was out the door again. Denise scrambled to belt her leg on and dressed quickly. She had to get around the mare's rump and climb down on a front wheel.

Outside none of the IRA men were in view. Johnny MacDonald was standing over a broken pram filling a churn at a standpipe. Just then a police car nosed into the lane and she saw Johnny accosted by the guards. She walked along to where they had stopped. It was the same inspector that had chivvied them at the Seventh Lock yesterday.

'What are you all doing down the lane here?' he asked, standing there tapping his swagger stick against his leg as a small crowd of Travellers collected around.

'We're splittin' up an' goin' our own ways,' she heard MacDonald assure him. 'There's none of us left above at the Seventh Lock.'

'You'd be well advised to get out in the country somewhere,' he told them, looking around at the apparently compliant faces. 'Well, go on then and just keep going.'

Evidently pleased with his little speech the inspector got back in the car. The engine was running and the car pulled smoothly away between the lines of wagons tightly parked within the confines of the lane, their ponies for the present idled in the shafts.

When Denise turned around, Steve was coming out of Bermingham's scrap yard with the Recruits. They were carrying sledgehammers and pickaxes. She recognised Frank McManus and little Eddie Logan; the one, she remembered, who had been flirting with Mary Riley.

She came up to Steve as the men mounted their bikes and hefting the heavy tools, rode off towards the Naas Road.

'What are they up to?'

'The IRA is going to open the park gate for us.'

It angered and disgusted her to see how chuffed he was. However, everyone and everything was now in motion and there was no time to talk. They went back together to their own wagon and within a short time were part of the column swinging and thumping at speed along the main road.

When they reached the Lansdowne Memorial Park, the guards came on the scene before the caravans had spread out between the flower beds. Infuriated at the sight of Tinkers occupying a public park, the officers ran about, batons in hand, looking for someone to blame.

In a pedantic English manner, irritating to the Irish ear, Steve pointed out that since the park was a public place no trespass was being committed. After some argument about Parks' Department bylaws, the outraged garda sergeant withdrew his men.

2 As Sam Caswell had predicated, a strike broke out in the Cleansing Department which partly paralysed Dublin Corporation. With rubbish piling up in the streets the City Manager had no time to take action against the Tinkers in the park.

In the Dail, Dr Noel Browne, a former Minister of Health, asked the Minister of Local Government Neil Blaney what he was doing, or intended to do, to implement the Report of the Commission on Itinerancy. Blaney replied only that the Government had the Commission's recommendations under consideration. Whereupon

Dr Browne rose to say, 'Is the Minister aware that Dublin Corporation is carrying on a cruel and inhuman hounding of itinerants in the area of this city?'

Aiken's article on the Travellers' campaign had been published in the Irish Times and even the British papers were beginning to follow the story. They had covered the parade and one had carried a picture of Dr Browne visiting the Travellers now under siege.

An open-air meeting in the Lansdowne Memorial Park brought together new adherents to the Travellers' cause, including students from Dublin's two universities.

A demonstration through the city was proposed to help sustain publicity during the current lull.

The long parade of wagons and carts wound slowly down to College Green, where the Travellers were joined by hundreds of undergraduates. O'Connell Street had never seen such a mob come breasting over the bridge. A jostling, jolly throng, it passed the GPO and around the Nelson Pillar, making its way finally to Kildare Street. Here the barrel-tops pulled up behind the slender iron gates of Leinster House.

Someone was playing an accordion and the front ranks, clutching their placards, began to sing. Joe Donohue, his black hair gleaming, passed a long envelope through the bars. The first Travellers' petition had been delivered to Dail Eirann.

Travellers' were calling for attention to their long neglected needs. They wanted recognition too for their way of life as a distinct people, the Travelling People.

3   'Do you know that you have an uncommon blood group?' the doctor said, looking at Denise Aiken's file.

'Yes, it's rhesus negative, I know that.'

'It can be a complication in pregnancy,' he said, 'and it seems from the blood test there's an added factor. You had a blood transfusion no doubt.

'Only a long time ago when I had my accident.'

'Yes, of course, Mrs Aiken.' He paused before saying, 'The analysis indicates that when they gave you blood the match was not exact. The probability is they gave you the wrong blood, in the emergency room perhaps.'

'I don't know what they did,' she replied, now fearing worse news.

'I have to tell you,' he went on, 'that your blood group and that of your baby are likely to be incompatible. You have a high chance of having a rhesus baby. That is one which has a haemolytic disorder, a blood disorder.'

'Can you save the baby?

'Mrs Aiken I'm only a general practitioner and you will need a specialist. But I can tell you what your options are. A rhesus negative baby needs a change of blood to enable it to survive. The usual procedure is to carry out a blood transfusion immediately after birth and I have to tell you that the success rate is not high.'

'You mean it's very risky?'

'Yes, speaking plainly it's difficult and risky.'

'What do you advise?'

'Here in Dublin they would in all probability recommend the post-birth transfusion. However, there is just the possibility of a second approach. Something very new. The British Medical Journal has a report by Professor William Liley on the first successful intrauterine transfusion. He has done a blood transfusion on an unborn baby.'

'Could I have it done?'

'All I have read is that this was done at a women's hospital in New Zealand. The procedure has not been tried here yet. In the event Professor Liley's work is taken up in London, or Liverpool for example, you might have a better chance by going to England. But I don't want to raise your hopes too much.'

'I'll go to England. I'll go to New Zealand. Anywhere to save my baby.'

'That's up to you and your husband. I don't know if cases are being accepted even in New Zealand. There would be a strict selection and the cost would be high.'

'What can I do?'

'Of course we've been talking about going to full-term with this pregnancy. I would not want to lead you in this matter. You could have a healthy baby. But I'm sorry to say the odds are slim. If you were to return to England you might have the option of a legal termination. Here in Ireland we are against abortion as you must be aware.'

Denise walked out knowing she was facing the hardest choices.

4 Back at the Meachen's apartment, Denise went another turn of the room and then collapsed into the armchair furthest from Steve.

'I want to go back to England. It's the only chance.'

'What, now? You're barely two months,' Steve retorted.

'I want you to come too.'

'I'd be arrested for desertion.'

'Nobody would know you were there.'

Steve was in a dilemma and searched for a compromise.

'We can contact some hospitals or this Professor Liley and you can go over later. If they agree to do a transfusion that is. But I don't want you to go yet. I don't want us to split up.'

'You don't want us to split up,' Denise said angrily, 'but you're not supporting me. You're thinking of the campaign and what's going to happen to the Travellers. Not what's going to happen to me – to me and the baby.'

'I'll find out for you,' said Tracey. 'I can make some calls to New Zealand if necessary.'

During the car ride back to the Lansdowne Memorial Park, the American couple talked about a Christmas party they were planning. Andrew wanted to invite the Fureys and other musicians. Behind them, Denise and Steve sat in silence. She took his hand and drawing it under her coat, pressed his reluctant fingers to her abdomen. Her heart beat for the baby now. He was something external but she did not want to lose him.

5 The Christmas Eve party was spectacular. An exclusively male company of Travellers trooped in bearing crates of stout. Andy Meachen, playing the Yankee host, had everyone downing shooters of his high-proof American vodka. The carpets were rolled back and soon everyone was cavorting together, all besotted with drink and each other. The younger Travelling men, rakish and gallant, flirted outlandishly with the bluestocking college girls.

Around them a lavish cold buffet awaited on the tables. The students fell on this food without compunction. The Travellers, following their own customs, almost ignored the edible refreshments.

Eddie Furey, the great piper, and his son Finbar, along with John and Paddy Keanan, came on from the Pipers' Club in Thomas Street. The four played endless reels and laments. The American was immensely proud to have the traditional musicians in his home.

None of the Civil Liberties bunch appeared. It seemed they had other places to go.

At one point, Pop's Johnny took centre stage giving the party his ballad about the Travellers' fight for rights. He ended it with these newly improvised lines:

Those students too, God bless them.
They did answer to our call.

Then Denise stepped forward and sang her blues, accompanying herself on a borrowed guitar. Seeing Old Pat Donohue there, she was saddened to be leaving the Travellers and sang for everyone in the camp; for all they had shared. She sang for her baby and the love of her man. It was her farewell performance. She was going back to England.

Afterwards, walking out abruptly on the applause, Denise headed for the Meachens' bedroom. Steve did not follow. Instead, he stayed with the Travellers, trying vicariously to share their pleasures. But he could not help remembering the first time he had heard her lilting voice, at the jazz club almost a year ago. So much more now bonded them; he could not believe they had come to the point of separation.

Denise had lain down alone with the lights off staring out through the long windows, homesick for England, sick for what she might be losing. She knew now that her childhood accident in addition to the loss of her leg might cost her the life of the baby she was carrying. Her fear was that if she could not save this one she might never be able to have a child of her own.

Tracey found her there and spread herself on the bed beside her. When the English girl glanced sideways Tracey had closed her eyes. Her long blond hair lay everywhere. She smelt of an expensive New York perfume.

'Steve won't like it on his own. He's sure to follow you,' said Tracey.

Denise sat up and blew her nose. 'The bloodiest thing is I admire him for what he's doing. I've never known anyone become so dedicated to other people. If it would just be to me.'

The American girl listened with growing sympathy as Denise explained her fears, allowing Denise in her desolation to nestle down against her ample bosom. Reluctantly, Tracey had to tell her that the new intrauterine transfusion procedure for rhesus babies was not yet generally available even in New Zealand.

Denise took this stoically, clinging to the hope that the new procedure might be taken up by a hospital in England before her baby was due.

'Anyway,' said Tracey, 'there's really no need for Steve to stay with the Travellers. Something big is going to be done for them. I'm not supposed to tell you this. Archbishop McQuaid is appointing a chaplain. He'll raise proper funds so that children can be collected from the roadside camps and taken to a special school. I know you have reservations about the nuns. But the Church can do so much.'

'I've told Steve the Travellers don't need him any more. They've got plenty of supporters now,' Denise commented, too concerned with herself at this moment to care what happened.

They could hear yet louder shrieks and stamping in the other room. The American girl said she thought the party was getting out of hand. 'I'd better get out there and protect the furniture.

There was rollicking fun through to the early hours. Finally, they all went home, leaving the devastation to the Meachens.

Some hours later, Andy and Tracey drove out to the camp. A hoary Christmas Day, the pots were on the fires. Displaying American largesse, the couple went the rounds giving out bars of chocolate to the children.

When they came to Steve's wagon, he and Denny were still in bed, tired, unhappy and hungover. Steve got up and lit the stove. The four drank black coffee together, listening to the church bells.

They were not in the mood to be impressed when Andrew told them that the Right Rev Thomas Fehily, Society of Jesus, was the new chaplain to itinerants.

Early on St Stephen's Day, the Dublin holidays were disturbed by an explosion. The huge blast, heard and felt over a wide area of the city, demolished part of the grandstand at the Leopardstown race course, upsetting the Christmas horse-race meeting.

It seemed to have been timed for when the stadium was empty and was clearly intended primarily as a message to the government. But the motive for vandalising this particular facility remained obscure to the general public. Nothing like it had happened for a long time. Since the IRA had ceased its activities it was not believed to have planned this bombing. In the press it was surmised to have been the work of an unnamed breakaway group.

6 In the New Year, to inconvenience the Travellers the Corporation closed the public lavatories next to the Lansdowne Memorial Park.

The dustmen's strike was over and Big Bill was out on his rounds again. Travellers had already been turned off at Ringsend and Coolock.

On a cold January morning Molloy, the Housing Manager, accompanied by Bill Redmond, paid a surprise visit to the Travellers in the park. They toured the camp seeking out anyone to whom they could preach their message. Sometimes only an elder child listened, cocking a numb, cold face.

'I've no quarrel with you people at all,' Molloy said, addressing Mary MacDonald. 'But the Corporation is getting a load of complaints. We cannot ignore the public.'

Mary leant her loose, flabby arms on the wagon door, looking down at Molloy, confused and disbelieving. 'It's the same all over, sir, is it not?'

'Well, you really topped it coming in here,' he said. 'And we've let you have a long stay. The Christmas included.'

Molloy, packed in a heavy coat, seemed to exude reasonableness. He told her in an almost amiable manner that no-one could flaunt authority indefinitely. For their own good, they should avoid a show-down and leave voluntarily

All the time something unsavoury smouldered at the edge of the MacDonalds' fire.

'I've come to make you an offer, Mrs MacDonald. You come out of this park and we'll not shift you for the rest of this winter. What d'you say to that?'

'Where would we go?'

'Anywhere that's not in the public eye. You know all the out-of-the-way spots.'

As they were speaking Maisie, her daughter-in-law, had crawled out of her tent and was listening to the talk. She sat cross-legged on the straw, her baby in her lap. The infant regarded the strangers dully, his wee pink mouth agape.

'Wack won't believe this,' said Maisie quietly. 'We've no call to move.'

'Have I ever broken my word?' Big Bill put in. 'Honestly now, Mary, and I've known you these years.'

'You were after terrorisin' us above at Walkinstown,' Maisie retorted. 'Didn't you break up this tent?'

'Well, consider it,' said Molloy more sharply. 'You won't get the same offer again.'

He and Redmond left them then and headed for the next fire.

Coming later to Denise, Maisie told the English girl what Molloy had said.

'I wouldn't listen. He said that to everybody and made the same promise at the Ring Road.'

'He did,' Maisie admitted, jogging her baby. 'Mary is that sick of it all.'

Denise took the baby from her while Maisie rolled herself a cigarette from some of Steve's tobacco. She had delayed going back to England, partly through lack of funds. She was in two minds when to leave.

When Steve came home from Kilmainham court he went straight to the MacDonalds' where Mary's husband John was seated by the fire, stitching a piece of harness.

'We've had a fair stop here, thanks to you and the students,' he said, without looking Aiken in the eye.

'Don't believe Molloy,' the young Englishman urged.

'Look at this place,' said John, indicating the mud. 'It's not fit.

Besides she's gettin' worse be the day. The asthma and her nerves.'

'Won't everywhere be the same in this weather?' Aiken was pleading now.

'Alright,' answered John, putting aside the leather. 'I'll tell you why we're leavin'. The IRA hangin' around Joe and that bombin'. One of those young lads is already braggin' they did it. Don't you know it's goin' to bring a whole lot of trouble? We'll be better out of it.'

Aiken withdrew defeated, worried for them and for himself.

It was drizzling, a miserable freezing rain, when the MacDonalds left. Maisie huddled down in Wack's trap, their few sticks and covers piled behind. She hugged little Tommy close to her in the shawl.

As old John MacDonald led them away, the clay clung to the wheels of his wagon, dropping a trail of muck along the Naas Road.

Their fire had died out, leaving a big empty patch in the park.

Two days later, word came that Bill Redmond had shifted the MacDonalds from Milltown. They moved in the rain to the banks of the Dodder and pursued there took refuge on Hungry Hill. Wack's leaky bender-tent now let in the weather and laying on sodden straw Maisie and Tommy took sick. The following week the three-month-old baby boy perished from pneumonia.

The MacDonalds trekked back to the Lansdowne Valley. The English couple went out to see them in. As the two wagons and the trap passed along by the park wall, they stood together in the rain waving a welcome. None of the MacDonalds waved back.

While Wack put up their sodden tent, Maisie, her lovely hair cropped short, told them how Tommy had died.

'He turned blue at the lips,' she said through her tears. 'I couldn't do nothing'. We was drownin' out there.'

Steve felt that what Bill Redmond had done was akin to murder. Denise too saw Tommy's death as a rank crime. It frightened her to realise just how easily a baby could succumb.

Maisie's tragedy drew them closer, yet she vowed to herself that she would get away from Ireland as soon as possible.

7 A crowd had gathered along the wall to watch the Tinkers evicted. The old wagons, towed out of the park by the Corporation tractors, caused a jam in the morning traffic.

After a futile delay and fearing for the safety of their children, the Travellers brought up their horses.

'We must go on,' said Donohue to Aiken, who himself was in low spirits. There was no sign of their supporters. The campaign had fallen to its lowest ebb.

Evening found them back at the side of the Long Mile Road.

❖

1 From the wagon door the Tilley lamp shone down on the darkened road, throwing moving rings of light and shadow over the empty shafts. A distance away in the cold crystal night, the flashlight of a bicycle, wavering rhythmically with the rider, approached steadily up the Long Mile Road.

Bent over the stove in the warmth of the caravan's interior, Denise was spooning baked beans onto an enamel plate.

As Steve took it from her, they heard the ring-rang of a bicycle bell outside. Denise put her plate on the bed and turning to the door took a peep.

'Looks like one of your Recruits,' she told him over her shoulder. She leaned out, showing herself to the visitor. 'You'd better come on up out of the cold.'

Propping the bike against the caravan and taking a packet off the carrier, he stepped over the shafts and climbed the steps.

'You don't have much room in here.'

'Three's a crowd already,' said Denise, as he sat down on the side bench, holding the packet against his body. The hot stove seemed to bother him.

'I'm Paul. We met in the Seventh Lock Lounge, yeah?'

'Nobody turned up at the park,' Steve commented, searching the other's face. He remembered now that this was Mitchell.

'Nobody told us. We'd have come if we'd known they were gettin' you out.' He paused and then said, 'I've come to ask you a big favour. And mind you, you owe us one. Right? The Special Branch is on our backs after Leopardstown,' he looked at each of them. 'You know about that, sure? '

To their astonishment Mitchell was them telling right off that he was here on IRA business. They wondered what was in the packet.

'We want you to look after somethin'. Just for a day or two like.' He grinned uncertainly, his fingers hesitating on the string. Then he tore open the newspaper exposing two yellowish waxed cylinders. 'Ammonal', he said, 'It's an explosive. The poor man's TNT. Some of what we had left over.'

Seated on the opposite bench, the pair looked on dumbfounded. Seeing their mistrust, Paul became more insistent.

'We've no-one else to ask at short notice. It had to be moved tonight. Now they won't come here that's for sure.'

'This is the worst place,' said Steve. 'We've got guards around us all the time.'

'Ah, we know that - but they're not lookin' for stuff like this are they?' He waited again and then went on, 'I'd have gone to Joe only he's not as level-headed as you.'

'Did Grady send you?'

'He trusts you, the Old Man does. Speaks well of you – yes he did. Of course he did.'

Steve was baffled yet sorely tempted. The dangers were unfathomable. But if this was a test of Grady's trust he did not want to fail it. On the roadside again, they needed the senator's commitment.

Keeping the opened parcel on his knees, Mitchell now reached into his greatcoat pocket. From it he hauled out a long, heavy revolver.

'Wouldn't Big Bill shit his draws if he saw this old blaster?' He raised the massive revolver. The barrel pointed at Denise. His finger was on the trigger.

Denise drew back from the weapon as if it were a deadly reptile.

'We just want this one favour. Don't be turnin' us down will you?'

'Just till Thursday?' said Steve, wanting that gun barrel off Denise.

'I'd appreciate it.' Mitchell spoke softly. 'Better for everyone. '

Turning to Denise, Steve said, 'It'll be alright just for these couple of days. Who will know?'

'Sure,' said the visitor. 'Good man.' He thrust the big revolver into Steve's hands. 'Mind, this is Frank's special. You have two rounds in it.'

While Steve held on to the weighty gun, Mitchell got up and put the ammonal on the bed. It sat between the plates of beans in their congealing tomato sauce.

'Don't worry, this stuff won't go off without a detonator. Only bear in mind it has to be returned. Army property. You can't just dump it or something.'

A minute later Mitchell was out the door and cycling away into the darkness.

Steve watched the disappearing red tail light; a danger signal that winked at his pretended calm. He unslung the Tilley lamp and turned it out.

Denise was lighting a candle, her face taut behind the flame.

'What are you going to do?'

'I'm going to hide this,' he said, holding up the big gun. 'Don't worry.'

'Get that bomb stuff out of here too. It could blow us up.'

He pulled on his jacket and putting the revolver into his pocket, took up the two sticks of ammonal in the newspaper, and got down onto the chilly road. His fear now was the fear of discovery.

The neighbouring caravan stood square against the night sky. Pop's Johnny and Catlin had long since gone to bed. Moving to the hedge, he lifted a strand of barbed-wire and ducked into the hilly ground that stretched in dim outline towards Walkinstown. Invisible on the far side laid the old camp.

Groping among the litter by the gorse bushes Aiken found an old paint tin. Into this he stuffed the newspaper and then carefully inserted the ammonal. As he climbed the slope, a cold, wet breeze blew on his face. He progressed at a crouch and for the last few yards crawled forward until he could see the spiky outline of the gorse at the top of the hill. Clinging here, more afraid than ever, he had a sense of falling, as if tipped at a dizzying angle the world was rotating under him.

Recovering himself and not wanting to be seen against the skyline, Aiken rolled between the prickly shrubs and lay on his back breathing hard. The grass was damp and the night-borne odour of the gorse pungent in his nostrils. The clouds looked as heavy and menacing as rock. Taking the gun from his pocket, he thrust it under the sharp foliage and with the tin placed on top, felt immediately relieved of the danger of possession. Accepting the gun and the explosives, he felt he had just made the biggest mistake in his life.

He was shivering when he got into bed.

'I've done a stupid thing,' he said in the dark.

'I'm worried sick. I don't want to know where you put it.'

'In a tin at the top of the hill.'

'What if Kitty goes up there and finds it? Any of the children?'

'That's what I'm afraid of.'

'Well, you'll have to move it.'

2   Aiken rose again while it was still dark, climbed the hill and pulled the tin from where he had hidden it the under the gorse. The revolver, when he groped for it, was wet and cold. He examined the weapon closely back in the caravan. The markings showed that it was an old British service pistol. It had a ring on the butt for a lanyard. He liked the weight of the gun in his hands. He felt empowered by it. When it was opened, bullets were revealed loaded into two of the six chambers, just as Mitchell had said. These he extracted and placed beside him on the bench. They rolled together with a little click. Then he closed it and raising the empty revolver pointed it at the door, squinted along the sights and pulled the trigger. The mechanism turned and the hammer rose and fell. He pulled again and then a third time like a boy with a new toy. He sensed its murderous potential, thinking of Big Bill.

Now he had to consider afresh what to do with the gun and the explosives. Mitchell had warned about it being IRA property. He thought of Liam Grady. The old man had stirred powerful feelings among the Travellers and proved a solid ally against Dublin

Corporation. Despite their early enmity, he did not want to let him down.

A subdued morning aura filled the caravan by the time Aiken had considered all this and decided on his next move. He extinguished the lamp and stowed the revolver in a basket, together with the ammonal, and touching Denny, awoke her from her sleep.

'I'm about to go,' he said, taking his peg-knife and adding that to the basket. 'I'll only be a couple of hours.'

'I want to come with you. Don't leave me on my own.' She was rubbing her eyes and feeling a sinking panic as she remembered the situation.

3 They were walking to the bus stop in Walkinstown Avenue. Aiken carried the raffia basket, weighted heavily at the bottom by the big revolver. A bus was already in sight when a police car came around the corner. They watched it prowl slowly past the caravans.

As it stopped on the far side of the road, a guard started to wind down the window. He shouted to them, something about leaving the lay-by.

'By the weekend,' Steve called back, realising the officer recognised him. 'Some might be going today.'

'Alright,' came the reply. 'But we can't let you stop there indefinitely.'

The car moved forward as the double-decker approached. They stepped onto it quickly.

The shock of this encounter still clung to them when they got off the bus and were mingling with the undergraduates in the quadrangle of Trinity College.

Steve left Denise in the refectory and went to find the hiding place he had in mind. She sat alone at the long table. Nearby, several young students were chatting and laughing. Denise eyed them. They had something to laugh about; for them this was an ordinary morning.

There were plenty of lockers in the halls of residence, as he had imagined. Old wooden lockers. But it was impossible to know which were empty. He waited in the tiny vestibule while students came up and down the stairs. At last, feeling rash, he thrust in the blade of his knife and succeeded in forcing a locker door. It swung open, spilling books and papers onto the floor.

Worried that someone would challenge him he grabbed up the basket and hurried out. He could not do what he had come to do. Not then anyway. He went back ignominiously to Denise.

'Let's go,' he said without sitting down. 'We'll go to the house.'

'What happened?'

'Too many people about.'

'This is getting worse,' she hissed. 'Let me go on my own. Nobody'll take any notice of me.'

He looked at her reluctant to let her go though knowing what she said made sense.

'Give me the basket!' She rose and took it from him and headed for the Ladies.

Denise locked herself in one of the lavatories and sat down on the seat. She had made up her mind to do this herself. Anything but hang about. Before last night she had been ready to leave Ireland alone. Now she passionately wanted them both to survive this day; she was sure she could persuade him to come with her. Unfastening her leg, she found that the two sticks of explosives would fit snugly into the hollow metal casing. She swathed them with lavatory paper and pushed them in. When she strapped it back on and lifted the leg it felt heavier. The small extra weight might unbalance her but it was manageable.

Looking into the basket, she transferred the peg-knife to her handbag. She squeezed in the gun, snapping the catch three times before it would close on the barrel. The handbag looked bulky and weighed a ton. That would not matter.

Full of fresh courage she came back to the door of the refectory and telling him to wait, left the empty basket and stalked away.

'Meet me in Trinity Library,' he called after her.

Divested of responsibility and at a loose end, Aiken headed towards the National Press Bureau. He could talk to Brendan and maybe ring Grady. He felt as guilty and furtive as a criminal, which it occurred to him he was.

'Denise is leaving Dublin? Get away out of that,' said Brendan

'She's pregnant and there're complications. She has to go to a specialist in England.'

'Have you fixed it up?'

'No but we've been told they can't help her here.'

Reading Aiken's worried face, Brendan said: 'Her leaving in a hurry wouldn't have anything to do with that Republican crowd? I told you you'd be in trouble.'

'I can't tell you, Brendan,' said Steve, sitting down now.

'Well, I can tell you,' said the other. 'If you're in trouble it's got something to do with Leopardstown hasn't it? '

'How would you know that?'

'Because I can put two and two together. Those Civil liberties lads were probably, in fact almost certainly, involved in the bombing weren't they? How they've involved you I don't know. But you're acting like a man on the run – running back to England. Is that it? You're leaving me in the lurch.'

'I'm not going back to England.'

'You'd be arrested over there, no?'

Brendan launched into a longer explanation. 'You've not an idea how they're connected have you? I'll tell you. It might help you to know,' he said, pointing a finger. 'First off, it's all about a cycle race.'

'Bicycles?'

'Yes, bicycle racing. I'm hankering after a story here. I've done some research. You may be able to fill in a few gaps.'

'Brendan, this is not about a good story. I'm in trouble, I admit. Please - explain it to me.'

'Okay. In 1953 a big cycle race was started. They call it the Tour of Ireland now. The fella who organised it was Joe Christle. In fact it was won by Colm Christle that first year. That's a matter of public record. Now Joe Christie lives a sort charmed double-life. He's a qualified barrister. Teaches law. At the same time he's a daredevil of the violent kind. An extreme Republican with his pockets full of bombs. Everybody in Seinn Fein knows it. Some hate him. More love him. He's at once a leader and an outcast of the IRA. Young Republicans led by Christle have dominated the sport of cycling for the past decade. Only now they're being elbowed out. Dropped from representing Ireland in races here and abroad. My guess is they've taken revenge by blowing up the new stadium at Leopardstown. Half daft and adolescent, it has all the hallmarks of a Joe Christle job.'

'The Civil Liberties picket. They always turn up on bikes.'

'Right. They're all followers of Joe Christle. That's my theory. I can't prove it. It couldn't be printed. But the guards know. They just haven't got the proof.'

'How did you come by this?'

'I got a bit of a start from Sam Caswell at the Seventh Lock Lounge that night. He mixes with these lefty Republican types.'

'D'you know anything about Paul Mitchell?

'Nothing. As far as I know he's just some minor scallywag.'

'I'm trying to get a grasp of what's going on. But don't ask me for details. I can't talk, Brendan,' his face was full of fear and apology.

'Alright. I get the picture.'

'I need to ring Grady.'

'Help yourself.'

Steve went to the desk and dialled Grady's number. He asked him if he had sent Mitchell. After a pause Grady replied, 'I did not.'

'Something's happened. Will you come over tonight?'

Instead of an answer the phone immediately went dead.

'Well?' asked Brendan.

'He put the phone down. But I think you can conclude he had nothing to do with it.'

'With what exactly?'

'With Leopardstown and getting me involved.'

Steve went to the door. 'I've got to meet Denny. Thanks Brendan. Thanks for everything.'

When Aiken got to Trinity Library in the big quadrangle Denise was still not back. He went to look at the Book of Kells and stood at the showcase in a kind of trance, mesmerised by the intricate Celtic pattern of the ancient manuscript. He was enmeshed in Ireland's troubles and desperate to get out. Most of all he was worrying about Denise. Letting her go to Irwin Street had been cowardly. He had got them into this mess.

4 There had been few passengers on the late morning bus on its outbound run to Ballyfermot. The lower deck was almost deserted. For the sake of warmth Denise sat near the front, enduring the throbbing engine and smell of diesel.

Inside the handbag on her lap, she felt the hard lump that was the huge revolver. A bout of heroics had set her on this mission; now she was frightened again. Already she had experienced difficulty concealing the gun from the conductor, while she fumbled for coins to pay the fare. Alone she thought with horror of the bomb in the metal casing of the leg below her stump. At each slothful advance and jolting of the bus, her insides weakened.

The smell of hot diesel was making her nauseous and she lowered her head, leaning her arm on the seat in front.

'Are you alright, love?' came a woman's voice from behind. A hand prodded her back.

Denise lifted her head. 'Just a touch of sickness,' she said. 'I'm expecting.'

'Oh dear. Well, you'll feel better when you get out in the air.'

The bell rang and the conductor called James Street.

Denise rose and with a wan smile to the woman moved up to the platform. The woman's kindly voice followed her, 'I hope it's a boy, God bless.'

When she looked up from the pavement, the other bobbed her head at the steamy window.

Bow Lane now sloped away in front of her, quiet and deserted. As the row of stone houses in Irwin came into view she stopped to rest on Bow Bridge. Then she took another look, surveying the empty wasteland where Pop's Johnny's hut had stood. There was a clear view as far as the shuttered-up Railway Tavern. No-one was watching. However she decided to avoid the street door, making instead for the shadow of the Railway Tavern. From the coach arch it was a short climb up the track to the back garden where the caravan had stood. Once there she was safe and out of sight.

Their abandoned garden, with its jumble of dead, sodden weeds and tumbled wall, was a forlorn sight. But she had no time to dwell on memories of their life here. Seating herself on a large stone, she got out the peg-knife and began to cut out a small square of the turf.

With the hole dug, she pulled the revolver from her bag and placed it inside the hole, pressing the turf down on top with her shoe. The result pleased her; its earthy tomb looked inconspicuous. However, for good measure she dragged the heavy rock forward until it rested over the buried weapon. She didn't care what happened to this gun, unprotected in the damp earth. It could rust and rot there undiscovered.

She started to unlace her artificial limb, feeling herself utterly helpless and vulnerable; if anyone approached now she could barely crawl away. Her anxiety mounted as she turned the leg upside down only to find the volatile packets of ammonal had jammed themselves tight inside the casing. Nervously she shook the metal prosthesis until the two cylinders slithered out onto the wet grass beside her. Some of the lavatory paper started to blow away out of reach.

In growing haste, Denise strapped the leg back on and got up to look about for a place to hide the ammonal. Her eyes alighted on the pile of firewood stacked close to where the caravan steps had rested. Stepping quickly to the spot, she laid the packets on the ground and covered them with sticks. Thoroughly scared, she did not care about anything any more, except that she and Steve leave Ireland before anyone found the cache.

5 Steve was standing at the door of Trinity Library when she got back. They clasped each other tight and she assured him the things were safely stashed

'I rang Grady. I've asked him to come up tonight and I'll tell him where you've put it. They can collect the stuff themselves.'

'Can't we just leave now? Get on a boat,' she asked, looking at him with desperate hope.

'I have to let them know first,' he said reluctantly. 'If Grady doesn't turn up, I'll go to Tommy Bowden. He lives somewhere in Palmerstown.'

The delay was agony to her but out in the crowded streets they felt anonymous and safe. Yet everything was changing and there was a sense of loss. Where recently the two had ridden their horse-drawn caravan in the Travellers' triumphant parade they walked now alone. They might be turning their backs on it all – the poverty, the mud, Big Bill and the IRA. The wet breeze off Dublin Bay smelt of the open sea and escape.

On top of the bus, Steve began talking about the cycle race and the link with the Leopardstown bombing. It didn't make any sense to Denise.

'Don't tell me any more. I don't want to hear it. Let's just collect our bags and leave.'

Steve said nothing. He had not yet agreed they should go and on that point was still struggling within himself.

The double-decker careered on past suburban streets where the Travelling women did their calling. Denise was keen to get off and peered ahead for their stop. As it crossed the Long Mile Road they were shocked to see that the lay-by was almost empty.

When they walked back to the corner only their own barrel-top and directly behind it Pop's Johnny's square wagon stood where they had left them that morning. Someway further down the lay-by, a flat-cart and a trap were being loaded. Except for the few Travellers engaged in this activity, the roadside was bare.

The couple stared along the road in disbelief, the more surprised because this sudden departure matched their own intention. Then they approached the old caravan. An alien, archaic thing, it seemed now to be resting there disowned.

Denise stepped up ahead of Steve, pulling herself onto the ledge. The caravan rocked in its familiar way as she got the door open. Inside was a jumble, the mattress on the floor, baskets and their contents strewn everywhere. Even the stove had been knocked out of place, leaving the chimney pipe at a crazy angle. A powdery grey peat-ash lay over everything.

They looked at it all in horror. And for an instant Denise thought that for some inexplicable reason Travellers had done this.

'Big kids!' she exclaimed.

'No. More likely the IRA looking for their stuff.'

Together they heaved the mattress back onto the bed. A suitcase and his haversack were underneath, opened and half emptied. As they squatted on the floor among their belongings, Pop's Johnny looked in.

'The shayds done it,' he told them, a twinkle in his eye. 'Come on out of it and I'll tell you what's after happenin'.'

The two turned to Johnny and followed him to his caravan, only too glad of a friend. Catlin had the tea made and in a minute they were seated around her new Delft.

'I've only got the condensed milk,' she apologised, pouring them some of her strong brew.

Kitty, rosie-cheeked and as bold as ever, handed round the sugar bowl and then ate a spoonful herself.

'Those Special Branch feins was here,' Johnny explained, grinning and unbothered despite the gravity of it. 'They began down at Joe's wagon and searched the whole lot – all down the line. For what I don't know. But didn't the boys take frit and before the guards had gone they start pullin' out, Joe an' all.'

His story was interrupted by the arrival of Pat Donohue. Johnny gave the old Traveller a hand up the steps. Pa said nothing to the company, only looked at the English girl, grief in his watery eyes.

'I think they knew the last one was yours and they spent the longest at it,' Johnny finished his account.

'I could hear them crashin' about in there,' said Catlin. 'I've only just cleared up me own mess, the divil take them.'

There was a silence then and Pat turned an enquiring face on Steve. He was the elder questioning a pair of youngsters.

'Well, what do you make of it?'

Steve rubbed his face, wanting so much to tell the truth. He hesitated a little longer and then said, 'An IRA man was up here last night.'

'Didn't I tell you?' said Johnny to Pat.

The young Englishman described Mitchell's visit, omitting to say where the gun and explosives were now stashed. For a long while no-one spoke. Catlin turned away to mind the children.

'You haven't put those things in the old house?'

Johnny's eyebrows went up.

'In the garden,' Denise stated simply.

'In the garden,' repeated Pat in a singsong. 'Aren't you the foolishest young people.' He shook his grey head, profoundly dismayed.

'I don't care who brought it – it's a plant,' said Johnny shortly.

'Of course it is,' Pat concurred. 'Docsn't make sense otherwise. They could have hidden it themselves – anywhere.' His face went flat and glum as he regarded the young couple. 'Don't you two see that?'

'There are ten thousand places,' commented Johnny. 'What if they did have a bit of explosives left over? Which I don't believe.'

'And the gun?' queried Steve.

'Sure, they've loads of old guns,' said Pat crossly.

Denise felt her anxiety returning as she took all this in. Pat's reasoning sounded only too plausible.

'We've got to leave,' she said to them, feeling now she was with three of the most loyal friends.

'You shouldn't be here now,' Pat responded hotly.

'I wanted to go this morning but Steve couldn't make up his mind.'

'For Godsakes go tonight!' Pat rasped out. 'Get out of this country quick.'

Catlin stood next to Denise at the little table. She put a hand on the girl's shoulder. 'We'll be terrible sorry to see you go.'

Another long unhappy silence followed. Steve, despite the danger, felt miserable that they should have to run. Their departure seemed ignoble.

Having lit his pipe, Old Pat lapsed into the corner by Johnny's stove. Outside an occasional lorry rumbled past in the fading light.

Everyone felt a finality, as if everything was ending with this day.

'We gave Big Bill a good run,' said Johnny. 'The boys won't give up either.'

Pat stood to leave. 'Thanks for all you've done. The school was the greatest thing.'

'I loved it,' replied Denise, suddenly sad. 'I love you all. Didn't last long enough did it.?'

'We'll remember you,' Pat said over his shoulder, hiding a tear.

Denise said goodbye to Catlin and they kissed each other. She gave Kitty a hug.

Johnny came outside with them. Behind them rose the dark hill, dim and insignificant.

'I'm going to pack,' said Denise leaving the two young men talking.

'What about the wagon?' Johnny asked.

'You can have it,' said Steve, wanting to make reparation for his desertion.

'I'll sell it and bring you the money when I come over. You can count on that.'

'We'll campaign in England – if they don't catch me and put me in uniform.'

'Why don't you get yourselves a little trailer? Go on the road with the Travellers. Nobody will know you.'

'I'd like to,' said Steve. 'I'd feel safer.'

'Go to the Speedway in Cardiff. The Prices are there. You'll get a trailer off 'em cheap and I'll meet you at that spot. You can stop there for weeks without no bother.'

'That's a great idea. Damn, I will. I'll see you in Cardiff. We'll get the boat to Holyhead in the morning.'

'God's speed,' said Johnny.

'Grady is supposed to come over. Keep an eye out for him, can you?'

'In his grand Mercedes-Benz,' said the other. 'He's the one to blame for this I'd say.'

Aiken tried to tell him otherwise but was still not sure himself when he left Connors.

'Up the tinmen!' said his friend, backing away and laughing, raising the young man's spirits as he had always done.

Discovering the two bullets in his pocket, Steve took them out and tossed them away into the grass beyond the barbed-wire. He wanted nothing more to do with guns.

Her baskets were all on the floor beside the battered rucksack and the suitcase. Eventually they lay on the bed too tired to wait up longer. But Steve did not undress.

'We ought to have gone to a hotel,' Denise said, yawning.

They cuddled together, close and warm under the bow-top roof. He was the old Steve again. The one for whom she had come to Ireland. She only had him.

The lorries had long since ceased and Aiken was drowsing when in the quiet night he heard the approach of a car. For a few seconds its white headlights lit up the front of the caravan. Denise felt him climb out of the bed.

6 They sat in the senator's car parked further down the lay-by with the heater on, talking in the light of a little low-watt bulb. Aiken told him what had happened.

'Paul Mitchell said you sent him up here.'

'That's not true,' said Grady. 'But listen laddy, I'm partly responsible for the situation you're in now. I got those lads to start the picket. But I want you to know this. I don't agree with what was done at Leopardstown. It was nothing to do with me. That's all I'll say on that score. But I will tell you something about Mitchell.'

'The Travellers think it's a set up,' Aiken interrupted.

'Him bringing you that gun was out of line,' Grady said and began to elaborate. 'Your Paul Mitchell has a job in the Forestry Department. Now those lads who were in the Curragh none of them got civil service places when they were released. They were in effect barred. Except Mitchell. That might not mean a whole lot but McManus does not like the man and we have reasons for not trusting him.'

Tired of theories, Aiken said, 'I'll hand the stuff back right now. Just drive me there. It's not ten minutes away.'

'I won't do that,' Grady retorted, now keen to end the meeting. 'But I'll pass the details on if you want me to.'

1 The dangers of yesterday had receded. They were almost safe now. The suitcase and haversack were packed and her baskets stood ready between them on the floor. In three hours they would be aboard the mail boat and far out to sea. A new beginning lay ahead of them in Wales.

But this new-found optimism was cut short by a voice outside the door. Although Aiken had never heard the voice before he recognised it at once. It was the voice a man on the run dreads to hear. He had heard it inside his head; a voice worse than the bark of a parade ground sergeant-major; more alarming than Big Bill's; the utterance of authority. In his subconscious Aiken, for all the bravado of his rebellious heart, had long accepted he would have to harken to it in the end.

Ironically, it was not the long arm of British law that had caught up with him, it was the Garda Siochana. But that made little difference; it was the police and they had come to take him.

'Alright,' Aiken called back in a voice alien to himself. He reached out both hands to the girl on the bed. Her slender arms came from under the covers. Her smooth, young face, her eyes so eager for life, now filled with anguish. Their eyes held and both knew now that they were lost. They grasped each other and held on in a desperate clinch. He could smell the tallow on her scalp; the smell of fear.

Only a while before, Aiken had stepped down to fill a kettle from the churn. He had noticed a small car pulled up on the opposite side of the road. There was nothing remarkable about the mud-spattered Volkswagen, nor the two men sitting in it. He had thought they were probably waiting to pick up a workmate. Yet their presence had increased his unease.

Other vehicles were passing up and down the Long Mile Road, rocking the caravan in their wake. When the parked car did not move he had become convinced they were being watched. He feared that he and Denise would be stopped before they reached the boat; or that Special Branch would be waiting on the quays. They were out there ready to arrest him the moment he made his move.

Not knowing why he hastened, he took his jacket and pushing open the door found himself looking down at two men waiting motionless by the shafts. Balanced a moment in the free air, he stepped down and, against all instinct, delivered himself meekly into their hands.

The handcuffs touched his wrists and closed.

One of them was talking to him as he was marched across the road. Aiken could not take in what the voice said. A hand pressed on his head and he was pushed into the car. Then Pop's Johnny was running up the verge. Johnny was shouting something.

The Volkswagen was moving and he caught a glimpse of the two caravans. He could not see Denise. Nothing more was said and in a while they were motoring down the Liffey embankment in a light drizzle, past the dome of the Four Courts.

Now he stood on the wet pavement outside the Bridewell. The fine rain darkened its fortress-like walls. His arm was gripped as the party waited to be admitted. Once inside the prisoner was halted before the long wooden counter where Eileen Ward had stood with her baby weeks before.

The two Special Branch hovered round him and the handcuffs were removed. This time he was able to pay attention to what they had to say.

'My name is Fleming. Sergeant Fleming. We're Special Branch officers. You've been arrested under the Offences Against the State Act on suspicion of being a member of an illegal organisation.'

'I'm not,' said Steve, gathering his wits.

'You'll have an opportunity later to answer any charges that may be brought against.'

'What charges?'

'You'll know soon enough.'

After a brief exchange with the station officers, the Special Branch men left.

Aiken was told to turn out his pockets and as he did so, another guard fished into his jacket. He found Aiken's knife and laid it on the counter. Everything was listed and slipped into a brown envelope and when this was completed he was led upstairs.

2 From the dark landing he was thrust forward alone into a drowning white light. The slam of the door behind him, the turn of a key, followed by the grating of a bolt spelt out his situation. The dense walls now cut him off from everyone and everything he knew; excluding the normal world. The air itself was imprisoned. For a moment, however, he would not look at the bare stone room; refused to acknowledge his surroundings.

Eventually, the cold in the cell, his isolation, compelled him look around to seek comfort. He lowered himself onto the metal bed and pulled the single, grey blanket around his shoulders. Still the chill spread through his body. He felt ill.

The hours passed. He did not know how many. In his solitude, the piled stonework of the prison bore down ever heavier. An anxiety, like a new phobia, took hold of his mind; the dread of sudden calamity about to happen. The Bridewell would fall in on itself and crush him.

Towards evening, the coldness of the cell increased and he sat up. For distraction he examined the four walls and found there some fading graffiti. There were obscenities and many undecipherable scratch marks. High up in the old paint someone had chiselled UP THE IRA. The words were meant no doubt to lend heart to successive Republican occupants.

He was not in the IRA but had associated with people who, according to Carey, had been ejected from it. If his handling of the gun and ammonal came to light, the police might consider that by helping them he had in effect joined Joe Christle' s mob. He had been arrested as such and classed with him. But as to the Leopardstown bombing and the issue around the cycling, he cared nothing. He had only got involved out of the mistaken belief he was doing something for Senator Grady. Only last night Grady had denied any part in Leopardstown; did not agree with it and had not sent Mitchell to him with the packet. So it was for Paul Mitchell that he had taken that colossal risk. Mitchell, he knew now, was not to be trusted; might possibly be an agent provocateur working for the Special Branch. He had in all probability been entrapped.

Here he was, he thought, a prisoner of the state; surely a political prisoner.

This reasoning helped him to conquer some of his fears, while arousing others. He needed to think logically and figure a way out. What his legal position might be Aiken did not know. He had no knowledge of the Offences Against the State Act. He had no way of gauging how serious it was to be accused of membership in an illegal organisation. Nor what the penalty might be. There had been no mention yet of his being an accomplice, of his accepting the gun and explosives and agreeing to hide them. That would be a more serious charge – if they could prove it. And they would be able prove it if the whole thing was simply a plant and Mitchell was their man. The conundrum tried his mind and his emotions. But a desire to survive this ordeal put a fresh edge on his efforts.

The big question was whether the Special Branch had found the cache at Irwin Street. Sgt. Fleming had made no mention of it. Aiken had no illusions however. They were certain to go to the old house and search.

And it struck him now that if they did find the gun his fingerprints were all over it. So, most likely, were Denise's.

The thought made him hope she had gone ahead and caught the boat to Holyhead. That would be the best news he could get. If any outside news was to reach him inside this medieval keep.

He wanted her to get away even though it meant he would not see her. He must now put her first.

What Denise had done had been under extreme duress and only to help him, not the IRA. She could not be blamed by anyone. Rightly, he was the one they had arrested and he alone would have to see this through.

Everything might depend on fingerprints evidence. In the light of this realisation he began to examine his right hand, looking closely at the whorls on his index finger and thumb. When he tilted his hand to the light, the lines and patterns stood out quite clearly. The sight of these means of identification filled him with dismay. His own flesh was going to betray him.

Aiken started to bite into the fleshy thumb pad. Ignoring the sharp, prickly pain, he gnawed off some of the skin, and spat little fragments onto the dirty floor. Soon his right thumb was raw and oozing. In a ferocious, panicky bid to destroy the living evidence, he went next for the index finger.

He looked at the result with satisfaction. He had devoured or spat out small areas of his own fingertips.

Then it occurred to his somewhat demented mind that the freshness of the little wounds would arouse suspicion. Without further thought or delay, he pinched up dust from the floor and rubbed it into them. Now they looked dark and nasty, the blood still coming through in tiny blobs. It would dry up presently, he told himself.

When the excitement of this self-mutilation had passed his fingers began to hurt. He clasped them hard, his eyes searching for a distraction. They stopped on the small, high window, recessed into the thick masonry. The iron grill and the grime on the glass barred most of the external light. But the window had a crack at the top to let in air. Through this small opening faint street noises reached into the cell. The cries of children at play somewhere and the distant rumble of a bus on the quays.

In his pain he thought of Denise. A few hours ago they had been together. It seemed a lifetime already. How long a separation lay ahead he could not tell. He tried to push it out of his mind. The long drama of the day had drained him. With a little difficulty because of his fingers, he got his shoes off and lay back under the coarse blanket turning his head from the light. All that he could do to save himself he had done. Now he must rest. In a twilight of shallow sleep the evening slipped away.

At some indeterminate hour the grating of the hatch in the door roused him. A tray was placed there with a plate and mug on it. There was a cheese sandwich which he ate hungrily. The cocoa was lukewarm and watery. After this small supper, he stood over the lavatory bowl, the presence of which had been offending him all day. Its ceramic nudity seemed designed to rob the prisoner of human dignity. Now he needed it.

Where the skin had been torn away on his thumb a blister had come up. Doing up his fly buttons was awkward. If queried about the fingers he decided to say that he had burned them on the caravan stove.

It came him now that while being admitted he should have asked to make a telephone call. He had heard that everyone brought to a police station had that right. He regretted that he had not had the wit to insist on it. So when a pair of white hands showed at the hatch, he flew to the door.

'Can I telephone somebody? I believe I'm allowed to do that.'

A pause and then the voice from the other side; 'I don't know about that. You'd have to ask when they bring you down.'

'When will that be?'

'Oh, not so long I suppose,' the other said in an indifferent tone.

The hatch banged shut and his jailer walked away. Aiken could hear him closing another further down the row. He listened intently for the prisoner's voice. He could hear nothing. But for a wild moment he believed Denise might be there.

The little strip of dark blue that had been visible in the high window had disappeared. The murky lower panes reflected only the electric light coming from the fitting in the ceiling. Night had arrived outside. Still he was not summoned. Eventually, it felt late and he knew he ought to be asleep. Instead he was stretched on the bed wide awake, continuing to speculate with sinking spirits on what might happen to him. It dawned on him that they were keeping him waiting through these long hours for a purpose. He was under subtle pressure. They were manipulating him. The anxious wait, the bright light preventing sleep; it was a strategy to weaken and break him down. He had not simply been locked up and forgotten. He was being prepared. The sinister intent, the implacable hostility, made him feel as menaced and frightened as he had been when arrested that morning.

3 Denise had suffered the first shock of Steve's arrest, staring in horror out the open door from where she lay on the bed. She watched propped up on one arm, helpless, unable to follow him because of her crippled leg. She heard Johnny's shout and pulled herself to the back curtain.

'Where have they taken him?' she called out of the window.

'I don't know. They wouldn't say.'

'Oh God, Johnny what am I to do?'

'We'll find him shortly. Don't be frettin'.'

'Let me get up then. Will you take me to the telephone?'

'I'll be waitin' on you.'

Denise strapped on her leg feeling in the lowest spirits. Catlin made her a cup of tea and she shared a little breakfast with them, while Johnny fetched his new pony from the hill. They drove to a kiosk outside the shops in Walkinstown.

Pressing in three pennies, she got through to Brendan Carey at the National Press Bureau. She told him about Steve's arrest.

'I'll phone around and call you back. I'm sure I can locate him. What's your number there?'

Encouraged, Denise dialled Tracey Meachen while she waited for Brendan. She had not seen her since Christmas Day.

'Good golly, that's awful.' Tracey's voice in the receiver sounded shrill. 'Let me know if there's anything we can do.'

Denise had Liam Grady's number but she hesitated to telephone him. She didn't trust him. She hated the idea of talking to any of them. They were to blame for what had happened. A further fifteen minutes passed before the telephone rang. Carey was apologetic. He had not been successful.

'The Special Branch is a law unto itself. They could have him anywhere. I've called the usual places but no-one will say.'

'Thanks for trying anyway.'

'Steve said you were to get the boat today. Will you still be leaving?'

'I must stay on and do what I can' she said. 'Thanks and come and see us when you can. We're still on the Long Mile Road.' She put down the receiver and through the squares of glass shook her head at Johnny on the cart.

The rest of the morning Denise spent with Catlin and Kitty, helping with the boys. Pop's Johnny went out collecting until four o' clock. When he came back they went again to the phone but Brendan had no news. She did some shopping in Walkinstown, feeling like a fugitive. She had begun to fear that the Special Branch would come back and arrest her. She told herself this was irrational as they would have taken her at the same time they took Steve.

Johnny pushed the wagon around so that the front faced Catlin's door. It gave Denise a little protection, and reassuring closeness with her only neighbours on the empty windswept lay-by. Evening descended and the traffic thinned out. Nobody came by, only a stray white dog who sniffed at the wagon wheels, lifted his leg and padded on. Now she was alone with a stub of a candle on a saucer where Steve ought to have been. She kept thinking, as she had all day, of

Mitchell's visit and the fatal packet he had brought. Just as Pat had said it had been a mistake to put those things in their own garden. Several times she had had the urge to go there again and move them. It was the biggest thing she could do to help Steve. But each time her fear had prevented her.

She had a horror of touching the ammonal. In any case she could not ask Johnny to go there. The police might be watching the house. By now it was possible, even likely, that her hasty hiding places had been discovered. Going to Irwin Street would be foolhardy. Her appearance there could provoke them into arresting her. She had to stay free in order to help Steve. Oh, it would have been easy for her to leave Ireland and run away from all this. But she could not abandon Steve not even knowing where he was.

Around midnight, Denise had to climb out of the wagon and go into the hedge. As she squatted in the free, cold air, she looked up at the pale, glittering slope where the ammonal and the revolver had first been concealed. The clouds had gone and a bright, crisp moon was rising in the rare clear sky, illuminating the frosty hill. Steve should have turned Mitchell down. They could have moved on with the others.

4   Aiken was at this time following the jangling keys of an old warden through an ill-lit labyrinth. He descended stairs and tracked low corridors somewhere deep inside the bowls of the Bastille-like Bridewell, anxiety mounting at every step. The young man was approaching close now to his first trial; a testing trial of wits by interrogation.

Inside the hot, bare office, the man at the table was of athletic build, like any old hurling player. His steel-rimmed glasses hooked onto round bruised ears, the greying hair cropped short. He indicated with a gesture that the prisoner seat himself on a chair close into the table. Aiken obeyed but this proximity to the big man immediately bothered him.

He was becoming aware of the queer warm, unpleasant odour that reeked over the place. As in his cell, there was here the faint smell of ancient, rotting mortar. A whiff of fresh carbolic had been added that only partially overrode a hint of human sweat. The air stank from tobacco smoke. Over all hung a night-time atmosphere of covert strife, of pending violence and violation.

He watched in wretched fascination as his interrogator took out a metal cigarette case, while continuing to peruse the papers in front of him. Then he was under the chief's hard blue eyes again, magnified through the glasses. He was being offered a cigarette.

'I'm Chief Inspector Cullan.' The chief addressed him in a cultured

Christian Brothers' voice.

The smoke came out of Aiken's mouth and nostrils as he slowly exhaled. He was pretending, under cover of the smoke collecting before his face, that he had not noticed what had been placed at the corner of the table; the two yellow sticks of ammonal explosives.

'Now Aiken, we know a lot more about you than you realise,' Cullan told him. 'You've been made a fool of by these Republican lads. They've made use of you haven't they? You're an intelligent person. You surely know you should never have associated with them.'

Steve could not meet his eyes and fought to calm himself. Cullan was observing the effect of this speech and the presence of the ammonal.

'You're in very deep water,' he went on. 'However, we're not particularly interested in you either way. We could have you locked up for a very long time. You could get seven to fourteen years for what you've done. But I'll tell you candidly, that's not the point of the exercise. We're interested in the people you've been helping.'

The young Englishman listened, puzzled and a little relieved. He took another drag on the cigarette. It had burned short and the heat was irritating the blister on his thumb. He changed the stub to his left hand and rested his sore fingers out of sight below the tabletop. He still said nothing.

'It's Christle we're after not you,' the chief said finally, looking hard at his prisoner.

Cullan seemed intent on cutting away any lingering loyalty Aiken might be harbouring towards the IRA men. Joe Christle was a man Aiken had not met and a name, he now realised, he had better forget. Not one fact had been introduced. No mention yet of the lethal mix of ammonium nitrate and TNT lying there within three feet of his elbow on a fragment of Trinity College lavatory paper.

Aiken was scratching his wrist. A red itchy line had appeared. He was being tempted to aid the Special Branch. With a clear hint that he could save himself, they were goading and manoeuvring him into becoming an informer. Only Cullan wanted a confession of his own involvement first.

'Why should I have anything to do with Republican politics?' Aiken declared. 'Me, an Englishman? You know I'm not going to join the IRA.'

'No we don't!' Cullan now waved his hand over the ammonal. 'This was found on your property. This is ammonal. Stolen some while back. We knew the IRA had it and now it turns up in your garden.'

Aiken offered no comment; his glance averted to a large ashtray that held an accumulation of cigarette ends in a bed of collapsing ash.

His head got a sharp cuff as another voice demanded from behind: 'Who gave it to you?'

But the Englishman had nothing to say.

'You'll have to tell us sooner or later,' Cullan shouted.

'What were you planning to do with it?' The second detective spoke close to his ear.

Aiken recognised that voice and twisted around. It was Sgt Fleming. He had entered the room as if on cue and was standing at the Englishman's shoulder. He smelt of aftershave. Perhaps he had been home.

The sergeant straightened up, his eyes on his chief.

Cullan made another bid, saying: 'It'll be better for you if you co-operate. We haven't charged you yet and maybe we won't – if you'll answer the questions and tell us what you know.'

An intricate game commenced. Cullan and Fleming alternated their approach. Fleming pressed the young man to implicate himself, while Cullan wanted to get from him any information he had about the IRA splinter group. He questioned him closely about the Leopardstown bombing. They obviously believed Joe Christle had organised it. From what Aiken knew they were right.

Twice when he faced around Aiken had seen a third man, with a notebook. As best he could tell the man had not yet written anything down. From this Aiken drew a little encouragement.

Aiken could not help dwelling on what Grady had told him about Mitchell. His goose might be cooked already. But he had to deny everything. In silence lay the one chance of getting himself out of this. At one stage he said carefully, 'I didn't go to them. They came to us.'

'Who came to you?'

'Senator Grady. He visited us at the Ring Road. He was concerned about the school and what's happening to the Travellers. I suppose you know the Corporation burnt the school down?'

'I'm not asking you about Grady and we're not interested in your itinerants. Who else came?'

'Members of the Irish Civil Liberties League.'

'Who are they?'

'The chairman is Frank McManus. I don't know them all by name.'

'Give us some more names,' Fleming said, jolting his chair with a sudden kick.

Aiken hesitated, confused in his own mind as to whether he was giving too much away. He knew what they were but he had to remind himself he was naming members of a legal organisation with legitimate activities.

'There's Paul Mitchell and a chap called Eddie, Eddie Logan.'

'When did you find out they're a bunch of extremists?

'All they did was picket at Walkinstown and then at the Seventh Lock. Your men saw them, so why ask me who they are?'

'That's not the whole story. You know quite a lot about Leopardstown don't you?'

'Yes, it was in the papers.'

'Don't try to be clever, Aiken. It won't help you,' said Cullen, himself smirking at the Englishman's duplicity. 'You still haven't explained this.'

Again he indicated the packets of explosives.

Aiken, who had now become cagey and obstinate, stared back at him. 'I'm a ban-the-bomber. I'm a pacifist. I came over to Ireland to keep out of the army. I don't agree with the military in any country and in any form. And that includes the IRA.'

'Maybe. But you've been helping these lads, right? You thought you owed them a favour.'

Cullan said nothing more and the fuggy room fell quiet. Fleming left his side and walked out the door. Aiken sensed some new development in the air.

The sergeant came back brandishing a newspaper and coming to the table spread it out flat between his chief and the prisoner. It was the Evening Press and the headlines announced RACETRACK BOMB ARREST. Next to the story was a picture of the house in Irwin Street.

Aiken bent over it, glad to hide his face for a moment. One paragraph read:

Following the arrest of a man at an itinerant camp, Special Branch detectives spent two hours searching a private house.

Under the table his thumb had begun to throb. He was very tired and wanted somehow to bring the interrogation to an end.

'I'm not a member of the IRA and I had nothing to do with what happened at Leopardstown,' he told them in the frankest tones. 'If you're going to go on trying to connect me with that madness, I don't intend to answer any more questions. Not without a lawyer here.'

'We'll get your lawyer here all in good time,' said Cullan, his hands flat on the table. 'What I have to say has to be got over now between me and you. All off the record if you like.' He paused before making his final offer, looking at the Englishman with an expression of patient condescension.

'If you'll just open up now and tell me what you know about these people, give us a full account of what they've been saying and doing, it's probable that you yourself won't be charged. We'll let you go. You can go back to your itinerant friends this morning.'

Leaning back in his chair, the chief again dangled the temptation before his victim. Then Cullan spoilt the effect he had so carefully created by adding with a note of disdain: 'And look at it this way. If we do charge you, which we should from what we've already got on you, your crusade for the itinerants will be over. You'll be discredited and behind bars.'

In the silence that followed Cullan kept his head very still. But he had given himself away. The Special Branch wanted to decapitate the Travellers' campaign. That's the message Aiken now got. No doubt Cullan was after the Leopardstown bombers. Only the build-up of evidence against Joe Christle was not the limit of his interest. The Special Branch had no great enthusiasm for obtaining Aiken as a state witness. The chief had spent the past three hours laying an elaborate trap baited with a false promise of freedom. The instant he implicated himself, by any admission, with Christle's group Aiken would be finished

'I've been a bloody nuisance to you, haven't I,' said Aiken quietly. 'Perhaps I've been a fool too. You've just opened my eyes to that. You say I've been mixing with criminals. But who are the real criminals? The real criminals are men like Bill Redmond, and Molloy, the Corporation Housing Manager who makes families homeless. Eviction is a dirty word in Ireland I hear. But nobody stops them from what they're doing. D'you know a baby died?'

Cullan began to shake his head and display his sarcastic smile. He saw the hardening resistance in Aikin's face and made no comment. Instead he looked at Fleming who had remained standing behind his prisoner. He gave him a nod. Unseen by Aiken, Fleming reached into his shoulder holster and pulled out his gun. Leaning over the prisoner, he laid the weapon with a clatter alongside the packets of explosives. It was a flat automatic.

'We know you've got one of these!' Cullan barked, watching Aiken closely.

The sight of the gun, although in no way similar to the big Webley service revolver, shook Steve. The possibility of physical violence hung in the smoke-filled room. Fleming was in motion, he could hear his boots on the wooden floor. The detective came back and gave the chair a kick that nearly unseated him. Out of the corner of his eye Steve saw Fleming lift his hand and instinctively ducked his head. The officer's fingers merely brushed through the boy's hair.

The touch was offensively familiar.

Fleming lowered his moustache to Aiken's ear. 'You're gonna get thin on top, lad. D'you know that?'

'About your girlfriend,' put in Cullan. 'I doubt your Miss Hanley will still be around if we put you away. The girls don't usually wait you know. You won't see her again.'

Fleming took his cue, speaking to the back of Aiken's head. 'She's expecting your baby, true? What d'you think will happen to them if you go inside. It's not only yourself you've got to think of is it?'

'Denise has done nothing wrong. She's only done good.'

'She'll suffer all the same and it will be your fault entirely, Aiken.'

'I want a lawyer here,' the Englishman said. He was holding tight to his sore thumb.

'Well, you won't get him here at three o'clock in the morning,' the chief said, sounding at last tired of it all.

'I'm not saying any more.'

For a moment Cullan looked provoked. But he pushed back his chair and stood up. 'Alright, you've had your chance,' he said with finality.

He called the warden and told him to take the prisoner back to his cell.

5   Relieved to be locked in and left alone, Steve sat on the low cot bed. The cell was his refuge now. His mind swam from the questioning and those questions of his own.

Feeling hot, he threw of his jacket. When he took his shirt off, he noticed that the red blotch on his wrist had extended itself along his forearm. The line, he saw, when he twisted his arm, extended right up under his bicep. There was a lump in his armpit. Putting a finger there he felt the swelling. The soreness and pulsing worried him. Before he could examine his arm further the light went off.

He lay under the blanket, trying to think against the pain, hand clasped to his wrist. Although dog-tired, he forced himself to go over the interrogation. Special Branch were concealing something. Fleming's play with the pistol gave a lot away. It threw additional suspicion on the role of Paul Mitchell in all this. He thought back to Mitchell's fatal visit. Then it struck him how odd it was that Fleming had arrested him at the Long Mile Road before the discovery of the explosives at Irwin Street. They must have picked him up then sent people to search the property. Yesterday's report in the Evening Press confirmed this.

It seemed to Steve now that immediately the gun and ammonal had been left with him, the Special Branch had been told. Not tipped off but told by someone working for them: Paul Mitchell. If that was the case they had certain knowledge of his guilt. Or, to put it the other way, his innocence. He had been set up. He was doubly convinced now.

As he continued to shiver and ponder, a bit of moonlight crept gradually across the floor. Steve got a glimpse of the white moon, like a silver sixpence, behind the grill. It had appeared like a messenger of hope.

There were questions in the affair that he could not satisfactorily answer. Perhaps he would never know the whole story. He was exhausted now and no longer thinking coherently. But he knew one thing for certain; nobody could tell them where the Webley revolver was hidden except Denise.

The dull ache under his arm persisted. His head was hot. His mind sped on in freefall, close to sleep. Finally he thought he had better tell someone he was ill. With an effort he stumbled to the door in the faint moonlight and called through the hatch. Then he took up one of his shoes and started banging on the steel door, until footsteps sounded on the landing. The hatch grated open.

'You've got a bell you know. What d'you want?' The guard sounded peeved.

'My arm hurts. I think it's poisonous.'

'What did you do then?'

'I burned my fingers on the stove at home. Now there're red marks up my arm and I've got a temperature.'

The cell light popped on and the guard unlocked the door. Aiken twisted his arm to show him the red line. He took the young Englishman's arm and looked at it for a moment.

'Okay so, I'll report this. But next time don't be hollerin' like that. See on the wall there? That's your bell.'

The door shut again and Aiken sat on the bed in a sort of trance of waiting and fatigue. An hour later, a police surgeon entered and put his bag there beside the prisoner. Through bleary eyes Aiken saw a little man with a pot belly and white hands. His right hand and arm were carefully examined.

'This is not a burn,' the doctor announced brusquely, glancing in the young man's face.

Aiken offered no explanation as he was examined further and the lymph glands pronounced to be abnormally swollen.

'There are definite indications of septicaemia.' The doctor addressed the warder. 'He needs treatment right away.'

As suddenly as he had arrived the doctor closed his bag and left. The warder pulled the door, leaving it half open. In a minute he came shuffling back.

'You better get dressed,' he said in his cheerless voice, pointing to Aiken's shoes.

Aiken was taken down to the well-lit lobby where a plainclothes officer was waiting. A moment later they were outside in the cold, dark shadows of the street. A freezing breeze blew along the pavement, swinging a street-lamp on its wire.

In a bigger car this time, Aiken was driven through the deserted, pre-dawn streets of Dublin to the Mater Hospital. He seemed to be alone in the world. Yet freedom was tantalisingly near.

His armed guard stood behind him as Aiken faced a fresh young nurse in the Casualty Department.

'I've no address. I'm living in a caravan in Walkinstown,' he informed her. She filled in the form, baffled by the presence of the Special Branch man.

Then an intern arrived, a youthful doctor not much older than Aiken. He looked like a medical student. When aware Aiken was in custody he assumed a serious expression and took his patient behind a green curtain.

'What have you been up to?' the junior doctor asked in a lowered voice, helping Aiken off with his jacket.

'They're holding me under the Offences Against the State Act.'

'Oh.' He paused his interested aroused. 'But you sound like an Englishman.' He was winding the pressure pad around Aiken's left arm.

'They won't let me contact anybody.'

'Is that so?' his attention was divided for the moment. 'Let me get you an injection. This is bad.'

'Would you ring someone for me?' Aiken whispered.

'I could.' He slid a notepad towards him.

Aiken took hold of a pencil and with his sore right thumb sticking up scribbled a number.

'Carey to call Grady.' Aiken told him. 'Just that message.'

After having the thumb cleaned and dressed, and the other fingers swabbed, Aiken re-emerged from behind the curtain. The intern informed his escort that the patient would have to be admitted.

'Without penicillin your man could've been dead within twenty-four hours,' he said, reproving the policeman.

Meanwhile, the nurse had taken charge of Aiken and was giving him the shot.

The general ward was asleep lit only by a dim night-light. A duty nurse walked quietly ahead, followed by Steve Aiken and his guard. Stopping at an empty bed, she sat him down on a chair and promptly swished away over the linoleum.

The Special Branch man waited, adrift in the middle of the ward. Steve eyed him, wondering if he would be left alone here. Presently the nurse came back with a set of hospital pyjamas.

He undressed fully for the first time since his arrest on the Long Mile Road and climbed gladly between the starched sheets. His arm ached but nothing now could keep him from sleep.

1 Emerging from the lavatory in the blue hospital pyjamas, he went to the row of basins and doused his face, between splashes glancing morosely in the mirror at his escort. The Special Branch was keeping Aiken under armed surveillance even in the bathroom.

Eventually the breakfast trolley arrived and sitting up against the pillows, he enjoyed a bowl of cornflakes. Long irked by the man's constant presence, he had decided to ignore the policeman seated by the bedside.

He was mildly startled when the detective addressed him.

'I'll be here the whole day so you might as well know who I am,' he said. 'The name's Barry.'

As if from nowhere, like a magician, he produced a large orange and handed up to Aiken.

'Thanks,' said his prisoner, further surprised by this small kindness.

The Englishman looked at the man's face. In his mid-thirties, he had tired, well-circled eyes and a harelip. Possibly treading water in mid-career he was there to see Aiken went nowhere.

Later in the morning, the two were exchanging a few sentences when into the ward strode a lawyer, dressed for court in a formal morning suit of black coat and pinstriped trousers. This opulent figure came on briskly, flashing a smile at the patient in the bed.

'Hello Mr Aiken, I'm Melvin Calhoun, barrister-at-law. I've been asked to represent you, if that's agreeable to you.'

He sat himself heavily on the bed, spreading waves of confidence.

'Is this fellow here all the time?' Calhoun asked in a mockingly lowered voice.

Aiken gave a reluctant nod, a little embarrassed by the affront to his new guard acquaintance. He started to scoop together some of the scattered orange peel.

Calhoun stretched back his sleeve and looked importantly at his watch. 'What time did they arrest you?'

'Bit before nine o'clock yesterday morning.'

'So, they've been holding you well over twenty-four hours and still haven't charged you. Well, they can go no longer than forty-eight. That's the maximum allowed by the Special Powers Act.'

'Will they let me go tomorrow?'

'I've no idea on that point. They could come in and charge you in here this afternoon.' Then turning around to Barry, hidden from Aiken's view by Calhoon's large bulk, the barrister said: 'Officer, d'you mind leaving us for a few minutes? I wish to speak to my client.'

When the Special Branch watch had moved away a distance to the ward door, Calhoun became confidential, his manner bordered on the conspiratorial.

'I've a fair idea as to what happened to you,' he said, his face assuming a knowing expression. 'Senator Grady called me late last night and asked if I would take on your case. We're personal friends you understand. Now is that what you want?'

Aiken assured him it was, glad to have such a weighty representative.

'I don't want you to tell me what you did. That could merely be embarrassing. Rather I need you to tell me what the Special Branch know. What you believe they know.'

'I've told them nothing,' said Steve hastily. 'I've signed nothing.'

'What did you tell them?' Calhoun persisted, less affable now.

'I said that Senator Grady came himself to our camp and later sent along members of the Irish Civil Liberties League to picket.'

'Did you mention any of their names?'

'Yes, I said Frank McManus is the chairman. I think I mentioned Logan.' Steve searched the barrister's face for a sign of approval.

Then he said slowly, 'Cullan, that's the Chief Inspector Cullan, said he'd let me go if I told him what I knew. He wanted me to turn informer but I'm certain it was a trick. I wasn't ready to go that route anyway. Too ashamed – and scared.'

'Did any other name come up?'

'Cullan said they wanted to get Joe Christle not me.'

'You wouldn't want to go repeating that name,' the lawyer warned. 'That's dynamite.'

After some further questions and discussion Calhoun offered his opinion.

'From what I know of the circumstances they've enough to justify charging you but possibly not the evidence to get a conviction. It's a borderline case.'

The State would rely entirely on the discovery of the explosives on Aiken's property. Somewhat unfortunately, he had paid off O'Keefe and was currently the freehold owner of 14 Irwin Street. By legal definition the ammonal had been in his possession. That was undeniable. Calhoun believed, however, that a jury might view the charge in a different light if the defence could create a reasonable doubt as to who put the two sticks of ammonal there.

Aiken hastened to impress on him how the land at the rear of the old house afforded an invisible approach. Anyone could roam over the plateau outside the walls Old Kilmainham Hospital without ever being seen from the street below.

'The garden is wide open,' Steve emphasised, seeking a shield for Denise. 'Nobody would be spotted slipping in there.'

'Then we'll invite the jury to inspect the location. They can form their own opinion.'

Finally, Calhoun had a query. 'If you were to be deported from the Republic you'd be picked up by the Military Police over there?'

'That's the danger, yes. I'm wanted for dodging National Service.'

'Alright then, we shouldn't attempt to strike a bargain along those lines.'

Calhoun lifted himself from the bed and took up his briefcase. 'I'm going now. But should they come and charge you I'll be here. They have to let me know.'

2 The sight of Denise, just ahead of Brendan Carey, cheered Steve. He lifted his arms to her and she stooped to meet his lips.

'You look awful,' she said, putting her basket on the bed.

'You get on that boat. They're going to charge me. I want you out of it.'

'Can't you shave?' Denise insisted, ignoring his remarks and glancing sideways at the Special Branch man.

'This is Barry.'

The two nodded at each other.

'Brendan brought me down here. He made that phone call for you. He showed me the news in the papers. I didn't know where you were.'

'Are you all right?'

'The both of us, yes.' Denise patted her belly. Then she touched his bandaged thumb. 'What happened?'

Using his good hand, he pulled her head down and whispered in her ear, adding in an ordinary voice, 'They're going to operate on it. Clean out the infection. I could have died.'

She wanted to utter a remonstrance but instead busied herself unloading the basket.

'Here's a few clean things. A decent shirt.'

'Have you got any cigarettes?'

'Right here. They're from Johnny. He and Catlin are really looking after me.'

'Are they all sticking together?'

'No, they've scattered all over the place. Joe Donohue has gone to Mullingar.'

The news confirmed his doubts. He feared the Travellers would break up.

'They'll be back,' Brendan said over her shoulder. 'Sure Dublin's their living.'

After a while the ward sister, a stern matron in a white cap, came to shoo them away. All morning Aiken was getting special visitors and she deemed it time to intervene.

'Off you go now, the doctor will be here on his rounds shortly,' She did not look at the guard at the bedside.

Carey bent forward, offering his left hand. 'I hope you'll be out of this soon. It's making a hell of a story.'

'Thanks for bringing her.'

3 That afternoon Pop's Johnny Connors moved the two caravans to the California Hills. He could not abide the isolation on the Long Mile Road.

Denise stood behind Dolly's lumbering, ample rump, the reins slack. She was letting the mare walk in the wake of Johnny's square wagon. Ahead hidden under horizontal clouds, the sun was setting unseen over the western edge of the city

She was gladdened by the sight of familiar faces. Children ran up clapping their hands. The Walls were back in the California Hills. It was like old times.

Among those to whom she was closest old Pat Donohue was missing. He had returned to the Seventh Lock. The MacDonalds had reassembled on the Back Road, a rural lane running through to Palmerstown. They were close to the Cherry Orchard fever hospital and not far from the shops at the Gala cinema.

4 At the Mater Hospital Steve Aiken was about to be wheeled into the operating theatre. Although a minor op it required a general anaesthetic. When he came round in the ward, two men were waiting at the bedside. It was official visiting time and they had drawn up chairs on the opposite side from Barry, his bored guard.

Steve lay groggily between the three of them while patients and their visitors ambled about the ward. The level of din in the long crowded room drowned the quiet talk of Joe Christle's men.

Frank McManus saw Aiken open his eyes and was the first to bend over him. 'Don't say anything. It's me Frank. I've brought you some ciggies.'

Steve looked with blurred vision into the pale blue eyes set in the shadowy, sinister face.

'D'you want a drink?' Eddie Logan peeped at him, small and boyish beside McManus.

'Water,' muttered Steve, turning his cheek to the pillow, confused by the attention.

As Eddie half rose from his chair, Barry passed him a carafe from the locker top. The Special Branch man inched closer hoping to be in on what was about to happen on the other side of the bed.

McManus bent again, very close to Aiken's ear. 'Did they get me gun?' His words were inaudible even to Eddie. But as a tease to the detective he said aloud, 'The papers said nothin' about that.'

Steve was shaking his head, doubt on his sickly face. McManus waited, glaring at the Special Branch man.

When Steve turned to him, licking his dry lips, Frank put an ear close to his mouth. 'Go on. The dummy won't hear.'

'Under a rock near the front of the garden,' Aiken murmured, his head still reeling.

'Okay.'

Frank winked at Eddie. Defeating the Special Branch on this one would be a treat. With new animation, the broad shoulders doubled once more and Steve had to strain to catch his next message. 'We can get you out of here. Fast car. You'd be over the border in a couple of hours.'

Aiken closed his drugged eyes. A pulse began to beat in his neck. He saw himself in Grady's Mercedes Benz dashing for Belfast. But the offer had a ring of hollow bravado about it. It also sounded insanely dangerous.

'What about your man?' he mouthed the words in the Dublin jargon.

'We'd take care of that.'

Aiken imagined the hue and cry that would inevitably follow. He was too stupefied and weary to cope with this. The risks were unacceptable.

'Melvin Calhoun was here,' he said, raising his voice to break the spell. 'He expects I'll be charged. He says I should go for a jury trial.'

McManus continued to look at him for an answer. Aiken shook his head. He had had enough of the cloak-and-dagger. It oppressed him.

5 That night Frank and Eddie toiled like grave robbers in the garden behind 14 Irwin Street. Wielding their bike lamps, the two probed among the dozens of large stones from the fallen wall. At last they found Frank's old Webley in its shallow rock tomb. It was wet and soiled.

'The witless wonders missed this,' McManus remarked, laying the big revolver in a handkerchief. He pocketed it inside his greatcoat.

Eddie Logan, misaiming the beam of his torch, was gazing over the marvellous spread of city lights.

'What's the next bit of crack?' he asked Frank, half in jest to a man higher ranked than himself. 'Big Bill or knockin' Nelson off the Pillar?'

'Never mind what Christle wants. We're gonna knock off Big Bill.'

6 At noon on the third day after his arrest, the guard was removed from Aiken's bedside in the Mater Hospital. Officially he was no longer a prisoner. However, a Special Branch officer loitered in the corridor outside the ward, keeping a close watch over the Englishman and his visitors.

Stephen Aiken was a now a man in the news. A Telefis Eireann crew did an interview in the ward. He spoke about the continuing plight of itinerant families around Dublin. But when the news item went out later in the day it was introduced with a slant that inflated the young man's notoriety:

'An Englishman, living at an itinerant camp, arrested this week in connection with the Leopardstown bombing, is now in the Mater Hospital...'

The sister on duty told Aiken he would be discharged after lunch which had put him in great spirits. Bolstered up in bed, eating a plate of braised beef swimming in gravy, he saw himself as a free man again.

Denise arrived bringing Tracey and Andy Meachen. The American couple were all smiles and ready to celebrate.

Propped shakily on the linoleum, Aiken got dressed. His three companions closed around and supported him out of the ward. As they negotiated the stairs, his confidence grew; Barry's replacement had gone and, as far as could be seen, the Special Branch detail inside the hospital had not been replaced.

But outside in the street a jovial Sgt Fleming awaited his approach. Denise held onto Steve's sleeve, striving against his being taken from her. Fumbling with the handcuffs on account of the girl's agitation, Fleming acknowledged the Englishman's convalescent state and changed his mind.

'Come on,' he said. 'We've only to take you back to the Bridewell.'

He let the young man, still leaning on her arm, follow him towards the police car. At the last moment, Denise let go and the door slammed, leaving her gazing in despair through the glass that now divided them.

Andy Meachen watched the arrest and did not like what he saw. The whole scene brought home the extent of Aiken's culpability. He had intended once more to befriend Steve and had got in some booze for a celebration. But this proximity of the Special Branch put him off. Tracey, her neck and face flushed crimson, stayed put beside her husband only out of decorum.

The two Americans shot across to their red Ford station wagon and climbed in. As the police car pulled away with Steve aboard, Denise was left alone on the pavement.

The sight of the red car's sudden departure galvanised her mind to immediate needs. Her limb cracked as she hastened back into the hospital. Soon a taxi carried her down O'Connell Street, past the Nelson Pillar and up the north quays, where she was dropped unceremoniously outside the Bridewell.

Inside, the large ledger-like charge book stood open on a lectern.

A barrister in morning suit had bellied up to it and was reading the fresh ink through his glasses.

She stood close to Steve as his entry document was given its final touches.

The reading over went on like an incantation. Aiken listened for every nuance. The charge alleged that on or about the 3rd of January 1966 Stephen Richard Aiken had under his possession a quantity of explosives with intent to injure or endanger persons or property. Calhoun at once drew his attention to the phrasing and advised his client that he could make a formal response now in the garda station, or wait to plead in open court.

Aiken steeled himself at the thought of standing trial. His mind however refused to clear and, looking at Calhoun for confidence, he had to wrestle to regain his reason. The height of his peril forced him to be honest. He was not innocent. Yet truthfully, his reluctant pact with Mitchell had not included plans to hurt anyone. Though Mitchell had made a comic, hostile jibe and he himself had toyed with the fantasy of shooting Bill Redmond. But that had involved the revolver which was outside this charge.

In an even voice he declared, 'I am not guilty of this charge.'

He was allowed a few minutes with Calhoun. There was not much to be said and the barrister remarked that the room was probably bugged. 'Apparently they have no reason to want your fingerprints,' Calhoun commented suavely.

When they came out he went to Denise and held her hand in both his.

'I needn't have done this,' he mouthed to her, wiggling his thumb. Then they clung to each other, her cheek wet. This little time together might be their last.

'Tell the lads I'll be out again.'

She nodded tearfully and he had to go with a guard up to the cells.

7 Confined in a different cell, Aiken paced about it, smoking one cigarette after another. Now a custody prisoner they had let him keep Johnny's supply. When promptly at ten the light went out, his current fag glowed between his scarred fingers, a little nub of red warmth in the chill dark of the Bridewell.

He had been charged; that was an irrevocable step. A trial was now inevitable. And possession of explosives, as Calhoun had explained, a serious felony offence. The political overtones of the case might help him but if convicted Aiken faced the possibility of a long prison sentence. That assessment appalled him. It was a steep price to pay for shielding the IRA.

The trial at the Central Criminal Court would be a humiliating exposure. Though having great faith in Melvin Calhoun, one of the brightest barristers in Ireland, he loathed the idea of being the subject of a legal contest however brilliant. He would be exhibited, poked with questions and most of the time ignored. He knew what court hearings were like. The knowledge that this night in the Bridewell might be extended into years inside some distant prison began to devour his courage.

This is what it was like without Denny; an emptiness with little to light it. Ahead stretched long years of separation, deprived of her happy voice, her warmth. In the shorter term, their child would be born in his absence. He was sorry now that while pretending downstairs incarceration left him undaunted his last message had been for the Travellers. To her he had said no word of comfort or farewell. He saw her face again as it had been in that moment, smooth, innocent, then puckered in pain. Try as he might now to look into those imagined eyes, the trick eluded him. Her cheek remained turned, her intimate self withheld. The frustration of this failure increased his anguish. Denny, he feared, might yet abandon him.

He got off the bed and walked about again, hoping to shake off these feelings of doubt and isolation. After a while, he stopped on his little peregrination and lifted his face to the high window. The night was just light enough to illuminate the bars. Words of pleading moved on his lips, involuntarily. He wanted to cry for help. Groping closer to the wall, he laid his hands on the cold, clammy stone. The white bandaged thumb alone stood out visible, like a flag of surrender. All he wanted was some presence, something palpable with which to communicate. As he lent there, breath checked, he was as good as praying to the masonry. He would have gone down on his knees to God, if he had believed, even a little, that he could solicit a response. But that spirit of rebellion which had got him where he was had not been quite extinguished. Aiken did not believe in God. So he swayed there alone, uncertain in the dark, needing help but having no-one to whom he could turn.

Suddenly over the knuckles of his bandaged hand he felt the fleeting brush of tiny legs. In horror he snatched his hand off the wall. Revealed in the flare of a match, a large brown, metallic cockroach crouched level with his face. Blindly it wavered its long feelers then dashed from the sudden heat. He struck another match to pursue and kill the insect. But it had gone and he moved back to the bed, wishing his own escape could be accomplished as swiftly.

His sleep through the remainder of the night was full of troubled dreams. He woke up crying for his mother.

8 It was still dark. Only the faint sound of traffic told him morning had come. When the cell light snapped on, Aiken stirred and got ready for his preliminary appearance in court.

Exercising a privilege of custody, he ordered breakfast to be brought in from a nearby café and, perched cross-legged on the cot bed, ate a plate of steak and chips, doused in HP sauce.

The warder brought him a safety razor and a change of clothes, by which he knew Denise Hanley had arrived downstairs. He put on the clothes and waited impatiently to be taken down, noticing as he smoked the last cigarette new nicotine stains on his fingers.

An odd assortment of other prisoners filled the basement detention room at Green Street courthouse. Men and women crowded together in a small shabby space amid much depression and human odour. There were some hungover drunks and girls who looked like prostitutes. They were loud, full of complaints and genuine good cheer.

When Melvin Calhoun swept into this den Steve almost expected applause.

'We're fortunate indeed. Up before Justice Donagh MacDonagh,' the affable barrister said as they conferred in a smoky corner. 'A most agreeable character. Didn't he write a book on the Tinkers a while back called God's Gentry? And he does not like the Special Powers Act.'

'What about their accusation that I'm a member of the IRA.'

'Oh that was only a ploy to hold you under Section 32.'

When he stood in the dock, Aiken had his arm in a black nylon sling, a touch suggested by Calhoun. A score of Travellers were hunched at the front of the public gallery. Pop's Johnny Connors raised a hand by way of encouragement. Brendan Carey sat among the reporters in the press box. He and Aiken regarded each other with mild embarrassment.

The robed figure of Justice MacDonagh glided in. Melvin Calhoun, already on his feet, greeted him with a respectful bow. Denise Hanley, seated behind the lawyers, could not shift her eyes from Steve.

After the formalities of the charge, the State Solicitor rose to oppose bail.

'Since coming to this country, your honour, this man has caused a deal of trouble. Now he stands indicted on a very serious charge which as I don't have to remind this court carries a heavy custodial sentence. Given the opportunity, the prisoner would very likely leave this jurisdiction. To put it bluntly, we believe Aiken would catch the next boat to England.'

MacDonagh's face remained sternly impartial. 'Mr Calhoun, what do you have to say?'

The bewigged barrister leaned his paunch into the front of the pew. 'Your honour, my client is a young Englishman who has for his own reasons taken up the cause of an unfortunate minority, the Tinkers. Properly described in official circles today, I believe, as itinerants. In this capacity, that is as their champion, he has become a well-known public figure.'

There was a splatter of clapping and calls from the public gallery. Justice MacDonagh eyed the Travellers for an instant over his glasses with tolerant amusement.

'Go on,' he directed, lifting his pencil.

'It is somewhat to the shame of Ireland, your honour, that it has taken a man like Mr Aiken, born in England, to make the plight of the itinerants a public issue.'

'Has he any previous record?' MacDonagh asked.

'No previous convictions whatsoever. He is perhaps I may say, in view of the task he has shouldered, a young man of exemplary character. He is anxious to stand trial and assures me he has no intention of letting down his friends, many of whom you see here present, by leaving Ireland.'

MacDonagh looked down judiciously at the legal men. 'I take the points you've both made. I am weighing this matter carefully.'

Then he inclined his head towards Aiken. 'I will grant you bail, Mr Aiken. But understand that I shall issue a warrant if you should fail to appear. The bond will be five hundred pounds.'

Steve bowed his head, hardly concealing a smile of relief. He was conscious that he had been favoured.

There followed some hand-signalling between Denise and Pop's Johnny. In a minute the young Traveller arrived at the front of the court with Black Johnny Wall, Catlin's father. He showed a wad of notes. They were directed to the clerk of the court's office.

Soon the main party was speeding towards the Gala in Black Johnny's motorvan. Steve sat wedged between Denise and Pop's Johnny. She had an arm around his shoulders.

'Me father-in-law put up half the money,' Johnny told him. 'The rest was collected last night from the boys in the California Hills.'

Warmly resuscitated by the blarney of triumphs to come, their newly-freed champion was borne home.

1 There had been much drinking on account of Steve Aiken's release on bail. Now the old crowd were here again in Hennessy's waking Pop's Johnny's departure.

The pickings in the scrap business around southside Dublin were thin. Pop's Johnny, like many others at this time, was not making any money. He was swapping away his lovely Newry wagon and going back across the sea, this time to South Wales. Black Johnny Wall, his father-in-law, had offered him the motorvan and some cash besides. In Cardiff or Swansea he could buy a second-hand trailer for a hundred pounds or less. With his new turnout Johnny would motor through the Welsh valleys to Merthyr Tydfil and Brynmaur, hoping to rebuild his fortunes.

'Can't be helped,' said Johnny, giving his impish grin. 'A man has to go for the main chance.'

'But you'll be back for the trial?' Denise asked, sitting with Steve, their backs to the big plate glass window. Their rendezvous with Johnny in Cardiff was cancelled.

'Sure I'm your bondsman aren't I?' He looked from one to the other, a question lurking in his twinkling brown eyes.

Everyone from the California Hills was in the pub, except some new arrivals up from Sligo who did not yet belong. Only Mikey Ward, still at the Seventh Lock Lounge with Pat and the others, was a drinker conspicuously absent.

The tables were covered in bottles and glasses, the air gritty with smoke. The youthful Finbar Furey, bent over his guitar, a pint at his feet, stood singing The House of the Rising Sun. His powerful voice lifted above the general din.

Denise, now content to stay and in swelling health, linked arms with Steve and listened to the singer. Happy that her man was free she began to sing along.

The whole room quietened to listen to the spontaneous duet. But Johnny was still waiting with his question.

'Will you tell us one thing in all honesty, Steve?'

Already boozed, the Englishman looked up complacently.

'Why did you ever let them cod you into takin' that stuff?'

'They asked me the exact same question in the Bridewell,' he laughed. 'Only I didn't give them the answer I'm giving you.'

Denise leaned forward and said for Johnny to hear, 'Mitchell had that gun out. He was pointing it at me. What else could Steve do?'

The youth shook his head. 'Yes, but that's not what persuaded me. I love guns, that's the truth. I wanted that revolver.'

'Helping gunmen,' said Denise to Johnny. 'And he's supposed to be a pacifist.'

'I'm not a pacifist when it comes to stopping Big Bill and the Corporation. I was one of those flung a rock or two at the Seventh Lock.'

'I always thought you were a harmless young fella,' Johnny mocked.

'But Molloy's lot are not,' Aiken responded. He spread his fingers on the table edge. The sheathed thumb stuck up, rather comic. Then he said, 'I'm going to start writing to a few people.'

'Who you talking about?' said Denise, herself tipsy.

'I'm thinking of writing to Bertrand Russell.'

'Whatever for?'

'The great philosopher and anti-war figurehead. That would be something for the jury.'

'He doesn't know you,' she said with a touch of indignation. 'Anyway, he must be close to ninety years old.'

'He might write a letter.'

Denise did not respond. Steve went quiet too but in a short while he seemed to shirk off doubts and his enthusiasm revived.

'I'll tell you what, Johnny. Lord Russell lives in Wales. You could go and see him.'

'Why not?' said Johnny, marvelling a little at himself. There was nothing he could not do, or try his hand at. If Steve Aiken said so he would visit the great man.

The drift of this discussion disturbed Denise. It upset her that Steve could use Pop's Connors for his own ends. He was manipulating the Traveller. But she kept her peace, beguiled by the thought that Russell's intervention might tip the balance in Steve's favour. She saw that in a bid to stay free a man might do anything. In that Steve was no different from most. He was her man and she would fight alongside him.

Besides, she argued silently, her good foot against his under the table, the Travellers owed them something too. She took up the next round of Guinness and tried to drown her own misgivings.

2 Curtains of icy rain swept over Ballyfermot, beating pitilessly upon the tents and wagons in the California Hills. The ceaseless water doused the fires and collected in brimming pools, where the raindrops danced on like devils.

Life for the bender-dwellers grew steadily more wretched as straw bedding soaked up the wet. Children lay sick from cold and hunger.

As long as the briquettes burned bright in the stove, Steve Aiken could ignore the quagmire around the caravan. He squatted at his typewriter for hours, hammering away at letters and articles to people and publications he thought might get involved in the Travellers' cause and his own defence. The two had become inextricably intertwined.

In this correspondence Aiken represented himself as an innocent pacifist framed by the Irish police because of his civil rights activities on behalf of the Travelling People.

Perhaps the youth was the victim of entrapment. But he knew he was playing a deception, simplifying or concealing facts to get people on his side. He was deliberately misleading his very idols in the anti-war movement. The whole thing was corroding and corrupting his integrity. Aiken had come to Ireland an angry young idealist. Lately he sounded like a cynic. Sometimes he winced at the abrupt change in himself. Guilty only weeks ago of aiding and abetting Republican bombers, his letters now displayed a flagrant dishonesty.

Though sensitive to the dishonour, Aiken went on justifying what he was doing as necessary to his own survival.

Whenever Denise tackled him, even obliquely, he got uptight.

'I can't see your letters making that much difference,' she said one evening, wearied by the hammering keys.

She looked at him from the bed, her eyes full of a deeper pleading. She was knitting a shawl for the baby.

He stopped and turned his head. The bright Tilley lamp at the door left his face half in shadow.

'Whoever's selected for the jury will be reading the papers won't they?'

'The judge won't be influenced. Publicity alone can't get you off.'

'Can't you be on my side?'

'I am,' she answered quietly, looking at the knitting needles. 'But I get so little of you.'

Her eyes glistened in the light, his remained rimmed in darkness. Aiken intended to hammer his way out of the jam and would not be deterred. In a moment, the clicking of her needles beat a furious counterpoint.

The California Hills attracted many strange Travellers, out-of-towners new to Dublin. No-one took much notice of the English couple any more. Some supposed they were down-and-out or beatniks, homeless buffers who had nowhere better to go. Absorbed in what felt to Aiken like a life-and-death struggle with Irish politics and the justice system, he temporarily forgot the Travellers; except as his abstract cause. Paradoxically, the teenage deserter became closer to the Walls and Connors than ever before.

Aiken had brought the barrel-top back to the very spot on which he had first seen it; to the land where the Travellers had first fired his naïve mind. A bonding had taken place in the course of all they had been through since the Ring Road and the burning of the school. Only that high-flying star sighted over the California Hills seemed now to have brought Aiken into a low and evil orbit. He didn't think less of the Travellers. He thought a lot less of himself. He was jinxed. Sometimes he felt desperately down and wanted to cut his wrists with that so-called lucky peg-knife.

Now that Aiken was awaiting trial, his Traveller friends expected nothing of him. The English couple more or less belonged to them and they were content to shelter the pair for as long as need be. His concern with self-preservation they regarded as entirely normal. Aiken for his part sensed their proprietorship and it gratified his need to belong. He might ultimately go back to England yet his feelings were rooted here with them. He was, as he had first discovered at Walkinstown, almost one of the clan.

Bored by the typewriter, Denise Hanley would retreat to Bridget Wall's wagon; share a cup of tea there, some motherly talk and camp gossip.

Aiken continued to do a day a week for Carey, covering the petty sessions at Kilmainham court. She and Steve would sometimes make the trip together as far as James Street Post Office. Though it brought them close to the old house a superstitious fear kept them away from Irwin Street.

Denise picked up a reply from a letter she had written to her former employer in England. Concerned to hear of the complications in her pregnancy, he promised to pass on anything they heard about the adoption of the intrauterine procedure by a hospital in Britain. Her old room at the farmhouse was now occupied by an au pair from Sweden. But the family would put her up temporarily if Steve went to prison.

3 During one of the frequent rainstorms, Big Bill showed up in the California Hills. He sloshed through the mud and puddles, doing the rounds and ordering everyone to leave.

With the camp awash nobody much cared. More water was draining in hourly from the end of the road, forming a muddy lake across the entrance and spilling over every level patch of land. It was no longer a fit place to stop and before the end of the day a few timorous souls packed up and left.

Luke Wall, a prominent figure among the California Hills Travellers, saw that the game was up. Bridget came and told Denise they were shifting. At the end of the week, the Walls yoked the wagon-horses which, descending into a foot of slop, hauled out onto the hard road at the edge of the Ballyfermot housing estate.

Steve Aiken got a lend of Dolly from Old Pop Connors and joined the waiting column. They went plodding past the long wall of Our Lady of the Angels Elementary, a string of five wet barrel-tops; a poor remnant of the great caravan that had invaded Walkinstown and only at Christmas had occupied the Lansdowne Memorial Park.

The California Hills was to be trenched and fenced off. Travellers would not be able to pull in there again. The land would be levelled and built over. Their departure marked the end of an era.

Under lowering clouds, the little wagon train passed the last council houses on Ballyfermot Avenue and a few yards further up crossed out of the city boundary. They were now in Dublin County.

On their left stood the squat asbestos buildings of the Cherry Orchard Isolation Hospital. To the right, behind bare hedges, glinted two yellow-grey fields, an empty expanse of dirty fallow acres stretching away to the near-distant houses of Palmerstown.

Little birds dashed across the hedge-tops, startled by the ponies while the procession slowed and turned into the Back Lane. Here Denise spied the smoking chimneys of caravans, and in a minute the dogs were running at Dolly's hocks. There were other tents and wagons all down the verge forcing the new arrivals to wait double-parked. The restive ponies, blowing into the chill air, jangling collars and harness, shook their heads as if in disbelief. A motorist edged down the carriageway, sounding his horn at the sight of the assembling Tinkers.

Wack MacDonald came up to the English couple, taking hold of Dolly's bridle. 'Not a whole lot of room,' he said by way of welcome. 'Don't be puttin' yourselves in the ditch.'

Maisie and Rosaleen were there and Ma Mary rose from her fire, watching them all arrive.

A full hour passed while the newcomers scotched their wagon wheels with stones and clods of turf. There was an old pump in the lane with a water trough. The meadow behind was full of cows

The next day Pat Donohue and his sons shifted over from the Seventh Lock. The puppies from his black lurcher bitch were now half-grown. The Wards arrived one afternoon pushing a pram. On to it they had loaded everything they owned, including infants. Paddy and Nan and the other bigger children walked behind.

Mikey put up his tent-contraption of plastic and sticks inside the meadow by the hedge. They were the first to enter this promised land.

Old Pat showed Steve Aiken the Enforcement Notices that had been served on them at the Seventh Lock.

'They're handing these out under the Sanitary Services Act,' Aiken said after studying the paper. 'Making us move because we don't have lavatories.'

Meanwhile, the guards had come from Palmerstown and summons were to be issued to several people in the lane. Prosecution threatened the owners of any vehicles which rested part-ways on the road surface. They tried to lift barrel-tops a few inches further onto the verge only to see inside wheels subside into the ditch.

'We'll have to go to court if we don't shift,' Luke Wall pronounced at a roadside meeting.

In the absence of Joe Donohue and Pop's Johnny Connors, collective leadership had passed to the Wall brothers.

'There's no goin' back into the city,' elder brother Jerry said, looking around at the dejected faces.

The little crowd was standing in the gateway of the big meadow. Close by a wafer of smoke rose serenely from Eileen Ward's fire. She sat with her brood of children unaffected by the bother in the lane.

'Let's take the field,' said Aiken, resting his hand on the five-barred gate.

'We'd best find out who it belongs to first,' Luke counselled. 'Don't want a farmer out here with a shotgun.'

So they waited while Aiken walked to two cottages at the corner with Ballyfermot Road. An old dame appeared, wiping her hands on her apron.

'Sure doesn't the land belong to the Corporation below?' she squawked, frail and uncertain.

'Are they going to build houses there?' the Englishman asked, unwittingly putting words into her mouth.

'I should think so, yes.' Her chin was quivering. 'They'll be puttin' the city right on my doorstep wouldn't you know it.'

'Good enough for me,' exclaimed Luke, unusually excited.

The men at the gate had waited impatiently. Now with a hefty shove they set the gate half-open, four of them walking it back into the hedge.

The first wagons bowled in, wheels pressing down the tall neglected grass. Ahead of them lay twenty-six acres, untouched by the plough for a decade; prime development land abutting the city boundary

4 On Sunday some of the men, led by the stout, wholesome figure of Luke Wall, trooped out of the opened gate and up the Back Road to Palmerstown. They were going to attend Mass in the parish church.

The parish however regarded these fellow Catholics as pariahs, an untouchable caste lower than the council tenants of nearby Ballyfermot.

Rumour had it that the Tinkers in the lane had vanished. Wherever these had sprung from they were not wanted.

Met by hostile looks from the pews, the Walls lurked self-consciously at the back of the chapel. Having dipped their fingers quickly in the holy water, they slipped out again before the parish priest had taken his place at the door to bid his congregation good day.

This failure to gain acceptance in the new neighbourhood bore heavily on their shoulders as Luke's small following went back across the fields, collecting up the others as they went. They gathered at the top gate opposite the fever hospital.

Here in front of the assembled camp, raising his arms like a prophet, Luke Wall suffered their attention.

'Listen fellas, a lot of places we're after bein' beaten out of. This old ground may be our last. Let's try to do things right. Right by ourselves that is.'

'Keep the place half-decent,' came his brother Martin's voice.

'Proper thing,' muttered Old Pop Connors.

'Try and burn your rubbish. Whatever you can,' Luke Wall told them. He had never asked so much of them in the California Hills.

The same afternoon, Jack MacAleer the wagon painter, crafted a sign for the front gate. On it he registered their claim and their intention: Cherry Orchard Settlement.

Hardened to Travellers' ways, Bridget Wall initially scoffed at her husband's efforts. Whatever they might say at a meeting, Travellers were not going to abide by anything. Every man would go his own road, as before.

'Rubbish is not the issue,' she chided him over the Sunday dinner. 'The greatest curse here is the drink. And you know it. Have them take the pledge. Haven't you taken it yourself.'

'How would I do that, woman?' he asked helplessly.

Luke Wall was no King of the Tinkers, no fighting man like Larry Ward of Loughrea. He would do his best and lead by example. He believed himself he was wrestling with the impossible trying to keep any sort of order on the field.

Almost as they spoke a loud quarrel broke out by the far hedge. Mikey Ward had been talking of leaving to find work in England. Eileen fiercely opposed his going, despite his drinking and dependence on her.

From their bender-tent close to the Back Lane gate, the row suddenly erupted onto the road. In a fit of desperation, Eileen had seized a chopper and was now running about the lane, demented.

Mikey got up and followed her, leaving Paddy and Nan shivering beside a dead fire. The roars of the little ones could be heard from the back of the tent.

Eileen bolted up the Back Lane, her hair streaming and the thing raised above her head like a battleaxe. Nobody could tackle her.

Her wails came back over the hedges as she disappeared from sight, 'Mikey, oh my Michael, oh my God!'

By the time Mikey caught up with his distraught wife, the chopper, with a ghastly crackle of glass, had gone through a cottage window. There hung Maggie in the garden, catching her breath. No sound issued from inside the cottage. Until all at once the same elderly creature that Steve Aiken had consulted appeared at the door. She was holding the chopper in a trembling hand, blood running down her face in a scarlet flow.

Seeing Eileen by the path, the frightful scar a-shimmer, the dame croaked out piteously, 'What've you done? Oh Lor', whatever have you done it for?'

Eileen seemed then to come to herself. Bare-armed and shawlless, she lifted her head and stared, shocked and unbelieving, at the blooded, ashen face.

Bridget Wall had by now hurried up Ballyfermot Road to the corner cottages and entered at the gate. Leaving Eileen to Mikey, she steered the elderly woman back into her home, calming her and attending to her cuts. She succeeded after a while in convincing the old woman no malice had been intended. Fortunately, she had been hit only by a splinter of glass.

'Please, missis,' said Bridget, bending over her. 'Don't call the guards or we'll all be put out. Sure we're not all bad are we? I have a man will come right away to fix the glass for you.'

The woman, holding Bridget's arm, her face puckered and forlorn, said shakily, 'I won't so. Aren't we all His children on this earth?'

'God bless you,' Bridget said. 'You're a very decent lady. May I bring you a soda loaf over tomorrow when I have mine baked?'

The very same evening Mikey was loitering outside the Gala stupid drunk.

Eileen, her bushy hair everywhere, squatted on her haunches under the window of Hennessy's Bar. In the folds of her shawl she jogged the smallest of her babies.

Paddy was cowering nearby when a squad car pulled up to the kerbside close to the swaying Mikey. Seeing the guards take hold of his father and propel him, lurching and mouthing towards the car, Patrick began an agitated dance.

The banging of the car doors sent the ragged boy into a final despairing frenzy. He was leaping in the air, clasping his hands and screaming, 'My daddy, daddy, my daddy.'

Eileen got to her feet, holding tight to the baby under the shawl. She waited by the wall until Paddy came to her.

'Why have they taken him?' Skipping and twisting, Patrick stared after the car then at his mother's face.

'The poor divil can't get off the drink,' she told him, regarding his tear-stained cheeks. 'Don't be frettin', son. He'll be back soon enough like a bad penny.'

Alcoholism was a topic to which Luke's camp committee often returned. Usually it was newcomers who broke the general peace. Pa McDonagh, an old Sligo man, on several nights returned to the field with his two grown sons, all of them drunk and bawling. Bottles were flung and Pop Connors insulted. Luke summoned Pa and his boys to a meeting but they failed to appear.

'Sure we all have drink taken on occasion,' said Mikey Ward, standing steady now in the gleam of Luke's fire. 'That's not including yourself.'

Mikey had been released by the guards and all forgiven. He startled the meeting with the news that the Wards from Loughrea were on the road to Cherry Orchard.

'There's drinkin' and there's drinkin',' remarked Pop. 'Those McDonaghs are makin' a show corin' forenenst the hospital.'

With some dissent, it was decided Pa must be chastised. Since he refused to come to them, the men would go down to him. A body of a dozen started in the failing light towards the bottom of the land. They intended by words to prevail upon the Sligo folk to reform their behaviour.

Hearing the posse approach, old Doreen McDonagh panicked. The mother rolled her pots and blankets into a hasty bundle, while her boys snatched up their tent and sticks. Dragging their donkey, Pa and the others dived out through a hole in the hedge and were swallowed into the dark funnel of the lane.

The long red sparks of Pa's abandoned fire blew up in their faces as Luke and the others gathered around, smirking in embarrassment at this unexpected result.

'We've done the poor critters an injustice. And that's all about it,' said Martin Wall, pouting his lip.

Not a week later the McDonaghs reappeared outside the top gate. A light sleet was falling. Standing there dejected, beside his ill-clothed boys, Old Pa McDonagh begged to be allowed to come on the ground again. Hadn't that Big Bill, he claimed, given Doreen a slap in the gob and kicked out their fire above at Balbrigggan?

'May I drop dead if I touch the drink agin so help me God.' Pa made oath they would cause no further bother.

His little grey ass plodded forward through the gate, stumbling on the frosty clods. Old Doreen followed shyly, steadying their rocking bundles with a thin, white arm.

5   The young Englishman, on bail to stand trial for possession of explosives, received a letter about this time from Bertrand Russell. His secretary wrote that while there was no possibility that the old, world-renowned philosopher, in failing health, could speak in court he would be writing to the Irish authorities.

Moreover, Lord Russell sent word that he was looking forward to receiving Johnny Connors at his home in North Wales. He enclosed a cheque for twenty-five pounds.

'We'll rebuild St Christopher's,' Steve Aiken said, coming home on the bus with Denise.

They found Luke Wall fixing up a kitchen hut and he paused to listen to them.

'We'd need to build something ten times as big as this,' said Denise pertly, regarding his little construction.

Several of the Wall children had sidled up and were hanging round the legs of their old teacher.

Big carts dispatched to a landfill at Ringsend, across from the power station on Dublin Bay, returned loaded high with Ford car-crates, the ponies and drivers ready to drop from the day-long haul. Nails, hinges and other fittings, and plastic sheeting for the sky-lights were purchased from a hardware store near the Gala. For a week hammers and saws rang out the glad news of St Christopher's approaching resurrection.

All over Cherry Orchard, in imitation of the school, more huts went up. Pat Donohue went one better and built his of corrugated iron.

By the time the school re-opened, Travellers were coming to Cherry Orchard from all over. The little school, short of teachers, was inundated and could not cope.

To alleviate the squeeze, parents sought to enter their children at Our Lady of the Angels Elementary in Ballyfermot. But when they fetched up at the office they were told no child from Cherry Orchard could be registered. The itinerant camp, it was claimed, fell outside the spread of the Angels' wings.

Since Aiken's arrest the American couple had withdrawn their support. In Archbishop McQuaid's book Aiken was now persona non grata and the Meachans had switched their efforts to helping Father

Fehily, Society of Jesus, the new chaplain to itinerants.

Despite this blackballing the Society of Friends kept to their commitment to aid St Christopher's. Quakers donated money collected at their Meeting House, and a County Dublin member brought milk for the children daily from her farm.

For the children of Cherry Orchard St Christopher's, often smoke-filled and draughty, became again the little temple of their aspirations.

Victor Bewley, the leading Dublin Quaker, came himself to the reopening party. Afterwards he sat in on a session of the camp committee. One outcome was Bewley's offer to give employment in his café to two teenage girls, Luke's daughter Ann and Theresa Maughan. The pale Ann, usually obedient, and the bold Theresa, wildly beautiful, both responded in the same way; neither could long stand the hours of confinement in the steamy kitchen and the endless washing brought to them from the restaurant. They quit within two weeks.

Luke Wall fretted over the failure of this try-out. Their mothers upbraided the two girls for chucking it in. Denise Hanley too felt they had let the side down.

'You should have stuck the job,' the English girl told them, when they came home defeated.

'Would you stand at a hot sink the whole day?' Theresa demanded, reddening in fury. 'I can earn better money gaigin.'

So she and Ann once more donned the Galway shawl and took their chances, calling at better-class houses or begging on O'Connell Bridge.

Meanwhile Father Fehily made an appeal for funds, to which there was an immediate public response.

When by a circuitous route the news of this reached Cherry Orchard, the camp committee put in a request for money to be spent on a bigger school building. Confident of a positive response, a Danish architect set about designing two low-cost alternatives. One was for a conventional rectangle and the other for a hexagon, either of which could be erected for a few hundred pounds.

The camp favoured the hexagonal school. They liked the canvas roof and open interior space. It would provide a community centre as well as classroom. The young people wanted to hold ceilis there.

But before the matter of a new building had been resolved a bus arrived one morning outside the hospital to take the children to a stopgap class arranged in the city.

Nuns went flapping over the land looking for youngsters for their school. They badmouthed the English people, saying the two were atheistic communists with no respect for the Holy Church, living in sin to boot.

'They call you a lame duck,' Bridget Wall told Denise.

The children, unused to school routine, found the nuns' ruler-rapping discipline cruel. Paddy came home crying and complained they had locked him in a cupboard. A rebellion followed in which a coterie of young teenagers ran off when the nuns, in a humiliating chase around the fields, tried to round them up.

'Ah, sure you can't blame the nuns,' Eileen Ward commented. 'They don't know no different.'

Such was the discontent over the money and the Little Sisters of Charity that Father Tom himself had at last to come to the camp.

6 Father Fehily, chauffeured up to Cherry Orchard in Andrew Meachen's red Ford station wagon, found himself welcomed at the school door by Luke and his brothers. They were surprised no-one else from the new Dublin Itinerant Settlement Committee had come to pay respects.

The stove had been lit and children let out early to make way for the meeting. They hung about drinking their milk, watching with curiosity as the priest, in gloves and highly-polished shoes picked his way through the potholes.

'Will the others be comin' along, Father?' Luke asked.

'No need at all,' said the chaplain, now at the low door. 'Mr and Mrs Meachen are here and will represent the rest. You wouldn't expect ladies and gentlemen to stoop down to this would you now?' he added, meaning his words as a joke.

Ushered in ahead, Fehily seated himself to chair the meeting. He was flanked by the American couple. Luke, who usually presided at the top table, had to find himself a place lower down.

'You've got it nice and warm in here,' he said, his back to the stove, burning hotly on briquettes supplied by the Quakers.

Steve and Denise, hunkered together at one of the small school desks, hugged their discontent to themselves. Denise had pinned her pupils' pictures onto the wooden walls, many showing the anguish of children living through violent evictions.

'Well now, I have some good news,' Father Fehily announced self-importantly. 'Mr Blaney, the Minister for Local Government, has accepted the main recommendations of the Commission on Itinerancy. This means that in due course sites will be provided for you. All of you. But of course it's going to take time. Our job then is to get local councils and more important local people to accept these sites. That is accept you people into their communities. Now we all know that's not going to be an easy task. We'll need to work together on it and that's why I'm here today. We want your support, all the co-operation you can give. That is for the Dublin committee and for the National Itinerant Settlement Committee which will be formed in due course. '

'Who's gonna represent us?' asked Martin Wall.

Before Fehily could formulate an answer, Pat Donohue stood up at the rear of the school. 'Wouldn't it be the proper thing for Luke here and me brother Joe to speak for Cherry Orchard?'

A cheerful murmur of approval met these words. Everyone assumed this proposal would go through on the nod.

'We want to hear everything you have to say', Fehily answered, smooth as altar silk. 'We want your suggestions. Any ideas you have you just come to me. Nothing will be done without your approval. I guarantee you that.'

It was months before Cherry Orchard learnt of the unpalatable reality; there would be no Travellers on the national itinerant committee.

As to the large sums raised none had come to Cherry Orchard. You had to go to the presbytery door to beg for a blanket. Yet all were reluctant to bring this up in Fehily's pink complacent presence.

'Father, we're thankful to the Archbishop over your appointment as our chaplain and we all appreciate what you are doin',' Luke told him, with dignity. 'As to this school here we all love it and we're proud of it because we built the place twice over, with our own hands. But as you see yourself, it's just not big enough for the numbers of children we have now in this camp. And there's more at the door every day.'

'We know that, Luke,' Fehily cut him short, 'and isn't that why I'm here? School is the most important thing. I know there's been some problems with the bigger children and I can tell you that we intend next year to start a proper permanent school.' He indicated Tracey. 'Mrs Meachen will be running this at Milltown.'

'Isn't that a long ways from here?' Joe Donohue said, newly reinstated and anxious to be heard.

'Transport will be arranged,' said Tracey Meachen. 'That's if you're still here.' She blushed at the all-male attention, avoiding the green eyes of Denise Hanley.

'Let me finish, young lady,' Luke remonstrated. 'We like havin' our school here so we can keep an eye on the children. Only this school is too small. We want to put up a bigger one. And at our last meeting in here we were lookin' at plans for it.'

Luke held up the blueprint for the hexagonal classroom. It was caught by a draught from the door and fell to the floor.

Fehily turned away and spoke into Andrew Meachen's ear. Taking his point the American said. 'Luke, I don't have to tell you that everything here is illegal. The huts, including this one, is an illegal structure. If you're asking for funding to put up a better school on this field the answer must be a straight no. I'm sorry. Father Tom's committee is getting recognition and funding from the government so everything we do has to be done within the law.' His brown eyes, once so sympathetic, jumped uncertainly from one face to another. 'You must understand that. You're trespassing. You've no security. No rights to put up anything.'

Crushed by these words Luke sat stunned. He could hardly credit Andy's change of attitude since the party at his home. Pat Donohue was incensed. This was betrayal. Everyone felt it, most of all Old Pat, who at the Ring Road had often smoked a pipe with the American.

Pat got to his feet, his face white: 'We've been illegal all our lives. What harm would it be to put up a temporary buildin'? Spend some of them pounds on Cherry Orchard? Would you be gettin' those donations if we hadn't of gone through all them evictions?'

'You're out of order, Patrick,' said Fehily, his neck hot. 'Whole point and purpose is to bring you people within the law. Get you all settled down and living proper lives. We don't want your children to go gallivanting around the countryside. That's over.'

His words provoked disbelief. The chaplain was advocating an end to the Travelling way of life. He was talking to them as if they were just a breed of failed settled people.

Dismay wreathed their road-weary faces. Only respect for the cloth kept other mouths clamped.

'Wasn't there a fine priest at Swords who'd have suited us better,' a calmer Pat reflected afterwards. He wondered had they demoted St Christopher himself just out of spite.

Aiken said nothing. This was a battle Travellers must win on their own. If not now, then later.

1 Frank McManus was in fresh digs in Terenure. His landlord was an old Sein Feiner so it was considered a safe house. The Special Branch knew where he was. However they had left off questioning him about the Leopardstown bombing. If now the guards did come to his new address and search, nothing would be found. And no-one in the house, being armchair admirers of Joe Christle's mob, would tell them anything.

Cullan and the Special Branch had to be satisfied with the arrest of the young Englishman.

McManus did not much like Aiken. He was xenophobic where the English were concerned. Nor did McManus care for Paul Mitchell, that cocky little civil servant who had got a government job by signing himself out of the Curragh camp. The man was unprincipled and untrustworthy. It rankled that Mitchell had been given a clerk's post in the Forestry Department while he dragged along in the lowest paid work as a warehouseman when he was not out on his arse and unemployed.

He thought Mitchell had been a fool, or worse, for handing over his cherished Webley. There was something not right about Paul.

Though as Frank now admitted to himself he had agreed to the idea. The panic had been on them after Leopardstown with de Valera's Praetorian Guard in hot pursuit.

Anyhow, it was back in his possession. The big Webley revolver, once his father's, lay on the white chest of drawers. Old Ted McManus, a Kerryman, had been a Volunteer in the fighting with the Black and Tans. It was a massive piece of artillery and a splendid inheritance. Of course, weapons were supposed to be collective property and he had endorsed that rule a while back. Only he still liked to keep this one in his private possession and nobody could challenge him over that.

Aiken had not given them away. That was to his credit. Though you had to believe Senator Grady when he said it was probably only on account of all the legal fuss made by Sean MacBride, no less, in the Gerry Lawless case, that the guards hadn't given him the full treatment. Lawless was beaten and pressed to turn informer; offered employment and pay if he'd work for the guards. Not that you could for a moment compare the two. Gerry Lawless was a fellow Volunteer in Christle's group. In the Curragh he had not signed out but applied to the Detention Commission. Sean MacBride, chair of Amnesty International, had argued for an order of habeas corpus and taken the issue of internment all the way to the European Commission of Human Rights.

Liam Grady had brought in Calhoun, an eminent Republican

lawyer, to defend Aiken. The senator could afford that; and it was odds-on Calhoun would get him off. Pulling that stunt with the sling in front of Donagh McDonagh had got him bail. No doubt the justice believed Aiken had been roughed up in the Bridewell. Almost the worst that could happen would be to have Aiken's dragging on for ever, like the Lawless case. No, McManus wanted the Aiken affair over soon and Aiken out of Ireland. The British Army were welcome to him. Any influence he had on Joe Donohue should be severed completely. Joe, a man with military knowledge and of great potential to the Republican movement, was asserting himself again as gaffer of the Southside Travellers.

Young Aiken had been led to believe he was helping the Dublin Brigade and was obviously in awe. Nevertheless, you had to see him as a weak link and, being an Englishman and a pacifist, hardly fit as any kind of associate in the larger Irish cause. Senator Grady was to McManus's thinking too soft on Aiken. In fact he had gone too soft altogether. Clann na Ploblachta was finished. And with all due respect, the man had gotten too old. McManus considered himself second to Joe Christle in operational matters. That was by dint of his physical force attitude. He had never bollixed up yet; not like Lawless in that aborted Ballintra bank raid. Chairman of the Civil Liberties League and next in line as OC. Not that they had voted any one in as commandant; nor given themselves a name. They were an anarchistic bunch, but still the most effective around. The only ones from this side of the Border doing anything; allied to Soar Uladh in the North. The Army Council had made a big mistake kicking Christle out. As to the IRA truce, that was a fucking disgrace.

Frank's lot would probably never call themselves Maoists. That sounded un-Irish and pompously intellectual. But the Maoist world view of the have-nots rising up against the rich appealed to McManus. Sure, Grady had prompted him into supporting the Tinkers. But he was developing a wider, wilder perception; the poorest Tinkers could become part of a guerrilla-led Maoist, or if you like Cuban-style Irish revolution. It was a stupendous idea. So he thought anyway after a few jars. Maybe it was just stupid.

Fact: in the past these selfsame Tinkers had given refuge to patriots on the run; his father had said the Travellers had oftentimes hidden Volunteers from the Tans. Didn't Christle himself agree they might be used to help move men and arms across the Border? Now with proper leadership and instruction, men like Joe could become an active auxiliary against the occupation of the Six Counties as well as playing their part in the eventual overthrow of the compromised and traitorous Lemass Government.

'We'll organise a trainin' camp in the Wicklow Mountains. Are yer for it!' Frank had said one night in Pat's new hut, popping his eyes and bringing laughter.

In the end it was all grist to justify the drinking, the slagging and the time-wasting they all indulged in up at Cherry Orchard. But for McManus his own particular – and peculiar – convictions and ambitions lent importance to his present mission.

2 Frank dragged his big frame off the bed and picked up the revolver. He broke it open and knocked the six shells out onto the candlewick bedcover. Then lifting the gun to eye level and turning it to the light, he squinted down the barrel. He was satisfied to see the electric bulb glint through the narrow tunnel.

He had twice cleaned and oiled the gun, meticulously, since it had lain in Aiken's back garden. That it had been wantonly left out in the rain and soiled was the cause of much of his resentment. He wanted it back in its former, near pristine condition. It was a matter of reverence to the memory of his father. He cared passionately for that memory, and for the old weapon.

Next he opened the top drawer of the white dresser and took out a role of black masking tape. With deliberate, slow twists of his large hands, he taped the handle of the Webley, giving it a surer grip. The kick of a thirty-eight called for a firm hold. After the job it could be stripped away. Finally, he slotted the rounds back, admiring how snugly they fitted into the six chambers. The ammunition was old, vintage stuff, marked with the arrow of the British War Department. Unsure of its reliability, Frank had taken the gun out this morning and fired one round as a test.

It was an hour since he had come in and he was still waiting for Eddie Logan's telephone call.

The slowdown of time became oppressive. Frank was impatient to get going. But he made himself lie back on the pillow and light up another cigarette, thinking over all the discussion that had gone on about this whole thing; the crack and the bragging, too much of it, with Joc Donohuc.

Meeting at Tommy Bowden's in Palmerstown, they'd held a sort of trial of Big Bill, in his absence. Since Redmond had once been in uniform a quasi-court martial was convened. It was a first for the group and they'd sworn a special oath of secrecy. Everyone had agreed on a kneecapping. That is except Christle himself who had not attended. An incapacitating wounding was in this case wholly justified and appropriate. But it galled him that Christle had stayed away. Perhaps he had bigger fish to fry, or more likely wanted no part in it. As expected, when it had come down to allocating the execution of this sentence, Frank had been alone in volunteering. He was the only man up to it. Eddie, an admirer of his prowess, was coming along as lookout. That was just to prove something, being the youngest and runt of the litter. Every one of them might be a self-sung hero, a Brennan-on-the-Moor. But Frank was the hard man, hard enough, maybe crazy enough, to shoot an unarmed man at close range. Though he did not think he was mad; no more nor less insane or psychopathic than the frontline British Tommy.

McManus had convinced himself that the successful completion of this assignment would bring him further renown within the Republican movement. Bill Redmond had an off-colour reputation; Corporation bailiff and former Blueshirt who had fought on Franco's side in the Spanish Civil War. Grady, for one, and Sean MacBride, founder of Clann na Poblachta, detested all those who had followed General Eoin O'Duffy to Spain. O'Duffy was the Irish Mussolini, a former head of the Garda Siochana. Grady had joined the Catalan anarchists and borne arms for the democratic Spanish Government. The old senator was a gut socialist and a bit of an anarchist at heart. He might have gone soft and senile, McManus thought, but Grady would recognise this as the settling of an old score.

A reprisal shooting, coming in the aftermath of Leopardstown, would bolster Frank's image. Certainly it was time to get on with it, time to snatch a little fame before a hot marksman fired on the Royal Navy destroyer due soon to visit Waterford. McManus expected to be on Christle's next big action, the blowing up of the Nelson Pillar. The Pillar was going to be dropped neatly onto O'Connell Street only hours before the parade for the fiftieth anniversary of the Easter Rising. That was in two months' time. Frank wanted to do something on his own before Nelson went up.

At last the telephone rang downstairs.

Little Eddie Logan, having spent a while at Cherry Orchard Camp, had come down to the Gala, with Paddy Ward loping along beside the bike. For an hour Eddie had gone off to watch Bill Redmond's house. Now he was back outside the cinema only to find Paddy still at his post. He looked at his watch; it was approximately ten o'clock. The film-goers would be out in a minute. He thought of Tommy and the others gathered in the cosy heat of Pat's hut, setting up an alibi for him and Frank. The minute book of the Irish Civil Liberties League would show there had been a formal meeting about the future of Dublin itinerants. They would all swear the two of them had stayed in the hut until past midnight. Joe Donohue and the other Travellers would say the same.

Usually unnoticed, Eddie had drawn attention to his presence this evening by giving a gift to Mrs Donohue.

'Remember you gave us tea above at the Seventh Lock? Your daughter Mary brought it over. And wasn't the mug broken when Big Bill tried to run us down.'

He saw by the Gypsy woman's face in the firelight that his gesture had gained him no favour with Mary's mother. The girl he was sweet on, though nearby, would probably never know where the six new porcelain mugs had come from.

'Your man's agreeable.' Eddie's voice went over the Molly Malone, using a pre-arranged phrase.

'Okay so,' answered Frank and hung up.

Having given the message and set the ball rolling whither it might go, Eddie was scared stiff of the coming action. Worse for him he had another while to wait.

Frank went back up to his room, socks padding noiselessly on the stairs. He put on his ex-army boots and laced them up, and shrugged into a heavy topcoat. The revolver found ample room in a deep outside pocket. It weighed down heavily on his right side. In the other pocket he stuffed a black balaclava. He was grinning to himself as he shut the street door behind him. He felt powerful. Yet he could not entirely dismiss the possibility that this affair would end in disaster. In the yard, wiping the damp from his bicycle saddle, he saw his puncture outfit had been nicked.

The negative aspects of the escapade loomed larger while he was on his bike and half way to Ballyfermot.

Since the Leopardstown do Christle's outfit had been under pressure. Not just from the Special Branch but from the IRA Army Council. Any activity being carried out without their explicit sanction was an affront. Especially something in the Republic. Even when it involved an individual like Redmond long on their blacklist. A git higher up on that list had recently been tarred-and feathered. They would get around to William Redmond soon enough. None other than Thomas MacCurtain, his commander in the Curragh, had reminded McManus that discipline was paramount and must be maintained. They had had an ugly argument. Frank knew that an unauthorised hit on a civilian in Dublin might precipitate retaliation against Joe Christle himself. That would put Frank smack in the shit; and very low in the popularity polls. It could mean a court martial.

Frank's courage was right off the boil as he and Eddie rode two abreast in cheerless silence through the dark, rain-haunted streets. Having counted on his hero's proverbial braggartism to sustain him, Eddie lapsed into a bear-pit of worry.

Few locals were out on the pavements of the unfinished Ballyfermot housing estate. A loose horse, like a shadow, clopped across their path and was left behind. Solitary headlights caught the riders at a wet intersection.

Over their heads a serene moon shone briefly exposing the approach of the flying column. As the bicycles slowed, the wind sunk and the two floated to a stop. They were near the house.

Eddie Logan loitered there astride his bike, while Frank pushed the low gate and stole up the path. In a moment his form had vanished into the hard black shadow at the side of the house. Over the angle of the roof turgid clouds moved swiftly on their nocturnal journey.

A few more steps took the gunman to the back yard for a recce. A light burned behind the kitchen curtains. A wireless was playing. Frank barely drew breath. Since coming up the garden path things had become unreal. His mind was fast unravelling; would not acknowledge what he was about to do. Frank had never shot anyone before.

He fumbled with the balaclava, bothered by the itchy fibre. Then his hand closed on the big revolver and he lifted it slowly from his pocket. Without further postponement he gave a rap on the dewy door.

A bright bulb came on above flooding the porch with a harsh white light.

Before McManus could recover from the sudden exposure, Redmond pulled open the door, saw the gun, uttered something unintelligible and slammed it closed again.

Panicking to the point of oblivion, McManus half-raised the Webley and pulled the trigger. The gun bucked in his hand, giving out an almighty bang. As he took off dazedly down the path, the man could be heard screaming on the other side of the door.

A small acrid cloud of smoke stood a moment in the air and began to drift away.

Riding like the wind the two whizzed up Ballyfermot Road, doubled into the unlit back road and hefted their bikes over the five-bar gate. They were now back on the sovereign territory of Tinkerland; the hut-covered fields of the Cherry Orchard Camp. Their machines bumping and rattling between the low nubs of the many fires, they pressed forward, shivering with shock and the cold, towards the singing in the Donohues' hut.

3 Bill Redmond sat on the kitchen floor gripping his thigh with both his meaty hands. The percussion of the shell still dinned in his head. Blood oozed through his trousers, sticking him to the brown lino.

His wife Yvonne, who had been bending close to assess the wound, now went to the door.

'I'm goin' out to phone.'

'No, don't be doin' that. I don't want the guards here. It's not that much, believe me.'

Yvonne came back to him, looking down at the sorry sight of her husband on the floor.

'Help me get me trousers off.'

When, with the help of a kitchen knife, she had the trouser leg removed and some of the blood wiped away, the wife saw that the damage was slight. The bullet had passed barely across the skin, cauterising the flesh. The slug was lodged somewhere under the sink. The door had the neatest little hole in it.

'What are you goin' ter do then?' she asked, having got him up and lying on the couch in the front room.

'I saw him,' said Bill. 'I know who the fellas are.'

He turned his eyes briefly to her, then screwed them shut. The pain and the throbbing had started.

'Listen, the best thing - the only thing I can do is hope they're satisfied with this, aaah! piece of idiocy what they've done to me.'

'I don't follow you.'

'If they've done what they wanted to do or think they have, they'll leave me alone. But if I fetch in the guards, sure they'll be back again to level up the score afresh.'

'There's somethin' in that,' Yvonne agreed doubtfully. 'Should get that crowd put away though. IRA madmen.'

She pondered what the neighbours would say, or ask, about the bang. But she decided not to bother the wounded man with that question just yet.

Redmond was feeling the burning now. It was as if a hot poker had been laid against his leg. By his own reckoning he was taking his punishment like a man. He was still Big Bill.

At the closing of the day, Joe's oddly painted wagon hove into view outside the hospital. There was Tiger, the familiar piebald, lifting his big head, nostrils flared, sniffing the sea salt on the Dublin air. For three days, Joe and Olivine and her daughter Mary had by turns led the wagon-horse onwards, following the Royal Canal for a good forty miles out of Mullingar.

All along the Ballyfermot Road, Joe had been glancing through the hedge at the great assemblage in the fields. Halted at the gate, he noted the camp sign and saw beyond Aiken's caravan. Further in was the reassuring sight of what he guessed to be Pat's hut. He looked ahead for a spot to pull on, no longer sure of his place among the Southside Travellers.

Pat showed himself tardily, meeting his brother with a brief handshake.

'How was it all above?' the elder brother asked of their home town, letting Tiger walk by.

'All played out wouldn't you know,' Joe called over his shoulder, feeling his age. He was not the same Joe as had left them on the Long Mile Road.

'Didn't Lawrence Ward pull in here last week,' said Pat, fondling one of his grown black puppies. 'Sure he's brought all his people from Loughrea. Must have come the same road as ye.'

Joe tugged on Tiger's bridle bringing the gelding to a sudden halt. 'The Wards? I'll not have him king over me anyways.'

He led Tiger on a little way behind the long corrugated-iron hut. He would stay close to the elder brother until he saw how the land lay. Dusk was already collecting in the field and the boys were waiting on supper.

Two nights later the sounds of revelry issued from Pat's long hut. Joe Donohue, accepting the company of the Recruits, had taken up the war-drum. McManus flattered him and this evening Eddie Logan had shown up with a set of porcelain mugs for Olivine.

Though saying nothing to his guests Joe was put out by the presence on the ground of Larry Ward and his people. They were gathered with Mikey Ward at the lower gate, a score of wagons and tents. Down there was a rival camp.

For Joe, the visits by the Republican lads were a bolster to his faltering prestige. Pat's sons loved these music-making evenings.

Denise lay listening in the caravan bothered by the noise and the atmosphere of dissension that had lately seized Cherry Orchard. Whilst she had resigned herself to remaining in Ireland the strife and the squalor of the camp were becoming intolerable to her.

Listening too, Steve said, 'That's Joe on his bodhran.'

'This is never going to stop,' Denise complained, putting her hands over her ears to shut out the aggressive rhythm that dinned through the back window.

'I'd rather be here than in some bedsitter waiting for my trial away from everybody.'

'Okay, Steve. But we need a bigger, warmer caravan.'

She was thrusting down the blankets on their cot-bed. Then her nightdress came up and she invited him to touch her belly. The sheen of her skin gleamed in the candlelight. The bulge rose and fell in slow modulation, as if it were the life beneath that moved. He placed his hand there over her distorted navel and felt the hardened muscle. Denise lay still under his exploration and devotion.

The beating of the drum and the skirl of the drunken singing went on long after they fell asleep.

Soon after first light Luke Wall came to the door with the news that Big Bill had been shot. The camp buzzed with it. Nobody knew yet if he was dead or alive. Jerry Wall was going to the Gala to fetch a newspaper.

Luke stood there in the cold, a ton of worry. 'The young Donohues are broadcasting it all over,' he said. 'Joe won't let on he knows anything at all.'

'You'd best be delayin' lessons,' he told Denise when she appeared at the door. 'We're havin' a meetin' in a minute.'

'This'll bring the shayds down on us in hundreds,' Bridget Wall complained when Luke went back to her.

The uproar in the school was unbelievable; incoherent shouts, one voice above another, angry accusations from all sides. In the midst of the tumult Chap Donohue, planted staunchly beside his father, was warding off verbal attacks that threatened at any moment to become physical.

Old Pat, so long the peace broker, looked ready to crown somebody. Pandemonium ruled. But the whole show was meant for his brother Joe. Everybody blamed the Gaffer for the new crisis. Some wanted him put out of the camp.

'Me uncle's not to blame, for Godsakes,' Chap shouted back.

'Bring him in here then,' a voice called.

'D'you think he runs the IRA?' the nephew answered, exasperated.

'Whether they run him or he runs them is immaterial,' Luke cut in. The babble died away. The faces turned in his direction were stiff and serious.

'For all we know right now murder was done last night in our name,' Luke pronounced slowly, looking from one to another.

'God help us,' Old Pop Connors murmured, wiping his eye.

A brazen voice came out of the pack: 'Serves Bill right. I'd have put him down meself.'

Wack MacDonald, abashed by the attention, pushed his way to the door. The meeting watched him leave sobered by his heedless temper.

Jerry Wall arrived to report that there was nothing in the morning papers about Bill.

The discussion had continued more quietly when suddenly the sound of a heavy engine broke above the voices. A fresh commotion ensued.

Wack reappeared with Denise close behind him.

'Lads, lads!' the wild young man shouted, his face fiercely agitated. 'Come out quick. They're goin' ter rip up the huts.'

Unable to believe this news, Steve looked to Denise for confirmation.

'It's a big bulldozer,' she said grimly.

All sallied forth and beheld the new menace. A huge yellow bull-dozer was tearing into the hedge along the front of the camp, leaving a mangle of mud and branches. Pat's hut and the school itself lay exposed in the path of destruction.

A gang of workmen had started to erect a wire mesh fence.

After much grunting and grinding, the bulldozer came to a halt. The driver had reached one end of the school.

Luke approached, his committee at his back. 'Keep away from that, d'you hear? That's our school.'

'Will ye leave those huts?' Chap Donohue said over his shoulder.

The driver pulled a wry face then swinging his leg over climbed down among the hostile Travellers.

'This is a Dublin County Council job,' he said easily. 'We're not here to put you out. We're supposed to be quellin' a rat infestation.'

Luke and Chap turned to each other, exchanging comic looks. They grinned at the council man.

'You're lettin' in a terrible draught,' Luke joked. 'We'll be blown out of here.'

'I won't touch the huts. Will that do?' the driver said and climbing back up to his seat resumed work.

At the end of the day a new wire fence closed off the top field from Ballyfermot Road. Luke went out with his two brothers and cut an entrance through the wire. They re-hung the camp's painted sign.

The earth mounds thrown up by the bulldozer provided Cherry Orchard with its first defences. Aiken urged them to level out a com-pound behind the school. The Walls dug ditches and had soon built a palisaded strongpoint large enough to run the wagons into if the camp was threatened with eviction.

It became clear to passers-by that here at Cherry Orchard the Travellers would make their final stand.

But the Wards, camped with Mikey at the bottom gate, were left out of this plan, inducing further division.

2 Because of legal action being taken by Dublin County Council against Ballyfermot Holdings, the owners of the land, Aiken was advised to move off their property. Melvin Calhoun warned that failure to do so would jeopardise his bail.

Prudently, he now placed his caravan on the verge of Ballyfermot Road outside the new fence. The night hours out on the exposed highway grew colder. Whenever the tiny stove died down, a wicked chill penetrated the wagon's thin cover. He and Denise wore their clothes in bed.

She reminded Steve of his promise to buy a new caravan and one morning they set out for North Dublin. Luke had told them of a Gypsy man in Finglas who had a touring trailer for sale.

A bus ride and fifteen minutes of walking brought them to a broad upward sloping green. Horses grazed slowly over the land and the sunlight played on a cream-coloured caravan standing against the hedge. Beside it were two old barrel-top wagons. The serenity of the scene contrasted sharply with the Ballyfermot camp. Denise wished they could move here.

As the two crossed the open ground, a young couple came up behind. Tightly arm in arm, they were also striding purposefully towards the little Finglas camp. The girl's headscarf, tied Gypsy-style, left strands of flaxen hair across her face. The husband, dark and unshaven, bowed to the wind.

The young Rom turned towards Steve as they came abreast.

'Is it me Uncle Johnny you want?'

'Yes, if he's selling the trailer.'

'That's Johnny Gray,' the other replied. 'You sound like an Englishman.'

The four were walking on together now.

'I'm stopping with the Travellers over in Ballyfermot.'

'We're from Rochdale,' said the young man.

They had come level with a neatly banked pile of scrap metal. A Bedford truck stood nearby. The door of the cream-coloured trailer opened and an older woman lent out.

'Tommy, come on in.' She held back the door, eyeing the strangers. 'You'll be wantin' a cup of tea.'

'He wants to buy the trailer, Agnes.' Tommy was helping Denise up the step.

'I'm expecting a baby,' she said, sitting on the edge of the double-bed, attempting to limit her invasion of their privacy. 'I'm not used to living in a wagon.'

'Well, they're hardly fit to live in,' Agnes said. 'You don't see nothin' like that in England no more. Over here we're behind the times aren't we?'

She was laying teacups on the table, taking china from a glass-fronted locker. 'The Corporation won't leave us alone,' she complained. 'How are you doin' on the Southside there?'

'Too many of us in the one place. They can't shift us.'

'What about Big Bill?'

Steve was not sure how to answer this. 'For one we're just outside the city. Not on his patch any more. We've just found out we're on private land. Belongs to speculators. I don't think they care we're there.'

'We'll move over to you,' said Tommy cheerfully. 'I might get your lot to stockpile the scrap as we doin'. Fetches the best price.'

'Could you help with the school?' Denise asked the girl.

'I will,' she said. 'If Tommy will let me.' She looked at her husband and seeing she had approval, added, 'Me name's Jessie. I was schooled in England.'

'I'll come to the point with you,' said Johnny Gray, speaking for the first time. 'You can have the trailer for two hundred and that's a fair price.'

'I can't go that far.' Steve knew he would have to bargain. 'Will you take my wagon and a hundred pounds?'

'I'll have to see it, young man.'

Agnes, helped by Tom's wife Jessie, began to move bedclothes and belongings by the armful to the nearest wagon. Johnny Gray went to fill up the petrol tank on his Bedford.

When the trailer was empty, the Gypsy man backed up the motor and the three of them squeezed into the cab. Coming through the city they passed a small crowd of Travellers on O'Connell Bridge.

'Would you want to join us?' Steve shouted above the engine noise. 'Plenty of room for all at Cherry Orchard.'

Johnny Gray smiled, concentrating on the traffic. 'I wouldn't come myself. We never stop on the Southside. But Tommy and Jessie'll give it a try.'

They turned west up the south quays. 'The Gala isn't it?' Johnny asked after a while.

He drew the trailer into the hospital forecourt and swung it around onto the verge near the school. The new fence, like a frontier, separated the camp from the road. The Walls' stockade looked like a little fort.

Standing on the verge, Johnny examined Steve's wagon. 'I'll give you forty-five pounds on it,' he said straightening up. 'And you can have the two gas bottles with the trailer.'

'Alright,' Steve agreed, eager to close the deal. Denise put in fifty pounds from her own savings and Johnny gave them two pounds back for luck.

When Steve and Denise had transferred their few things, the old barrel-top, with the help of two planks and some extra hands, was run up onto the back of the Bedford. Johnny Gray took off slowly down Ballyfermot Road.

The young English couple stayed on the road watching the lorry diminish. Their old wagon, swaying on its springs, faded quickly from sight. Part of their life together, a unique experience, was disappearing with it.

Denise had sometimes loved, more often hated, the wooden caravan. She was immediately in love with her new home.

'I'll stoke up this stove and let it burn through the night,' she told Steve, turning a pirouette in the spacious interior.

After eating their supper they let down the double bed.

3 The children had fallen so quiet Denny could hear the murmuring voices of the men outside. They had been in the compound all morning sorting and weighing scrap. Half the camp had joined Tommy Clarke's co-operative, pooling upwards of forty tons of old iron and steel. It was noon and they were waiting for the foundry lorry.

'They'll get top price for a big load like that,' Jessie told her as they warmed themselves at the school stove.

Denise had taken to the Lancashire girl and the atmosphere in St Christopher's II was almost always congenial. Everything Jessie did chimed with the children. They all loved Denny but Jessie was one of them.

This morning the children were drawing pictures of home life; the insides of huts and outside fires. Most were putting the violence of the evictions behind them.

Tuckerlaly, Mary MacDonald's nine-year-old, a veteran of the Ring Road school, chewed on his crayon, deep in concentration. The plastic skylight flapped above his head unnoticed.

The Quakers' milk had been delivered and cocoa would be made at the end of the period.

Louder voices could be heard now on the hospital side of the building; the movement of many feet. Then an engine flared into life. It was loud enough to be a bulldozer. Denise guessed the County

Council had returned to finish the fence. It irritated her that they might have to argue again about the school. Meanwhile the noise was disturbing the tranquillity of the class.

Old Pop Connors put his head in the door, 'Sorry to interrupt an' all,' he said, his one eye gleaming. 'The guards are out here. They want your man.'

'Isn't Steve out there?' she said, hiding her alarm. 'Knock on the trailer.'

The men in the compound had stopped talking. A dog yapped and barked.

'I'll go see,' said Jessie. She returned to report that there were coachloads of police and workmen out on the road.

The children were no longer intent on their drawings. Denny moved behind them, trying to restore the calm. Their faces had grown doleful.

A smell of acrid smoke seeped through the skylight. It smelt like burning rubber.

Denise directed Paddy Ward to bring the churn to the front. He filled a tin pan and started making the cocoa.

When she next glanced at Tuckerlaly, the boy's head was up. He was listening to the noises from outside, his lips quivering with self-whispered words.

She spoke soothingly but the pitch of the engine made her heart quake. Looking over Tuckerlaly's shoulder she saw he had drawn the outline of a baby in blue. As she watched he added in a thick blue mouth. He was remembering the death of Maisie's Macdonald's baby.

Transfixed by those cold blue lips she was reminded with pain that she would almost certainly give birth to a blue baby.

She summoned the front row and guided by Jessie five little ones slithered off their seats and came clutching at her dress. Tucker had his thumb in his mouth. One shoe had dropped to the floor under the desk.

Nan, in the back row, her black hair scattered, kept pumping her arm in the air.

'What?' said Denise.

'Please miss, is it Big Bill?' The girl's eyes were all agitation.

'I don't know.' she said, unnerved by the fear in the children's eyes. 'No, of course it's not. He's not coming here. We're out of his area. And you know he's been shot. '

'Me bruther Wack is goin' to kill 'im,' said Tuckerlaly, cheering up.

'Well, he's not dead yet,' Denise responded, not wanting to escalate this conversation.

'Are they puttin' us out?' Nan asked, coming out of her desk and going for the door.

'Don't you go out,' Jessie scolded her. 'You must all stay in here.'

Commotion followed her words as if a gun had been fired. There was a rush for the door. But Nan, older than the rest, held it closed.

All turned their haunted faces on Denise. Big Bill, the bogeyman of nightmares, might not be out there. But something was. And it had the power to tear their lives apart. The terror had returned.

4 A crowd of policemen, their eyes looking every which way but at the huge encampment opposite, shuffled into companies beside a row of navy-blue coaches. Marshalling the centipede-like lines was that same tall inspector familiar from other confrontations.

Less inhibited were the stares of a loose flock of men who waited close by, uncertain of their orders. These, poorly dressed for the cold, bareheaded most of them, had been bussed in fresh from the Labour Exchange.

It was clear the guards were not going to fraternise with the unemployed riff-raff, some no doubt from the houses in Ballyfermot. These blew on their hands, cold and uneasy, the uncertainty playing on their nerves.

The yellow bulldozer which had rooted up the hedges, stood driverless alongside the fence. Inside the curtain of wire a handful of Travellers had mounted a picket. A brazier burned, sending up early red flames.

Aiken was gratified to see there the figure of Joe Donohue among the picketers. The Gaffer, imitating the Civil Liberties League, had brought out posters from Pat's hut and rallied his nephews, who at this moment were hanging out the big Irish tricolour in full view of the guards.

These few picketers were the sole defenders in view. Most of the men, gathered for the scrap weigh-in, were out of sight in the compound beside the school.

Deep down the land, indistinct in the moist air, some children could be seen on their way up to the school for the afternoon class.

The tall officer walked over to where Aiken stood watching on the verge by his caravan.

'You know you're trespassing,' he said, speaking down to the youth. 'You can't be left here. The owners have been ordered by the courts to move you off.'

'I'm not parked on their land,' Aiken responded. 'I've just been dealing with the company's letters.'

The officer turned as two black-coated businessmen stepped up beside him.

'These two gentlemen are from Ballyfermot Holdings.'

The parleying went on at the side of the road. The guards were massed only a dozen yards away. It was a relief that their arrival had nothing to do with the shooting of Bill Redmond. But Aiken could not tell whether the Cherry Orchard men would stand their ground should the ranks of guards be ordered to advance into the camp.

Glancing around however he saw that more people were coming up to the fence, women among them.

The bulldozer chugged backwards towards the Ballyfermot houses, away from the smoke of burning tyres that crept like poison gas across the road.

'This caravan will be removed,' the garda officer insisted.

'Where to?'

'Out of the way,' He pointed with his stick towards the Gala.

'I can't be held responsible if these gentlemen block the road with my caravan,' said Aiken.

'The caravan will be pounded,' the officer retorted in frustration. He strode away with the company men and they conferred on their own behind the blue ranks

Seeing his opportunity Aiken called to Joe Donohue. Helped by Pat's boys they rolled Steve's trailer forward across the gap, hoping the police would believe it was being pushed out of the way. Chap was removing a wheel when the inspector came hurrying back.

'Your caravan will be taken to the pound,' he warned the Englishman. 'A low-loader is being ordered for the job.'

'Okay,' said Steve, knowing it would not be okay with Denise.

The caravan was standing tilted on one wheel.

Aiken climbed in at the side door looking for food. Having found himself a piece of cheese he wedged himself at the table and watched out the window. Big Bill's operations had barely prepared him for the scale of this eviction. He had never seen so many policemen. The bulldozer stood squared up ready. The whole settlement had been condemned by court order. It could crush the huts and the school in no time. The rule of law; the insanity of it maddened him. He went to the door and locked it determined to stay inside and defy them. Jackboot justice. He would pervert the course of this so-called justice if he could.

The first catcalls and the sound of breaking glass on the road told Aiken the camp was now intent on resisting. He could see through the end window that people were coming out of their huts. They were hauling several wagons towards the safety of the compound.

The two directors, ignoring the heckling Travellers, recrossed the road and knocked on the caravan.

'We have to order you off,' one of them said, almost apologizing. They had three policemen with them.

Aiken opened a window and said, 'Everyone here's been evicted before. Many times over. They're unlikely to leave. They know they'll be evicted from the next place.'

He could see the company might be reluctant to use force. Yet it was there behind in ample quantity. Even while he spoke the tall officer was scanning the activity with a keen, assessing eye.

The two company directors looked back nervously at the crowd behind the wire as they returned to the police lines. Aiken shivered and lit himself a cigarette.

After a time he noticed that the police were heeding a new commotion towards their left. The labourers were craning that way too. Something out of view from Aiken was drawing their attention.

The lofty officer came to the window and said urgently, 'Mr Aiken, you must tell those people to stay peaceful.'

Aiken nodded a mute assent and unlocked the door. Standing on the road he saw some of the young men had armed themselves with iron bars. Independent of Joe's picket, they had gathered by the huts and were chanting and waving their weapons. But there were many in the lower field still hanging back.

In the compound behind St Christopher's, figures were on the move. An old gate was lifted; a steel pole rose in the air. The barrel-tops had been packed close. Those gathered for the scrap sale were now yelling too. Boys were running up and down the trenches rolling rubber tyres onto a fire. He wondered how Denny and Jessie were bearing up inside the school.

It was obvious to those outside that the camp was preparing a second line of defence in a well-trenched position.

Realising the power of this impression, Aiken decided to bluff the guards. He walked along the front of the fence egging on the resistance, urging those there to make a war-like show of defiance. The police had seen the affray at the Seventh Lock. They must believe the Tinkers would fight.

The little conference on the forecourt looked startled by the new round of yelling. The guards kept glancing towards their chief, like a pack of reluctant runners under starter's orders for a marathon.

Meanwhile, exposed to a cruel wind, the defenders dragged out brazier stoves from huts and fed them the uprooted hedges. The Donohue boys moved among the growing cohorts, keeping up an appearance of violent resolve.

The billowing black smoke continued to percolate through the fence and drift down the road.

For a while it obscured the hired crews and when visible again they had dissolved into chattering groups. A few individuals had climbed back on the buses, showing their pallid faces at the windows. They looked like raw reserves that hope not to be thrown into an unwinnable battle.

Up the road again clanked the yellow bulldozer advancing with noisy purpose between the opposing lines. Busy with the levers, the driver disregarded the menace from the camp. He cut the engine and stopped close to the company representatives, awaiting instructions.

Then he was on the move with one track halted, scraping around to point the huge blade at the Cherry Orchard side. The bulldozer slowly lumbered forward. There were barely ten yards to the fence. Bodies of guards formed on either flank. As the machine nosed up to the wire several Travellers backed away. Others dug their fingers into the mesh and held on. The shovel lifted a foot and inched forward, threatening fence and defenders.

A burning stick sailed into the air and broke in sparks against the blade. Two more followed making scorching black whorls on the yellow paint. The great steel blade rose higher and hovered in the air, as the driver tried to shield himself from the missiles. A bottle went smash. Another flew passed his head. The guards, stopped by the fence, fell back. Again the bulldozer engine cut. The driver, now frightened, climbed down and disappeared among the policeman.

Losing patience, the officer advanced with a sergeant at his side.

'I won't stand this, Mr Aiken. I'll start making arrests shortly if your people continue.'

He looked along the line of Travellers out of reach beyond the wire. Realising the delicacy of the situation he changed his tone.

'I need to properly assess what to advise here. Will you allow me to come in there and just take a look. I'll come by myself.'

Leaving the sergeant, the officer crossed the verge and squeezed past Aiken's toppled trailer. The Englishman waited while he counted the picketers and then escorted him over the field towards the compound.

Without a word of welcome Luke met the guard at the barricade and permitted him to sidle through.

'I'm Inspector Collins,' he said. No hand was offered. 'I just want to take a look.'

'What you see here, sir, is about eight hundred pounds' worth of scrap. That's the livin' of the whole lot of us. We was expectin' the foundry lorry when yous arrived.'

Collins looked into Luke's red face hardly knowing what he was talking about.

The men and women in the compound, surrounded by their wagons, opened ranks to let him move forward. He noted the strength of the barricades behind which all had waited these hours in a sullen crowd. The people here were unarmed but weapons and missiles were plentiful among the high banks of scrap metal.

'Will you open the school door?' he asked.

'There's a class in there,' said Aiken. 'This is as far as you need come. If Ballyfermot Holdings sends in the bulldozer you can imagine the outcome for yourself.'

The inspector nodded. He had been present at the Ring Road when the school had been barricaded.

'Is Senator Grady not here today?" he asked, ready now to leave the redoubt.

'It's just ourselves. Ourselves alone,' said Luke Wall.

The officer shouldered his way out, saluting those he passed with his cane.

Shortly after, the foundry lorry arrived and pulled onto the verge in front of St. Christopher's. The big eight-wheeler nosed forward until the cab was close behind Aiken's immobilised caravan.

Tommy Clarke went out to explain the situation to the driver. While they talked a green double-decker bus edged towards the hospital bus stop.

5 Climbing to the upper deck of this bus Inspector Collins continued his recce. A sighting of the whole camp through the drifting smoke and over the heads of the Tinkers along the fence revealed a large body of people coming up the land.

He saw the cloth caps and tartan shawls and pricking above them numerous sticks and bars. Heading his way was a substantial reinforcement armed for a donnybrook.

What Collins could not know was that many of the womenfolk, some with babies in their shawls, wished only to catch the bus into town. New in Dublin, the Wards had just learnt women of their sort could spend a lucrative day down on O'Connell Bridge.

The big man leading them, bare-fist champion King Ward, was unknown to the Dublin policeman. But as they floundered forward to join those at the fence, Collins heard the great cheer that greeted Larry and the men of the West.

The mood of these swollen ranks, flushed with new confidence, finally convinced Inspector Collins that an eviction, if attempted, would be violent.

'I was watchin' the back door,' said Larry by way of excuse for his late arrival at the front.

'It's all bin talk so far.' Joe Donohue answered, still sour towards the Wards.

For the Donohue boys, who at noon had stood almost alone, and for the Walls watching from the redoubt, this closing together came as a great relief. It was like the answer to a prayer none had dared utter. Everyone down to the smallest boy and girl sensed the significance of it. At Cherry Orchard the Travellers of Ireland were uniting in common cause. True nomads, they had entered here only to bivouac upon this land. No-one among them owned it nor claimed ownership of any part. But forced to fight they felt themselves in possession of something they needed. This was their encampment and they would not be driven from it.

A pugilist with a reputation, Ward believed himself and his people unbeatable. They would hold the fence line until nightfall.

None of this, perhaps, was understood by the businessmen of Ballyfermot Holdings. But staring out at the mob opposite from within the safety of the police cordon, they might have come to recognise themselves as cardinal transgressors. To go in there meant to trespass into a hundred homes.

'We'll not leave without we spill yer blood, yer inhuman divils,' cried a voice from the wad of Connaught women. Throwing back their shawls they prepared to loose themselves in a headlong charge. Raising sticks, some were seeking a way through the wire when the King called them back.

Eileen Ward, with others already out on the road, hesitated to return. She needed bread from the shops. Seeing her there, Aiken beckoned her to his caravan. Three young women crushed in behind her curious, as much as anything, to see the inside of this newfangled living-van.

'Will you just sit down?' said the young Englishman. 'A sit-down will stop them moving this trailer.'

'What's a sit-down?' said on of the Ward girls, giggling.

The young women sat along the sloping bed, amusing themselves with chatter. Larry Ward came to the window saying, 'The buffers are not able for it. Begob, the boys are squarin' up to 'em.'

Not to be left out, Joe Donohue stepped into the trailer and Ward followed him. There were now seven for the sit-in. Conscious of the mild impropriety of the girls, the three men hunched together united in their male embarrassment.

All the early uncertainty had gone. The police presence no longer fazed them. In Aiken's mind this was a moment of pure revolt. He saw it in the faces and the gestures along the fence. Today it was no hit-or-miss defiance; no-one was going to lie down under a humiliating eviction of the sort inflicted at the Ring Road and Landsdowne Valley. Here the Travellers had broken out of the old apathy and found a valour all their own which in a few short hours had turned into an insurrection.

Cold, appraising eyes played over the rebels and both sides knew the odds had altered.

Better prepared for negotiation, the three went out into the drifting smoke in front of Aiken's trailer. Fire sticks smouldered at their feet.

Seeing them, Collins in his long blue coat came with lank strides to meet the trio.

'Who is the spokesman here?' the inspector asked, his stinging eyes averted from the close crush of agitated heads now roaring for buffer blood.

'You met the camp chairman in the compound there,' Aiken said, indicating the stockade. 'That's Luke Wall. I can ask him to come over.'

'All right. No matter,' Collins said, finding himself in a situation so precarious he could afford no delay. 'You three here appear to be leading this. I want an answer and I want it now without any blarney or explanations. Just a plain yes or no.'

He looked first at Larry Ward and then Joe. 'Will you tell your people to back off that fence and stand back from the gate?' Then to Steve he said: 'Mr Aiken, get those ladies out of your trailer. It's going into the pound.'

The light of the afternoon was failing. The low-loader had not arrived.

The two Travelling men turned uneasily to each other. Ward's hard jaw levelled with the nose of the Southside Gaffer. They answered to different constituents; different clans. The breadth of Ireland separated them. But circumstances demanded a single voice. Both knew the fate of Cherry Orchard as well as their personal prestige hung on their response. Aiken owned no part of this. He could only watch and listen.

At that moment people came streaming out of the compound. Luke could no longer hold them back. Everyone wanted to see what was happening. They stood on the mounds and crowded beside Aiken's trailer. Ward and Donohue spoke in the gammon, a rapid exchange that the Englishman could not follow.

Only two words he recognised, gredi karib. Which he took to mean keep up the fight.

Before they had delivered an answer to the police officer one of the company directors stepped in.

'Ballyfermot Holdings needs a clear statement from you,' he said, waving his gloves. 'Are you going to vacate this land?'

When both hesitated, Aiken ventured to respond: 'None of us can answer for the whole camp. Least myself. There's maybe a thousand people here. These are the only homes they have. We want to keep running the school. You can see how worked up everyone is. We've been evicted ten times this winter. That's not your doing but there's going to be people hurt if you come in here. This field isn't being used. It can't do you any harm if we stay on a while longer. We need it until another ground is found. That's been promised us by the Minister, Mr Neil Blaney.'

Cutting short the English lad, Donohue interjected: 'Sir, you've asked for a plain answer. We're none of us leavin'.'

'We mean no harm to ye,' Ward said with dignity, raising his huge hands. 'All the same we can't let ye do harm to us and ours. D'you understand us, sir?'

Without further word the company man and the inspector retired to safe ground on the far side of the road.

The three climbed back into the caravan and settled in the tilted seats. Eileen handed round Denise's biscuits as they waited for the verdict.

The fulsome voices of the people outside went on unabated. More bottles smashed and an iron bar went into the air and rattled across the road to the feet of the workmen. Another bus arrived and passengers disembarked for the afternoon hospital visit.

Finally, the ringleaders were called out and went together to the forecourt. There they were told in low voices that the eviction was being called off.

Larry Ward walked back towards the fence. Nobody inside had heard a word. He raised his arms, smiling, signalling to all for quiet so that he could convey the news.

'The day is won,' Ward said. 'A darp talosk. A great day it is for us Travellers.'

Up at the fence, he and Joe were clasping hands with the picketers who had stood so long through the afternoon.

Already many of the young fellows were breaking out onto the road as the ranks of guards swivelled abruptly and began a slow tramp down the Ballyfermot Road.

The jobless walked after them in a rabble, glad to depart unscathed. The coaches awaited further down.

The women surged over to the bus stop to watch them pass away, amazed that the whole confrontation was at an end.

A few youths ran down the road, jeering at their retreating enemies. A pebble or two was flung, bouncing harmlessly off the tarmac.

Against the stream of this chaotic, animated throng, Steve Aiken pushed his way towards St Christopher's. A cheer went up and hands reached to clap his shoulders. The congratulations rang in his ears. He was a hero.

'May I hope to die the shayds are runnin',' exclaimed old Mick O'Brien.

'We'd have fought an' all,' said Luke, watching the last police car pull away.

The bulldozer was now surrounded by girls. They patted its sides, eager to feel the metal of this monster that they had tamed.

Pat Donohue was in tears of relief and joy. Old Pop Connors, dazzled by what he had seen, muttered several times under his breath, 'Be the Holy!'

Mothers, who had stayed with children inside the huts, now came out laughing. They laughed with relief and a determination to wring from this rare victory every bit of pleasure they could. Tears were running down Mary Macdonald's cheeks. Holding Tuckerlaly's hand she was gasping with the elation of it all.

The other children let late out of class went leaping and clapping down the field as if at a fair.

In a minute Denise came out of St Christopher's and was hanging on Steve's arm in the joy of this dull grey evening.

1 A week later Kilmainham District Court sat again on the adjourned case of Dublin County Council versus Ballyfermot Holdings. Reporting for the National Press Bureau, Aiken heard a lawyer for the company explain why the squatters had not been cleared from the land.

'The order for the workmen to go in was not given,' said the solicitor for the defendants. 'It was determined by the senior garda officer present that to do so would have provoked a civil riot. He wisely advised against it.'

The district judge was content to accept further assurances from the company that every effort was being made to find an alternative for the people at Cherry Orchard. He said the Minister for Local Government had promised financial assistance to local authorities to help meet the cost of what were referred to as sites for itinerants.

He explained that the new deal also included an offer of aid to voluntary bodies set up to encourage 'the long-term integration of itinerants.' The court was told a Dublin Itinerant Settlement Committee, chaired by the Rt Rev Thomas Fehily, had raised considerable funds for the purpose.

At a meeting in the school Luke Wall told the camp: 'We've won this ground fair and square. Nobody is goin' to bother us further. Big Bill's out of it and the government's against any eviction here.'

To his surprise this reiteration of the security they had won brought no applause. Only blank faces showed around the school desks. The mood of victory had changed within a few days to a rankling new discontent.

'What!' said Luke, 'Are you not satisfied?'

Nobody wanted to show disrespect for Luke's efforts. Yet something had to be said.

'You've told us yourself enough times,' said Old Pop Connors. 'This whole place is a pigsty. Not fit to live in. We can stay here, sure. But the chillin'll be dyin' on us if sommut isn't done.'

In the middle of the meeting Andrew Meachen arrived in his red station wagon. He had come to find out for Father Fehily what the camp was up to and sat listening at the back puffing on his briar pipe. Nobody had expected to see him again.

The men were pledging a big clear-up of the accumulated rubbish.

Luke next broached the subject of Fehily's committee and the recent television appeal for money.

'Is it right ten thousand pounds has come in?' he asked Andrew, his face roasting with annoyance.

'Around that,' Andrew answered. 'Of course every penny will be accounted for. You can trust Father Tom, can't you?'

'Trust the priest, yes,' said Joe Donohue. Only there's somethin' amiss. Be rights we should have a say. A great lot of money has been raised in our name.'

'Didn't we face a whole battalion of guards to get stoppin' here,' said Chap Donohue. 'Why wasn't our chaplain out there on the road with us that day?'

'What I want to know is will the Government give us the same support?' said Luke.

Meachen made a stabbing gesture with his pipe, saying: 'I can tell you categorically that the Dublin Itinerant Settlement Committee has received no government funding.'

'As yet,' Aiken put in, as irked as everybody else.

'Fair enough,' said Luke. 'Can we apply for help since we're doin' the job already here?'

A queer look came into Meachen's face. Unable to look around at the men he said what he felt compelled to say. 'You may apply, sure. But you can take it from me the government is not going to give a grant to a Travellers' committee.' His eyes engaged them now as he added through his beard, 'To Tinkers?'

The faint sneer was bitter to see. But they knew he was right.

It was cold enough for snow when Andrew Meachen drove away and no-one was happy. They were being robbed of much of their victory. Nevertheless, the clean-up commenced next day. A great bonfire, fed by cartloads of rubbish from all corners of the two fields, burned day and night.

Aiken pitched in with the others to reduce the uncollected rubbish. As a result he caught an infection and his urine turned red. Denise saw with alarm that his eyes were discoloured and his scalp a mustard yellow. Aiken felt exhausted. He was going down with jaundice.

'You've got to see a doctor,' she pleaded.

'I can't,' he told her. 'The council could start health proceedings against the camp. Everyone would be summoned and forced to leave or pay big fines. I can't let that happen.'

'Yeah but what if I catch it? You can't do this. If I get hepatitis on top of the blood thing the baby won't have a chance.'

'First we've got to keep mugs, cutlery – everything separate,' he said. 'I will see a doctor if I get worse.'

Too tired and dispirited to go into the city he lay down on the bed. Denise went to seek advice from Bridget Wall.

'Keep him on the plain food. No grease, butter, fat. Nothin' like that. Apples, salad anythin' green. Fruit and vegetables. No milk.'

So Denise nursed him and after a few days on a strict regime Aiken was a little better. She herself showed no symptoms of the jaundice.

2 'Me Uncle Larry is takin' us to the pictures,' said Paddy, dancing on the fine snow outside the Gala cinema. 'They'll be along in a tick.'

His sister Nan, shaking a sugaring of snow from her hair, smiled shyly at Denise. Steve came out of the hardware shop, humping a bale of peat briquettes.

He gave the young ones sixpence each and the couple walked away, the snowflakes bumping in their faces. A silent blizzard had started to blow. At the lighted hospital forecourt, Lawrence Ward and a whole party were on their way down the road. The snow swirled about them. Footmarks led across the white verge and into the silent camp.

Pat's hut was already a grey-white blur and beyond other huts and wagons stood as if crudely whitewashed. Peering from under the hood of her duffel coat, Denise could just make out in the distant landscape the white and black humps of bender-tents. Red fires still burned, one bigger than the rest.

Inside, their caravan was wonderfully warm and giving way to his fatigue Steve got into bed.

'How we'll all survive I don't know,' said Denise. 'Nobody should be in a tent in this cold.'

'I should have told Paddy and Nan to come in with us after the films.'

But he was too sick to worry longer and after they had eaten fell asleep. Denise kept the gas burning and started to read, trying to ignore the ceaseless buffeting on the curtained windows. Outside the snowstorm was pasting the aluminium panels with specks of frozen moisture. Finally, the snowflakes caught and began to settle on the roof. Beyond the laced white fence the encampment was lost in the winter night.

Denise was deep in the narrative of her paperback when there came a quick rat-tat at the window. It sounded like a coin striking the glass. Alarmed she jogged Steve with her knee but he didn't stir. Pulling herself up she drew back the curtain.

Pressed close to the pane was the cold white face of Frank McManus.

In horror she dropped the curtain. Steve was struggling out of sleep when the sharp tapping sounded again just above their heads.

'It's McManus,' she moaned. 'For Godsake don't open the door.'

'It's not locked.'

That knowledge precipitated her panic and she clung to him. They both listened intently but nothing further was heard above the muffled blowing of the storm.

All at once the door clanged open, the caravan rocked and with a rush of cold air and snow, in stepped McManus. In his hand he held the long Webley revolver.

'You'll fuckin' leave Ireland,' he shouted as he advanced to the end of the bed and stood over the prostrate couple, who were now clutching the bedclothes.

They sat up, scared and helpless, the barrel menacingly close. Steve stared yellow-eyed at the intruder.

'I could blow your fuckin' heads off,' the gunman sang out. 'Nobody'd hear in this storm.' His voice cracked in mid-phrase, their predicament looked comic.

'Frank for Christ's sake – sit down.' Steve said to him, a weariness in his plea.

Aiken's sick demeanour had a calming effect on McManus. He backed over to the table and lowered himself onto the seat, the big snow-flecked collar of his coat standing up around his neck. His red nose glistened in the gas light.

His rage, it seemed, had been simulated. He had been faking all the bluster; the gun, in the presence of such vulnerable victims, now superfluous. He laid it on the table. McManus was man enough to deliver his message without it.

'We want you out of here. D'you hear the pair of you?' More peevish than angry, he kept looking at the two frightened faces. They struck him as too funny and his expression changed to a smirk.

'I can't leave. I've got to stand trial.'

'You'll leave this camp. I don't care where you go.'

'Steve is going to prison for you people. Doesn't that mean something?' Denise said, finding her voice.

'You've done it all wrong,' McManus waved his hand dismissively. 'For what in the hell did you involve your fuckin' Lord Russell?'

'I think he's done some good,' Steve said, sounding ridiculously reasonable.

'Some good? You're coddin'. Didn't that Lord Russell, his grandfather, your Prime Minister, just let a million people starve in this country? D'you think we forget the famine? D'you think we forgive? We don't like him. His a fuckin' atheist and he's screwing up the Travellers' campaign. And that's your doin' – and you're goin'.'

McManus was getting some colour back in his face from the heat of the stove. There was a pool of melted snow at his feet.

'We can't leave this place because of Steve's bail,' Denise told him, feeling a pain in her gut from the tension.

She and Steve, sitting up in the bed, were working in tandem to placate the gunman. She wished urgently he would go. In her abdomen a cramp gripped her and would not release itself.

Before McManus made any answer the door opened again and the icy draught carried a voice from the dark outside.

'Haven't you finished your man off yet? I thought you were gonna shoot him?'

The floor canted and Tommy Bowden entered, grinning at the other. 'I won't stand out there longer freezin' like a fool.'

He had cycled through the snow from his home in Palmerstown.

'It's too friggen hot in here,' said McManus, going at last for the buttons on his coat.

Bowden stood in the middle of the floor, his snowy back to the bed. He joked some more with McManus, putting his tongue between his teeth and giggling wickedly. Then he got out cigarettes and offered the packet around, shaking out two onto the blankets. The pair in the bed let him light them up.

As the four puffed away together the atmosphere of tension between them subsided. But Denise Hanley, under cover of the blankets, was holding her hand to her stomach. Every now and again came the griping, contraction-like pain. It frightened her now more than the presence of the IRA men.

Presently, from out on the road they heard the approach of singing voices. The sound, barely penetrating the flurries of snow, came slowly nearer. Larry Ward and the other Galway Travellers were returning from the Gala. They had probably bought a few bottles from Hennessy's Bar.

Frank McManus got up, bowing his head under the thin, low ceiling. The revolver went back into his pocket and he made for the door pushing Bowden, his lookout man, ahead of him.

'We mean it.' His raised finger threatened them. 'Out of here or you'll get it.'

Angry, Steve could not at the last resist needling him.

'You sound like Big Bill only worse.'

'You'll get what Big Bill got only a lot worse,' McManus turned, clenching his fist.

They left the door swinging; a black chasm sucking in the freezing snow.

This had nothing to do with Grady, Aiken assured himself as he went to close the door. This was just pure mad McManus. But there was Tommy Bowden's part. Perhaps they held him in contempt, all of the Republican crowd.

Not two minutes later, with boisterous sweeps of his arm, Larry Ward was banging on the side of the caravan.

'Are yous alright in there?' he called at the lighted window.

'We're okay,' Steve said, showing himself at the door. Paddy and Nan were out there. 'Come on up. Bring the children in.'

'No, we won't bother you. Don't worry about us. Eileen has the biggest fire built beyond.' Then knocking the snow off his cap he said, 'We saw those fellas comin' away in a hurry like.'

Larry Ward sung out a cheerful goodnight and the Ward party went on their way down the dark snowy field towards their fires.

3 The cramps had subsided and Denise hopped about with her leg still off, straightening the bed. She dropped four briquettes into the stove. She hoped that the crisis in her belly was over and settled back down with Steve.

Outside the wind had died away, the light snow now descending vertically. When Steve cupped his hand on the window to look out a final time, he could see nothing but a white wall. The night had closed around everything, putting down its infinite peace.

Both soon fell asleep.

A long time passed before Denise was again woken by the pains. Having waited, clenched and hurting, for the spasm to fade, she rolled off the bed and stood on her one foot. She had to go to the lavatory. The flannel nightdress brushed across the damp floor as she reached to steady herself. Light as she was, her first awkward hop shook the room. Glancing back, she saw by the ghostly, jumping firelight that Steve did not move.

A few short shuffles brought her to the door of the tiny closet. Once inside, having lifted the lavatory lid she seated herself astride the basin. Alone, poised for the onset of the next gut-clutching jab, she waited anxiously in the dark holding by her fingertips to the cold window-jamb. Her hair sunk forward exposing her neck.

She began to believe it was over when another contraction gripped her. Her hand tightened on the folds of her nightdress. The stink of the closet chemical brought her close to vomiting. She fought back the waves of pain and nausea. All at once came a powerful downward movement as though her bowels had opened. In trepidation, she put two fingers between her legs and felt there a wetness. Warm, flowing blood. She knew then she must be aborting the baby.

Her cries of panic brought Steve to her side. She was gasping, the sweat breaking out, hot and cold, on her body; the extremity of the crisis had come.

'I'm losing blood. Get a towel quick.' Her face was pressed sideways against him.

She made an effort to stay on the seat while he moved away. When he returned she thrust the towel under her and the two of them staggered back to the bed. The towel was soaked in blood.

While Denise collapsed back on the blankets, panting and moaning, Steve squatted beside her, helpless. His proximity irritated her and she waved him away. When he went to light the gas she shook her head vehemently. The pains grew closer, her grunts and cries louder until she was writhing and pushing, kicking away the bedclothes. At last the ordeal was over and she subsided on the pillows, her face wet, her eyes screwed shut.

He turned on the gas, leaving a bud of flame popping in the mantel.

She looked at him out of a pale, stricken face.

'I've lost the baby, Steve,' she said, the tears trickling down her cheeks.

She was the most forlorn sight he had ever seen. Worse than his mother on her deathbed. But he was in too much shock to cry.

Hardly able to keep his sanity, weak from jaundice, Steve forced himself to act. He started tugging the bloody bedclothes from her and she lifted herself to assist. A tiny discoloured thing less than the length of his finger lay with a mass of liverish afterbirth. Wrapping all in a fresh towel, he carried the bundle to the kitchen out of her sight.

After he had helped her clean herself they lay on the bed under coats. Both drifted into fitful sleep. It was the dead zone of the night and outside the snow, in endless tumbling wafers, piled down upon the silent caravan.

4 Somewhere near dawn Aiken awoke. An intense blue-white hush engulfed the caravan. The snow had stopped. He knew he had to get up and deal with the bundle in the kitchen. That necessity oppressed him and for a full minute he sat up shivering, aware of the morbid lighting coming from behind the curtains. The snow outside had an eerie presence.

His watch showed four hours had passed. He crawled off the bed leaving Denise in slumber. Helpless in the night he would now spare her the distressful job that had to be done. He crept to the kitchen and lit an oil-lamp, feeling his actions to be ugly and wrong. The bloody sheets and blankets rested in a heap on the draining board. When he unwrapped them the embryo lay stuck to the towel, the umbilical cord twisted in a corkscrew. Out of a horrid compulsion, he moved the little body with his thumb wanting to see whether it had the jaundice of a rhesus baby which the doctor had warned about. But in the yellow light it was impossible to tell. Moved to pity, he laid his palm over it. Cold to his fingers, the little head was hard like a walnut. Hardly knowing what he did, Aiken lifted his hand away and smelt his fingers. Poor wee mite, he thought.

He dressed quietly and banked up the stove; fetched the bundle from the kitchen and put it into a basket, together with a few things he needed. Then he opened the door to a wash of freezing air and stepped down into the snow.

The long road and the blanched houses lined up cold and dead towards the city. Only from the white-capped hedge beside the school issued a sign of life, the stirring of small birds. He wondered how in their little bodies they could survive. High above in the dim primordial blue a single rook flew onwards. Hearing its melancholy call, Aiken glanced upward and saw its wings touched beneath by the first pale light of dawn.

He passed the white mounds and barricades, pierced here and there by black stakes, like crosses in a snowy cemetery. The trenches of the redoubt had filled with soft drifts. As he tramped forward with his load, the land stretched ahead in a silvery smudge. Wagons, huts and tents loomed whitely, without full form. Two horses were moored, silent and still, in the lee of Pat's long shack, the snow at their hooves mashed and stained yellow.

At the centre of the shrouded land lay the humped grey embers of the fire which had burned there since the great clean-up. The falling snow, kept at bay by the heat, had settled in a ring about the perimeter of deep ash, allowing its glowing bowls to survive the night. Here Aiken stopped and put down the basket. Taking a stick and stirring the wads of half-burned debris, he drew together the drier under-layer. On these he laid the kindling and the peat briquettes he had brought and, with reverent care, set over them the basket with its bundle. Atop the pyre he placed the Gypsy peg-knife.

The knife had been Aiken's talisman since meeting the Travellers. It had been with him in prison. Its sacrifice filled his need for some ritual, for an act of contrition. Mournfully he emptied the oil lamp over everything and dropped a lighted match.

The flaring paraffin forced him to step back. He watched the flames licking like living demons over the surfaces. The tartan blanket, purchased for Denise in such happy days, gave off the stench of scorching wool. There was an awful fascination in the way the sheet, shredded by the hungry blaze, quickly blackened and disintegrated. Rising in black billows before his face was the love child he had made with Denise. The loss of the child broke his heart. He looked on in horror. Then remorse and shame compelled him to avert his eyes. He too wanted to be consumed and wished somehow the dead child could know this.

Finally Steve was crying, the tears tumbling freely down his frozen cheeks. All his own fault, his heart wailed. He had brought Denise Hanley only grief. Why had he asked her to come to Ireland? Better they had bided their time. The hardships she had borne because of him! Worst of all he'd caused that madman McManus to come to their door last night. That had killed the baby. She might have bled to death. He had been a young fool.

After a while, in the midst of his afflictions, Aiken said in a clear, keen voice, as if to someone there in the furnace of the flames, 'Goodbye, Little One, Goodbye.'

Those words rode in the frosty air and in an instant slipped away. Hearing himself utter them brought forth fresh weeping. He knelt now in the white comfort of the snow, the fire receding from his consciousness. Left behind was all awareness of where he was. He cried with an intensity he had not known since childhood. Strangely, he could hear his voice but faintly as if it were something distinct from himself and yet familiar. An uncanny wailing came from an emptiness inside him; the crying of an infant, lost and long forgotten.

Aiken felt better when it was all over and got up from his knees. His mind was clear, his vision sharper. The fire had grown a heart of red and beyond, all across the hoary field hung a veil of smoke. He had no idea how much time had passed only that during this solitary wake all his sorrow had spilled out. He wondered at this, pondered as he crouched to warm his body. He had been transported in his feelings to a place where he had not been before. Now he felt lightheaded, liberated; he had rediscovered himself. The experience could only be compared with the way he and Denise had found each other, all in an instant and the twinkling of an eye. His face was lit by an extraordinary triumph as he turned for home. The virgin snow, the blue heaven over him, life itself was a glory.

Looking back over the snowy vastness of the landscape, Aiken saw his square caravan out on the road, glistening in the early morning light. Nearby the white roof of St Christopher's School and the barrel-tops and the white-topped huts, and behind them the snow-laden hedges drooping under their load. Low over the snow-hushed city, in the eastern sky, a rose-edged cloud floated, shot through with the rays of the rising sun. As he watched, the sky whitened and then bloomed pink again. Finally the sun itself crowned, a watery blood red rim, climbing quickly. Everything looked pink-fresh and clean. The sight of the clear new day pleased him immensely.

He started off towards the compound, his old steps in the crystalline white carpet were there to follow. He stepped lightly, feeling his youth. A great burden was off him. He believed at this moment that if he went to prison it would not matter. He'd regained himself. Perhaps he had to suffer because of his wrongdoings. He would accept punishment for the grief he had caused Denise. It might be his salvation.

When he peeped, Denise was still miraculously asleep. Her head had slipped half off the pillow and sunk into the wad of red hair. Her cheeks were colourless in the light from the edges of the curtains. The sight of her made him suddenly hate McManus. How he had admired the IRA he could not credit. But he was not sorry Big Bill had been shot. The Travellers had to fight the evictions. Children were dying. He would oppose bad law and the men that upheld it.

He stripped off his damp outer clothes and heated water on the stove to wash his grimy hands. Then set about cleaning up the caravan. When this was finished he sat on the end of the bed waiting for Denise to wake up. Sleep was what she needed but Aiken was now impatient to communicate to her some of what he had just gone through at the fire.

Voices were calling and out on the snow a horse whinnied. There came the clang of Luke's water churn. For a long while yet however she remained unaware. Aiken went to the table and rested his head in his arms. Some of the tiredness had returned. It was a full hour later when she raised her head, giving a low moan. He stepped to the bedside watching her. The tip of her tongue moved at the corner of her mouth before she opened her eyes.

5 Denise looked up into his face. She felt limp and broken but his closeness soothed her and she shut her eyes again, glad that he was there. She heard him say some words but unable yet to concentrate did not know what he said, only that his voice was different.

Something in him had changed. When she studied him, frowning with the effort, she saw how full of feeling he was. Withdrawing her arms from the covering of coats she rose to him. They held each other close. She was crying, slender arms tightened about his neck. In that moment of sorrow and acknowledgment everything between them deepened. All that he had wanted to say, all that was essential, they said in this embrace.

'I stopped bleeding,' she said quietly.

'Thank God.'

'But it hurts to pee.'

Then she let go of him and drew breath. Her next words came out in a choking cry: 'My baby, Steve, my baby.'

'It was a tiny thing,' he said, alarmed. 'Just a wee thing, Denny.'

After a minute she lay back, still on the pillows, looking with stricken eyes into his face.

'I want to see it,' she pleaded.

Not knowing what to do or say, Steve backed away from the bed. Then he turned to her: 'I cleared all the blood and stuff out. I thought it would upset you more to see it.'

'Where?' She said, struggling to sit up. She was as persistent as a child.

'I'll tell you later.'

'No – I better know now.' She kept her smarting eyes on him, waiting.

Steve took a step to the window and with a sweep drew back the curtain. The light jumping into the room dazzled her. Outside the glassy sun swam on the sparkling surface of the snow. Some ponies were trotting over the field. One gave a little leap and darted forward with its shadow. Beyond them smoke still rose in dirty flattened billows from the distant fire. Denise stared at the scene beyond the window. The baby she had conceived and nurtured under her heart was now a discarded thing, going up in smoke with the camp garbage.

Her hands went to her face as she sobbed out, 'I wanted to hold my baby, that's all. I need to hold my baby just once, once, Steve.'

He came to her his eyes brimming with tears. 'I know I've been neglecting you. Solving everybody else's problems. Trying to change the world. But it all feels wrong now. I could have lost you last night. Christ, you could have bled to death.'

After a while he held her away from him and said; 'I deserve to go to prison. I want to go. I thought I did, anyway, when I was at the fire.'

'Then I'll be left alone. I'll lose you too.'

'We've got to face that. Will you wait?'

Denise saw his remorse. 'I'll wait, yes. You know I will wait. I'm scared for you, that's all.'

But she was tired and their conversation weighed on her and she lay back to rest.

Much later there was a rap on the door. Steve found Luke Wall outside knocking the snow off his boots. They spoke in low voices in the kitchen.

'We lost the baby last night,' Aiken told him. 'That McManus frightened the life out of her.'

'Oh God, that's awful. Will I send Bridget over?'

'She'd better sleep on now.'

But Bridget Wall came all the same and she told Denise she must go to the hospital.

'I won't,' said Denise. 'They'll ask questions. They'll treat me like a slut. You know we're not married.'

'Don't be so soft. Think of your health and the next baby you have.'

'I doubt I'll be able to have another, Bridget. My blood is all mixed up on account of my leg and the transfusion they gave me. Anyway, I'm okay now. I just need the rest.'

'Well, please yourself,' said Bridget, not at all pleased herself.

She returned later with a plate of hot dinner for the two of them.

1   Aiken had been told his trial would come on at short notice. Twenty-four hours was all he could expect. This warning from the solicitors instructing Melvin Calhoun, the Republican-leaning barrister defending him, made the Englishman feel suddenly trapped. For weeks his arraignment in the Central Criminal Court had remained a distant event. He had accepted his guilt. He was guilty of possession of explosives; if not of intention to use them. Additionally there was the gun, and only luck or police incompetence had saved him from facing a further charge on that account.

Melvin Calhoun was one of the brightest young barristers practising at the Irish bar. But the Englishman doubted Calhoun could get him off. He feared the barrister's known Republican sympathies would count against him however well contrived the defence. Calhoun's part in the Jerry Lawless case, on the legal team with Sean McBride, had incensed the Irish Government.

Pop's Johnny Connors had arrived back for the trial, bringing with him from Wales an old Sprite touring caravan which he drove onto the Cherry Orchard camp. Convinced his mission to Bertram Russell would save his friend, Johnny was full of optimism.

'A lovely man,' said Johnny. 'Didn't his wife pour the tea for me and Catlin.'

'They're mad as hell here over Bertrand Russell,' Steve told him, bringing out some cuttings. 'That Frank McManus wants to run me out of Ireland.'

'Ah, but we've got Lemass worried. He doesn't like all this pother about Pavis.' Then he pulled some papers out of his coat pocket. 'We had a meetin' with the students in Cardiff. They all signed the petition for Cherry Orchard.'

The petition calling for immediate implementation of the recommendations of the Commission on Itinerancy had been signed by Canon Collins of CND. According to one press report it was circulating among Members of Parliament and had on it the names of Labour MP Barbara Castle and Norman Dodds, an MP championing the cause of Gypsies. A Peace News item said there had been a rally at Hyde Park Corner and a march to the Irish Embassy demanding an end to evictions and the dropping of charges against Steve Aiken.

The next morning Steve and Denise went to the Green Street court house. A score of Travellers accompanied them. Inside the court the affable Melvin Calhoun took charge, sending the Travellers upstairs to the public gallery and guiding the couple through the pack of lawyers. He indicated the bench directly behind his own.

'No reason why you shouldn't sit here together,' Calhoun said, giving comfort to them. 'I can tell you this is not going to take long.'

He winked mysteriously, heaving his black gown. The barrister's wig perched atop his round pink head glinted in the electric light as he bent now to his books.

Denise clasped her hands tight in her lap but the presence of Calhoun close in front and his brief unexplained words, intimated that hope was not gone.

At last the court rose and the robed judge took his seat above them.

When everyone had sat down the clerk read from his list, glancing over his glasses at the lawyers. 'The case of the State versus Stephen Richard Aiken.'

'My client is present, your honour.' Calhoun bowed then laying his arm along the bench, whispered over his shoulder, 'It's going to be alright.'

The prosecuting council, a large gaunt man, was now on his feet.

'If it pleases your honour, after taking due consideration of all the circumstances of this case, the state wishes to enter a nolle prosequi.'

Listening intently to this short crucial statement, Steve had no idea what the two last words meant. He had to prod Calhoun's back and leaning close to the wig he asked anxiously, 'What's happening?'

The judge was in the midst of speaking but when he stopped, Calhoun twisted around to say, 'They've entered an indefinite stay of proceedings.' He enunciated each word and hissed at the Englishman, 'You're free. Now get out of here but quietly.'

Aiken was too surprised to move. He could not believe it was all over in so few minutes. It was an anticlimax. Almost a disappointment. His nerves demanded more. He turned to Denise Hanley and only then, seeing her face flushed with relief, could he properly register what had happened. He had been let off; his life given back. In another minute they were ducking out of the court, like two children released early from school.

The Travellers met them in the vestibule.

'What was that about for Godsakes?' asked Johnny, grinning, also unsure of the finer points.

The couple stood in front of them, Denny's arm linked into Steve's.

'They've as good as dropped the charges,' Aiken said, his face finally lightening.

'Didn't I tell you?' Johnny turned in triumph to the others. ''Twas me and Lord Russell accomplished this. The man will be delighted.'

Melvin Calhoun was now at Aiken's shoulder listening with amusement. 'They knew they lacked the evidence for a conviction,' he commented, smiling at the group. 'Your young man here was fortunate.'

2 'Wasn't it on the wireless just now,' Johnny Connors told the English couple one evening. 'Dublin Corporation will be buildin' a site for us. At the Seventh Lock. Would you believe that?'

'The Dublin campaign is really won then,' Aiken said, glad for himself and the camp.

'Oh, they'll have us waitin' a long while yet.' Then he thought. 'Won't other Travellers in other places stand up for themselves after this. Begob, I'll start somethin' meself when I go back over.'

'I hope we'll join up with you, Johnny, when we can and wherever you are.'

There was a meditative pause in which the three were united. Absently, Denise was screwing the gold ring on her finger. Steve turned to her. 'When its clear for us to go back. I won't risk two years in a glasshouse.'

'I wouldn't mind travelling with Catlin and Johnny,' she said. 'It would be a whole new life.' Looking at Johnny she said, 'You'd have to show us the ropes over there as you did here.'

'You'll come and stand with us then?' Johnny said to Steve, his face lighting up.

'If Denny will,' said Steve. 'You know that's what I want.'

The two men fixed their eyes on the girl. Raising her head bravely she said, 'If I can't have a baby this is the next best thing for me. I'm willing to go with you, yes.'

When Johnny had gone Steve disappeared into the kitchen to make them something to eat. They had travelled but a little way these past months. Yet had come so far. He knew now they would stay together with the Travelling people.

3 When the snow had melted and spring finally arrived the Wards prepared to leave Cherry Orchard. Larry Ward had secured an assurance from the National Itinerant Settlement Committee that his people would eventually get a piece of land to live on in their hometown of Loughrea. There would be a tigeen, or kitchen-hut, for each family.

His epic trek to Dublin had brought both triumph and humiliation. The King had come to back up his people. They had fought and won the battle for Cherry Orchard. Ward had expected a voice on the buffers' national committee. That was denied him. No Travellers were included. However, he had no wish to rub the unpleasantness of this in their faces, nor his own. He would return to Galway.

While the wagons were on the road outside the hospital, Larry went to have a last word with Luke Wall, and thank those who had been running the school.

'We'll get no respect for what we stand for,' said Larry, 'unless we speak out.'

'We need an organization,' said Luke. 'Like what we started here.'

'I'll see yis all at Ballinasloe Fair then. I'll book the town hall. We'll have the biggest meetin' yet.'

A few days after Ward left, a letter from France was delivered to the camp mailbox. Luke brought it to the English couple at a meeting in the school asking if they could translate it.

'It's from a Romany organization. Vaida Voivod, the head of it. Wants to visit Cherry Orchard,' Denise said, giving the gist of the message. 'By all means let him come,' said Luke, pleased that their fame had spread so far. 'Best he'd be over here for the Ballinasloe do.'

'He says here they're planning a world congress and hopes some of you will go to that.'

'All the Travellers united,' Pop's Johnny exclaimed. 'Course we want to be part of it.'

'Let's see that,' said Jessie Clarke. She took the letter from Denise and scanned it. 'See how he signs off? Pral. That's kushti. That means brother. Yes, I'd go if I could.'

4 Mikey Ward had left for England and Paddy and Nan were not coming up to the school anymore. Denise found the children one morning in their hut near the bottom gate. Eileen had gone downtown and the grub-box was empty. She took some of the Quakers' school milk to the hut and gave the children what food she had.

The next day, Denise set off for a second visit. The hut stood alone on ground unoccupied since the departure of Lawrence Ward. In the long, shallow hollow of fresh grass, the horses had collected to graze. As she reached the broken line of dividing hedge, Denise saw them on the move.

About twenty animals had started to canter around the field in a loose pack, frisking and whinnying as they gathered momentum. At the far side they turned, a fluid bank of muscular flanks, and led by a heavy cob, tore up the soft turf, hooves whirling. A rousing sight, it was a salute to spring. But she watched with misgiving.

The herd slowed momentarily and then the wilful cob, tossing his big head, gave a sharp snort and dashed ahead in another direction, bringing the rest behind him. Denise halted too, to see her own way safe. She felt the ground jolt as they stretched away in a gallop along the level towards the lower gate. She heard the click of metal, hoof upon plated hoof.

The speeding rumps were heading towards Mikey's hut. Denise saw a girl emerge. All at once she was under the hooves and down. Horrified, Denise hurried to the spot behind the retreating herd and found Nan. Putting down her bag, she raised the girl up. Paddy came out and they carried her into the hut. Nan lay limp in Denny's arms, blood soaking her long black hair. Denise could feel her heart against her own pumping out the life of her.

Paddy ran as fast as he could to fetch Steve. He got down to the hut and in the gloomy light saw Nan's prostrate body in the warren of old clothes. Denise sat beside her now, and the small children, hushed by his entrance, huddled around their senseless sister. Denise raised Nan again and cradled her body. Patrick believed his sister must be dead. His face contorted into tears.

'She's hurt bad,' Steve told him. 'We've got to get her up to the hospital.'

Steve moved to take her from Denise and bearing the weight of the girl, backed out of the hut. Fighting to keep his feelings in check, he hastened up the field. People appeared in their path, there were cries of alarm, but he raced passed them towards the hospital gate.

Inside the hut, Denise stood among the children hearing their sobs. Paddy sat on the mattress holding the smallest infant, waiting in forlorn expectation. Denise did not know how to console them.

'Fetch my bag and get the grub-box, Paddy, I'll cut you some bread,' she said quietly.

Patrick set up the empty box and the children closed in around her as Denise began to prepare the food she had brought.

5 Aiken was standing beside Nan as she lay on an examination table. The doctor who, with some reluctance, had agreed to look at her, was now gingerly lifting each of her limbs in turn. She was breathing but her eyes stayed closed.

'You must hold her arms,' the doctor told Steve, bending with a swab to probe the head wound.

Steve held on to the girl, his face coming close to hers, while the doctor methodically cleaned and stitched. He could not avert his eyes from the crescent gash, in the midst of which white bone showed through. The blood, the parted flesh and the smell of chlorine made his head swim.

Nan writhed into consciousness from the pricking of the needle. Within a short time she seemed miraculously to have recovered and was able to speak. The doctor, having heard some details from Aiken, asked how it had happened.

'I don't rightly know,' said Nan. 'I came all over faint with the hunger. I heard the ponies but I wasn't seein' them like. I can't recall at all.'

'Alright,' said the doctor, finishing the bandaging of her head. 'Can you walk?'

Nan let herself slowly off the table and stood on unsteady feet. Then she took a step or two, holding tight to Steve's arm. Then sudden dizziness forced her to collapse into a chair where she sat holding her head in her hands.

No nurse came to the small surgery and the doctor wanted to leave. In the end he left them to make their own way out.

'Me ma's goin' to kill me over this,' Nan said, as they walked slowly down the corridor.

'No she's not, Nan. She'll be glad you're alive. We all are.'

'This is goin' to be the biggest bump.'

Nan forced a smile, looking up at him with her wide, black eyes. Then she tugged at the tangled locks that straggled below the white bandage, said cheerfully, 'He didn't have to cut me hair any road.'

When they reached the hut it was filled with a fusty heat. Paddy had found something to burn. Nan looked a sorry sight squatting on the edge of the mattress. She took a tin mug of hot sweet tea and a piece of bread and butter from Denise and it revived her.

Seeing her eating, the little ones grew calmer. Only Larry, the youngest infant, continued to whimper. Denise lifted the tot in her arms and comforted him as if he were her own. The weight of his round, living body rested lightly against her breasts. Snuffling and wheezing in laboured breathing, the babe kept his eyes squeezed shut. His loose swaddling was damp.

'May I feed him?' Denise asked humbly.

Nan nodded her throbbing, bandaged head.

Steve heated milk on the stove while Paddy found a bottle. Then Steve stood watching; the mothering and the care. On the road ahead, in every encounter, he only hoped his courage would match hers. His feelings were very exposed, tender towards them all.

———